Renewal

Renewal

Howard Lewis

Matador
9 Priory Business Park
Kibworth Beauchamp
Leicestershire LE8 0RX, UK
Tel: (+44) 116 279 2299
Fax: (+44) 116 279 2277
Email: books@troubador.co.uk
Web: www.troubador.co.uk/matador

ISBN 978-1783062-904

British Library Cataloguing in Publication Data.
A catalogue record for this book is available from the British Library.

Typeset in Aldine by Troubador Publishing Ltd
Printed and bound in the UK by TJ International, Padstow, Cornwall

Matador is an imprint of Troubador Publishing Ltd

For Sue

CHAPTER ONE

His sleeping form was slumped in the chair, head resting atop the sturdy pine table. He snored lightly as the reluctant tendrils of a misty November dawn crept sulkily across the cluttered farmyard to slowly illuminate the grimy kitchen window as the blackness of a cold night, like a mortally wounded animal, slunk away.

As the light gradually increased, it revealed the broken shotgun lying on the table, with a handful of unspent cartridges in an untidy heap beside its polished wooden stock. A greasy smudged tumbler stood there also, accompanied by an empty bottle of Scotch, a small amount of the amber spirit still pooling above its thick glass base. Thin mean brown-stained butt ends clogged an ashtray nearby to overflowing.

The uneven flaky slate flagstoned floor was filthy and the worktops and sink were piled high with dirty crockery, cutlery and all manner of cooking utensils. An old range, once the heart of a warm and welcoming room, sat disconsolately against the shabby wall, a thin layer of grey dust bedecking its once shiny black enamelled surface. A small amount of powdery ash had fallen from its half-open fire door, bearing testament to the fact that it had been a long time since it had been cleaned out, and an even longer while since it had been lit to spread warmth and cheer throughout the whole house.

He stirred. Lifting his head, his rheumy eyes bit by bit took in the depressing scene. He groaned.

Leaning back in the chair, he brushed unkempt locks of straggly hair from his face and groggily rubbed his watery eyes before running rough palms down his stubbly cheeks. He stared at the gun for a few seconds before woozily focussing his gaze on some neglected photographs on the pine dresser.

"Well there you are, dear," he said bitterly. "Couldn't even get that right, could I?"

The chair agonisingly scraped the floor as he stood. He wandered unsteadily to the sink, filled a grubby electric kettle and plugged it in. He separated one of the many unwashed mugs from its companions and half-heartedly swilled it under the cold tap before shovelling a couple of spoons of coffee granules and a generously heaped spoonful of sugar into it.

Having downed the coffee, he left the cold kitchen. In the dim hall, he shuffled on his donkey jacket and slipped out of the door into the harsh chill air of the late autumn morning, gently dropping the latch behind him. As he had singularly failed to carry out his plan of the previous evening to end his miserable life, he drifted aimlessly around the empty farm buildings where at one time not that far in the past he had been a happy and successful farmer. Drawing open the sliding wooden door of the milking parlour, he stared morosely at the deserted scene.

On dry dusty wooden beams above the milking jars and other associated paraphernalia there still remained rosettes won by him and his father for one or other of their prize-winning Jersey cows. Stabbed into the crumbly wood with rusted old drawing-pins they gazed down forlornly at him, curled faded frilly edges dusty and despondent in the dim light. He sighed once more. What was he going to do now? Try again? No, he knew he wouldn't be able to do it. A single tear tracked down his cheek to dangle from his craggy chin. How could everything have gone so wrong so quickly?

After his father had died, followed in cruel speedy succession by his mother, he found himself totally alone. But he'd risen to the challenge, carrying on the business by himself and had made a good fist of it. It was hard on him – of course it was. The desolate feeling of loneliness was at first all but intolerable, it gnawed away at him; but he got through. Then he'd met her, the answer, so he thought, to all his prayers. *Marry in haste: repent at leisure.* Yes, that was about the size of it. He realised too late just what she was. A fair weather wife was how he'd come to describe her later. When the going got tough, and the profits from the farm started to fall back, her support was non-existent. Furthermore, coupled with falling milk prices and strangulating milk quotas came the added woes of the BSE crisis.

"I don't know why you just don't get rid of the whole lot of them!" she bawled at him one evening. "Why do you insist on carrying on pouring money down the drain: it's just!" she shrieked, desperately trying to find the right words, "it's just…bloody ridiculous! We never have a holiday! I never get any nice new clothes, or…or a new car! I tell you Frankie, I'm sick of it!"

It was at that moment that his love for her suddenly morphed into a bitter and irreversible hatred. "You don't see it, do you?" he shouted right back, starting to tremble with rage. "There's generations of breeding gone into this herd – my grandfather built it up from scratch; talk about blood, toil, tears and sweat! And you want me to throw it all away because you want a new car! Christ Isabel, you really are…you really are… God, you're unbelievable!" he spluttered.

3

So that was the point of no return: just one short month later she packed her bags and left. He soldiered on for a couple more years before disaster struck. Foot and Mouth disease was spreading inexorably across his county of Devon, and one unforgettable morning he found the nightmarish lesions in the mouth of one of his beloved cows. By the end of that same day every animal on the farm had been destroyed. First they were anaesthetized and then dispatched one by tragic one with a pistol where they'd dropped. The sounds of the shots would haunt him for the rest of his life. To add insult to injury, the foul bloated animals were left littered around the yard for over a week before their rotting stinking carcases were removed for incineration. The stench even now lingered in his nostrils. Maybe if he'd had the support of a good wife he'd have been able to pick himself up and start again. Or maybe if he'd had a son to inherit the business it would have spurred him on. But no, he'd sunk into a deepening abyss, finding himself more often than not staring with unseeing eyes into the bottom of a glass of whisky. No doubt if Isabel had stayed with him she'd have been delighted to see the demise of his dairy herd – after all, the compensation paid by the government was generous. Needless to say, replacing such well-bred stock would have been nigh on impossible.

He slid the door shut and walked back towards the house.

"Frank? Are you there?" The postman had already ventured into the farmhouse and poked his head around the kitchen door. Realising Frank wasn't inside, he'd come to look for him. "Frank!" he yelled again, leaning on the metal gate, "you about?"

"Alright, alright, I'm coming." He reached the gate. "What's up?"

"Got one here recorded delivery – needs your moniker."

He waved a clipboard at him. Frank took it and scrawled his signature beside his name whilst the postman took in his shabby appearance. Bearing in mind what he'd seen on the kitchen table, he asked if everything was okay.

"Eh? Yeah, I'm fine; just a bit peaky, that's all. In fact, I was just about to see if I could go and pop off a few bunnies: a bit of fresh air'll probably do me the world of good."

"Oh right," came the unconvinced reply. "Well, thanks for that anyway." The postman thrust a bundle of mail into Frank's arms and jumped back into his van. The wheels spun on the slippery road surface as he sped off up the lane, leaving Frank to wonder, not for the first time, why Royal Mail employees had to drive so bloody fast.

Inside, he flumped the post onto the table and refilled the kettle. As he waited for it to boil, he picked up the letter he'd signed for and inspected it suspiciously. He couldn't decipher the blurred postmark, and it was addressed in a spidery hand he didn't recognise. He dropped it carelessly back down and made himself a cup of coffee. Then he pulled up a chair and grabbing the envelope once more, with grimy fingers ripped it open.

Dear Mr Anderson,

I have recently discovered, after a good deal of searching and with the corroboration of others, something which I believe you are bound, if you are who I think you are, to find at the very least startling. My name is Dan Hussey, and I think some years ago you knew my mother Sally: then Sally Ward.

Sally? Yes, he remembered little Sally. He'd been her boyfriend for a while before he tired of her, as he inevitably did with all of his many girlfriends when younger. Hadn't she gone to Australia? Married a sheep farmer or something, he thought. He read on.

Tragically, both my parents were killed six months ago in a road accident. My mother had a secret she kept from my father for obvious reasons. She left a letter with her solicitor to be opened only in the unlikely event of her and dad unexpectedly losing their lives at the same time. There's no easy way of communicating this news, but it would appear that my dad was not my biological father; you are.

He stared dumbstruck at those last two words for a while. Was it possible? He seemed to recollect that Sally had left the country only a short while after the pair of them had split up. Everybody had said that it couldn't possibly last, that she was on the rebound. An Aussie sheep farmer? It would never work out: apparently it had.

I wouldn't be writing to you if I wasn't 99% sure of this, but if you're not that Frankie Anderson, please forgive me. I've no idea how you might greet this explosive revelation, and if you wish not to pursue the matter further then I fully understand – no doubt you have your own family to consider. For my part, I am more than curious to meet you, and may be contacted at the above address. I shall be staying in London for a month or so to be near my grandmother – mum's mother. She is quite frail and not expected to last more than a few weeks and I intend to stay with until the end; she has no one else, poor soul. If I don't hear from you in the next week or so I will not pester you again.
Yours sincerely,
Dan.

He stared at the letter in disbelief. He read it through slowly twice more, while his untouched coffee cooled in the chipped mug. Then he just sat there staring into space for a few minutes, feeling knocked for six. He read it yet again before folding the sheets and sliding them back into the torn envelope. He rose from the chair, scraped up the loose cartridges with one hand and picked up the shotgun with the other. He walked out into the hall and locked the whole lot away in the gun cabinet.

It was certainly a shock, he thought, as he leant against the cold stone wall, but a good shock nevertheless. He had a son! And how old would he be? He did a quick bit of mental arithmetic. He'd be twenty-seven. He wondered if the boy had a girlfriend, or maybe a wife. Christ, he could be a grandfather – at forty-seven! To say this put a different perspective on things would have been a gross understatement. He hardly dared to believe it, but there it was, in black and white, Sally had said so; she wouldn't have made it up. This was it; this was the news that would get his life back on track.

He strode outside; his first task was to get the range burning again, then he could start cleaning up the pigsty he'd been living in for the past few months. After that, he'd have a nice long soak in the bath and shave that fungus off his face. And after that, if he could think how to go about it, he'd write back to his son. His son!

But as things panned out, he failed to put pen to paper that day. He was exhausted by the evening, and after a relaxing bath, went straight to bed, determined to write the next morning. However, despite his weariness, he spent a restless night; there was too much going on inside his head. He rose a good hour before dawn, shivering in the cold bathroom as he washed, the night again coal black and cold beyond the ill-fitting sash window.

By nine o'clock he'd spent the best part of an hour trying to pen a missive to Dan when yet again he screwed up the paper into a tight ball and hurled it at the wastepaper basket. It missed, ricocheting off the wicker side and landing at his feet. He made himself a coffee and had another go at it.

> *Dear Dan,*
>
> *Suffice to say, I was bowled over by your letter, arriving as it did like a bolt from the blue, and yes, I am that Frank Anderson. I was very sorry to hear of your tragic loss, and that your grandmother is so poorly. I also have to tell you that I would be very happy to meet you wherever and whenever you may wish. Please forgive me for the blunt formality of this letter, but I find myself in a (happy) state of shock. I look forward to your reply.*
>
> *Yours most sincerely,*
> *Frank.*

There. It was done. It wasn't particularly pretty, but it would have to do. Anyway, short and sweet should get the message across. He yawned expansively, stretched, and sealing the envelope got up from the table in search of a stamp. Having no success in locating one, he decided to walk down to the village Post Office.

He stepped into a silvery world outside. Although the sun was indeed shining valiantly down from a cloudless sky, there was little warmth in its pallid rays at this time of year. He pulled up the worn collar of his jacket and headed briskly up the narrow lane flanked on both sides by high steep Devon banks. The countryside was deathly still, the only noise to disturb the calm came from a couple of quarrelsome crows squawking in the uppermost branches of an enormous beech tree dominating a small sloping field on the higher side of the lane; its sweeping skeletal limbs filtering the weak sunlight onto the frosted white grass. Behind him, in pastures below the farmhouse beside the brook, a delicate mist was wafting upwards from the water, languidly floating sylph-like through purple-tinged bare boughs of towering bank-side alders.

The bell jangled excitedly as he shoved the door open and pushed inside. The postmistress appeared from somewhere deep within the bowels of the shop.

"Oh, hello, Frank," she greeted him, failing spectacularly to disguise the surprise in her voice. "How are you? We haven't seen you for a while. Everything alright up at the farm, is it?"

"Yes, absolutely fine, thank you Anne," he replied gruffly. "I just popped in for some stamps."

"Right you are - did you want first or second class?"

"Better have a book of each. And can you start delivering my paper again?"

"Of course; 'The Times', wasn't it?"

Once he'd gone she scampered off to find her husband.

"You'll never guess who that was, Gerald."

"Probably not," he answered with little interest, "but no doubt you're going to tell me."

"Only Frank Anderson," she continued enthusiastically, choosing to ignore his disappointing lack of curiosity. "He looked like he'd tidied himself up a bit as well; he was clutching a letter and…"

"Fancy that, eh? Someone coming into a Post Office with a letter. Whatever next?"

She scowled crossly at him. "Alright, but you know full

well what I mean. He's been holed up in that farm for months now; ever since he lost his cows…something must have happened. I wonder if he's met somebody. Perhaps he's got a girlfriend, or maybe Isabel's come back."

"No chance of that, he'd never have her back again - no way."

"Well *something's* going on; I can tell. He wants a paper delivered again as well. What's that all about?"

The bell jingled again, breaking off her fanciful musings.

"Hadn't you better go and see who that is, dear? You never know who it might be – perhaps it's somebody with a parcel this time."

She opened her mouth to protest, but thinking better of it turned on her heel and went to attend to the customer.

Frank popped the letter into the box in the wall outside and wandered back down the lane. He determined to spend the rest of the day tidying up the house, and getting some washing done. Kicking off his boots inside the door, he trotted upstairs to strip the bed; a task that was well overdue.

During the next few days he kept himself busy, although his heart leapt every time the postman called, and sank when he saw there was no word from his son.

"Are you expecting something important then, Frank?"

"What? Oh no, just some stuff from DEFRA, that's all… nothing important, Joe."

But Joe remained unconvinced and said as much to Anne. "What's going on down at Willow Farm then?"

"What are you driving at, Joe?"

"Well, Frank almost comes running out to snatch the mail off me; and 'e's cleaning the place up – even the yard; that's a first! Not only that, 'e's shaved and got 'is hair cut. Can only be one explanation as far as I can see – 'e's got himself a woman!"

"Have you seen anybody else there?" she asked eagerly.

"Well no, but what else could it be?"

She could think of no satisfactory answer to this.

Nearly a whole week passed before Frank received a reply from Dan, and he was beginning to become a bit edgy. When the letter arrived with a smudged London postmark in the familiar spidery hand, he hastily slipped a forefinger under the glued flap of the envelope and tore it open.

> *Dear Frank,*
>
> *I'm sorry not to have written to you sooner, but I've been a bit preoccupied with my grandmother. The consensus among the doctors is that she can't last much longer. I'm very pleased (and rather nervous as you are I guess) that you want to meet me. May I suggest that you come up to London? I would come to you but I'm sure you understand that the current situation demands that I stay here.*
>
> *We could either meet at the above address, or anywhere else that you may prefer.*
>
> *I look forward to hearing from you soon.*
> *Yours sincerely,*
> *Dan.*

Frank surmised correctly that the *above address* would be the boy's grandmother's house, and he naturally felt uncomfortable about meeting his son there. He'd never been to his capital city in his life, and after he'd phoned the local train booking office and got himself a day return to London which cost him, in his mind, a ludicrously large sum of money, he wrote back saying he'd be coming up in a week's time, and that he'd like it if they could meet in the foyer of the Natural History Museum.

He received a reply by return. The date was fixed.

Throughout the following week, Frank worked tirelessly in the house and farmyard, thoroughly cleaning windows, re-hanging gates and doors and generally tidying up. He immersed himself in all manner of neglected tasks in an attempt to smother his growing nervousness and apprehension and to pass the time more quickly.

CHAPTER TWO

Frank gazed blankly out of the carriage window and stifled a yawn. Outside, drops of rain jagged haphazardly down the dirty glass as the miserable wet landscape flashed by, the speeding train all the while hurtling inexorably towards its destination. He turned to glance briefly at his travelling companions on the other side of the small table opposite him. An earnest-looking young man was annoyingly still tap-tapping away on the keyboard of a shiny blue laptop, totally oblivious to his surroundings. Next to him, a seriously overweight woman was tearing open a jumbo-sized packet of crisps. She then proceeded to shovel handfuls of them into her capacious mouth, regularly plunging a fat mitt into the crinkly bag with gusto to ensure a continuous supply. He hastily looked away. On the other side of the carriage a scruffy lad, presumably one of the many of the great unwashed that made up the student fraternity, was squinting at some magazine through thick-lensed glasses whilst an indefinable tinny noise emanated from headphones clamped tightly across his greasy uncombed locks. By his side, mouth agape, an elderly shrewish woman was sound asleep. Her head had slumped against the tartan headrest, and was gently rocking to the rhythm of the moving train. He shut his eyes and tried unsuccessfully to doze.

After a couple of hours the train reached the large

conurbations on the outskirts of London, and slowly snaked its way into Paddington station, where it juddered with a protesting squeal of brakes to a halt. Once he'd clambered down onto the platform, he was carried along in the flood of hurrying humanity to the exits. He glanced at his watch; it was ten past one, the train had actually arrived a few minutes early. Feeling a bit peckish, he decided to grab a bite to eat at the pub in the station before heading off for his rendezvous. Outside the concourse half an hour later, he felt increasingly overwhelmed by the unfamiliar rushing tearing atmosphere as he fought to get a taxi.

Marvelling at the massive cathedral-like edifice, he climbed the steps of the Natural History Museum and walked through the huge arched doorway into the central hall. He decided to wait for his son by the impressive skeleton of the dinosaur *Diplodocus*. He'd not been there long before his mirror image came tripping into the hall. It had to be Dan, for apart from the fair hair the similarities were striking, no *unmistakable* he thought as his heart pounded against his ribcage. Tall, like him. He had his father's eyes, his chin, even his high forehead.

Oh my God!

"Mr Anderson?" A polite enquiry with that attractive sing-song Australian accent.

"Er yes. It's Dan is it?"

"It is; good to meet you." He extended his hand confidently; a nervous smile dancing on the edge of his lips.

"Pleased to meet you too," Frank rejoined a little stiffly as he stretched out his arm. They shook hands firmly.

"Look, call me Frank, would you? Or Frankie if you like: I don't mind which."

"Of course; no worries… Frank." He laughed nervously.

"Shall we go and see if we can grab a coffee or something somewhere a little less…frenetic?"

A group of schoolchildren were tearing round and round the sombre-looking dinosaur skeleton.

"Sounds like a plan to me."

They found the café, which at this time wasn't very busy and having furnished themselves with a cup of coffee each, planted themselves at a quiet table in the corner. Frank enquired first as to the health of the boy's grandmother.

"Actually, she erm…she's no longer with us, she died in the night," came the blunt reply.

"What, last night?"

"Er, yeah."

"Oh, I'm sorry." Frank was somewhat taken aback. "You should have let me know – I'd have come up another time."

"Oh no, that's okay. It wasn't as if it was sudden or unexpected or anything. I'm afraid the old dear was pretty gaga. I guess it was a blessing really that she didn't suffer any more; she had no quality of life at all."

"Yes, I suppose." He took a sip of his coffee and carefully replaced the cup in its white saucer. A short awkward silence ensued.

"I'd better tell you a bit about myself," Frank ventured after a few moments. "Not that there's much to tell really. Before I start, I want you to know that your mother was a lovely girl and I'm afraid I treated her rather badly. I was a stupid selfish young buck when we started seeing each other and I finished with her just because I fancied another pair of legs. That's how I was at that time: I suppose it took me a while to grow up. I always thought afterwards that if we'd first met each other when I was older and less bloody stupid, we might well have been happy together: but there you are, that's

15

life as they say. As it transpired, when I eventually did tie the knot, it was with a totally self-centred woman whom I was glad in the end to be rid of. She never loved me – or perhaps she did a little bit to start with, who knows? She was essentially a gold-digger: it was my own fault, everybody else knew what she was like but I blindly and bull-headedly ignored their warnings and disregarded their sound advice."

"Ah well, love's blind. Isn't that what they say?" Dan replied, somewhat taken aback by the other's candour.

"Yes, well it was certainly true in my case. Anyway, she wouldn't countenance the idea of having children and when the farm began to get into difficulties and became less profitable she turned against me instead of trying to support and encourage me when I needed her most."

"And so then you split up?"

"Yes, I divorced her about a year ago. I won't bore you with the tawdry details, but fortunately she didn't ruin me financially – not for any lack of trying, mind you; she wouldn't have cared one jot if I'd had to sell the farm to pay her off. Luckily for me we were married for only a short while, and her settlement wasn't that huge."

"Oh right. So do you have any other family? Cousins or brothers and sisters?"

"No, my parents each had a brother; funnily enough they would have been about the same age. But they were both killed in the war. I had one sister, but she was fatally run over on the farm by my dad when I was a baby; she was only a toddler and I can't say I remember her at all. I don't think my father ever forgave himself although he was in no way to blame, and my mother definitely never thought it was his fault; it was just one of those terrible tragedies."

"Do you mind if I ask how it happened?"

"No, I believe she slipped out of the house into the yard when he was reversing a hay trailer and the back wheel went over her. It was instant; at least that's what I was told in later years."

"Bloody hell, that's awful."

"Yes, but tragically accidents like that happen all too often on farms."

The two of them sat in quiet reflection for a moment or two.

"So what about you, Dan? Do you have any siblings?"

"Yup, I've got a kid sister, Jane. I don't see a lot of her these days. She got married and moved away to Brizzy, sorry Brisbane about…let me see, five years ago now. She's busy making babies, three girls and another on the way. Her hubby Wayne's got some fancy overpaid job in IT; we haven't got much in common."

"Sounds as if you don't like him much."

"Oh no, I wouldn't say that at all. It's just he's, well, boring really. Still, my sister's happy with him; I guess that's all that matters."

"Yeah I guess it is. Any other relatives?"

"There's uncle Ned, that's dad's brother. He runs the family cattle and sheep station near Bulloo."

Frank regarded him quizzically.

"Sorry, do you know Australia at all?"

"Not really; well not at all actually. I'm not what you'd call well travelled, and I took scant interest in anything at school."

"No worries. Right, well Bulloo's in Queensland which is on the right-hand side of the country if you like, about halfway up, above New South Wales. It sits in the bottom left-hand corner of the territory, whereas Brisbane's in the bottom right, south of the Sunshine Coast."

"Oh I see," said Frank, who didn't see at all and made a quick mental note to consult his old atlas when he got home. "I suppose it's quite a big spread, is it?"

"It's a little under three thousand acres, so it's big compared to most farms over here but it needs to be to carry a profitable number of animals. There's always some disaster waiting in the wings, such as flood or drought. The sheep don't make much since the global collapse of the wool market, but the cattle do pretty good. There's a big healthy export trade, and Australia's got the advantage of never having had a single case of BSE."

He paused to take a swallow of coffee before continuing. "Uncle Ned's married to my aunt Kate and they've got two sons, Billy and Mike. Billy's thirty-one and Mike's thirty-three; they both work full-time on the station. Apart from that, my only living relative is mum's brother James, the black sheep of the family."

"Every family's got one," Frank grinned. He picked up his cup, and a drop of black coffee fell into his lap. "So what's his story?"

"Well, I don't know really; I've never met him, you see. Mum and he were never close; he's a good five or six years older than her, and as far as I'm aware they've not seen each other or been in touch at all for years and years. Funnily enough, he lives down in your neck of the woods, in a town called Dartmouth – or at least he used to. He never even came over for the funeral, so God knows what's happened to him or where he is."

"Mmm, sounds intriguing. So are you going to try and trace him while you're in England?"

"Nah, I hadn't thought to. Like I say, he's taken no interest in us over the years, so why should I bother?"

"But he might be dead, or I don't know - in prison or something. Aren't you even slightly curious to know why he stayed out of touch with his entire family for such a long time?"

"Like I already said, him and mum were estranged for a long time; he means nothing to me."

Frank considered it prudent not to pursue the matter further. Instead, he rose from his chair and offered to fetch them both another drink. A few minutes later, he returned to the table with two fresh cups of steaming coffee, sat down and tore open a sachet of sugar. The white granules toppled into his cup and he stirred the liquid briskly.

"So," Dan asked, "what do you farm at your place?" He took a tentative sip from his cup.

"We've kept a dairy herd since my grandfather's day. Unfortunately, that all came to an abrupt end with the Foot and Mouth outbreak back in the spring. Ironically we were the last farm in the area to catch the disease. Everything was killed out in March."

"'Struth, that must have been awful. So are you going to rebuild?"

"I don't know. To tell the truth, I'm sort of in limbo. Losing the herd knocked me sideways – I couldn't bear to go through that ever again. The other problem is that Bovine TB is running amok in the West Country, with no commitment by the Government to tackle it: the situation's getting worse and worse by the day."

"It doesn't sound much like a good country to be farming in."

"You're not wrong there. But never mind all that, what are *your* plans for the future? I suppose you'll be going back to Oz a bit sooner than you reckoned now, will you?"

"I'm not sure; I think I might stick around for a while longer. I've come a long way – I might as well see a bit of England now I'm here. After all, there's no reason why I should rush back to Queensland."

"Oh, so there's no one special waiting for you there then?"

"No," he grinned, "no one special."

"But aren't you needed back at the station?"

"What? Oh no, I don't work there all the time, nor did dad. Mum met him when he was over in this country. Back in those days he used to go around the world shearing sheep. They got hitched and moved back to Australia: that put paid to his travels. He set up an agricultural contracting business, although he still carried on shearing – I don't think he could bring himself to stop completely." He smiled. "He had no stake in the station, although we both lent a hand in busy times."

He stole a glance at his watch.

"Oh I'm sorry," Frank interjected, "you must have a lot of stuff to sort out, what with your grandmother…"

"No, no, that's okay," Dan reassured him. "It's just I'm meeting the undertakers at four, you know, to sort things out…"

"Yes, yes, of course, I understand. Look, you'd better get on; I don't want to detain you."

"It's alright; we've got another hour yet. Are you staying up here tonight?"

"Oh no, I only got a day return; my train leaves at four fifteen."

"Oh, okay." Another short awkward silence followed.

"You know, you're probably right; I ought to try and trace James, even if it's just to tell him his mother died."

"It seems odd that he lost touch with his own mother. She said nothing to you before she died?"

"He was never mentioned; she made it quite clear to me she was entirely on her own."

"There must have been a serious falling out, for him to disappear off the radar like that."

"If there was, nobody told me."

"Oh well, another of life's little mysteries, I guess. Listen, there's one other thing I'm curious about…"

"Oh?"

"It's well, it's slightly difficult. Have you told your sister that, you know, you're…"

"…only her half-brother?" Dan finished for him.

"Well I wasn't going to put it quite like that, but yes."

"Yes, she knows, and so do the rest of the family. I can't say the lot of them weren't shocked, it was hard to believe that mum kept it to herself for so long. I think once it had sunk in and they all realised that I was still the same Dan I'd always been, they understood that nothing had changed between us. Jane made it quite clear that I might have a different father physically, but as far as she was concerned my real dad died when he pulled out his pick-up truck into the path of that road train."

"And she's quite right of course," Frank was quick to assure him. "I wouldn't want you thinking any different. Your father is the man who raised you and made you who you are."

He said this because he thought it was what his son wanted to hear. It wasn't what he himself believed in his heart.

Dan's fair complexion coloured slightly. "Thank you for that," he muttered quietly.

"Look, while we're here why don't we wander round the exhibits for the half-hour or so we've got left. I could do with stretching my legs before getting back on that cramped train."

"Good idea. Where shall we start?"

21

They traipsed around the building, being suitably impressed by the skeletal remains and models in the Large Mammals Hall. The pickled exhibits in the Darwin centre held a morbid fascination for both of them. They retraced their footsteps down the grand staircase, and made their way past the dinosaur skeleton out into the fresh air.

The earlier rain had by now blown over, leaving the wet streets and pavements shining in the ebbing sunlight and growing amber glow of the capital's streetlights. A continuous stream of traffic roared by, spray swirling off black glossy tyres. The scoured sky was a milky orange, with occasional puffy cotton wool clouds scudding across its washed sickly surface. Frank stopped at the bottom of the imposing flight of stone steps and proffered his hand.

"I'm really glad to have met you," he said, a shade formally. "I'd like to see you again before you shoot off home – that is, if you want to of course."

"Yeah, I'd like that. Look, give me a week or so to sort out my grandmother's stuff. When the funeral's over and everything I'll be in touch. Is that okay?"

"Yes, that's absolutely fine; just write or give me a ring when you're ready. I'm looking forward to getting to know you a bit better, now we've broken the ice so to speak."

They shook hands firmly.

"Yeah sure, me too. Good to meet you at last."

"And if you feel the need to search out your elusive uncle, you're more than welcome to come and stay with me – if that's any help at all."

"Thanks, I'll bear it in mind."

Frank's travelling companions on his return journey proved no more salubrious than those accompanying him on his outward trip. When he boarded his train and found his seat, he was less than enthused to see slumped opposite a grossly overweight middle-aged man in a blue pinstripe suit, the discarded jacket of which lay in a crumpled heap on the table in front of him. The fellow had clearly enjoyed a first-rate and no doubt extended lunch. Frank smelt the sweet aroma of wine about his persona, noting also the beads of sweat on his flushed face, and the wet stains pasting his shirt to his flabby armpits. *How delightful.* In the seat beside this disgusting individual sat a forlorn-looking skinny youth who was raptly fiddling with his mobile phone. The seats on the other side of the carriage housed a heavily pregnant girl in her twenties who seemed to be a total stranger to shampoo. Sitting beside her, pressed against the window, were two toddlers intent on squabbling over a plethora of sweets which she had disgorged from her huge handbag onto the table.

"Right you two: stay there, and stop fighting or I'll put those sweets back in my bag and you won't get any at all!" she threatened noisily. "I'm going for a fag." She rose to her swollen feet with some difficulty and clutching the enormous bag, waddled off down the centre aisle. The two little terrors stuck their tongues out at Frank. He glared back at them.

A few minutes later the engine pulled away with a sudden jarring jolt, urgently snatching the carriage forward. The children, now both sporting melting twin candles of snot from dirty nostrils, continued to quarrel, but their mother no longer tried to chastise them, choosing instead to bury her head in some trashy book whilst they ran up and down the passageway. The fat man, his head now lolling against the window, breath from his open mouth fogging the glass, began to snore loudly. Frank could stand no more. He stood up. If he had to stand outside the doorway for the whole journey it would be preferable to this torture.

He was relieved when the train pulled up at Newton Abbot a couple of hours later. He tumbled onto the platform and strode off to retrieve his battered old Land Rover from the car park. A fine rain had started to fall, and he carefully drove homewards, poorly guided by the skewed yellowy beams of his inadequate headlights.

It had been months since he'd stepped into his local for a drink, but that evening he decided to do just that. A couple of pints before he went back to his cold lonely farmhouse with the fish and chips he'd just bought was just what he needed. Pushing open the door to the public bar of The Golden Fleece, a wave of welcoming warmth and cheer washed over him as he absorbed the comforting aroma of tobacco and beer. For a weekday, the place was surprisingly busy. He was disappointed, nevertheless, to see that the postmaster and his nosy wife were propping up the bar.

"Evening, Frank. Pint of Guinness, is it?" If the landlord was surprised to see him after such a long while, he hid his natural inquisitiveness with a practised expertise.

"Er, yes please, Pete."

He nodded a curt greeting to one or two familiar faces across the smoky bar, and once he had his drink retreated to a quiet table in the corner and turned his attention to rolling a cigarette. Barely had he popped the lid off his tobacco tin, when he was accosted by the two people he least wanted to talk to in the whole pub.

"Do you mind if Gerald and I join you?" a female voice enquired sweetly.

"What? Oh, Anne. No, of course not, please do."

She plonked herself down in a chair opposite, beckoning her husband to sit beside her, and sighed theatrically.

"Ah, that's better; it's getting a bit noisy and crowded up there."

Frank thought uncharitably that the any increase in noise at the bar could only have been attributable to her boisterous presence. He took a deep draught of his stout, then flicked his lighter and lit his smoke. She regarded him with a thinly veiled air of disapproval.

"We haven't seen you in here for a while, have we Gerald?" she said brightly.

"Er no, not recently anyway," he replied dutifully. She threw him a reproving look. He took the hint and asked,

"Erm, how are things now? On the farm, I mean." He immediately felt embarrassed and awkward.

"Yes, absolutely fine – thank you for asking. I was thinking it's about time I restocked the place actually."

"Oh really?" Anne jumped in. "Is that where you've been today?"

"Sorry? I'm not sure I get your drift."

"It's just that Sylvia saw you earlier – going through town."

"Oh right. No, I've been in London actually."

"London?" This time the woman was barely able to contain much less cover her curiosity.

"Yes, I had a bit of family business to sort out, that's all – nothing very exciting." He volunteered no more information, but merely continued to pull on his pint and draw on his roll-up.

Family business? Her mind was whirling. *But he hasn't got any family. What on earth is the man talking about?*

Frank drained his pint and got up to go.

"Can I get you a refill?" Gerald asked hopefully.

"No thanks," he replied brusquely. "I'd better make a move before my fish and chips get completely cold. Nice chatting to you both." He stubbed out his fag and with a wave of acknowledgement in the landlord's direction, left the cosy hostelry.

"Come on, Gerald, let's go back to the bar." Anne emptied her wineglass and eying the wisp of blue smoke still rising from the crushed butt in the ashtray in front of her hurriedly got up from the table.

"So what's Frank up to then?" Pete asked, as Anne hoicked herself up on a vacant bar stool.

"Well, he told us he was thinking about restocking the farm."

"Is that all? Blimey Anne love, you're not going to set the world on fire with that juicy snippet of information."

"No, but there's a bit more to it than that," her husband broke in, coming to her defence. "He's been in London all day."

The landlord raised his eyebrows. "London!" he exclaimed. "Does he even know where the place is? I mean, he hasn't ever been out of the county, has he?"

"I doubt if he's been further east than Exeter market," Anne commented scornfully.

"But what was he doing up in the smoke? You can't buy animals up there; apart from dead ones at Smithfield of course!" The tubby licensee chuckled at his own feeble joke. "There must be a woman involved," Anne surmised, "there has to be; just look at the evidence. He cleans himself up, and the house: he even tidies up the farmyard, and that was *always* a mess. And then he goes up to London on so-called family business – but as we all know, he hasn't got any family! You know what I reckon? I reckon he went to meet someone, probably from one of those dating agencies. There're loads of them about these days."

"But why go all the way up there? Surely if he was meeting someone for a date, he'd arrange it a bit nearer home, wouldn't he?" Pete asked. "Hey, maybe he went up there for a bit of fun, you know, in one of them clubs. Or maybe he went down Soho."

"Oh really Pete!"

"What?"

"Well, think about it," Anne said dismissively. "It's not very likely, is it? Do you honestly think that that man would spend that sort of money just for a bit of how's your father? We all know how tight he is."

"Can't argue with that."

"He's had a couple of letters from there recently," Gerald offered, keen to stay in the conversation. "Handwritten as well; Joe told us."

"Then maybe some distant relative's traced him," Pete speculated. "It's all the rage now, people tracing their ancestry. Or maybe he's been left something in a will or something."

"Or maybe some illegitimate child from his murky past's tracked him down," the postmistress quipped.

"Now we really are getting into the realms of fantasy."

"Quite," agreed Gerald. "I agree with Anne. Somehow or other, Frank's got himself involved with a woman: let's hope for his sake she's not like the last one he tangled with."

"Amen to that."

Frank lay in bed that night, cocooned in freshly laundered cotton sheets, reliving his encounter with his son. He felt it had gone well and was hoping the boy would be in touch again soon.

He might just bugger off back to Australia – after all, they'd met up, he'd satisfied his curiosity, his grandmother was dead, so why would he want to hang around? He might never see the boy again.

He tried to dispel this frightening thought. It was odd to think that that he'd only known of Dan's existence for a very short time, but yet couldn't bear the thought that he might never see him again. No, it was no good going down that road, the lad had told him he'd be in touch and that he was going to stay around for a while yet. The only thing to be done was to wait as patiently as he could to be contacted again. He sighed and rolled over on his side, pulling the bedclothes on top of him. Somewhere outside in the impenetrable syrupy darkness an owl hooted, answered a few seconds later by another some distance away. With the soothing waves of sleep failing to wash over him, he turned onto his back and lay there in the cloying silence until eventually he drifted into a disquieting ragged slumber, punctuated with haunting confused images of his ex-wife, broadly grinning son, and the skeletal remains of his dairy herd. He was violently wrenched from these disturbing dreams an hour or so before the long night gradually began to withdraw, to be replaced by yet another dishevelled and depressing grey dawn.

CHAPTER THREE

Four days later, Frank had just poured himself a second cup of coffee and was on the cusp of (optimistically) tackling 'The Times' crossword, when he was rudely interrupted by the insistent shrill ringing of the telephone. He lifted the phone from its base unit, instantly stilling its harsh cries.

"Hello," he growled gruffly.

"Hi. Mr Anderson?" The unmistakable Australian twang flew down the line.

"Dan? Yes, it's me. How's it all going? And for God's sake call me Frank, will you?"

"Yeah sure; sorry Frank. Things aren't too bad this end. My gran's funeral was yesterday and as you can imagine, it was a pretty quiet and simple affair. She specified in her will exactly how she wanted the order of service, so that was straightforward enough. She also asked for her ashes to be scattered on Chepstow racecourse: she was a keen follower of the gee-gees apparently, that's something about her I never knew."

Frank's heart skipped a beat. "So you'll be coming down to the West Country then? Or at least as far as Bristol."

"Once I've got things sorted out here, yes. I've spoken to Janey, and she's entrusted me to clear gran's house and do what's needed to put it on the market - which isn't much. She didn't own anything of any real value, but obviously I need to go through everything and want to keep any family mementoes and jewellery. I've obviously met her solicitor and read through the will with him. It was quite straightforward, she left her entire estate to mum…"

"Oh, so she didn't change it after…"

"No, but it doesn't matter. Everything will just automatically pass to me and my sister in equal parts."

"Right. So no mention of your errant uncle, then?"

"No, none at all."

Frank's heart sank. "So you'll not be coming down to this neck of the woods to search for him?"

"I think it's best to let sleeping uncles lie, don't you? I mean, I know I said I'd try and track him down, if only to tell him that his mother's died, but it's not as simple as that, is it? I don't want to know what made the whole family fall out with him. What would be the point of opening up a can of worms, when…when mum…well, she's not here anymore, is she? Do you understand?"

"Yes, I think so. Did you er, did you place an announcement in any paper? About your grandmother, I mean."

"Oh yes. In 'The Daily Telegraph'."

"Oh well, perhaps he'll notice it."

"Perhaps."

"So, it won't be that long before you'll be on your way home then?"

"Like I said before, I'm in no rush to get back. I guess I'll be up here at least a week sorting the house out, and then it depends how long it'll take to get probate granted. According to the solicitor, it should only take a week or ten days. I've already got a valuation of her entire estate to them, so hopefully it won't take too long."

"Huh," scoffed Frank, "you obviously haven't had many

30

dealings with the legal profession. They'll drag it out as long as they can to justify their extortionate fees, don't you worry."

"Let's hope not, eh?"

"So," Frank was feeling increasingly nervous and his heart was thumping in his chest. He took a deep breath before continuing. "I'd like us to meet up again, if you're willing that is, whenever suits you," he burbled.

"Actually, I was kind of thinking...say if you disagree."

"Yes, yes, thinking what?" The impatience was evident in his tone.

"Well, as you know, I've got to come as far as Chepstow, and I thought I might come a little further west and maybe stay with you for a few days, explore Devon a bit. After all, it was where mum was brought up. Obviously I don't have to stay with you, I..."

"No, no, I'd love to have you stay, I really would."

"Are you sure? You're not just saying that?" Dan asked tentatively.

"Of course not – don't be daft." *You're my son, for Christ's sake!*

"Okay, well that's great. I'll give you a call a few days before, shall I? Give you a bit of notice."

"Sure, no probs, like you might say."

"Right, I'll speak to you in a bit. Bye for now."

"Bye Dan. Take care."

As Frank replaced the phone, a wave of elation washed over him. His son was actually coming to stay under his roof and with any luck he'd stay for a while. They'd have the opportunity to get to know each other properly; maybe even work on the farm together. Dan would provide him with the perfect incentive to restock and restructure his business. He wouldn't bother with milking again, oh no; that was far too

31

much hassle. A beef herd, that'd be the way ahead: less work, but still providing a reasonable income.

And, who knows, maybe his son would stay on in England with him, the two of them working happily side by side on his farm together. Why not? Dan had already stated that he was in no immediate rush to return to the Antipodes. Would it be so far-fetched to envisage the lad settling down and marrying a local girl? Who knows, in a few years from now he might not only have a son in his life, but a daughter-in-law as well and perhaps several grandchildren too: that would bring the tired old farmhouse back to life. But hang on a minute, he was getting ahead of himself; he shouldn't let any fanciful ideas run away with him. For now, his main concern must be the boy's impending visit. It was time to give the spare bedroom a good clean - and a lick of paint on the old plastered walls wouldn't hurt either, come to that.

He trotted up the stairs and walked along the drab landing. Pushing open the door to the neglected spare bedroom, he cast a critical eye over the dusty interior. It was certainly a long time since anyone had bothered to do anything remotely resembling housework in here. Faded floral curtains hung dispiritedly on either side of the dirty window panes, their plastic runners liberally spotted with dried faecal remains left by several generations of houseflies. Desiccated husks of long dead bluebottles littered the windowsill, the insects having turned turtle in their death throes. *Why do flies always die on their backs?* he wondered pointlessly. There were a few morose dark patches of damp at the foot of the north-facing wall, and a particularly unpleasant stale musty smell oozed upwards between the mouldy floorboards and crept from the underside of the jaded peeling wallpaper. The room seemed, in its miserable abandoned state, to be in a worse condition than it really was. His eyes came to rest on a sagging stained mattress sprawling across an ancient iron bedstead. It was, without doubt, time to grasp the nettle.

Frank set about the task with grim determination by initially ripping down the curtains and their fixings. It took him the remainder of the morning to clean off all the mould and rid the place of spiders, their numerous filthy webs, and the dead flies. He also disposed of the bed and stripped the walls of their paper. This he tore off easily, some of it coming away in whole sheets, the paste long since having lifted from the dry old plaster beneath it. When his rumbling stomach hinted it was nearing time for lunch, the room was cleared and clean; the bare wiped-down walls stood ready to be decorated and shone faintly in the pale sunlight which was now able to penetrate the previously fogged window.

Three hours later, with the dying sun's orange rays gently kissing the bare crowns of tall beech trees higher up the eastern slopes of the valley and a cutting coldness rushing into the hollows, the farmhouse door flew open and Frank staggered inside, weighed down with several tins of paint which he gratefully set down on the floor. With a grunt, he straightened up and flicked on the light before going back to the Land Rover to retrieve the rest of the booty he'd garnered from the local DIY store.

He awoke the next day with an uncharacteristic feeling of joie de vivre and uplifting enthusiasm that he hadn't experienced in a very long time. Despite the dawn being damp and dreary, and the day soon turning wet and windy, he remained in buoyant mood. After a hasty breakfast, he set about painting the bedroom, covering the jaundiced and in places sagging plaster on the ceiling with a fresh bright coat of brilliant white emulsion, whose distinctive clean smell spread along the shabby landing, seeping into the other upstairs' rooms. As he ran the roller back and forth, a fine white drizzle settled on his arms and speckled his hair. He was happy in his work, snug and dry inside whilst the wind rattled the panes in the ill-fitting sash window, ice-cold raindrops tracking chaotically down the glass in the dismal depressing dankness outside.

By one o'clock he'd covered all the walls and the ceiling and was rather satisfied with the result. He'd stop for a bite to eat, by which time the paint would have dried enough to apply another coat to the walls. He squinted upwards at the ceiling, noting that it too would benefit from another going over. He glanced at the small amount of white emulsion remaining in the bottom of the tin and realised with dismay that there wasn't enough there. That being the case and being by nature a man careful with his money, Frank soon decided that the ceiling looked okay; after all, who would notice? Besides, it was still a hundred times better than before.

By the end of the afternoon he'd applied a second coat to the walls and they were now shining wetly in the jaundiced light emitted by the single bare bulb hanging in its fitting in the middle of the ceiling. He wasn't too sure of the colour, it was perhaps a bit *too* yellow, but the paint had been half-price, so it would do fine. After dousing the brushes and rollers under the kitchen tap, he left them to drain in the crazed, chipped Belfast sink.

He made a half-hearted attempt to wash the worst of the dried paint from his skin, and then, grabbing his jacket from a hook in the hall, made his way once more to his Land Rover. He reckoned he'd earned a pint.

If the landlord was surprised to see him for the second time after such a long absence, he didn't show it.

"Evening Frank, pint of the black stuff, is it?"

"Yes please, Pete." For his part, Frank was pleased to see that the place was practically empty. He nodded politely to the solitary customer at the bar to his left. The fellow barely acknowledged him; instead he gloomily contemplated the last inch or so of lager in the bottom of his glass. The only other patrons were a young couple whom Frank did not recognise sitting by the fire, their golden Labrador blissfully stretched out in front of it.

He climbed onto a stool and with exaggerated concentration started to roll himself a smoke.

"I'd make the most of it if I were you; you won't be able to do that next year."

"Eh?"

"Smoke. They're going to ban it in all public places, and that means pubs as well."

"Nah, it'll never happen; not in this country."

"Oh yes it will, they've already banned it in some places abroad, you just wait and see. It'll kill my trade, I know that much." With that, the landlord disconsolately plonked Frank's drink on the washed out frayed bar towel in front of him. A blob of creamy yellow foam meandered down the glistening cold glass.

"That'll be two-seventy, please."

"Two pounds seventy? Blimey Pete, never mind smoking; your prices will kill your trade long before any ban." He dug deep into the front pocket of his paint-bedecked trousers and yanked out a grimy and crumpled five-pound note which he handed over.

"There you go, two-thirty change."

"Ta." He pocketed the coins and lit his cigarette, inhaled deeply, exhaling the blue smoke luxuriantly a few seconds later.

"Been decorating, have you then?" Pete asked, in as casual a manner as he could muster.

"Well, sort of, I suppose. I just thought I'd tidy the place up really – it was beginning to get me down actually. To tell the truth, I've kind of let things slip a bit since…well, you know."

And so he did. *Since that bitch of a wife of yours abandoned you in your hour of need, you poor bugger.*

"Yeah, well it's good to freshen things up every now and then. Just look at the state of this place; it's about time I did some interior decorating myself."

Frank looked around the bar, taking in the faded stained carpet and the walls festooned with old ragged-looking beer-mats beneath a beamed ceiling whose plaster was not only yellowed with age and nicotine, but also wood smoke from the sometimes recalcitrant open fire.

"I wouldn't worry about it mate. I reckon it adds character to the pub. I mean, it would look horrible all shiny and white; it's taken years to perfect this kind of lived-in ambience, don't you think?"

The chubby landlord grunted noncommittally. "You're not taking the piss, are you?"

Frank smiled. "No, not at all - well maybe just a tad." He swiftly downed the rest of his pint.

"Refill?"

"Yes please; then I'd better make tracks. Oh no," he groaned, "not her again."

Pete chuckled to himself as he set another glass under the Guinness tap and easing the lever downward gently teased the smooth dark velvety liquid down its inside. "Good evening, Anne!" he greeted her with overstated ebullience, "you on your own tonight?"

"Oh no," came the coy reply, "Gerald's right behind me. Hello Frank, how nice to see you in here again so soon. We *are* honoured."

He smiled weakly at the dreadful woman.

"You look like you've been busy. Doing the old place up, are you?"

"Well no, hardly. Just a bit of titivating, that's all, nothing major."

"Well good for you anyway. You should take a leaf out of Frank's book, Peter. This pub is way overdue for a make-over. When was the last time these walls felt a paintbrush?"

"Well not for a while, that's for sure."

"No, quite a long while I'd say; wouldn't you, darling?"

Her hapless husband had now entered the bar, but seemed reluctant to be drawn in by her. "Oh I don't know, it looks alright to me. Gives the place a bit of atmosphere, don't you think? You know, character…"

"Ambience?"

"Yes Frank, that's it: ambience."

After the unwelcome appearance of the postmistress, Frank drank his second pint in haste, anxious to get away before the woman was able to start interrogating him again. Sliding off his stool, he mumbled goodbye to the company and with some relief left the pub.

Some time later, after an unsatisfactory supper of cheap sausages (which he'd burned badly) and mashed potatoes (conversely undercooked and lumpy), he dumped his empty plate in the sink and poured himself a generous measure of Scotch. Sitting back down, his nicotine-stained fingers dextrously fashioned a cigarette. As the rather too dry tobacco rustled in the thin paper, strands of it escaped from the open ends, scattering brown threads on the table beneath his spade-like hands. He lit the monstrosity, and leaning back in the chair, his long legs stretched out in front of him, gazed disinterestedly through the stark naked smudged glass of the kitchen window at the jet black nothingness outside. He inhaled a lungful of smoke, absent-mindedly tapping a small smattering of ash from the glowing end of his roll-up into the emptied out but still filthy heavy glass ashtray. Taking a soothing sip of whisky, his thoughts turned to the time, way back, when he'd been going out with Sally. He'd met her parents on a few occasions. Her mother, he recalled, seemed rather demure; rather like her daughter. Her father appeared to him to be very much 'of the old school', polite and pleasant, but also conveying an air of being somewhat baffled and bemused by the ways and workings of the modern world. Frank had certainly never met James. In fact, as he sifted through his memory he was sure there was never any mention of him by any member of the family; at least not in his presence. When he'd finished his fag, he ground the butt out in the thin layer of grey ash glued doggedly to the bottom of the ashtray like compacted fine volcanic sand, and knocked back the rest of his drink. Yawning expansively, he made his way upstairs to his cold bed. Once between the sheets, he was soon fast asleep.

Suddenly he was wide awake. It seemed to him that he'd only just dropped off, but a quick glance at the bedside clock told him that he'd been in the land of Nod for a good two and a half hours. What had wrenched him so violently from his slumber? Had he heard something? A shot perhaps? Poachers in the wood? He lay there with ears pricked, the inky darkness pressing in on him. No noise came to him in the still of the thick dark night.

After a few moments, he drifted off again. His sleep was

fitful, however: punctuated by disturbing images of dead cows and the scornful selfish rants of his ex-wife, berating him for being fool enough to persist in his vain attempts to save his beloved dairy herd. *Well they're gone NOW!* she screamed, spittle flying from her spiteful mouth. *So that was a total waste of time and effort! All by yourself now as well, aren't you? Aren't you! And stewing in your own stinking juices! Good, because you bloody deserve it!*

Once again he woke with a jolt, but was relieved this time to see a grey light framing the window. He lay there for a minute or two, whilst he tried to rid his fuddled mind of all the night's distressing scenes. Despite the dreams having upset him, he told himself that's all they were. Furthermore, he wasn't on his own now, was he? *See Isabel, I've got a son – and thank Christ he's not yours!*

He flicked on the light, whipped the bedclothes off, and started to get dressed.

He'd barely reached the foot of the stairs when he heard a loud rapping on the door. He flicked a switch in the hallway and weak yellow light from a solitary bulb strove valiantly to illuminate the dim corridor. He strode up to the solid old door and slipping the bolt, yanked it open. It shimmied inwards, scraping noisily on grey and uneven dirty flagstones. He made a mental note that although he'd swept the floor somewhat desultorily, it could really do with a good scrubbing. He also conceded, a little despondently, that the walls down here would also benefit from a lick of paint.

"Mr Anderson?" The cheerful enquiry distracted him immediately from his reverie.

"Yes?"

"One bed, antique pine finish, four foot six, complete with two matching bedside cabinets – also in antique pine.

Well they would be, wouldn't they? Can I have your autograph sir? In that little box at the bottom, if you wouldn't mind."

A delivery note clamped to a battered clipboard was thrust under his nose. "Here, you can use my pen."

"I ordered a mattress for it as well," Frank informed the lad as he scrawled his signature on the thin pink paper. "Don't you have that?"

"Mattresses are soft furnishings sir," replied the driver. "Different department. Be with you tomorrow I expect, or perhaps later on today if they're coming this way."

Frank noted the condescending tone in the young man's reply, but chose to ignore it. "Just leave it all here would you? I'll sort it out later."

Right, sure, anything you say, guv. And thanks for the offer to help. With the cheery smile wiped from his pock-marked face, the delivery driver returned to his van and crossly pulled open its sliding side-door.

After a leisurely breakfast, Frank clumped upstairs with the various packaged pieces of bed and cabinets, and set about putting them together on the bare floorboards in the bedroom. He'd initially thought to lay a fitted carpet in the room, but had since been deterred by the cost. After all, his son was a tough Aussie: a rug each side of the bed would suffice. He'd managed to fix the headboard loosely to the frame when he heard the sound of his daily paper flumping onto the floor downstairs, having been unceremoniously and forcibly thrust through the too small letterbox. *Time for a coffee.*

CHAPTER FOUR

The shop bell jangled irritably as Frank pulled the glass-panelled door open. There seemed an inordinate amount of women inside, and they all stopped talking as he entered.

"Morning ladies; not a bad one is it?" They stared at him as if he were mad. Anne could contain herself no longer.

"You haven't heard then?" she blurted out, a little too quickly.

"Heard what?"

"About *Tom*," a buxom woman interjected. Frank recognized her as the well-fleshed wife of a weasel-faced sourpuss of a man whose farm straddled the main road to the east of the village.

"Tom?"

"Tom Sanger!" She answered. Frank's blank face registered no sign of recognition. "Bob's boy, you know, a bit..."

"Oh yes!" It had suddenly dawned on him who the subject of their gossip was. Tom had always been a bit simple and rumours had abounded for years as to the cause. Sally, the woman now conversing with him, was convinced that he'd been dropped on his head as a baby. *"You may snigger, but it does happen – and more often than you'd credit, I reckon."* Anne took a more intelligent stance on the matter; she reasoned the lad's mother had endured a long and traumatic labour, resulting in the infant being starved of oxygen for a while and causing damage to his brain. Mrs. Manning, who sold fresh

41

eggs and milk from her farm on the edge of the village and who was also in all probability the biggest wind bag of them all, blamed the boy's lack of intelligence on his parents. *"There's some that shouldn't have children, and some that should, that's all I'll say about it,"* she let slip enigmatically whenever the subject was raised. She had no idea why she said this, save that it pleased her to sound as if she knew more than she was willing to divulge. Truth to tell, none of them had any idea why the child had turned out the way he had. Bob was a man who very much kept himself to himself; as for his wife Elizabeth, she had tragically died when her son was just five years old after succumbing quickly to breast cancer. Her husband had up to now not remarried, and it looked increasingly likely that he never would. To many it was a miracle he'd ever got hitched at all. He'd never been a sociable fellow; he'd in fact employed his future wife for a few months during the summer when she was a student to help with the harvest. She'd subsequently lost her education, but he gained a pretty young bride.

"Anyway," Sally continued before any of the others could butt in and steal her thunder, "seems like he's shot himself."

"What, you mean..."

"Now we don't know that for sure," interrupted the postmistress, "none of us know exactly what happened."

"Except he's dead," Sally speedily riposted.

"Dead?" Frank uttered in astonishment. "Are you sure?"

"Absolutely positive. Bob told you himself, didn't he Marge?" the plump woman proclaimed triumphantly.

"Yes, I'm afraid he did," Mrs. Manning confirmed sadly. "He came round about eight and told me Tom had had an accident with his gun - he found him himself in the woods near your place Frank. There was nothing to be done."

"Good God, poor bugger," he muttered, and then they were all silent for a moment or two.

"So, what can I get you, Frank?" Anne piped up.

"What? Oh, I just need a small loaf please - that one's fine," he said pointing. "And I'd better have a packet of baccy as well."

"Of course," replied Anne, smiling broadly. "Golden Virginia, isn't it?"

"That's right." Frank squeezed past the ladies to the counter, and proferred a ten-pound note. Anne handed over the goods then turned to get his change. This she counted back to him, dropping the coins into his dirt-engrained palm. She couldn't quite hide the feeling of disgust she felt as she noticed his black ragged fingernails and the yellow nicotine-stained skin on his fingers.

"Lovely job, thanks very much." Once more the bell jingled belligerently as he yanked the door open. "You will let me know, won't you, about the arrangements for the funeral?" he asked.

Anne was quick to answer. "Yes of course, Frank. We'll let you know as soon as we hear anything."

"Thank you." He closed the door behind him and pulled up his collar against the fat cold raindrops starting to slant down from the flat featureless blanket of slate-grey cloud.

As he walked along the road, the rain began to spatter on the surface, turning it darker. Very soon it was raining steadily, the water running in an ever-expanding rivulet along the sides of the highway, rushing away down the occasional steel grid of a drain, or shooting off at a tangent into channels cut through the earth banks. *So I wasn't dreaming then,* he mused, *when I heard the shot in the night it must have been poor old Tom. Maybe he just tripped over something and the gun went off. God knows, enough of those sorts of accidents happen all the time.* But for some reason, he had the certain feeling deep inside that this was not the case, that in fact the poor boy had ended his life in a desperate moment of dark despair. Perhaps he knew this because he'd almost managed to pull the same stunt himself. Maybe he was sure this was no accident because he too had contemplated suicide: was that possible? His train of thoughts was interrupted by a white transit van beeping at his back. He squeezed into the dripping hedge to let it go past, then an old red Volvo pulled up beside him, speckling his calves with drops of muddy water. The windscreen wipers swished noisily back and forth as the driver's window wound down squeakily.

"Morning, Frank, I suppose you've heard about poor Tom?" Pete asked.

"Yes, I've just come from the Post Office. I was actually wondering if I should go and see Bob, not that I really know the man well - what do you reckon? You know him better than me."

"Hardly - God knows when he came in the pub last - certainly not since his missus died; she was the one that used to drag him out occasionally." He chuckled softly. "I remember them coming in years ago; she'd shamed him into taking her out for a meal. When she asked what he was going to eat he said he wasn't that hungry. She had a right old go at him - she knew, you see, that he was really trying to avoid spending his money. She ordered a starter, mains, and a pud while he sat there miserably with his steak and chips."

"Oh."

"Any road up, I'd leave Bob alone - he won't thank you for your concern. And don't expect any announcements about a funeral; it'll be a private affair, on the q.t."

"Perhaps I'll write him a note, just to show I'm thinking of him."

"Yeah, that'd be a good idea. Anyway, must scoot - time to open up. See you soon." He wound up the window and pulled away, leaving a small blue cloud of exhaust gas hanging sullenly above the ground. Frank quickened his step as the rain started to fall harder, thinking that his former bright idea earlier that morning of a brisk walk to the village was not one of his wisest.

By the time he reached the lane to the farmhouse, water was coursing along the verges under the high Devon banks. His feet were thoroughly soaked and his shabby leather shoes squelched as he hurried along. The rain had set in, heavy and persistent. Cold water seeped beneath his collar, making him shiver involuntarily as it trickled down his spine. He brusquely pulled the lapels of his grubby donkey jacket together. Holding them tight in his clenched fist and stooping slightly against the foul weather, he trotted the last hundred yards or so to his front door. As cold fingers fumbled for a key in a soggy pocket, he glimpsed something in the corner of his eye, tucked behind the decrepit wooden door of one of the outhouses which stood ajar, leaning drunkenly at an angle, due to the absence of its upper hinge. It was the mattress he'd ordered for the bed, wrapped in a plastic sheet and propped against the wall. He unlocked the door, leaving a trail of wet footprints on his way into the kitchen. Dumping his shopping on the table, he turned and made his way outside again to retrieve it. With little enthusiasm, he decided to have a bite of lunch and then tackle the construction of the bed and cabinets anew.

Darkness had fallen by the time Frank finally had all the bedroom furniture assembled. Groaning, he stiffly raised himself up from his knees and ripped the plastic cover from the mattress, unceremoniously heaving it onto the frame of the bed. *There, thank Christ that's done.* He considered he'd earned a pint. Scrunching up the plastic sheet, he gathered it under one arm and descended the stairs. On reaching the bottom, he flung it to the back of the hallway, in the general direction of the little-used lounge, where it lay in the gloom, crinkling as it slowly unfurled, like a lethargic serpent uncoiling in the rising heat of the summer sun. He banked up the range in the kitchen, gathered the keys to the Land Rover, stuffed a couple of ten-pound notes from the cluttered table drawer into his trouser pocket, and shrugging on his warm donkey jacket that had by now dried on the back of a chair, he went out into the cold night, firmly shutting the door behind him. The rain had ceased falling an hour or so since, and beneath the clear night sky the temperature was rapidly plummeting. He could clearly see his way across the concrete to the spot where his Land Rover was parked, the green paintwork shining like wet gloss paint under the pale ghostly light of a full moon and a myriad of twinkling white stars strewn across the black heavens. He pulled up his coat collar against the penetrating cold. Approaching the vehicle, his warm breath rolling in front of him and curling away spookily into the night, he noticed that the dirt-smeared windscreen was already turning opaque; glazing over like a dead creature's eyes as a hard frost began to take hold. He felt a momentary pang as he was reminded of the horrific spectacle of his dead cattle lying in grotesque bloated lumps, their malodorous corpses dotted higgledy-piggledy across the bleached concrete of his farmyard in the warm spring air. The shiver that fleetingly ran through him was not due entirely to the weather. Climbing into the driver's seat, he slammed the door noisily and wiped the grubby windscreen with the back of his hand.

Firing up the engine, he turned on the demister fan full bore and engaged the wipers to melt away the frost. He drove carefully up the lane, peering through the dome-shaped gap on the misty glass, which steadily fanned outwards like the bursting brightness of a June sunrise. The ineffective yellowy beams of the vehicle's headlights feebly illuminated the way. He pulled up on the patchy tarmac of The Golden Fleece's car park and extricated himself from the uncomfortable vehicle. The glass in the driver's window rattled in protest as he slammed the door shut and hurried towards the welcoming warmth of the saloon bar. Closing the door firmly behind him, he was surprised to see so many people in there. The homely fire was roaring in the background, the occasional puff of wood smoke escaping the draw of the chimney and blowing out into the room to add to the hazy atmosphere. Frank, rather than be comforted by the conviviality the hubbub and chatter fashioned, instead felt disconcerted.

"Evening Frank, be with you in a minute! Pint of the black stuff, is it?"

"Oh...yes please, Pete," the other replied a little wanly. Finding a small gap at the bar, Frank deposited his tobacco tin and set about rolling himself a cigarette. Unsettled by the number of people around him, once he had his pint he backed off to a small unoccupied table in the far corner. Looking about him at the company, he was disappointed to see that Anne and her sycophantic husband were once again present, deep in conversation with a young couple he did not recognize on the other side of the room. At least they had not appeared to notice him. Even above the babble of the other punters, Frank could occasionally catch snatches of conversation, mainly thanks to the volume of Anne's aggravating voice, and it was clear to him where her main topic for tittle-tattle lay.

"Yes, well that's right, that's what we thought, didn't we, Gerald? I mean, he was never right...wouldn't be surprised if he'd..." Her long-suffering husband sat by her side, every now and then nodding in agreement as well as stifling more than one yawn as she gabbled on excitedly, poor Tom unwittingly providing her with one of the best targets for gossip she'd had for some time.

Poor bloody lad - well at least the bitch's leaving me alone.

"Hello Frank! How are you? You're practically a stranger!" A huge man sporting a brown checked trilby emerged from the door leading to the Gents and towered over him, head practically brushing the dirty ceiling. Frank pulled himself to his feet and extended his hand, hoping vaguely that the other, considering where he'd just come from, had washed his. Long fat fingers curled around his own digits, clasping him in a firm handshake which made his arm quake right up to the shoulder blade.

"You restocked yet?" And before he had a chance to respond, "Mind you, dairy cows are making good money - but still, you got paid out well enough for yours I suppose, didn't you?"

"Yes I did," Frank replied with a hint of indignation, thinking of adding that he'd rather have his animals than any amount of compensation, but deciding against it. "Actually Toby, I was thinking of starting a beef herd - but not before the spring," he added hastily.

"Oh right! Well I might be able to help you there." The dealer glanced at Frank's near-empty glass. "Can I get you another?"

"Erm, thank you, yes; Guinness please."

"Right you are." Toby lumbered off to the bar. Although Frank was wary of doing business with the cattle dealer, he wasn't about to pass up the opportunity for a free drink. In any case, it would do no harm to put out some feelers by letting the man know he was on the lookout for some animals.

"There you go." Toby handed him the brimming pint glass, creamy froth sliding slug-like down its side forming bearded black droplets on its base which dripped despondently onto the polished wooden tabletop. He plonked another slopping pint onto it and, looking round, dragged a chair from the neighbouring table, gratefully setting his unwieldy bulk upon it.

"Well, cheers then, good health."

"Yes, cheers."

The dealer took an enormous draught of beer and put down the half-empty glass, wiping his upper lip with the hairy back of his hand in appreciation. "That's better. Now, do you have any idea what breed you might want to go for, and how many? I know of some nice Aberdeen Angus coming on the market soon; I'm sure they'd suit very well - just right for what you want."

Frank thought it best to curb the man's enthusiasm. "I actually haven't given it much thought yet. Like I said, I don't intend to set anything up before next spring." He grasped his mug by its meaty glass handle, and drank some of the opaque black liquid.

"Well, whatever and whenever you decide what you want, give me a call, eh? I may well be able to help." The bulky trader devoured the rest of his beer in one huge swallow, and with palms firmly placed on the table before him, heaved his considerable frame onto equally considerable feet.

"Another pint?" Frank asked apprehensively.

"Oh no, no; that's me done - better get on, I'm already late."

"Right. Well thanks for the drink; I'll let you know about the cattle."

"You do that. You've got one of my cards haven't you?"

"Er yes…somewhere."

"Here," he poked two fat fingers into the breast pocket of his tweed jacket and prised out a rather aged and dog-eared business card. "I know what you blokes are like," he grinned, "probably lost the one I gave you before."

Mumbling his thanks Frank pocketed the offering, then bade him goodbye. Watching Toby trundle heavily past the bar towards the exit, he realized that Anne was regarding him quizzically. Hastily he gulped down the remainder of his beer. Yellow froth slothfully oozed down the inside of the empty glass as he placed it on the table and rose purposefully to go. Suddenly the postmistress was there, blocking his path.

"Good evening Frank, did you get your delivery alright?"

"Sorry?"

"This morning, just after you left the shop, I gave the man directions. Did he find you alright with the, er, whatever it was he had for you?"

"Oh yes, he did. In fact the item was there when I got back, thank you." *Item? Well, he was buggered if he was going to tell the nosey cow what it was.*

"Oh good. Something else for your home improvements, was it?"

"Yes Anne, something like that." He attempted to edge past her, but as he tried to do so she leaned across and whispered hotly and urgently in his ear.

"Have you seen anything of Bob?"

"Bob? No. Why? Should I have?" he asked, already irked by her conspiratorial manner.

"Oh no, no reason, it's just I thought, well, you know, you

50

might have heard more about how poor old Tom...apparently it *was* suicide you know."

"Really?" he replied testily, before continuing swiftly: "To be perfectly honest Anne, I've got better things to do with my time than listen to idle tittle-tattle and…"

"Oh yes of course, I quite agree. I didn't mean, you know…" she flustered, "…it would just be nice to find out for sure what actually happened."

"Well I'm sorry but I can't help you," he snapped, prohibiting any further probing by the ghastly woman on the subject. He strode past her and edged his way through the throng at the bar to the exit. It was with some relief that he found himself outside in the cold night air. *Bloody bitch of a woman,* he thought angrily as he crossed the glossy tarmac under the unforgiving glare of two ferocious halogen spotlights perched high on the pub's white wall. He retrieved Toby's card then used it to scrape away the haze of frost which was already clouding the Land Rover's windscreen. Pouching it once more, he climbed into the old vehicle and drove off, leaving a faint blue puff of exhaust smoke hanging lazily above the ground. This slowly and languidly began to thin out, stealing into the wider night, dissolving beneath the pale milky light of a watery moon.

Pete was to be proved right. A week passed, and no one was any the wiser as to the cause of Tom's demise, although the favourite theory amongst the locals was one of suicide. There were no announcements in any newspaper referring to the boy's death, national or local. (Anne was thorough in her hawk-like scanning of these pages every day in all the various publications.) Bob had spoken to nobody about the incident and even the gossip-mongering postmistress was not brazen enough to broach the subject personally with him.

On yet another cold evening, starless and moonless under a dense covering of cloud and black as a cow's guts, Frank had just finished another unsatisfactory supper when there was a timid knock on his front door. Pushing his cleared plate aside, he rose to his feet with a grunt to see who could possibly want to see him at this time of night. Dragging the heavy door inwards, he was more than surprised and somewhat disconcerted to see Bob on the step.

"Bob! How are you?" he enquired with genuine concern in his voice. "Sorry – stupid question. Come in, come in." He ushered his neighbour into the kitchen. "Sit down. Can I get you a drink? Scotch maybe?"

"Thanks Frank, that'd be good." He pulled out a chair and fell heavily into it, wordlessly watching as the other poured two generous shots of whisky into two greasy-looking tumblers that had clearly been previously washed up in a far less than thorough manner.

"There we go then. Water?"

"Just a drop." Frank passed Bob his drink and took a seat opposite him. They sat, not in a companionable but more in an awkward silence. Frank waited for Bob to open the conversation, but after a few minutes the tension was getting too much and prompted by the Dutch courage afforded him from the Scotch, he said purposefully: "I was really sorry to hear about your boy, Bob."

"Yeah, well, thanks for writing."

The other dismissed this with a wave of his hand. "Don't be daft; it was the least I could do."

Bob took a mouthful of the malt, swilled it round thoughtfully and then swallowed noisily. "Look Frank, I know we're not close buddies or anything, but we've known each other a long time and, well…I need you to do something for me."

"Of course," he replied calmly as a wave of dread swept through his stomach. "Fire away."

Bob sighed deeply. "Thing is, I'm getting pissed off with all this tittle-tattle. Whenever I see anyone in the village, I know they're all wondering about what happened to Tom. I can't face them. I want *you* to tell them the truth, then perhaps they'll find something or somebody else to gossip about and we can all move on."

"Right, sure," Frank answered with a confidence he didn't even remotely feel. "Can I get you a refill?"

Once more a deathly silence enveloped them, broken this time by Bob.

"You can tell them that Tom took his own life..."

"Oh Bob."

"Let me just get this out - please."

"Sorry."

"I guess the poor boy had just had enough. You know about his problems - I think they just overtook him. He was certainly more withdrawn than usual in the days before, but I never in my wildest dreams imagined he'd..." His voice trailed off and his chin began to wobble. Reaching for his glass, he swirled the contents around distractedly then knocked back a generous mouthful of whisky. "Anyway," he continued, "without going into details there's little doubt he intended to take his life." His voice cracked on this last word as his eyes welled with tears. Sniffing noisily, he resolutely blinked them back.

"I see," said Frank quietly, "so was there, um, a note or something?"

"No, but apparently that's not all that unusual..."

"Oh." A fleeting flashback jumped into his head as he remembered his own botched attempt to end his life. Silence wrapped itself around them once more and Frank wondered if he ought to pour some more drinks. He quickly decided against it. The man had already downed two generous measures, and he had to drive home. In his mental state, another one would do more harm than good. Besides, there wasn't much left in the bottle, and he'd want a tot himself after his unwanted visitor had gone. Time to get rid of him.

"Right Bob, I'll do that for you first thing tomorrow, and thanks for coming to me." This latter remark immediately seemed out of place, and he suddenly felt embarrassed. Bob drained the last small drop of his whisky and rose to leave. Frank solemnly shook hands with his misanthropic neighbour at the door.

"Mind how you go now."

"Yes. Thank you."

Frank stood and watched as the beams from Bob's headlights lit up the gloom between the high Devon banks as his car snaked steadily up the hill. When it reached the top and turned out of sight, with these bars of light appearing to stab manically at the impenetrably black heavens, Frank pushed the unwieldy heavy oak door firmly shut, locking out the chill night. No sooner had he drawn the sturdy steel bolt across the top than the telephone broke the stillness with its shrill insistent ringing, petulantly demanding his immediate attention. He strode crossly down the hall and snatched the receiver from the cradle, swiftly cutting off its persistent cries.

"Yes?" he all but shouted into the mouthpiece.

"Oh, er hi Frank – is this a bad time?"

His heart leapt when he heard his son's voice on the end of the line. "Hello Dan: no, not at all. Are you okay? How're things going up there in the Smoke? Sorting everything out alright?"

"Yeah, yeah, pretty good. Might be one little hiccup, but I'll explain that later. Er look, I was planning to come down your way next week - probably Thursday or Friday, if that's still cool with you."

Cool? "Yes of course it is - let me know what time the train gets in and I'll pick you up at the station."

"There's really no need to do that, I'm sure I can find my own way to the f…"

"Don't be daft, it's no trouble at all," his father interrupted.

"Well if you're sure, that'd be great. Thanks."

"No worries, as you 'Strines might say," Frank replied, with an ill-conceived attempt at humour. He abruptly changed tack. "So what's this little hiccup, then?"

"What? Oh, like I said, I'll explain when I see you. It's probably nothing; just solicitors drawing things out like you said, trying to justify their exorbitant charges."

"Right, well they're certainly good at that."

The two of them chatted amicably for a while before Dan hung up. Frank emptied the last of the Scotch into his glass, dropped onto a chair in the warm kitchen and rolled a cigarette, meanly pinching out the ends and returning a few wispy strands of tobacco to his tin. He flicked a lighter, leaned back and inhaled deeply. As he exhaled, he tried to occupy his mind with the pleasant prospect of having his son to stay, but his thoughts remained stubbornly fixed on the tragic plight of Tom, and his own reluctant undertaking to confirm to the locals the tragic cause of his death. After a while, he stubbed out his smoke, gulped down his drink, and trudged up the bare wooden treads of the stairs to his cold bed. Despite the initial soporific effect of the alcohol, he awoke after only a few hours, spending the rest of the night dozing fitfully. Around six o'clock he gave up all notion of a decent sleep, pushed away his blankets, and shuffled downstairs in search of a soothing cup of tea.

Five minutes before eight found him sitting in his Land Rover outside the village shop. Fingers drummed nervously on the dashboard as he waited for it to open. To distract himself, he switched on the radio.

"Randy Crawford there with 'One day I'll fly away' or was it 'One day I'll weigh a fly?' I'm never sure which," the Irishman burbled pleasantly.

Frank started when suddenly with bell jingling the shop door flew open. The postmistress latched it to a hook in the wall, bent to pick up a bundle of newspapers dumped on the tarmac, and scuttled back inside, stooping slightly under its weight. He hurriedly pushed a button on the radio, cutting off the inane banter in its tracks. Slamming the vehicle's door shut, he followed her into the shop. He was about to make her day.

CHAPTER FIVE

James hurled the phone onto the table in disgust. Landing on its end, the plastic cover flicking off, it bounced into the air disgorging its gold and black batteries before falling to the dirty carpeted floor. He sat fuming for a while, oblivious to the irritating squawking of herring-gulls outside the grimy casement windows of his third floor flat.

He'd only heard that his mother had died by chance a week or so ago. One of his drinking cronies in the dive he regularly frequented had seen the announcement in 'The Daily Telegraph'. He'd managed to eventually establish that he'd not been provided for in her will by correctly guessing that she would have still used the same firm of solicitors to draw it up as he knew she and his father had employed when he was a child. How could she have denied him his inheritance? It was his by right! Especially now his little sister was dead too. All because of something stupid that happened years before; something silly that he bore the full brunt of blame for – not her, the little bitch, oh no. Daddy's blue-eyed little girl could get away with murder in his eyes. He'd hoped at the time that his mother might have been more sympathetic towards him; but no, obviously not. And time apparently hadn't altered her view either. Instead, she'd cut him off without a penny. He had figured he'd a good chance of contesting the will successfully but the conversation that had just finished between himself and a so-called legal expert, enthusiastically recommended to him by his own solicitor, proved more than disappointing: it appeared he'd have little chance of seeing a judgment in his favour - and of course, whatever the outcome, it would cost a lot of money.

"But surely, *surely,*" he'd insisted over the phone, "I'm *entitled.* Anyone can see that."

"I'm sorry, Mr. Ward, but I have to say that I can't share your confidence. Your mother was clearly of a sound mind when she drew up the document, and there are obviously no grounds to suspect coercion by your sister as she was on the other side of the world at the time..."

"But I'm *entitled,*" he repeated again in stubborn desperation. "Can't we contest that I was...I don't know...just overlooked or something?" His anger was increasing by the second.

"Well...there has been limited success along those lines in a few cases - but I must stress I think we'd be on pretty thin ice if we tried that approach here."

"So that's it then, is it? Everything due to me goes to her boy, does it? That's just dandy!"

"And his sister as I understand it...Mr. Ward, I'm only giving you my professional opinion. Of course, if you wish me to act on your behalf, I would be glad to receive your instructions, but as I've already said..."

James' fury overwhelmed him at that point. "Right, well thank you very fucking much for your valuable time and help!" he yelled into the phone before flinging it down.

He sat sullenly for a while, trying to calm down and think of some other way of getting his hands on what he erroneously thought to be his rightful legacy. Eventually he could see no way of achieving this, and so he decided that the best thing to do, as he had before when faced with seemingly insurmountable problems - and there had been more than a few such occasions - was to go and have a drink. That would help him think; do him good. Of course it would.

Four hours later saw him stagger across the hall and struggle for several minutes to unlock his door. He fell inside, clumsily dropped the latch, and supporting himself against the wall, tottered to his bedroom where he collapsed, fully clothed, onto the unmade bed. Within seconds, the whole flat reverberated to the sound of his porcine snores.

The sun had long since struggled above the grey horizon into a cloudless pale washed winter sky and was shedding feeble rays of light through the opaque panes of the bedroom window by the time James awoke the following morning. He felt pretty rough after the previous day's drinking, but this was hardly unusual. He had for some time now considered that life had dealt him a bad hand, failing to see that all of his woes were due entirely to his own shortcomings. Overweight and unattractive, he took little pride in his appearance and although he was not unintelligent, his career had never progressed further than a minor hack for a small provincial newspaper. This was not only because of his obsession that everybody had it in for him, but was also due to the irrefutable fact that his social skills were all but non-existent. All through his life he'd had few friends, no one ever that he'd describe as close, and women in particular found him odious and in some cases frightening. He yanked off his creased faded tweed sports jacket, patched at the elbows, and lobbed it over the foot of the bedstead. After pulling off the rest of his clothes, he abandoned them in an unruly heap on the floor and stomped off naked to the bathroom. As it was now Saturday, he opined that a shower would be in order before he readied himself for another long lunch in the grubby bar where he felt most at ease. No doubt the dubious company he kept there would be sympathetic when told of yet another misfortune to befall him.

It occurred to him as he stepped out of the shower a little later that it might be possible to approach his sister's boy himself and plead his case. Perhaps, if he were to meet with him in person, he could appeal to his better nature, and make the boy see that his uncle was at the very least entitled to something from his own mother's estate. But it was still a daunting task. He briskly rubbed himself down with a somewhat damp-smelling towel that to most people's minds should have been washed some time since, and chucked it unceremoniously into the corner of the bathroom. He peered at his rotund face in the small pitted shaving mirror on the stained sill above the grubby basin. A shave wouldn't have come amiss, but he couldn't be bothered with that today. Rummaging through the most recent pile of unironed laundry he found socks, a shirt and one pair of underpants. He shrugged the clothes on, vaguely thinking that he ought really do a load of washing. Instead, he scooped up some pound coins together with a few crumpled banknotes on the side and went out. There was little point in preparing any breakfast himself; the milk would undoubtedly be off by now and he hadn't bought a loaf of bread in several days. He'd grab a bite to eat somewhere - or more likely than not have a liquid lunch.

It was half past eleven when he pushed open the door into the dimly lit bar. Cigarette smoke idly drifted beneath the nicotine-stained ceiling, hideously bedecked, as were the walls, with dark plastic beams.

Surprisingly, even at this early hour, the pub was doing a brisk trade.

"Morning, James, usual?"

"Please," he replied curtly, settling onto a tatty washed out red bar stool and shaking his newspaper open.

"Alright Jimmy?" a small voice questioned beside him. He failed to respond. He didn't like to be called Jimmy.

"Only you seem a bit hacked off..." the voice trailed away. James folded up the paper noisily and flung it on the sticky melamine surface of the bar. He took a swig of beer.

"Well you could say that, Robby. But then, anyone would be in my position."

"Oh." The other was beginning to wish he hadn't asked. What sort of mess had he got himself into this time? he wondered. Doubtless he was about to be enlightened. James explained his predicament - at length.

When he'd finished recounting his tale of woe, his friend sat quietly, trying to think of a suitable response. After a minute or so, he responded as aptly as he could.

"Well you could try talking to him I suppose, but from what you've just told me, I don't think you've got a cat's chance in hell."

"Oh thanks, that makes me feel a whole lot better, mate."

"Okay, let's look at the facts. You fell out years ago, right? Over something you say was trivial - but you won't tell me what. Whatever happened back then, obviously your mother and sister took it much more seriously. I mean, none of you've spoken to each other since - you've never even met your nephew - and here you are, actually considering asking him to concede that you have some right to part of his inheritance! I'm sorry Jim, but I don't see it: I don't see it at all."

"But don't you realize - he's getting what's rightfully mine!"

Robby sighed. "I wouldn't think like that if I were you,

because whether he is or whether he isn't, you ain't gonna get a penny from him, not to my way of thinking, unless the boy's a complete fool and takes pity on you or something. That's hardly likely though, is it? I mean, what's his mother told him about you, eh? Nothing very flattering, that's for sure."

"I must admit, it is a bit of a long shot."

"More than a bit, I'd say. Best to forget all about it, part of life's rich tapestry and all that. Come on, I'll get you another beer."

"Yeah okay, thanks." He drained his glass expertly. "I still think it's worth a try - after all, I've got nothing to lose, have I? It isn't as if us falling out's going to make any difference to our lives, is it? And Sally wouldn't have slagged me off to the boy, I'm sure of that. She'd not have said anything to him, it wouldn't have been her style. She was one for the quiet life. No, I still think it's worth a try..."

"So you're going to tear off to Oz, are you, on a hopeless mission?"

"Oh no," he smiled, "the lad's still over here in London, came over to care for his gran in her last days, bless him."

Robby passed him his beer, shaking his head in disbelief at the foolishness of his friend. "You're just heading for more upset Jim: you really shouldn't go looking for him, you really shouldn't."

But James had made up his mind.

Mandy turned the burnished brass knob and slipped through the imposing glossy front door, past a mahogany umbrella stand and the obligatory palm in a pot. The large Georgian town house lay in a quiet leafy cul-de-sac in one of the more salubrious parts of south London. Approached by a short flight of stone steps, decorated either side with lustrous black iron railings whose candy-twist spikes glistened with fresh gold paint, the building sported three polished brass plaques on its brick façade, informing whosoever arrived there of the business occupants on the first three floors. The girl briskly walked along the rather grand reception hall, the colourful Victorian floor tiles of which still shone wetly from their recent swabbing, and unlocked a door on the right. The slightly pompous inscription above, again on a brass plate, bore the proud legend: HUTCHISON, SMEETH AND HUTCHISON. SOLICITORS. EST 1898. FIRST FOR FAMILY LAW.

She flicked on the light, shrugged off her skimpy faux fur coat and hung it on a hook behind the door, then gathered the mail that had spewed onto the floor, piling it on her desk. As she opened the blinds on the huge sash windows the phone began to ring. Glancing at the wall behind her, she saw that it was barely nine o'clock. Mandy ignored the relentless clamour. She plugged in the drinks machine, flicked it on, then sat down and began sorting through the post. The phone stopped after a short while. It started up again a few moments later. She tut-tutted and lifted the receiver to her ear.

"H.S.H Solicitors…Good morning, how may I help you?"

A ragged voice from the end of the line -

"Oh, good morning. Is ,er, I mean, could I perhaps speak to Mr. Hutchison please?"

"Mr. Andrew or Mr. Clive?" She inspected the fingernails on her left hand with a critical eye.

"I'm sorry, what?…Oh, I don't know, Mr. Hutchison senior, I suppose."

"That would be Mr. Andrew."

"Oh, right."

"I'm afraid he's not in the office yet, he usually gets in

63

around nine forty-five. Can I take a message? Or ask him to call you back?"

"Erm, well it *is* sort of personal..."

"Of course, ask him to call you back then, shall I?"

"Yes, thank you."

"Right. So it's Mr...? Right, I see, as in hospital. And can I tell him what you might be ringing in connection with? Oh yes, your mother. I see. I'll make sure he gets in touch. Thank you Mr. Ward." Sighing, she rose from her chair to see if the drinks dispenser might be ready to furnish her with a cup of hot coffee.

Nearly two long hours passed, and James was on the cusp of ringing again when his telephone burst merrily into life. He snatched it from its housing.

"Mr. Ward? Andrew Hutchison. I'm sorry to take so long returning your call - one of those days, I'm afraid." A brief chortle floated down the line. "How may I be of assistance?"

James plunged recklessly in. "I want to get in touch with Dan, have you got his contact details?"

A slight pause at the other end, then, "Well yes, of course I have them. May I ask why? I mean, only this morning I've received a letter from a Mr. Atkinson. On your behalf he informs me that you no longer wish to contest your mother's will. Is that the current position, or are you telling me something different?"

"Oh no, no, that's right...only I just wanted to meet him, to...well...I thought, if I don't contest the will, he may, sort of *consider* me."

Mr. Hutchison senior did not like the way in which this conversation was heading. He felt his anger rising.

"Mr. Ward, if you feel aggrieved, then you must pursue the matter through the proper channels. Am I correct in assuming that the reason you have decided not to do this is a direct result of sound legal advice? In fact, to put it bluntly, that you have no realistic chance of success?"

"No, well not exactly…that is, I just thought…"

"I've a pretty shrewd idea of what you're thinking Mr. Ward. I'll inform Mr. Hussey of this conversation and what you wish from him. As his solicitor, I will naturally offer him my advice if it is sought. Obviously this will be entirely to his advantage. I trust this makes the matter plain to you."

"Oh yes, it's certainly that. Thank you for your time."

"A pleasure, good day Mr…" But there was no need to continue the exchange. Mr. Hutchison could only hear the monotonous dull dialling tone in his ear. He replaced the phone in its base unit, and pressed a button on his intercom with a perfectly manicured finger, admiring for the nth time the chunky 18 carat gold cufflinks his wife had given him on the occasion of their thirtieth wedding anniversary a couple of months before.

"Mandy? Has Mr. Simons arrived yet?"

"Not yet, it's not quite half past."

"Good, then I've got time for a quick cup of coffee. I feel in need of a boost. Can you be a dear and fetch me one? And do I have his file?"

"Yes. I have it here. I'll bring it through with the coffee."

Later that same day, Dan received a call from the advocate detailing the conversation he'd had with his estranged uncle.

"Blimey," the boy uttered at the end of it. "I've never even met the guy. He suddenly appears out of nowhere after God knows how many years, contests his mother's will, drops his claim, and now this. I don't know what to think. Maybe I should let him have a few thousand once the house is sold, just to get him off my back."

"Mr. Hussey, far be it for me to influence any decision you might arrive at in this matter. If your natural honesty and good nature, shall we say, suggests you give the man some form of remuneration, so be it. However, let me stress that in the eyes of the law he is due not one single penny, attested by the fact that both your mother and grandmother severed all connections with him some time ago for I'm told some serious misdemeanour, the nature of which neither one of them chose to make me privy to."

"Are you telling me that my grandmother *specifically* told you that she didn't want to leave her only son a bean?"

"Clearly, whatever dialogue took place between us at the drawing up of the will remains, and will remain, confidential. Her wishes are expressed quite visibly within it. But, like I said, if your conscience is pricked, then you should act as you see fit. I would warn you, however, that the man has a history and I seriously doubt once he got in contact with you that you'd be able to shrug him off that easily, even with a generous cash gift."

"Oh...perhaps I'd better leave that particular viper's nest undisturbed then."

"Very wise." *And a pretty accurate analogy.* "Obviously now we have written notice of intent not to proceed against you as rightful legatee, we can start working towards probate. Your grandmother kept her affairs in order, and we should achieve this hopefully in three or four weeks. I'll naturally keep you informed as to progress."

"Right. I'm actually going down to Devon for a bit. I can let you have an address and phone number where I'm staying if you like; just in case I can't get a signal on my mobile."

"Yes alright, that may well be useful. In the back of beyond, some of those places down there."

Dan gave the man his father's contact details as suggested, but before hanging up asked him another question.

"You say he has a *history*. What exactly do you mean?" There followed a long pause on the other end of the line whilst the solicitor considered his response. Then he spoke with calculated deliberation.

"Some might describe your uncle as the black sheep of the family. This probably is the most complimentary portrayal you'll hear from anyone who knows him. Those who've had, shall we say, more intimate dealings with the man, would be unlikely to be so generous in their use of metaphor. He is someone who very definitely looks after number One, and he would not hesitate in taking advantage of anybody to further his own ends."

"Oh, I see." Although he didn't. He really wanted to find out more about his uncle's transgressions, particularly the incident that was serious enough to result in his disinheritance, but could tell that Mr. Hutchison was unwilling to divulge any further details. He thanked him politely for his help, and ended the call.

The next morning, around ten o'clock, saw him spilling from the underground and being poured with his fellow travellers onto the huge concourse at Paddington railway station. He had a good half an hour to wait for his train, and slumped into one of the many chairs at one of the numerous cafés, gratefully shedding the crammed shabby khaki rucksack from his back.

At the same time in the ozone-enriched skies above Dartmouth, seagulls were screeching and wheeling as James was dragged from yet another alcohol-induced torpor by the shrill bleeping of his alarm clock. Coincidentally, he was that same day going to travel up to London in search of his nephew. His train was due to leave Totnes at twelve thirty-five. Somewhere between Exeter and Taunton, unbeknownst to either of them, they would pass within feet of each other.

CHAPTER SIX

Once Frank had enlightened the postmistress with the truth about Tom's tragic demise, the village gossips again turned their attention towards him, noting with unrestrained curiosity not only his change in disposition, but also his change in appearance as the day of his son's arrival drew nearer. Whenever he was spotted in the locality, he was seen to be clean-shaven and tidily dressed. Gone was the scruffy donkey jacket that had clung to him for months. Instead he sported an almost stylish tweed jacket over a checked brushed cotton shirt which even on occasion boasted a tie. He'd had his hair cut short: furthermore it was quite evidently no longer a stranger to a comb.

"Must be a woman," Anne whispered under her breath to Mrs. Manning one morning as Frank left the shop, leaving a faint subtle trace of soft soapy fragrance lingering in the air. "And that jacket, that's proper Harris tweed, that is. That doesn't come cheap." She was actually only half right in her assertion, since the man had bought his entire new wardrobe from various charity shops, and had even succeeded in haggling down the marked price on many of the items. His deeply engrained caution when parting with money was manifestly extremely difficult to shift.

When the big day arrived he was feeling inexplicably nervous. He swallowed his cup of tea and snapped the radio off. Christmas was just a few short weeks away, and the usual plethora of moronic and irritating Yuletide songs swamped the airwaves. *Same old rubbish every year. Santa's a Scotsman - for God's sake!*

It was a stunningly beautiful winter's morning. He stepped outside and inhaled deeply, holding the sharp fresh air in the pit of his lungs as if it were some exotic luxurious smoke. Exhaling, his breath roiled out in a billowing cloud. The moment was then marred by a brief coughing fit. After recovering from this, he decided to go for a stroll around the farm; he felt it would settle him as well as killing an hour or so. An image of his father shot suddenly into his mind. *"Farmer's boots boy, farmer's boots."* That had been the old man's way of stressing to his son the importance of regular close inspection of crops and livestock. With a wry smile he crossed the yard and unlatched a warped wooden gate beside the dark damp mossy trunk of a huge lofty beech tree, from whose twisted, gnarled and spiralling boughs large drops of melt water fell, plopping onto the concrete and splattering on his head. The top bar of the gate, shaded from the sun, was prickled white with frost. He absent-mindedly brushed this away, revealing wet malodorous lichen beneath that stained his palm a deep greenish black. Shutting the gate behind him, he wiped the slime on his trousers, and continued his way across the field. His boots scuffed through the tussocky ill-managed grass, flicking off bristles of hoary frost on the individual blades as he walked. This formed a white crust, a crystalline sugary arc across his wellingtons. A pale but nevertheless benign sun shone down from a cloudless stark blue sky, whose only occupants appeared to be a solitary rook whispering past high up, and higher still an airliner, no doubt whisking away its cargo of tourists to warmer climes. Soundlessly it tracked across the empty firmament, puffing behind it twin vapour trails, which slowly drifted apart and thinned to nothing. At the far end of the meadow an insipid mist hung over the chirruping stream. It coiled itself around the riparian alders, not a breath of wind in the air to disperse it. As he made his way across the farm, the warming sun burned off the frost, and by the time he'd returned to the farmhouse it had been banished to all but the shadowy spots beneath high banks and behind the cold north-facing stone wall of the old dwelling. He changed into clean clothes, gulped down a cup of coffee, and then, still feeling somewhat apprehensive, climbed into his Land Rover and fired it up.

Gaudy Christmas lights and illuminated decorations criss-crossed the street on looping wires above his head as he crept along in the heavy traffic. There issued, it seemed from every shop doorway, ghastly tinned Christmas 'muzak.' He wondered how the staff could put up with this torture for weeks on end. He wondered more, once he'd left the town centre and was heading for the railway station, how on earth anyone could bring themselves to plaster the whole of the outsides of their houses, and stuff their gardens, with plastic Santas, hundreds of lights, snowmen, elves, sleighs, reindeer and all the other pointless - not to mention tasteless - tat that somehow had something to do with the most important religious festival in the Christian calendar: not that he had any sort of religious fervour at all, but like so many others, he was, every year, more saddened by the increasing commercialism that surrounded the occasion. With a little uncharacteristic nostalgia, he began to think of Christmases past, when he was a child; happy family gatherings. He was brutally snapped back to the present by the blaring of a car's horn behind, not realizing that the lights had changed. *Alright alright; keep your hair on.*

He swung into the station car park only to see a Volvo

almost as ancient as his Land Rover reversing into the sole unoccupied space in the short-term parking bays. *Bugger,* that would mean he'd not only have to park further from the entrance, but he'd have to pay as well. He glanced at his watch: the train wasn't due in for another ten minutes or so. He pulled up behind the parked cars and switched off the chattering engine. With any luck someone would leave if he waited a moment or two. He rolled a cigarette and looked across to the large shiny sliding glass doors. Once he'd lit up he wound down the window and the fragrant smoke rolled out, languorously drifting away in the still air. Some passengers now started to trickle out of the station, although most of them seemed to be heading for the taxi rank, heavy cases hanging at the end of tired arms, or being dragged behind their owners on chunky plastic wheels.

"You can't park there."

Frank had failed to notice the self-important uniformed attendant who'd limped over to his Land Rover from apparently nowhere.

"You'll 'ave to move; you're causing an obstruction."

"Yes, but all the spaces are full, I was just waiting for somebody to go, so's I could..."

"Plenty of spaces down the far end, sir - you can't park there," the annoying little man reiterated.

"But I'm just waiting; I'm not causing an obstruction. I'll move if..."

"Move *now* please, sir." Frank swore under his breath, and started the engine. Driving slowly along, he noticed reversing lights come on in one of the bays, and stopped to let the car back out. He could see in the smeared and blurry glass of his cock-eyed wing mirror that the car park attendant had seen him come to a halt, and not realising that another car was coming out, was once more hobbling hurriedly across the tarmac towards him to move him on. *Bloody jobsworth.* Frank drove smartly into the vacated space. Coming abruptly to a halt, he jumped out and slammed the door shut without bothering to lock it. Making his way towards the automatic doors glinting prettily as they reflected the low rays of the winter sun, he noticed from the corner of his eye the attendant scowling at him. Nonchalantly, he flicked his cigarette butt behind him, where it came to earth, still smouldering, almost under the feet of his pursuer. The officious employee extinguished it angrily with an exaggerated twist under the worn sole of his scuffed black boot.

The television screens on the platform informed Frank that the London train was on time, and that it would be arriving at platform five in four minutes. A great wave of apprehension washed through his stomach. In order to still it, he took a deep breath and turned to climb the stairs. He briskly crossed the footbridge over the line, and trotted down the iron staircase on the other side, vaguely wondering as he did, why railway stations always seem to smell not just of diesel, which would of course appear obvious, but also of that shiny, medicated and unforgiving toilet paper that he remembered from childhood. Or was it more like Jeyes fluid?

"The train now approaching platform five is the 13.46 to Penzance, calling at Totnes, Plymouth and Penzance. Passengers for Totnes are reminded to take a seat in one of the central carriages," the announcer's voice boomed from the loudspeaker directly above Frank, making him jump. It bounced off the walls, and echoed discordantly throughout the concourse. Up the line, the engine was now just gliding smoothly into view. The train snaked almost gracefully along the curved track, coming slowly to rest beside him, where it sat, quietly fuming, as if resenting

being forced to break its long journey. Steel doors flew open and passengers poured out, Frank looking anxiously up and down as he tried to pick out his son. Heads bobbed and bodies hurried past him. It was only when doors were slamming noisily shut that he noticed Dan bearing down on him from one of the further carriages. They shook hands a little awkwardly, whilst Dan joggled the rucksack on his back.

"Welcome to Devon. Did you have a good trip?"

"Yes, no worries, thanks."

"Well it looks like you brought the sunshine with you."

"You mean it's not always like this?" the young man grinned.

"Believe it or not, the trains *have* been known to be late, and rain *has* been known to fall in this part of the world."

"Oh right, you don't say!"

Outside, the pale midwinter sun was sinking fast towards the western horizon, wallowing in a wishy-washy sky. Chill air was beginning to wipe out its wan warmth, promising another cold frosty night. Dan lobbed his rucksack in the back of the Land Rover, and the two men climbed in.

"How far away's the farm?"

"Oh, about nine miles; we'll be there in about half an hour or so. Have you eaten? I've got a stew for later, but we could stop for fish and chips or something now, if you want."

"No, no, I'm fine thanks. I had one of your delicious British Rail sandwiches on the way."

"Oh lucky you: I should have warned you about them."

"No, really it was okay - apart from the price that is. Three pounds fifty of my hard-earned cash."

"Good God, talk about daylight robbery!"

The dusky amber rays of the fast falling sun struck the smeared windscreen of the Land Rover as they bowled along

74

the country lanes, having left the congested streets of the town behind. Frank pulled the dusty visor down to prevent himself being dazzled. He squinted through the dirty glass. The high Devon hedgerows cast long darkening shadows, ever stretching eastwards across verdant fertile pastures, here and there dotted with a scattering of sheep. Now and then, the glossy deep rich red of a ploughed field appeared like an island in the sea of green.

"It's certainly a lovely part of the world," Dan noted appreciatively. "It's every bit as beautiful as mum said."

"Did she miss England?"

"Oh yes. I mean, the station's a great place to live, but a hard place as well. Month upon month of unbearable heat, flies and orange dust everywhere can be a bit wearing. It sometimes feels like living in the middle of nowhere, it's hard to describe the feeling of isolation: it takes some getting used to. In fact, our part of Oz is often called The Forgotten Corner."

"It must have been one hell of a culture shock for her, when she first got there."

"You'd better believe it."

When they arrived at the farm, Frank showed Dan his room and clattered downstairs to the kitchen, filling the kettle and placing it onto the range's hotplate.

"I'll make us a cup of tea, and get supper on the go, then I'll show you quickly round the farm if you like, before it gets dark!" he shouted in the general direction of the stairs.

"Great, I could do with some fresh air!" came the enthusiastic reply.

The westering sun had slipped below the horizon when they went outside again, lighting up the sky all around in a soft orange glow. However, the ambient temperature fell rapidly as father and son walked briskly across the shadowy landscape, cold air clutching at them, taking a firm grip as night began to fall. It was very nearly dark when they returned to the house, the toppled sun's ghostly glow barely visible on the dark grey horizon. A myriad of twinkling stars already peppered the black heavens.

Some while later, they sat in the warmth of the kitchen, remains of their supper on willow-pattern plates before them. Frank rolled a cigarette, stuck it in the corner of his mouth, and lit up.

"Sorry about that, I'm afraid I'm not much of a one for cooking - don't really bother just for myself, you see..."

"No, that's okay. I guess I wasn't that hungry anyway."

"Just as well, that was near enough the worst meal I've ever tasted."

"Aw come on. It wasn't that bad."

"What, you mean apart from the chewy meat, insipid gravy, crunchy onions, and practically raw carrots?"

"It just needed a bit more time to cook; long and slow's the secret to a good stew. Also, if you fry off the onions first for ten minutes or so, that'll soften them. Oh, and fry the beef as well, to seal in the juices. I coat the pieces with flour too – that thickens up the gravy."

"Oh, right. So you're a bit of a dab hand in the kitchen then are you – a bit of a galloping gourmet?"

"Ah no, not at all!" he laughed. "My mum was a pretty good cook, it just rubbed off I suppose."

"Well, if you're willing to rustle up a few meals while you're here, don't let *me* stop you..."

"Sure, it'd be my pleasure."

Frank propped his smoking butt in the ashtray and rose from the table. "Fancy a snifter before retiring?"

"Sorry?"

"I mean a drink."

"Yeah, sure."

Frank poured two uncharacteristically generous measures of Scotch.

"Cheers."

"Cheers."

"Do you have any idea as to how long you might be staying? I mean, I'm not trying to get rid of you already, but have you made any plans since we last spoke?"

"No, I can't say I have. I'm in no rush to get back - if that's alright with you."

"Yes of course it is, stay as long as you like: after all, we've got a lot of catching up to do, haven't we?"

"Yep, certainly have."

A short silence followed. Frank drilled his cigarette-end into the base of the glass ashtray, extinguishing it in a swirl of blue smoke.

"So, is everything sorted out? With your grandmother's affairs, I mean."

"Yeah, or at least it should be soon."

"You said on the phone there might be a glitch."

"Sorry?"

"A hiccup."

"Oh yes. It's all sorted now. It was James."

"James? What, your uncle?"

"The very same. He was threatening to contest the will. He decided against it apparently. He actually tried to persuade my solicitor to put him in touch with me, see if he could cajole me into giving him some money."

"Bloody hell! What a cheek. I hope you didn't."

"No, although I *did* consider it to start with, I sort of felt sorry for him. I was... dissuaded."

"I should hope so; you don't owe him any favours. Besides, once he'd got something out of you he wouldn't leave you alone, he'd be back for more sooner or later."

"That's what Hutchison, the solicitor, said. James has a history apparently, whatever that means."

"Does he indeed? Top up?"

"Eh?" Frank pointed to his glass.

"Oh yes, go on then, but just a small one, then I'm off to bed if you don't mind, I feel pretty bushed."

"Sure." The glasses replenished, Frank engaged himself in rolling another cigarette. Dan took a swig of whisky, carefully replacing the glass on the table. "Once probate comes through in a couple of weeks' time, I'll put the place on the market."

"You could rent it out, earn a little money from it."

"Yeah," he answered thoughtfully, "I'd considered that, but I don't want the hassle and I know Jane wants to sell - with all her kids she's always short of cash."

"You've obviously looked into the tax implications, or rather your solicitor has."

"Yep, that's no problem. Gran didn't have much else apart from the house. Once the proceeds are split two ways, the amount will be well below the Inheritance Tax threshold. Granddad suffered a long illness before he died; caring for him took most of their nest egg."

"Oh, that's sad."

"Yeah, well at least she never had to sell the house herself; although mum said if he'd lived much longer she would have had to."

"I don't know, you work hard all your life, paying your taxes and scrimping and saving for what should be an enjoyable retirement, then something like that happens. I tell you, this country's going to the dogs. And to think, our National Health Service was the envy of the rest of the civilised world not so long ago!"

Dan quickly gulped down the remainder of his drink. He was tired, and the last thing he wanted to do was indulge in a political debate.

"Well if you'll excuse me, I'm going on up. Thanks for the drink, and thanks for picking me up from the station and er, thanks for putting me up," he added rather awkwardly.

"Don't be silly, it's a pleasure. I'll see you in the morning; sleep well."

"Right. Good night then, Frank."

"Good night, Dan."

He rose to go and then hesitated. "It's alright to call you Frank, is it? I mean..."

"Of course, I hardly expect you to call me daddy!" He grinned widely, briefly exposing discoloured nicotine-stained teeth.

"No, well that's fine. I'll see you tomorrow then. Oh, and I'll cook breakfast, shall I?" It was his turn to grin broadly, revealing an even set of pristine white incisors.

"Yes, that's probably for the best."

Dan slept like a log that night, the dark dense night gripping him in its deathly torpor. No fox barked, no owl screeched to break the soupy silence. He awoke with a jolt at eight-thirty the following morning, for a moment confused by his strange surroundings. He dressed quickly, and throwing a towel thoughtfully left at the end of his bed over his left shoulder, trotted off to the bathroom, noting on the way that his father's bedroom door lay ajar, the room obviously already vacated.

There was a note on the kitchen table, pinned underneath

a large glass ashtray, already bedecked with the remnants of the day's first cigarette.

Tea in pot. Gone to shop for bread and baccy. Won't be long. Everything for breakfast in fridge, the barely decipherable scrawl read. Dan scrunched up the missive and threw it in the bin, then armed with a large mug of tea, he set about preparing a fry up. Barely five minutes into the task, he heard the front door slam, and Frank appeared in the room.

"Something smells nice. Bacon and eggs, is it?"

"Er, yeah. It would have been sausages as well, only I chucked them - they were a little green round the edges."

"Really? I only bought them a few days ago...oh well, never mind. Toast or bread?"

"Toast I think."

"Right-o: and I'll make a fresh pot, shall I?"

"Best way to start the day." Frank pushed his cleared plate away. He splashed some milk into his empty mug, and filled it with steaming tea. Dropping in two generously heaped spoons of sugar, he stirred it expansively, before sitting back and rolling a cigarette. Lighting the finished article, he inhaled deeply and exhaled luxuriantly. Smoke comfortingly floated across the kitchen in a faint blue haze.

"Any plans for today?"

"I thought I'd take a look around the town maybe. I'll need some more clothes sooner or later, and I ought to think about finding some work if I'm going to be around a while."

"Oh. What sort of work?"

"I don't know. Bar work maybe or something. There must be a few seasonal jobs going, aren't there? With Christmas just round the corner I mean."

"Perhaps."

"I just need a bit of beer money you know; and besides, you don't want me hanging around here all day getting under your feet, do you?"

Frank considered this for a minute or two, before deciding to plunge in.

"It depends really."

"Depends? On what exactly?"

"Well...on how long you're staying, for instance."

"Why?"

Frank sighed. "Because if you're planning to be about for a while, I could use a hand around here."

"Oh, well like I said, I'm not in any hurry to go back to Oz, so..."

"You see," Frank interrupted, seizing his chance, "it's time I got this place straightened up and started farming again."

"Oh, and you'd like me to help; is that it?"

"If you're willing to: yes. Look, if you don't fancy the idea, that's fine, I won't be offended. I only thought that working together might be a good way to get to know each other."

"Yeah, right. Er, I don't know what to say."

"Sorry, I have rather sprung it on you, I know. Never mind, like I said it's only an idea."

An awkward silence ensued. Frank pushed back his chair and rose from the table. "Right, if you need to go clothes shopping we'd best go into Exeter; there's more choice there."

"There's no need for you to drive me in, I can get the bus."

"No, no. You'd have to wait for ages; and it goes all round the houses to almost every village between here and there. It'll take you half a day to get there and back. No, I'll take you in, it's no bother. We may as well do a food shop too: I need to stock up on most things."

"Okay, thanks. I'll just wash these bits up, then I'm ready."

"Fancy a pint and a sandwich before we go back?" Frank asked as he dumped the laden shopping bags in the back of the Land Rover. Dan threw the plastic carriers of clothes on top.

"Why not? I think we've earned one, don't you?"

"Bloody right."

Dan edged his way past the throng at the bar, beer spilling from the two pint glasses he clutched, and slid down in the seat opposite Frank. He set the drinks down on the small oak table and peered at the plastic snack menu card that his father handed him.

"There's Specials on the board too, if you're hungry."

"Right. No, a baguette'll do me - ham salad."

"Right. I'll go and order." Frank squeezed out from behind the table, knocking it with his knee as he went, slopping more beer onto its lacquered dark surface.

Having eaten his fill some minutes later, Dan drained his glass and belched pleasantly.

"Oops, pardon me. I guess I haven't got used to your warm English beer yet."

"It's got to be better than that lager stuff you Ozzies knock back, full of gas and chemicals. Shall we have another?"

The light was fading rapidly as they drove back to the farm. Angry black-bellied clouds were scudding across the sky from the west, the sinking sun shyly peeping between their billowing dark borders as they rolled menacingly eastwards.

"Looks like it's going to absolutely tip down later," Frank observed as the first random raindrops spotted the windscreen. He flicked the headlights on. Very soon, more drops of rain began to crowd together. Like a mass gathering of insects, they tracked across it. The arthritic wiper blades wheezed asthmatically as they tracked stiffly back and forth.

"About what you said this morning," Dan began with some uncertainty, "you know, about us working together. I'd like to give it a go; so long as I know just what my role is."

"Really? Right, like I said, I want to get the farm back on its feet again. So...what I want you to do is to help me repair and possibly extend and alter some of the buildings, sort out the fencing and broken gates, troughs, all that sort of thing: kind of estate maintenance if you like. Then in the spring, I want to establish a beef suckler herd."

"Ah, I see. Sounds good." The whole sky was now one dark mass of plumped-up cloud behind which the sun had disappeared completely. It was practically night outside, and the rain was setting in, drumming persistently and noisily on the roof of the old vehicle, slanting downwards through the yellowy beams of its sombre headlights.

"So, are we on then?" Frank had to raise his voice to be heard above the noise. "Obviously I'll pay the going rate - after board and lodging of course."

"Of course." Dan considered this for a moment. This could be a golden opportunity for him, for although he'd told his father he was in no immediate hurry to return to the country of his birth, in truth he felt no compunction to go back at all. So what did he have to lose?

"Okay, you're on."

"Good." Frank smiled. *Good.*

CHAPTER SEVEN

As he most certainly would have put it himself, James was seriously *pissed off.* Clearly, this was not an infrequent sensation for a man with a chip, or more accurately chips, on his shoulder. At the start of his expedition he was reasonably confident of a satisfactory outcome, but now felt totally thwarted and devoid of any further ideas. He'd been in the capital for nearly a week, hanging around his mother's neat brick semi, every day thinking that tomorrow he would be bound to see his sister's brat, confident of his ability when he did to wheedle some money out of him. He'd seen no one come or go, not even the postman. The time had come for him to abandon his search and return to Devon. Moreover, he'd been staying with Colin whose friendship could at best be described as tenuous, the two of them sharing the occasional companionable drunken evening many years ago at university before James was unceremoniously asked to leave. Colin's wife had been frosty from the start of his sojourn in London, and hadn't warmed at all to him as the days tediously passed.

"James! It's half nine! You don't want to miss your train, do you?" the voice of the perfect wife flew upstairs to him.

"Okay, I'm just coming!" he shouted back. He flung off the duvet, pulled on the clothes abandoned in a creased heap on the floor the previous evening, and making no attempt to leave the bedroom in a tidy state, bundled the rest of his belongings carelessly into his hold-all. He thought of showering, but instead collected his wash bag from the bathroom without making any use of its contents.

The sooner he was out of here the better.

"I've made you some breakfast," Colin's wife Carla said indifferently. "Here." She casually plonked the plate on the table in front of him. Greasy eggs swimming in bacon fat and accompanied by a couple of mournful-looking soggy pink chipolatas stared up at him.

"Thanks," he replied, not meaning it, "you really shouldn't have bothered," meaning it.

"You ought to have something inside you if you're travelling; besides, after all that wine you poured down your neck last night I thought you could do with some solids," she added coldly.

Gritting his teeth, he tackled the food as quickly as he dared, swallowed a cup of tea, and hurriedly left the house. He ran down the road to the main street, where he stood at the kerb in the sheeting rain, looking up and down, trying to spot a taxi for hire through the hazy curtains of spray.

Meanwhile, at more or less the same time two hundred odd miles away in Devon, Frank was chatting with the postman, who stood on the glistening, puddle-speckled concrete surface of the farmyard, his mail tucked under his arm, leaning with the other on the roof of the van. The heavy rain that had thundered down during the night had cleared away eastwards, leaving a sodden dejected landscape. Water steadily dripped from the huge limbs of the beech trees in the field opposite, and the discoloured sodden dead foliage of blackthorn and hazel littered the black tarmac in the lane. The few remaining mottled leaves still clinging desperately to the branches drooped miserably in midwinter's pallid weak watery light. A large sycamore stood a bit further up the hill, its blotchy and pockmarked leaves completely stripped from its boughs. They piled beneath in a great soggy ungainly heap, clogging up the drainage ditch by the roadside. Some had been washed into the centre of the lane, lying like drifts of sand shaped by the tide on some far-off sun–soaked beach.

"And you 'ad no idea?"

"None at all. The letter came out of the blue, and now my boy's here."

"Blimey, must 'ave been a bit of a shock though, coming unexpected like that."

"I suppose so, but a good one none the less. Wouldn't you be pleased if you found there was a little Steve out there somewhere?"

"Christ, I don't know about that: I know one thing though, the missus wouldn't. We've got enough on our plate with the two girls."

"Yeah I bet, but still, a son..."

"No," Steve said, starting up the van, "I'm quite 'appy as we are thank you. I don't want no surprises from my past turning up on the doorstep. Not that there would be any of course," he added with a grin.

"Of course," replied Frank. "See you Steve, go careful now." The postman sped away up the hill as Frank made his way across the yard to the house. He opened the door and a rush of warm air greeted him, carrying on its wings the soothing scent and sizzling sound of frying bacon.

"That's good timing! I was just about to put your eggs on. You ready for breakfast?"

"Certainly am." Frank came into the kitchen, picked up a

86

knife from the table and after dumping the mail on top, began to rip open the various letters. "Blimey, most of this is just junk, it must cost these companies a fortune! Look at this, what makes these people think I need a stair-lift for Christ's sake - or come to that, a cruise around the Mediterranean?"

"Is that all there is?"

"Apart from the electricity bill, yes. Why, were you expecting something?"

"No, not really; well actually I thought they might have sorted probate out by now. Still, there's no hurry, I suppose." He placed a plate of bacon, eggs and golden fried bread in front of his father. "Watch out, it's hot."

"Oh, thanks. There's not much chance of that before Christmas. I expect they're already on their extended festive break. Your Mr. Hutchison's probably dipping his toes in the Caribbean as we speak: I'd be surprised if you hear anything before the end of January," he added as he eagerly sliced an egg in half. Thick creamy golden yolk oozed across the fried bread and sluggishly slid onto the plate. Frank cut off a corner of bread and shovelled egg and bacon onto it. Spearing the load with his fork, he crammed it into his mouth. He chewed noisily, before washing the food down with a mouthful of tea. Dan tried not to notice.

"So you told him, did you?"

"Eh?" Frank answered; he was clearly more interested in gobbling up his food than holding any sort of conversation.

"The postman, you know, about me."

"Oh yes, it'll be all round the village by lunch-time." He paused, suddenly concerned, knife waving in the air. "That's alright, isn't it? You're happy with that, aren't you?"

"Yeah, yeah; the sooner everyone knows the better."

"Good. God knows what rumours that bloody postmistress

has been spreading, probably that you're my live-in lover or something equally sordid."

"She's not that bad is she, surely?"

"Humph. I wouldn't put much past her. She lives on tittle-tattle. I've even heard it said she's been known to steam open people's private correspondence when her insatiable curiosity gets too much for her."

"Oh right. Well I'll bear that in mind. Hey maybe I'll write a few salacious letters to myself, something really lurid - d'you think she'd like that? We'd know if she was opening the mail then alright."

"Mmm. That may be a little over the top: it's an idea though, if she gets too much out of hand."

Dan grinned. "Anyway, never mind that. Did you get a look at the fence you wanted sorting in the lower meadows?"

"Yes, it's in a worse state than I first thought. Mind you, they always are," he added despondently. He'd been hoping to salvage it by banging in a few more posts and retightening the wire, but having inspected it that morning, he saw that this option was denied him. Even those posts still upright were either loose or snapped like kindling with the slightest pressure. It didn't seem that long ago that, together with his father, he'd put this stretch up one mild spring week in April. In fact, it was nearly twenty years since. He sighed; it all needed redoing, and that meant spending money.

"If you go down there and take down the top two strands of wire, we can use them again. Don't bother about the other two, they're broken and rusted - just as well leave them to get grown over. I'll go out and get a load of stakes from Gill's and we'll replace the whole lot."

The sun was warm on his back as Dan strode across the soaked pastures of the lower meadows, his new wellington boots squelching on the waterlogged unkempt grass. The brook snaked through the middle of the flat field, a living scar slicing it jaggedly in half. The whole valley steamed lazily in the sunshine. The world was still and quiet, the only sound the enthusiastic rushing of the water in the swollen stream; the only sight the occasional treecreeper scurrying up the tall trunk of an alder in its interminable quest for scarce grubs under the rough scaly bark. Dan reached the far corner of the field, and began his task. Once he'd wrenched the old rusty but surprisingly stubborn staples from the spent posts, he carefully pulled the wire away, leaving it in a neat line on the ground at the base of the hedge. He'd only just finished freeing the second strand, when he saw the laden Land Rover coming through the gate. As the vehicle approached, it left twin muddy tracks in the long grass behind it.

"Jump in the back," Frank instructed. "Then you can chuck out the stakes as I drive along - big strainer and strut first then about one every four yards, okay?"

"Okay. No worries." Dan clambered tentatively into the back of the Land Rover. Maintaining his balance wasn't easy and he rocked around a bit as it rolled along beside the hedgerow. However, he managed to complete the task without mishap. By lunch-time between them they'd sunk all the posts in a straight row from corner to corner.

"Can you string the wire up this afternoon?" Frank asked his son. "Only I ought to catch up with some bookwork: might as well bung that reel of wire out while we're here too. If you tack two strands up under the two you've salvaged, that should keep the hedge shockproof – and if it's as tight as a piano wire, nothing will think of trying it."

"Right-o, this old barbed is sure vicious stuff, no wonder the cowboys hated it so much."

"Eh?"

"The cowboys: you know, the Wild West and all that."

"I'm sorry, you've lost me there."

"Barbed wire was invented by a fella in America, and used widely by settlers to fence off their land, carving up the plains and preventing the ranchers from running their cattle and droving them those vast distances to the railheads. It was their downfall. Apparently, the amount of wire used in just a few years would've spanned the globe…"

"Really?"

"…three times."

"Good God, well there you go: you learn something new every day, don't you?" Frank retorted with more than a hint of irony. "Now shall we go and get some lunch?"

Anne could barely believe her ears. "Are you absolutely *sure* of that Steve?"

"Look, I'm only telling you what 'e told me."

"You haven't got it wrong, have you? I mean, it just seems so very, I don't know..."

"Far-fetched? Unlikely?"

"Well yes, I suppose so."

"I don't see why. We was all young once, why should Frank be any different?"

"I suppose; but even so, a love child! Frank Anderson!"

"I think you're being a bit overdramatic. It's something that could 'appen to any bloke. My old man said it went on all the time during the war when them Yanks was over 'ere. 'E reckoned 'alf the girls in the village was at it with 'em while their poor 'usbands and boyfriends was away fighting for King and Country - and we all know about Mary-Jane."

"Yes, yes, let's not trawl through all that again." It was

accepted as fact locally that Mary-Jane had been the product of an intimate liaison between a local farmer's daughter and a young good-looking American serviceman, although this had always been denied by her and her family. Even her husband stood steadfast by her, a quite extraordinary show of fealty considering Mary-Jane bore no resemblance at all to her other family members, being tall, willowy and dark-featured, in contrast to her parents' and indeed her two younger brothers' shared small stocky build and rather banal and unremarkable appearance.

"So is the lad staying long then?" Anne asked, trying to steer the conversation back to its original topic.

"Don't know, Frank said 'e was doing some work for 'im on the farm, fencing and that."

"Oh, I see. And did you see him then?"

"Who?"

"Oh, for heaven's sake, his son of course; Sam, was it?"

"Dan. Yeah, I've seen 'im a couple of times."

"And?"

"And what?"

"Ye Gods, it's like drawing teeth! What's he like? And by that I mean does he look as if he could be Frank's son?"

The postman considered this for a minute or two.

"Well," he started with exaggerated deliberation, his sole intention to aggravate the postmistress further.

"'E's tall like 'im, but fair..."

"He might have got that from his mother - was she a blonde?"

"'Ow on earth would *I* know!" he riposted indignantly.

"Alright, no need to fly off the handle. What else?"

"Erm, I don't know really. 'E's got that kind of lean look about 'im like Frank, but maybe not the sort of 'ardness about 'im…mind you, that could just be 'cos 'e's still young I s'pose."

"So if you were to see the two of them together, would you assume them to be father and son?" Anne persisted.

Steve paused once again for theatrical effect, seeming to mull the question over in his mind. After a suitably drawn out length of time he said decisively: "Yes, you might well think that."

"Well, I never would have imagined, not in my wildest dreams…talk about a dark horse."

"Right, well, I'd better get going. Is that it then?"

"Is what it then?"

"All the post to go. Just those two parcels?"

"Yes, that's it - oh, and this." Anne pulled a large bulging Jiffy bag from under the counter. "Mr. Harris's regular mystery package to London." She smirked conspiratorially as Steve scooped it up together with the two parcels and strode out of the shop.

The weather leading up to Christmas continued to be wet, and at times very windy. Although rain was not uncommon in winter (or any other season) in this part of the country, the amount of it was, as was the ferocity and frequency of the damaging storms trekking across the landscape. Normally benign tinkling streams and ambling winding rivers turned rapidly into swollen ugly muddied torrents, toppling trees with their feet in the water by washing away the earth foundation securing their naked roots. The odd corpse of some unfortunate sheep was occasionally spotted bobbing along like a soggy woollen balloon, caught unawares somewhere upstream and whisked away by the boiling waters. Dan was once again preparing breakfast when he heard the door down the hall open, followed by the now familiar sound of his father pulling off his boots. Frank appeared in stockinged feet in the kitchen. He wrenched off his soaked donkey jacket and draped it over a chair which he dragged noisily to the side of the range. It hung heavily there, dripping disconsolately onto the flags, then began to stealthily steam, releasing as it did a rather unpleasant pungent odour. Dan regarded it suspiciously.

"I don't know why you don't get rid of that," he said, "it stinks. Why don't I get you a new one for Christmas, a nice waterproof waxy jacket and maybe a good old Ozzie Drizabone hat?"

"I'm quite happy with that one, thanks - and don't you go wasting your money on expensive Christmas presents for me, understand?"

"Yeah, sure. Scrambled or fried?"

"What?"

"Eggs."

"Oh, scrambled please."

"Coming up."

"That big oak's come down, the one by the stream out the front."

"That's a pity."

"Yeah, looks like the bank's collapsed in, and the water's undermined the roots. I suppose that wind last night did the rest."

"Shame."

"Oh well, gives us a bit more firewood anyway, doesn't it?" He picked a half smoked cigarette from the rim of the ashtray, and pressing it between his lips, lit it, wordlessly puffing on it whilst watching his son effortlessly and dexterously stirring his eggs in the pan as they gently cooked. Once ready, they were presented to him heaped on top of a round of golden buttered toast, accompanied by two rashers of bacon.

"There you go."

"Thanks." He scrunched his butt out in the ashtray, and attacked his breakfast.

"This is good."

"Thanks."

Frank chewed thoughtfully on his food. "Look, say no if you like, but do you fancy going out to the local tonight? Just for a jar or two."

"Yeah, sure, sounds like a great idea."

"Really? Only..."

"Look, it's okay, honestly. I'm sure I'll get one or two looks, but I'm not bothered by it. Anyway, you'll be in the limelight as well, won't you?"

"Well yes, but they've all seen my ugly mug before."

"Don't worry, I can handle a few yokels staring at me: besides, once they've all seen what I'm like, they'll lose interest pretty quick, not that I'm uninteresting or anything..." he grinned.

"No, I know what you mean – and I'm sure you're right. We'll go along about six then, shall we?"

"Fine, I'll pop a casserole in to cook before we go, then all I've got to do is get it out of the range when we get back, okay?"

"Perfect."

By the time the two of them were ready to leave for the pub that evening, the heavens had once again opened, heavy rain-clouds tipping their unwanted load onto the already saturated ground. Drops of water dashed this way and that down the outside of the kitchen window, like excited children ducking and dodging one another in the playground. In the blackness, rain hammered down remorselessly on the metal sheeted roofs of the farm buildings, rushing along the overflowing gutters and cascading from downpipes, pouring over blocked drain griddles and pooling on the surface of the yard before the daisy-chains of puddles joined together to form a stream which zigzagged its way to the lip of the concrete, and gurgled over the edge, out into the meadow, flattening a path through the grass as it made its way towards the ever-swelling brook.

Frank roughly yanked the kitchen window's old curtains together.

"Another bloody filthy night," he muttered to himself. He stubbed out his cigarette in the ashtray, and opening the door of the range, emptied its contents inside. Hearing his son clattering down the stairs, he pulled his tweed jacket from the back of a chair and shrugged it on as he flicked off the light, leaving the room in darkness.

"Are we ready then?"

"I reckon. Shall I leave the light on?" Dan asked as Frank opened the front door.

"Why?"

"Well, I don't know. Burglars or something?"

"I shouldn't worry about that, boy. There's not much worth nicking. Besides, they'd have to be pretty desperate to trawl all the way down here on a night like this, wouldn't they?"

It was coming down like stair-rods when they got to the pub, and they splashed hurriedly across the puddly tarmac to the sanctuary of the bar. The place was totally deserted, save for the barmaid standing in front of the roaring fire, her hands behind her back hitching up her skirt to warm her bottom in front of the dancing flames.

"Oh, hello Frank." Completely flustered, she hastily dropped the folds of her skirt and hastened back behind the bar. "What can I get you two gentlemen?"

"A pint of Guinness for me please Susie, and…?"

"Erm, a pint of lager please."

"Certainly; which would you prefer?"

"Which would you recommend?" Dan answered with a boyish grin.

"Well as I want to keep my job, I'd have to say both of them," she replied with a coquettish smile. "Except perhaps that one," she added, patting a chrome tap, "we don't sell much of that."

"I'd better have a pint of the other then, if I may."

"Of course."

"Susie, this is Dan, he's staying with me up at the farm for a bit - helping me get the place straight, actually. He's come over from Australia."

"Really? Wow! I've always wanted to go there. What part are you from?"

"Bulloo."

"Never heard of it."

"You're not alone in that. It's in Queensland."

"Oh, okay. Nice part of the country." This was a total stab in the dark because the girl, although she'd heard of that state, had no idea of where it was either.

"Yes, it is. At least, there're worse places in Australia."

"It must be lovely out there, all those long sandy beaches and sunny weather…"

"…and flies and heat and choking dust and drought and bush fires," he finished for her.

"Yeah, but it's got to better than living here with rain day in day out."

"Perhaps."

"Shall we sit by the fire, Dan?" his father interrupted, "or are you happy at the bar?"

"I don't mind. We'll go down by the fire if you like." He picked up his drink and turned to go.

"Nice meeting you Dan."

"Likewise Susie," he replied a little coyly.

Once settled by the comforting warmth of the fire, Frank rolled himself a cigarette. He lit it, drew in a lungful of smoke, and exhaled slowly.

"We'd better clean the gutters out and unblock the drains next dry day we get, especially if the weather's going to go on like this."

The two of them amicably discussed other jobs that were best done before winter really set in as they drank.

"Must get the water-pipes in the loft checked too," Frank said thoughtfully. "If we get a hard winter, and they're not lagged properly, we could find ourselves in real trouble."

"Right. That's not something we'd normally have to worry about back home. Another pint?"

"Please."

Dan carried the empty glasses to the still deserted bar, behind which the barmaid was wiping the optics in a somewhat desultory manner.

"Same again?"

"Yes please."

"So what do you do in Australia? Are you a sheep shearer?"

"No, and I don't wrestle crocs, either."

"Sorry?"

He felt himself redden. "Never mind. Actually you're not far off. My dad was a shearer - travelled the world. In fact, that's how he met mum."

"How romantic! So how long are you over here for then?"

"Oh I don't know really. For a while anyway, I guess. I'll

probably..." there was a sudden whooshing of froth accompanied by a gurgling and retching noise from the lager-pipe.

"Great, looks like it's gone. I'll have to change the barrel I'm afraid."

"That's okay, I'll have a pint of the other."

"Sure?"

"Yeah, no worries. It can't be that bad, can it?"

Dan took the drinks back to the table while Susie went off to change the barrel. "It's quiet in here tonight; is it always like this?"

Frank yawned. "Hardly. Whenever I come down here, it's heaving. It's probably because it's Saturday - a lot of people come out later, maybe have a bite to eat. Plus there's no one dropping in for a swift pint or two on their way home from work."

As if to immediately prove his hypothesis wrong the bar door swung inwards, and a tall scruffy man entered, with a Jack Russell terrier tucked under his arm.

"Evening Frank, not seen you in here for a while. Everything okay up at the farm?"

"Hello Bill. Yes, everything's tickety-boo, thank you."

"Good, good." He placed the dog carefully on the floor where the animal gratefully shook itself, besprinkling the worn carpet with droplets of rainwater. He then shrugged off his shabby wet raincoat, shaking it vigorously before hanging it on a peg behind the door. Over baggy grubby jeans he wore a moth-eaten woollen faded red jumper over a checked brushed cotton shirt with a crumpled, threadbare, sweat-stained collar.

"Bit quiet in here, isn't it? It's like the Marie Celeste," he observed. "Must be the weather I suppose. Where's Pete?"

"I don't know, Susie's just gone to change a barrel. I'm sure she'll be back in a minute or two. Oh, I'm sorry, I should have said: this is Dan - he's staying with me for a bit."

"Hello Dan, nice to meet you."

"And you, Bill."

"You're Australian, is that right?"

"Yep."

"Hmm, not a country I've ever fancied visiting, I must say. I'm not very good in the heat see...the sun doesn't agree with me."

"Really? Well you're better off here then, for sure - so long as you don't mind the rain."

"Oh no, I can cope with that. You see, it's like my father always said, '*you can only get wet once.*'" He chuckled softly.

At this point, Dan was rescued from any further conversation by the reappearance of the barmaid.

"Sorry to keep you, Bill. Usual, is it?"

"Oh yes please Susie. And what do you have on the Specials board tonight?"

"Er, cottage pie, curry and lasagne. Any good?"

"Are they big portions? Only I'm quite hungry, you see." Before she could answer, the door flew in again and a raucous crowd poured into the bar. Frank groaned.

"Evening, Susie! Hello, Frank!" The loud voice catapulted itself across the room, shattering the peace. "How are you? Haven't seen you in a while. How's farming these days? Are you still farming in fact?"

Before he had a chance to respond, the newcomer turned his attention to the girl behind the bar.

"Now then Susie, four pints of *Director's* please and is it vodka and tonics for the girls, George?" His companion nodded.

"I'll be with you in a minute, John. I'm serving Bill at the moment," the barmaid replied a little testily.

"Oops, sorry, didn't realise – sorry, Bill. I've actually got a table booked in the lounge for eight - that's for eight o'clock and a party of eight. We thought we'd have a drink in here first, that's okay is it?" John gabbled on.

"Yes, of course... Bill? Are you ready to order? And to answer your question - yes, the portions are very generous."

"In that case, I'll have the cottage pie please."

"Certainly."

Bill tactfully retreated from the bar, sitting down on a settle not far from the fire. His dog jumped up beside him. "I'll have to eat in here, not allowed to go in the lounge with the dog."

"Would you want to eat in there, with that lot?" Frank asked quietly, a mischievous smirk creasing his face.

"No, probably not; well definitely not, actually."

At the other end of the bar, the 'girls' in John's party had gathered around a table, and were talking animatedly about their recent skiing trip, whilst the 'boys' were clustered around the bar on stools, in effect preventing anyone else from getting near it. John sat amongst his friends, stool tipped back on two legs, with the sole of his foot pressed firmly halfway up the counter. Although he was clearly enjoying holding court with them, he nonetheless occasionally surreptitiously cast his beady eye towards Frank and his son.

"Another pint, Dan, or shall we make a move?"

"Up to you; I'm quite happy here in the warm." He smiled at Susie as she crossed the floor. She plucked a log from the brass bucket on the edge of the hearth and lobbed it onto the glowing embers. A shower of red and orange sparks leapt into the air, some immediately dying, others darting chaotically into the room or up the chimney, like a myriad of dancing gnats frolicking in the burnt tawny rays of a summer sunset.

"It's okay, I'll bring them over," she said, gathering up their empty glasses.

"Oh thanks." Frank flopped back into his chair.

"That's alright; it'll get me away from that lot for a minute or two." At that moment a roar of laughter exploded from the bar, no doubt fuelled by one of John's wisecracks. A short while later, with another round of drinks inside them, the sound levels from the 'boys' and 'girls' began to climb even higher.

"Right, shall we go?" Frank asked.

"Right."

They edged past the four men at the bar and out into the Stygian night, where the rain had at last ceased.

"Who was that guy?" Dan asked.

"Which one?"

"The fella with the dog. He looked like he'd just crawled out of a hedge - backwards."

"Ah, well Bill would regard himself as a sort of artisan. He lives in a caravan down near the old mill. I suppose you might say he's something of an eccentric. He scrapes a living working with wood. He makes bowls, furniture, garden ornaments, anything that anyone wants really. He carved a couple of mushrooms for Mrs. Massey back in the summer, they were really quite good."

"Wooden mushrooms?"

"Yes, she put them on her lawn; they looked rather attractive - in a funny sort of way."

"Did they? It sounds to me like he's not the only one around here who might be a bit eccentric."

"The loud bloke was John Chester. He's actually a decent sort, just likes to lord it a bit when he's out with his friends. He's also incredibly nosey - not as bad as Anne, though."

"Anne?"

"The postmistress: you'll find out soon enough."

Inside the pub, Mr. Chester was living up to his reputation for nosiness.

"Was that him, Susie?" He demanded, the minute the door had closed.

"Was that who?"

"Frank's boy - you know, the one he's just found out about."

"Yes, he's Dan. Rather good-looking, don't you think? Would you like to go through? Your table's ready."

That night, despite being tired, and despite having downed a large Scotch before retiring, Dan found himself unable to get to sleep. Truth to tell, his outwardly easygoing nature notwithstanding, he was painfully shy in the company of women. Yes, he'd chatted effortlessly to Susie in the pub, but he feared that if he were ever to find himself on his own with her, he would very quickly become panicky and tongue-tied.

He had good reason: he'd only dated a few girls and without exception, every one of those occasions had ended disastrously. In fact, the thought of any physical kind of relationship filled him with an inexplicable, irrational fear and sickening dread.

He rolled onto his side and crossly plumped his pillow up. What on earth was wrong with him? Filling with angst, he rolled onto his back and stared into the cloying darkness. He could hear his father's muffled snores through the walls.

Maybe, he reasoned, maybe his inherent coyness was due to the fact that he just hadn't met Miss Right yet. Perhaps, he tried to reassure himself, perhaps when he did it would all be different and everything would fall neatly into place; he'd be able to happily settle down and have a normal relationship like any other red-bloodied male.

He was being stupid, making mountains out of molehills, he told himself. His former reticence was probably just part of growing up. Hadn't he read that in some lads' magazine somewhere?

Eventually he drifted into an uneasy, troubled sleep; his dreams flecked with images of his mother's smiling face and the dry and dusty homeland that he'd left behind.

CHAPTER EIGHT

With his left hand tightly grasping the top rung of the ladder, Dan reached out his right arm and ran his fingers along the inside of the gutter. Stinking freezing cold brown water choked with rotting leaves slopped over the plastic rim, trickling along his arm to dribble off his elbow. He scooped out the sludge before clambering down the ladder and moving it along to clear the next stretch. He stood momentarily in the yard, rubbing his red palms together to dispel the numbness already creeping into his chilled fingertips.

The door of the house scraped open.

"I've just made coffee if you want some!" his father shouted.

"Thanks, be right there; I'll just finish cleaning out the gutter!" he shouted across the yard. Frank turned to go back inside, flicking his cigarette butt in an arc to his left. Dan gratefully followed him in a couple of minutes later. Once in the warm kitchen, he backed up to the stove, curling his cold fingers around the towel-rail and warming his bottom on the hot enamel.

"How are you getting on?"

"All done." He reluctantly abandoned his comfortable post to retrieve his mug of coffee from the table, which he cradled in his hands, feeling the soothing fragrant steam waft onto his face.

"You look cold."

"You don't say - I'm glad to finish the job."

"I noticed you looked a bit, how shall I say, *ill at ease* up the ladder."

"Bloody terrified more like: me and heights don't get on."

"Oh well, never mind, now you've done that you can start on the blocked drains on the ground, you'll be happier there. Heights never bother me much; you must get the fear from your mother."

Dan considered suggesting that if Frank was so bloody intrepid, then perhaps he should be the one up there. But instead he wordlessly sipped his coffee.

"Reminds me of when I was about your age - actually no, I must have been a few years younger than that at the time..." Frank trailed off vaguely.

"Sorry?"

"I was working on a farm not far away at the time, helping with the hay harvest. Harvey his name was, Frank Harvey funnily enough, been dead many years now. Anyway, we were poking these hay bales right up under the eaves in his loft, which we reached by climbing up a ladder from the outside. He was generally a grumpy old sod, and he loved giving people the benefit of his advice. As I was coming down the ladder, absolutely knackered at the end of a long sweaty evening's work, he thought he'd let me be the next to benefit from his worldly wisdom. *'You know son,'* he barked in his thick accent for all to hear, *'you should always come down a ladder the same way as you go up.'* The words suddenly sprang out of my mouth; it was too good an opportunity. *'What, you mean headfirst?'* I spat at him. Of course, the other three lads fell about laughing. Needless to say, he never offered any advice to me again: even today, it somehow still brings a smirk to my face when I think of it."

Dan forced a smile. "It's good, isn't it, when something spontaneous like that happens?"

"Well that certainly was, the old bugger had no answer to it."

"Did you ever work for him again after that?"

"Oh yes, more than once. I think probably, deep down somewhere, he could see the funny side; though of course he'd never admit it. He liked people to think him bad-tempered and curmudgeonly: it was his sort of shield against the world most likely. I actually got him to laugh - once. It was a freezing cold dark dismal day in November and I was helping him pull swedes with two other lads - one of those days when it never seems to get light properly. A hard frost had followed a day of relentless driving rain, and the miserable damp steadily and persistently seeped through our clothes and skin. I was beginning to lose any sensation in my fingers as I walked half stooped along the rows of swedes, ripping them from the half-frozen ground, topping and tailing them with my billhook, and lobbing them into nets strategically dotted around the field. God, it was gruelling work. We were all continually wiping cloying cold mud from our caked gloves on our trousers, to get some grip on the slippery wooden handles. Our boots were getting heavier by the minute, plastered in the slick red clay soil. Conversation had petered out by mid-afternoon; we were becoming increasingly morose. Old man Harvey was a couple of rows away from me, doggedly plodding along, having done this job countless times before. Suddenly he threw down his hook, stood up straight, and hands on hips, stretched his aching back.

'What a buggerin' job, I 'ates it, 'bout time I stopped doin' it. Don't know 'ow, though. Any of you boys got any ideas?'

Again, the words were just there. *'How about not sowing 'em?'* I shouted across to him.

'Not sowing 'em!' He started laughing wheezily. 'That's it boy, don't sow 'em in the first place, eh? Ha, ha, ha! If I don't sow 'em, then I don't 'ave to 'arvest the beggars, do I?'

For some reason, and to this day I don't know why, he seemed to find my suggestion highly amusing. For the rest of that dismal afternoon, we could hear him, every so often chuckling away to himself and muttering under his breath 'don't sow 'em, don't sow 'em.'

Nearly every time I saw him after that, he mentioned my advice to him re swede growing. 'Do you remember what you told me, eh boy? Don't sow 'em , you said, don't sow 'em.'"

Dan swilled out his empty mug under the tap and upturned it on the drainer. "Right, I'd better get back to it I suppose," he uttered without much enthusiasm.

"Tell you what," Frank said, recognising that his son was more than a little down in the dumps, "shall we go to the pub later? Be good to get out for a while, don't you think? We could have a bite to eat as well, if you want. Make an evening of it."

"Yeah, that'd be great." Once again the young man cracked an unconvincing smile before heading back to the yard. Frank sighed heavily after he'd heard the front door latch shut, then reached for the comfort of his tobacco tin. He may well have been an insensitive character at times, but his heart now went out to his boy. He knew that he was suffering the pain of his loss at the moment, and at this particular time of year that pain was bound to be severe. With Christmas fast approaching, past memories of joyous times would be flooding back, stacking up in his mind and cruelly stabbing him in the heart, one by agonising one. The worst thing, the *worst* thing - was he, his natural father, could find no way to comfort him, nor alleviate his aching feeling of grief. He planted his cigarette in the corner of his mouth and lit it. He then shrugged on his donkey jacket, pulled on his boots, and made his way outside, where a weak winter sun was struggling in vain to pierce the cold thin maudlin veil of low grey seamless cloud that floated motionless above.

"Hang on boy, I'll find the outfall."

"Sorry?" Dan was on all fours, his forearm buried inside the drain. It's metal grid lay beside him on the wet concrete.

"The pipe comes out in the field, over near the corner somewhere. It's probably blocked there. Hang on, I'll go and have a look." Frank scooped up the spade leaning against the wall and strode off into the field. After a few minutes of exploration, he found the outfall, and, seeing it choked, cleared the accumulated silt and earth that was causing the blockage. Dan watched as the water level fell quickly in the sump of the drain, then suddenly disappeared down the pipe with a satisfying whoosh.

"I should have told you," Frank said, reappearing in the yard, "most likely the outlet would be blocked. There isn't much fall you see, and what with animals and such trampling about, the pipe tends to silt up that end. It's a job should be done before every winter, but, well, you know...I've sort of neglected it recently." He smiled guiltily.

"Well it's done now. What else is there to unblock, apart from the one from the dairy?"

"Erm, there're two more on the lower side of the Dutch barn. Come on, I'll give you a hand: that way with any luck we'll be finished by one."

Some hours later, Dan was luxuriating in the bath, lying up to his shoulders in hot soapy water. His knees protruded above the sudsy water's surface, steaming gently. The air in the damp bathroom was fuggy; the small window completely glazed over with condensation. And despite the bare boards on the floor and faded wallpaper curling at the edges adding to the general air of neglect and squalor, after being miserably cold all day, he now felt warm and relaxed at last.

"Are you still soaking in that tub? I'm just about ready to go!" his father shouted from the far end of the landing.

Dan sighed before shouting back. "Give me five minutes! I've only just got the feeling back in my fingers!"

"What are you going to do when winter proper arrives?" Frank yelled. "Okay, five minutes more, then I'm going; I'm spitting feathers!"

Reluctantly, Dan extricated himself from the bathtub. Standing on the small shabby bath mat he grabbed the frayed and worn towel hanging on the (thankfully) heated towel-rail and vigorously rubbed himself dry. He tied the towel around his lean midriff and trotted to his bedroom where he quickly pulled on his clothes before the chill air upstairs could get to him.

They were hit by a blast of warm air as they entered the public bar of the pub. At the far end, logs burned brightly in the old fireplace, crackling merrily. Tall orange and yellow tongues of flame danced in the grate, licking the back of the chimney, casting flickering shadows on the walls opposite. The subdued lighting seeping through the dusky faded shades on the wall brackets added to the overall feeling of comfort and cosiness. Dan was pleased to see that Susie was once more behind the bar.

"Good evening, Susie," his father said breezily, "now that's what I *call* a fire. Pete's obviously not about; he'd choke on his ale if he saw the amount of wood you were burning."

She laughed prettily, being just as pleased to see Dan again. "No Frank, Pete's out the back trying to organize the draw for tonight. Did you buy any tickets? There are still a few spaces left on the last card if you're interested. One pound for twelve - and some great prizes."

"Don't tell me; amongst which are several out of date items kindly provided by our charitable postmistress no doubt."

"Such cynicism! Actually, I don't think Pete's got anything from the shop this year."

"That'll please her. So what do we stand to win from our investment then?"

"Oh, the usual stuff. You know, booze, choccies, meat – and there's a duck, couple of pheasants, and I think a goose as well. There should be over a hundred prizes: we've sold a lot of tickets this time."

"Right, well can I have a pint of Guinness and a pint of lager first? Then we'll consider it." Frank wandered off and parked himself in a chair next to the fire. He popped open his tobacco tin and studiously began to roll himself a smoke.

"I'll have a couple of quid's worth," Dan offered, picking up the drinks.

"Thanks, I'll bring the card over and you can fill in the squares you want."

"Great, and can we have a bar menu as well please?"

"Course you can; I'll bring that over as well. Specials are on the board."

"Right, thanks." Much to her surprise, his boyish grin immediately melted her heart, and caused a mild flutter in her stomach. Dan picked up the freshly poured drinks, and carefully carried the brimming glasses to his father who now sat with his long legs stretched out in front of him, soaking up the soothing heat from the blazing logs. Thin layers of wispy blue smoke hovered in the air above him and a lit cigarette smouldered in an ashtray on the table by his side.

"There you go."

"Oh, cheers." Frank took a deep draught of his porter, and set down the half empty pint. "That hit the spot."

The barmaid appeared carrying two menus in one hand, and also a large cardboard sheet tucked under her arm. She tidily placed one menu in front of each of them, and laid the sheet on a vacant table nearby.

"I'm sorry, but there aren't any Specials tonight, because of the draw, so you've only got these to choose from. I think there're about twenty-five squares left on the card, so if you fill them all in we'll call it two pounds – fair enough?"

"Sounds fair to me," Dan replied with a grin. Not for the first time he noticed how attractive the girl was, especially when she smiled. Her hazel eyes seemed to twinkle mischievously, and the swirling tips of her soft brown long hair bobbed gently, dusting the top of her neat cleavage seductively. As she walked back to the bar, he couldn't fail to appreciate the swaying movement of her rounded hips in her tight jeans. Neither could his father.

"Pretty girl, don't you think?"

"Sorry?"

"Don't tell me you're not attracted to her, it's written all over your face," he teased.

"Yeah well, she is kind of…"

"A word to the wise," Frank interrupted, lowering his voice. "She's a bit fragile is our Susie, although by her manner you wouldn't guess it. A not uncommon story, I'm afraid. She fell for a married man who swore to her he'd leave his wife and kids. He didn't of course; after the initial infatuation had cooled, he left her high and dry and scuttled back to his wife with his tail between his legs. Her father was furious, disowned her and chucked her out. She's been living at the pub ever since."

"Poor girl. What about her mother, couldn't she talk him round, or did she side with him?"

"Frankly the woman's a doormat. She won't stand up for herself. I wouldn't be surprised if he knocked her about, but for Christ's sake don't go spreading that around."

"Sounds like she's better off out of it to me."

"Probably is, though I doubt if the girl would agree: she loves her dad. Anyway, enough of all that; I'm hungry." He quickly perused the bar menu. "I'll have sausage and chips, please – and ketchup – don't forget that. Here…" He grubbed in his pocket and fished out a crumpled twenty-pound note. "You can pay for the food out of this; but don't forget it's your round next."

Smiling broadly, he settled back in his chair and with his tobacco tin resting on his stomach, set about the serious business of rolling another cigarette.

They remained ensconced in the bar longer than anticipated, and were on the point of leaving when the landlord announced to the by then packed pub the imminent start of the Christmas draw.

"Might as well have another, seeing as we've got some tickets."

Dan didn't argue. He grabbed the empties and squeezed through the noisy throng jostling for position at the busy bar. After one more pint and when the prizes had all been claimed, Frank was ready to surrender his warm spot by the fire and face the elements.

"Well that was worth waiting for, I don't think," he complained as they crossed the car park.

"It was a bit of a laugh though, wasn't it? I mean, it could have been worse, we might have won those hair curlers instead of that poor fella, what was his name?"

"Nigel, yeah that was funny, I admit. "Especially," this slightly slurred, "'specially as he bought God knows how many tickets, and that's all he came out with. Ha! Serves him right."

"Anyhow, I don't know why you're so disgruntled; it was me who paid for the bloody things anyway."

Once back at the farmhouse Frank poured two measures of Scotch, and gestured to his son to sit at the table opposite him.

"Oh, I think I'd sooner just have a coffee if..."

"Come on, one won't hurt, and I want to say something to you now, while I'm slightly oiled; it'd be easier."

"Oh right. I guess one won't do any harm." He pulled up a chair and took a sip of the drink, wincing somewhat. Whisky really wasn't his tipple.

Frank rolled himself a smoke, having to concentrate with great deliberation on the task due to the befuddling effect of a little too much alcohol. He lit it carefully, took a tentative drag, and reached for his drink with it clasped between two fingers.

"I noticed you seemed a little low recently," he plunged in, "and want you to know I understand, and I sympathise. I know how you feel – I've been there, you see."

"Frank, it's..."

"I know," the other rushed on. "It's Christmas, isn't it? It brings it all back. Not only that, it's your first without your parents; you're bound to find it an emotional and stressful time. All I can tell you is it *does* get better with time, or at least less raw."

"Does it? Only sometimes, I feel like it happened

yesterday and I'm overwhelmed and feel like my whole world's crumbling…"

"Well if you want to crumble, crumble on me; or if you just want a chat, or to talk about them, that's fine with me too. I can be a miserable old sod, God knows: but I'm a good listener. It'll be painful for you to talk about them, of course, but it'll help as well. For heaven's sake don't go and bottle it all up; there's nothing worse you could do."

"Okay, thanks." Dan smiled weakly, looking at his father through eyes beginning to mist with tears.

"Right, good," Frank replied a little self-consciously. He resumed his assault on his roll-up, and for a short while silence reigned between them.

"How do you get on with your sister?"

"Janey? Fine. Like I said, we don't have that much contact; our lives have sort of gone in different directions I guess."

"Why don't you give her a call sometime? She'll be hurting too, for sure. Hell, she'll know exactly what you're going through, because *she's* going through the same thing. It'll help. But don't phone her peak times, will you? It'll cost me a fortune!" He grinned. Dan reciprocated. Frank drained his glass, and scrunched out his butt in the choked ashtray.

"Bedtime for me I think." He rose a tad unsteadily from the chair, and feeling slightly awkward, patted his son on the shoulder as he made his way to the door.

"Good night boy."

"Good night."

Frank paused at the door and turned. "Oh, and while I'm dishing out all this sound advice, there's one more thing."

"What's that?"

"Susie."

"What about her?"

114

"What about her? Ask her out of course."

"But you said she…"

"I know what I said, just be mindful of what she's been through, that's all. It's patently obvious that the girl won't say no to a date with you, even to an old fool like me."

Dan was thoughtful for a minute or two as he listened to his father clump up the stairs and walk heavily along the squeaky bare boards of the landing to his dark cold bedroom. Then he rose from the table, leaving his barely touched whisky in the glass. He crossed the kitchen, turned off the light, and made his way upstairs. He normally fell sound asleep as soon as his head hit the pillow, but as in the previous night, despite the anaesthetizing effect of the alcohol he'd taken, sleep eluded him. He lay there in the gloom, listening to the sound of his father's snores once more roll along the passage and ooze under his bedroom door. Although he felt a frisson of excitement at the prospect of a date with Susie, the old feelings of anxiety nibbled away at him. Perhaps he ought not to bother after all – especially as the girl was damaged. But then, a lot of people were, weren't they? To some extent anyway. He himself was hardly without emotional problems. *Issues.* Isn't that how a psychiatrist would put it? Or was that a psychologist? With these thoughts skittering through his rather addled brain, he eventually nodded off. Bizarre muddled images floated in and out of his dreams. However, when he awoke the next morning in the cold half-light of another drab December day, he had made his mind up. He'd already decided to start his life afresh in England, and that's exactly what he would do.

"Should I take a driving test?"

"What?" Frank asked, a little annoyed at his concentration

being broken whilst he was reading his morning paper. "Haven't you got an Australian licence?"

"Well yeah, but I can't drive on that indefinitely can I? If I'm staying over here, might as well take the test sooner rather than later, eh?"

"And are you?"

"Am I what?"

Frank plucked his glasses from the bridge of his nose and looked over the top of his broadsheet. "Staying here, of course."

"Ah."

"Bloody hell boy, what does *ah* mean?"

"Sorry, I suppose it means yes - as far as I can tell, that is."

"As far as you can tell?"

"Do you want me to? I mean, I know you said you'd like me to help sort the farm out, but what then?"

His father regarded him quizzically.

"How can I put this?" Dan struggled. "Will you still want me around?"

Frank wanted to tell his son that he wanted him to stay, that it was the most important thing to him in the world at that moment; that he wanted more than anything else for the boy to get married and settle, to inherit his business and prosper, to provide him with a family to cherish. But he didn't, he thought it would be too much weight to dump on his young shoulders. He considered his reply, and answered with deliberation.

"You've only been here a short while; can you be sure that you'll still want to be around *me*?"

Dan felt rather hurt by this response. "We seem to be getting on alright so far, don't we? I see what you're saying, and I wasn't trying to butt in on your life, but..."

"Whoa, whoa. You're not butting in: I'm just trying to be realistic, that's all. Let's just see how it goes, shall we? A lot can happen in a few weeks…"

"Is your glass always half empty?" Dan cut in, rising angrily to his feet.

"What…?" Frank was clearly taken aback.

"Well, if you just want me to help you get back on your feet that's fine, so long as I know that's all there is to it. I'll do that then I'll bugger off out of it."

"Dan! That's not what I'm saying at all!"

"Then what *are* you trying to say?"

"I'm only trying to… I don't know, I'm not the easiest person to live with, and…"

"You think I haven't noticed?"

It was Frank's turn to be stung. "I'm sorry, I suppose I've been on my own too long…"

"…and you can't get used to someone else being around," his son finished for him.

"No! That's not it. Look, I don't want you to go anywhere, any time. Nothing would make me happier or prouder than if you were to stay on here and be my son, take over my business, fall in love, give me grandchildren; all the usual family stuff."

His answer stunned Dan for a few seconds.

"Then why are you so reticent? Or am I getting the wrong vibes?"

"No," he sighed. "I'm being cowardly. I'm frightened it'll all go tits up. I'm frightened that if I balls it up, and I'm good at ballsing things up, believe me, that I'll be miserable and lonely for the rest of my life. Your turning up out of the blue has really meant that much to me."

Dan considered this for a while before responding.

"I don't think anything that's happened to you has been your fault: not from what I've heard anyway."

Frank harrumphed dismissively.

"Well? Was it down to you that you had BSE? Or Foot and Mouth? Or that your wife couldn't or wouldn't support you in your hour of need?"

"I wasn't exactly the perfect husband."

"No, I don't reckon you were, but you didn't deserve to be treated like that. Stop beating yourself up and let's just get on with it. And if we don't get along, it'll be my doing as much as yours: agreed?"

"Yes, yes, agreed."

"Right, good. So, as it's for some strange reason not raining today, why don't we get that fencing finished?"

"Yes, let's do that; you go on and get the gear together, I've just got a quick phone call to make."

Once his son had gone out into the yard, he dug out the telephone directory and thumbed through the dog-eared pages in search of the number of the local driving test centre. Outside, Dan threw the fencing equipment into the back of the Land Rover with little care. Whilst on the one hand he was deeply touched by his natural father's wish to see him settle and one day take over the farming business, on the other he had detected in him a fragility that he'd not noticed before. This was disquieting. Would he do something stupid if the two of them were to fall out? Would losing his newly discovered son push him over the edge once he realized the likelihood of spending the rest of his days in loneliness? Furthermore, he felt guilty that he was betraying the man who'd brought him up so lovingly. He told himself that Frank had reassured him that he didn't wish to take his dad's place, but somewhere inside he feared this was just what the man wanted. These notions so crowded his mind that he failed to notice Frank approaching, and he made him visibly jump.

"Have we got everything?"

"I reckon," Dan replied tersely.

They both climbed into the cab and Frank twisted the ignition key. The engine turned with painful sluggishness. *Come on, come on.* Suddenly it roared into life, blowing a great cloud of diesel smoke out of the exhaust, which billowed across the yard like a huge sail unfurling. They rattled up to the field in uncomfortable silence and went about their work with little to say to each other.

"I shouldn't have asked you to be my son," Frank blurted out from nowhere as they headed home. The jaundiced beams from the Land Rover's woefully feeble headlights bucked along the bumpy ground. Yellow overgrown unruly clumps of withered grass threw long shadows before them as the daylight rapidly faded; the sky on the western horizon a red smear, sole testament to a gloriously sunny winter's day ended. "I have no right to ask you that, and I never will again, I'm so sorry."

"That's okay. Look, let's just put it all behind us, shall we?"

"Good idea. By the way, I booked you a driving test; fifteenth of January, if that suits."

"Yeah, sure, thanks…only what am I going to take it in?"

"What's wrong with the Land Rover?"

"Well, yeah, I suppose I could…but I was actually thinking of buying a car, nothing fancy of course," he added hastily. "It'd make it a lot easier for me to get around independently; if you get my drift."

"Yeah, I can see that; but can you afford it?"

"Well not at the moment, no. But once probate comes through…"

"That could take weeks. Look, don't fly off the handle, but I can lend you some money until your grandmother's estate's settled - so long as you don't want a Maserati, that is."

CHAPTER NINE

"What was the number?"

"Seventy-five."

"It's got to be further on, look that's only fifty-five there."

"Alright, we'll keep going then. What was it again?"

"Er, white Astra, P reg - the blokey said we'd see it parked up in front the house," Dan added helpfully.

They soon found number seventy-five with the vehicle, as promised, on its driveway. Frank pulled up on the other side of the road and killed the engine.

"If you like it don't let on. Try and comment on its bad points and if it comes to buying it, let me do the talking, alright?"

"Sure, no worries." Looking around the street whilst his son pressed the doorbell, Frank couldn't help but notice how out of place his Land Rover looked in this urban environment. The door was cautiously opened by a short and slight man who was clearly of pensionable age.

"We've come to look at the car?" Dan said in his naturally amiable manner. "I'm Dan, and this is my...this is Frank."

"Right, I'll just get the keys."

A while later, having meticulously examined the car from top to toe, and after a thorough road test, the two of them were unable to find anything seriously at fault with the vehicle. The only criticism that might have been levelled at the owner was his overzealous use of car stickers which plastered a large part of both the rear and the front screens.

"Seems to be genuine, he's obviously looked after it. Do you like it?" Frank asked Dan quietly.

"Yup, I reckon you're right: it'll suit me fine," he answered equally quietly.

"I've got the service history inside, and all the other paperwork – if you'd like to see it, that is," the little man offered hopefully.

"Thank you, we'd like that."

In the kitchen the vendor's wife had made tea, which she presented on a tray whilst her husband fetched the car's documents. "Do help yourselves; the biscuits are still warm, I've not long baked them."

Frank scrutinized the paperwork. Occasionally, to his son's disgust, he dunked a biscuit in his tea before cramming it half soggy into his mouth.

"Yes, well we like the car, and you've obviously looked after it, but we can't give what you're asking for it, I'm afraid." Dan felt further embarrassed as he noticed the old man's face drop. He would've given the guy what he wanted, and got the hell out of there. He wished his seat would swallow him up.

"Six hundred seems about right to me."

"Oh, but that's a hundred and fifty less than we're asking! Can't you go a bit more?"

"Not really, though I tell you what…we'll give you six hundred and fifty cash in hand, now. There." Frank placed a wad of notes on the table in front of him. "What do you say?" The old fellow glanced at his wife before replying. "Is that the best you can offer? I paid nearly twice as much as that for it when I bought it, barely two years ago, from Harrison's garage."

"Yes, but look. Cash, no hassle and the deal's done."

The wife now piped up. "You might as well take what he's offering dear: it's done then, isn't it?"

"I suppose so," he said wearily, "you've got yourselves a deal." He stretched out a shaky skinny arm and Frank shook his hand firmly before enthusiastically counting out the money.

Dan reached the farmhouse in his new acquisition first, and was looking over it when his father pulled up beside him in the yard. Frank heaved himself out of the Land Rover and slammed the door.

"You got back alright then; any problems?"

"Nope, she drove like a dream."

"She?"

"Yeah, didn't you know? All cars are female."

"Oh, is that a fact? We got a good deal though, don't you think?"

"I guess. Truth is, I felt a bit uncomfortable, you know, haggling with the old fella like that. I reckon it was well worth what he wanted, what with the regular servicing and all – and there's still five months' tax on it."

"Yes, I noticed that too, he must have forgotten about it. Still, he was happy enough. And in any case, if he didn't like what he was offered, he didn't have to sell it, did he?"

"I thought he told you he'd had a stroke and couldn't drive?"

"Yes, he did. What I meant was he didn't have to sell it to *us*." Dan appeared unconvinced. "Look, it's a hard world out there, and he clearly paid over the top for it in the first place. If we had such a bargain, how come there weren't more people interested in it? No, he had a good enough deal, and cash as well: that always does the trick."

Dan however still harboured the uncomfortable feeling that his father had treated the old couple unfairly, and despite being pleased to have his own set of wheels, this stuck in his craw. However, he considered it prudent and diplomatic to let the matter rest.

By this time, Christmas was a scant two weeks away and Dan raised the matter of the impending celebrations a couple of evenings later whilst Frank was settled in the warm kitchen, drink in one hand, fag in the other, after a satisfying chicken casserole his son had cooked for supper.

"Do you have any plans for Christmas?" he remarked casually.

"Plans? What do you mean?" Frank rejoined swiftly.

"Oh I don't know, I guess I mean do you do anything special like parties, or anything like that?"

"Nope, never…oh, except once when my wife insisted on having a *drinks party*. It was a total fiasco: me pretending to enjoy the company of people I'd nothing in common with, and her becoming more and more pissed, glaring at me for not liking her awful friends. Most of the guests left early, no doubt embarrassed by her increasingly drunken state and the icy atmosphere between the two of us."

"Oh."

"Obviously since she left I haven't bothered much."

"Right." A pause in conversation followed, the only sounds being the clanking and clattering of plates and cutlery as Dan washed them, up to his elbows in steaming suds at the sink. "I was thinking it might be nice to do out the front room. Get a tree, put a few deccys up, that sort of thing," he soldiered on. Frank exhaled a long plume of smoke.

"Well," he opined thoughtfully, "it would cheer the old

place up a bit, make a change from being in here all the time; but it's in a bit of a state – it's a while since it's been lived in."

"Yeah, but nothing that a good clean and a lick of paint wouldn't sort out, eh?"

"No, I suppose not. It should be warm enough, the fire draws lovely in there. I'll tell you what, I'll get some paint tomorrow, and you can make a start. And since you're offering to smarten it up, I'll even let you choose the colour, how's that?"

Dan couldn't recall at what point in the conversation he'd volunteered to undertake the whole task, but chose to let this go and instead stuck his neck out further. "That old telly, does it work?"

"That old thing? I don't know, it ought to; at least it did last time I switched it on, but that was ages ago. I'll have a look in Benson's while I'm in town; see if I can't pick up a new one for a reasonable price," he added, overcome suddenly by a largesse so uncharacteristic that the plate Dan was stacking on the drainer nearly slipped from his grasp. Regaining his composure he replied,

"Great - should be something worth watching over Christmas."

"I wouldn't bank on it – unless you like the idea of trawling through three tedious hours or more of *The Great Escape,* or even worse one of those great biblical epics with Charlton Heston or Christmas Specials of so-called comedy programmes that were never funny in the first place, and have no chance of being in the slightest bit entertaining," Frank declared, every word slickly coated with a raw cynicism. Dan nudged the conversation away from this topic.

"So are we going to have a turkey, or what?"

"I hadn't really thought…"

"Only if we are," his son interrupted, "don't you think we'd better order it now? There are only a couple of weeks left to get one. Mrs Manning says she can put a bird back for us, but she needs to know soon."

"Alright, then I'll pop in and see her on my way out tomorrow," Frank answered, a note of irritability creeping into his voice. "And before you ask I'll see the butcher as well, and order a ham to go with it; though God knows how we'll eat it all."

"Don't worry about that, there's plenty of different meals I can make with the leftovers."

"Fine, so long as we're still not eating turkey at Easter," Frank retorted grumpily.

"We won't be, so long as you don't buy a monster. I'll make some mince pies as well, shall I? And what about presents? What do you need?"

"Oh please don't bother about me; I've got everything I want." Dan glanced dubiously at his father.

"What about a shirt, or maybe a coat?"

"I'll tell you what, why don't you get me a shirt *you* like, and I'll get you a shirt *I* like as well. That way, when we exchange presents, we can simply swap them over if they don't suit."

"I can't really argue with that, can I?"

The next morning, after a very satisfactory breakfast, Frank gulped down the last of his tea and dropped the empty mug into the foamy warm water. It bobbed on the surface for a few agonizing seconds before plummeting to the bottom of the sink, emitting a dull thud as it came to rest. "Have you made up your mind yet?"

"Yes, this one I think." Dan rose from the table with a paint catalogue folded in his hand, and showed his father the colour he'd selected. "Evening primrose."

"Aha." Frank noted with some dissatisfaction that the paint selected was one of the more expensive brands, but refrained from making a comment.

"Make sure you get the matt finish, won't you? Ten litres should do it."

"Ten?"

"Yup, those walls will need at least two coats to make the job a good'un."

"Oh, okay then," he replied resignedly.

"I'll make a start cleaning the place up. I'll bung the curtains in the washing-machine first, then give the ceiling a coat of white – there's enough here to do that, isn't there?"

"Yes, yes, plenty," Frank replied hastily.

"But can you get some white undercoat and gloss for the door and window? And we'll need two or three decent brushes and a couple of new rollers – oh, and some cleaner and masking tape."

"Right; well I'll be off then."

Frank had barely shut the door behind him when the phone rang. It was Mr. Hutchison.

"...so you see," he said, at last coming to the point, "I am thus able to inform you that we have reached a figure for probate. As I intoned before, you, and consequently your sister, have no fear of incurring any Inheritance Tax liabilities. I have divvied up, if I may put it so crudely, your grandmother's estate between you as far as I am able, less of course our fees for so doing, and as we speak a cheque will be winging its way to you – fortuitously, some might say, considering the time of year. You both inherit her house in equal part: the same naturally

127

applying to liquid capital in her Lloyds bank account, and the house contents. And that's it, pretty straightforward. I've also received from her – your sister that is – written confirmation of her wishes to sell the property, and that she is happy for you to appoint a suitable estate agent and also to dispose of the contents in any way you deem fit. I trust you've spoken to her, and are in accord with these arrangements?"

"Oh yes, absolutely."

"Good, then the only thing remaining for me is to wish you compliments of the season, and to add that naturally we'd be delighted to act for you should you wish to instruct us on any other matter."

"Thanks." Dan replaced the phone on its base, wondering why the legal profession had to make such a meal out of such a relatively easy undertaking. When he was in receipt of the payment, a couple of days later, he was also given to wondering how they justified such an exorbitant charge for their services. He said as much to Frank.

"They're all a bunch of thieving bastards, I'm afraid," he replied succinctly, "but doubtless the London firms are the worst. You're not going to let them do the conveyancing on your grandmother's house, are you?"

"I haven't really thought that far ahead."

"Well don't. I'll have a word with my fellow Dawkins. I won't say it'll save you a lot of money, but at least he'll have a chat on the phone with you without charging you a hundred pounds for the privilege, and he's contactable; by that I mean he spends more of the working day in the office than he does on the golf course – usually anyway."

"What do you think of the colour?" Dan had by now painted the front room, and was rehanging the curtains.

"Well it's certainly cheered the place up, and it's quite a

subtle shade too, not yellow yellow, if you see what I mean. You made a good choice - it's surprising what a lick of paint can do," he added with genuine appreciation.

"Thanks, I must say I'm pretty pleased with it as well."

"So all you've got to do now is set up the new goggle-box, is it?"

"Yup, only that's gonna have to wait a while, unless you want to do it. I'd better get into town and open up a bank account first, and deposit this money safely inside before I lose it somewhere. Then I'll be able to pay you for the car."

"Good, I'm all for that."

Much to his surprise, when Dan returned from the bank armed to the teeth with paperwork some time later, he found that Frank had managed to install the television and had even more surprisingly, successfully tuned it in to all four stations. The quality of the picture was however disappointingly poor.

"Look at that," his father said mournfully, flicking through the channels. "Every one's the same." He stared disconsolately at the snowy screen.

"Must be the aerial then, or the cable's deteriorated."

"Perhaps you could shimmy up the ladder, see if there's a loose connection or something?" he asked optimistically.

"Er, sorry but no chance. It's way too high for me. You'll have to call in a pro, I'm afraid. Hang on a minute, have you checked the connector on the end of the cable?"

"Yes of course I have, I'm not *completely* daft you know."

"And the wall socket?"

"Yes, yes." Dan wandered out into the yard and walking backwards away from the house, eyes shielded against the dazzling slanting rays of the setting sun, squinted at the aerial fixed high up on the side of the stone chimney.

"Looks a bit cock-eyed to me," he opined as Frank approached. "How long's it been there?"

"Donkey's years I should think." He sighed. "Oh well, like you say, I'd better get somebody out – God knows what that'll cost." He plunged his hands into the deep pockets of his corduroy trousers and disconsolately turned to go.

"I could help, if you want."

"Sorry?"

"With the aerial… I mean you've bought the telly, and I've got some money now."

Just for a moment or two, Frank was sorely tempted to take him up on his offer. Then common sense kicked in. What *can* he have been thinking of?

"No, I won't hear of it. It's kind of you, but I can't accept your money; thank you anyway."

"Well if you're sure…"

"Absolutely positive. Come on let's have a cup of tea while I delve into the Yellow Pages again." Dan meekly followed his father inside.

"I saw Susie in town," Dan mentioned casually as he gently stirred his tea. Frank looked up from his search in the Yellow Pages, dumped two heaped teaspoons of sugar in his own drink, and whisked it vigorously. As the teaspoon clinked noisily against the sides of the mug, the tea slopped over its rim, trickling down to pool around it.

"Really?" He dropped the spoon unceremoniously and picked up the mug. A couple of drips fell and splattered onto the table's wooden surface. A third hung undecided from its base.

"In the bank actually."

"Oh."

"We had a coffee and a chat – I'm seeing her tomorrow night in fact," he added, doing his best to sound nonchalant.

★

"You look nice," he complimented her as she climbed into the front seat of the car.

"Thanks, you don't look so bad yourself."

"Do you fancy going anywhere in particular?" he asked, stupidly feeling a bit nervous.

"Erm, no; it'll just be nice getting away from here for a few hours. Don't get me wrong, Pete and Margaret have been great, but it's, you know…"

"I know, living on the job."

"That's it. Because I'm always there, they assume I'm always available."

"Yeah, I know what you mean. Well, I thought we might have a bite to eat at the Maltsters Arms. The food's quite good there I've been told."

"Blimey, it's a while since I was in that place!"

"Do you want to go somewhere else then? Like the Bell, maybe?"

"Oh no," she replied a bit too hastily. "I'm sorry, but my dad drinks in there sometimes, and I sort of don't want to see him. I'm sure the Maltsters will be lovely."

And it was. The two of them sat near the comforting fire in an intimate corner of the comfortable snug. The pub wasn't that busy, with a few locals perched on tall bar stools pleasantly and quietly chatting to one another, their flickering shadows cast from the flames creating wavering silhouettes onto the thickly plastered aged walls.

"I hate to admit it, but that was one of the best steaks I've ever tasted," Dan said appreciatively as he pushed his knife and fork together on the empty oval plate.

"Why do you hate to say it?"

"Isn't that obvious? I'd have to admit that you Poms have

131

got better beef than us Aussies. That would never do." He smiled boyishly.

"Oh no, heaven forbid." A brief silence followed between them. Susie gently swirled the last remnants of the red wine in her glass before swallowing it.

"Would you like another? That is, if I can tear myself away from the fire."

"Yes please."

"How are you getting on with Frank, if you don't mind me asking?" she enquired once Dan had settled back into his seat opposite.

"No I don't mind you asking at all. I suppose you know that he's my…"

"…father," she pre-empted him. "Yes everyone knows, you can't keep secrets in *this* village, not with Anne as postmistress. Mind you," she added vaguely, "I expect every village in the country's the same."

"Undoubtedly. To answer your question, we're rubbing along together alright most of the time: but he's not the easiest person to live with."

"No, I don't suppose he is."

"I mean," Dan continued, warming to his subject, "he lets me get on with the work without much interference; and he clearly made an effort to tidy the place up a bit before I arrived…"

"And himself too."

"Really?"

"Oh yes, we hardly ever saw him in the village; and when anybody did spot him, it was clear that neither personal hygiene nor the state of his dress featured highly on his list of priorities."

"But then, life had dealt him a few blows by then, what with his animals being wiped out and his wife leaving."

"Yes it had. But some would say that the reasons for his demise go back further than that."

"Oh? He's said nothing to me."

"Well, he wouldn't. And anyway, it's only a rumour."

"What is? Come on, you're intriguing me."

"Do you know Bob?"

"Up the road, yes. He lost his son not long back."

"The very same. Well, rumour has it that his wife and your dad were having an affair."

"But she died didn't she?"

"That's right, but apparently their fling was over long before she found out she had cancer; it finished even before Tom was born."

He looked into her bright hazel eyes, waiting for her to carry on. But before she could, he suddenly interjected: "Are you telling me that Tom could have been Frank's son?"

"That's the gist of it."

"But there's no proof. What about Bob?"

"Nobody thought he suspected the boy wasn't his, or at least if he did, he certainly never let on."

"So why the rumour?"

"They were seen together, only a couple of times admittedly. And his Land Rover was spotted parked up at the farm when Bob was at market on more than one occasion."

"But there could be any number of innocent explanations for that. They were neighbours for God's sake!" Dan protested.

"Absolutely. Like I said, it's probably just spiteful malicious chit-chat. I tell you, I hear stuff behind that bar that'd make your hair stand on end! Take no notice."

Dan heeded her advice and changed the subject. "So what are you doing for Christmas?"

"Nothing exciting, that's for sure. Pulling pints probably. No doubt you've heard about my family situation."

"Er, yes. You haven't got any other relations you can spend it with then?"

"No, my father was the youngest of three sons, one was killed in the war, and the other, Uncle Gordon, died about ten years ago. My mother has a sister in Dartmouth. She's nice - but I can't stand her husband. Mum's parents are still alive but in a home, I'm afraid. It'll be okay, we'll have a nice meal at the pub. Like I said, they look after me."

"I almost envy you the company. It'll just be the two of us for Christmas dinner; and we'd probably be eating bread and cheese if it was up to Frank, he's not exactly the type to be brimming over with Christmas spirit."

"No, I can well believe that," she grinned.

"Oh well, never mind, it's only for a day, everything will be back to normal afterwards." They sat in companionable silence for a little while, appreciating the crackling fire and warm ambience.

"Last orders, gentlemen, please!" The Landlord's booming voice knocked Dan from his reverie.

"Blimey, I didn't realize it was so late. Do you want another?"

"No thanks, I'm fine. That was a lovely meal, I enjoyed it," Susie replied demurely.

"Good, perhaps we can do it again, soon."

"That'd be nice, but I've only got a few more evenings off before Christmas."

"Then we'd better make the most of them hadn't we?"

Back outside The Golden Fleece, Dan stopped the car's engine and switched off the headlights.

"I'll see you on Friday then," Susie said, one hand resting

on the door handle. He stretched over and gave her a chaste kiss on the cheek, catching as he did so an evocative whiff of her subtle perfume.

"I'm looking forward to it."

"Me too." She climbed out, shutting the door behind her with a soft click.

As Dan drifted off to sleep that night, it started to rain. As the long dark night dragged tediously on, the rain got heavier. It was still drumming on the roof slates when he awoke at seven o'clock, the dawn reluctant to break and throw its grey half-light on the miserable scene. He pattered barefoot downstairs, with the intention of making a brew and taking a mug up to Frank. But his father was already up and dressed. A thin wavy line of smoke from his first cigarette of the day gently spiralled up from where it rested on the lip of the ashtray.

"Morning boy, tea's in the pot. How was your date last night?"

"Er, morning. Yeah, it was fine thanks, we went to the Maltsters; the food was really good." Reclaiming a mug from the draining board, he slopped in some milk and splashed in the golden tea.

"I haven't been there for years: mind you, it was more a spit and sawdust kind of establishment then."

"Well it certainly isn't like that now." He stirred the hot drink before taking a tentative sip.

"Good, and I'm glad you both had a good time. Any plans for today?" he asked, suddenly changing the subject, "because if you haven't, and I would suggest you haven't in view of the shitty weather," he continued before Dan had a chance to answer, "we could go into town and get a few things for Christmas. Look, I've already started making up a list." He tapped a piece of paper on the table with his index finger.

135

Dan peered at it, then read out loud:

"Mince pies, Christmas pudding, wine, port, brandy, crackers, cheeses…"

He was clearly taken by surprise. "But I thought you..."

"Yes, but you're right. I've decided to make a bit of an effort. It's only once a year, after all. Can you think of anything else we should get. I've ordered all the meat, so it's only…I know - celery, that's always nice with a lump of stilton: and do you think we should have a bottle of single malt too?"

"Well I don't…"

"I'll put it on the list then. What else?" He retrieved his half smoked cigarette and took a deep drag. Tiny petals of grey paper ash fluttered onto the table from its glowing tip.

"What about Brussel sprouts?"

"Ah yes, Bru…are you being funny?"

"Only a little bit…"

"I know! Christmas tree. Better not forget that. Right, are you going to go and get dressed? Only the earlier we get in there the better to avoid the hordes. Besides, I'm hoping the man from Bradford's coming this afternoon, to sort out the aerial."

"In this weather?" Dan asked, trying not to sound too sceptical.

"It'll have stopped raining by then," Frank confidently replied.

"Yeah? How can you be so sure?"

"Rain before seven, fine by eleven, that's what my father used to reckon, and he was right - most of the time anyway."

"No doubt we'll find out if he was soon enough."

It didn't take them long to buy everything on the list, plus of course a shirt for each other. Dan also got a pair of earrings and a bottle of perfume for Susie. As they walked back to his car through sodden streets, the heavy rain-clouds peeled away to reveal a pallid washed blue sky. A watery sun beamed down benevolently on them, its light reflecting in the water chirruping down the roadside gutters, and bouncing dazzlingly off the numerous shop windows. A bus whooshed past on the wet tarmac, its wheels throwing a fine spray into the air, where momentarily the colours of the rainbow hovered tenuously before dissolving into nothing.

"There you are, what did I tell you?" Frank pronounced triumphantly. "Just look at that glorious blue sky."

"I can only bow to your superior knowledge," his son answered with mock reverence. "I suppose that means I've got to buy you a pint now?"

"Much as I'd love to take you up on your generous offer, I'm going to have to decline. In any case, that particular pearl of wisdom came from my father, not me. We'd better get back; Bradfords said they'd send a van out any time after twelve."

"Oh right – I'd forgotten all about that."

By the time they'd got home, a white van with an array of different sized ladders stacked on the roof was parked in the yard. Two neat figures clad in clean blue overalls stood by the house, staring up at the aerial on its precarious perch.

"Good morning," Frank greeted them cordially, stepping from the car and, much to Dan's annoyance, slamming the door brutishly behind him. "What do you think?"

"I can't really tell from the ground," the smaller man peevishly replied. From his demeanour, he was obviously in charge. "Although even from here it looks like it's had its day. Do you know when it was fitted?"

"Some time ago, probably twenty years or so."

"Then you haven't done too bad out of it." He began unlashing the longest set of ladders.

"Can I get you gents a cup of tea, or coffee maybe?" Dan asked. *Might even cheer you up a bit.*

"No thanks, we're fine," the same man answered without consulting his workmate, adding sullenly: "I never touch caffeine."

"Oh right." Dan threw his father a sidelong glance.

"We'll let you chaps get on with it then."

Ten minutes later there was a knock at the door. "I'll get it," Frank offered. "That'll be happy Harry I expect."

He was right. "I've been up and had a look," the dour man said sombrely, "and the strap fixing the aerial to the chimney stack has broken. The whole thing is rusting away and needs replacing I'm afraid."

"Oh, and what's that going to cost me?"

"Probably about two hundred and fifty quid for the whole job."

"Have you got an aerial with you?"

"Yes, we can get it done now."

"Well you'd better replace it then."

When Frank reappeared in the kitchen, he began rifling through one of the drawers in the heavy oak sideboard, pulling out various dog-eared documents and envelopes and massing them untidily on top.

"What are you looking for?" Dan enquired.

"Insurance: ah, here it is." He extricated a battered manila folder, and setting himself at the table, started to pore through the various papers inside.

"I thought so," he muttered, scanning the policy he'd been searching for.

"Thought what?"

"Listen. *The word Contents shall mean…any fittings which do not form part of the structure of the Buildings, including television and radio aerials…*"

"So?"

"So it means that the aerial's covered under the House Contents."

"But it's just knackered, isn't that what Happy said? The insurance won't cover that, will it?"

"Ah, no," Frank continued craftily, "but they will pay out if it was wrecked in a storm."

"Eh?"

"The man said the strap was broken. And with a broken fixing on a windy night, waving around and banging against the chimney, who knows what damage it could suffer?"

"Isn't that a bit risky?" What if they find out?"

"How?"

"I don't know, but…"

"Nah, they won't bother to query it – not for the sake of a couple of hundred pounds anyway. I'll give 'em a ring later, get a claim form sent out. I tell you what, all the money the buggers have had off me over the years, it'll be nice to claw a bit back."

Dan said nothing to this, but for the second time in as many weeks, he felt discomforted by his father's penny-pinching ways.

CHAPTER TEN

"This is nice." Susie sipped her wine appreciatively. Dan slipped his arm around her, drawing them closer together on the elm settle beside the cheery fire.

"Good, I was afraid you might want to go somewhere else other than a pub."

"Oh no, I like it here. Go on, you were telling me about your shopping trip."

"Yeah, well like I was saying, you could have knocked me down with a feather. Out of the blue, he suddenly produces this list of all the stuff he wants to buy. It's so out of character, I don't understand it. He's tight as a duck's arse normally – pardon the language."

"Perhaps he's got a side to him that you've not seen before; or maybe you're a good influence on him."

"I think that's pretty unlikely," he scoffed. "In any case, his generous mood didn't last very long. He decided to wangle a new aerial off his insurance."

She laughed. "That sounds more like the Frank I know. And at least you won't be having bread and cheese on Christmas Day."

"That's true. Actually, I was wondering if you'd like to join us."

"What? Oh I…"

"I won't be offended if you'd rather not," he added hastily,

140

"only I thought it might make a change for you, that's all: plus I'll be doing the cooking, so naturally the food will be delicious."

"So that's it."

"Sorry?" he said, looking perplexed.

She chuckled again, to him her light tinkling laughter seemed seductive, even a touch erotic.

"Don't you see?" Dan stared at her with a completely blank expression. "Okay, was it his idea to invite me?"

"No not really. I mean he may have mentioned it in passing."

"There you are then. He's obviously matchmaking."

"Oh," Dan replied, a little hurt. "I'm sorry, I didn't realize. Forget I even asked."

"Don't be daft; I'd love to join you both. We can't disappoint Frank, can we?"

Later on, Dan pulled up at the spot where he had dropped her off the previous night.

"Thank you for another lovely evening." Susie unclipped her seat-belt and leaning across kissed him tenderly on the lips. He responded in kind, pushing his tongue slowly into her opening mouth. They snogged for a while and he tenderly placed a hand on her breast, massaging it lovingly in his palm. Her hand wandered into his crotch, her lithe fingers tracing the outline of his erection through his jeans.

"You can come in if you want," she offered, between somewhat ragged breaths.

"I don't know if…" he answered huskily.

"It's alright, we can go up the back stairs; we won't have to go through the bar."

The old panic immediately struck, and he felt a great wave of fear wash over him. "Better not, eh? I mean, if anybody sees us," he added hurriedly, "I wouldn't want them gossiping about you. Besides, Frank'll wonder where I am."

"Oh, alright then, fine." Disheartened, Susie sat up and briefly checked her image in the rear view mirror. Dan kissed her once more on the lips.

"Night Susie, see you tomorrow."

The girl stepped out of the car and watched as, with a brief wave, Dan drove away into the blackness. Padding softly up the stairs to her room, she wondered what on earth was wrong with him.

To his irritation, Frank was still up when his son returned. "Is that you, boy?" he shouted from his armchair in front of the new television. "Pour yourself a drink and join me!"

He helped himself to a small shot of Scotch and took it into the sitting-room. The fire had just about died down, but the room was warm and the television was blaring out, credits scrolling down the screen denoting the end of some ghastly film. Frank zapped the remote control, extinguishing noise and picture simultaneously. The television stood, crackling quietly, dark and sullen as if sulking after being so humiliatingly and precipitously snuffed out.

"Did you have a good evening?"

"Er, yeah. Great thanks."

"And?"

"And what?"

"God, it's like drawing teeth with you sometimes…did you ask her about Christmas?"

"Yeah I did. She said she'd like to come over here."

"Good, so why the long face?"

"Nothing - I'm a bit whacked, that's all."

Susie was drinking coffee the next morning, elbows on the

bar, the steaming mug clasped in her cupped hands. Her friend and work colleague Tricia was briskly polishing the tables in front of her.

"Did you have a good time last night? By that I mean, of course, did he live up to expectations?"

"We had a lovely evening at the Maltsters…"

"Do I sense a but coming?"

"Well I don't know really. We were getting on fine, but then he suddenly backed off."

"Oh, so you think what? That maybe he doesn't fancy you after all?"

"No, I'm not saying that. He was definitely *up* for it, if you get my drift," she smirked mischievously.

Tricia giggled. "He's probably just shy then. Hey, he could still be a virgin! Or maybe he's a closet gay – or maybe he's got a really small one…"

"Trish! I can safely say that isn't the case."

"Oh, so you got somewhere with him."

"Yes…"

"Look, I wouldn't worry about it. He might even be a gentleman. Have you considered that? God knows that would make a refreshing change around here."

"Yeah, you're most likely right. I'll have to polish up my seduction techniques."

"I'd let him do the chasing if I were you: you don't want to frighten him off, do you?"

After giving this some thought, Susie realised that her friend's advice was sound.

At the end of that evening's date, she gave Dan a brief kiss on the lips, and made to get out of the car.

"Hang on a minute," he said. "Have I done something wrong? Only you seem a bit…distant."

"No, no, of course not. It's Christmas Eve tomorrow, that's all; and I'm working all day."

"Oh. Look, I didn't…last night…" he stumbled over the words.

"Honestly, it really doesn't matter…"

"It matters to me. Look I want you to know that I really like you, but I don't want you to think I'm just after one thing." He leaned across and planted a lingering kiss on her glossy lips.

"I really like you too Dan."

"Good." He kissed her again, before letting her go. "What time shall I pick you up on Christmas Day?"

"Any time after ten."

"Great. Eleven o'clock okay?"

"Fine."

"You're not going to pop in for a pint tomorrow then?"

"I wasn't going to," he answered cautiously, "the place'll be packed out, won't it?"

"Bound to be, I'd stay away if I were you."

Christmas Day dawned bright and sunny, and surprisingly mild. Dan had been up early to put the bird in the oven, and then set about preparing the vegetables - a task his uncle, a mere twenty odd miles away, had never undertaken in his life. James would rise reluctantly around ten. He'd yet – in his adult life at least – to wake clear-headed on the 25th December. To him, this was the worst day of the year, as most of his drinking cronies were committed to spending time *en famille* whilst the majority of pubs closed in the evening, and only opened their doors at lunch-time for an hour or so. Whilst his nephew jumped into his car to fetch his girlfriend, he was preparing to follow a route around the town which afforded him the longest overall drinking time in the greatest number of establishments. Traditionally, he'd be furnished with a free drink in each one, and that should render him nicely drunk for an afternoon snooze before finding the one or two that opened their doors for the evening session. A couple of his friends had invited him to join them for lunch, but he'd declined their offers. He couldn't be bothered to go. Besides, he knew that they were just being polite, or possibly kind-hearted. He was pretty certain that none of them craved his company around their festive tables, and even if one or two might, their wives most certainly would not. Besides, he'd have to be on his best behaviour and worse, there would never be enough drink to meet his demand.

As Susie was putting the finishing touches to her make-up, and Dan accepted a glass of punch from Pete, James sidled around the saloon door of his first port of call, The Sportsman's Arms.

When they entered the farmhouse, Dan could hear whiny American accents spewing loudly from the television, a sure sign of some ghastly sugary Disney film being broadcast.

"Frank!" he shouted above the din. Immediately the noise ceased, Frank hastily turning off the set. "How's the turkey doing? Have you basted it like I said?"

"Just about to," replied his father, appearing at the door of the front room.

"What were you watching?" asked Dan, slightly annoyed that his old man was becoming something of a telly addict.

"Oh nothing, I was just seeing what was on, that's all," he answered guiltily. "Alright, I know I was watching a load of old rubbish, and I know what I said about that, but I was just passing time before you two got back, that's all. I'll stick the kettle on, shall I? What's so funny?" He suddenly noticed that Susie was grinning from ear to ear like a Cheshire cat.

"You reminded me of something dad said, that's all," she remarked, slipping off her coat.

"Oh yes?"

"Well some years ago, when I was about, I don't know, probably only a few months old, my uncle, dad's brother, stayed with us for a while. He was in the army - I think he'd just come back from Malaya, and dad had recently bought our first television. Heaping scorn on this interloper in the family home, uncle Gordon vowed never to look at it, convinced that it represented the death of all things civilized. He stayed for a couple of weeks, and dad told me that when the time came for him to leave, he was hooked. He'd sit in front of it from the time transmission started until it finished with the National Anthem at night, whatever rubbish was on."

"Just goes to show the power of the media, I suppose. Now, let's have that coffee, shall we? Then we can open our prezzies." Dan strode purposefully into the kitchen.

Sometime later, after the exchange of shirts and other gifts, and after a sumptuous lunch, the three of them were in the front room, the fire blazing away cheerfully in the old hearth. In the overheated atmosphere, satiated with rich festive food, they were all finding it difficult to keep their eyes open.

"Fancy a spot of fresh air?" Dan asked Susie. "Only if I stay in this chair much longer, I'll fall asleep."

"Yeah alright; only I don't want to go too far. I'll just pop to the loo first." She rose reluctantly from the soft comfort of the settee and left the room.

"That's a good idea," Frank muttered, "I can have forty winks while you two are out. By the way, is Susie staying tonight?"

"What? Well, I don't know, I haven't really thought that far ahead…" his son blustered.

"Only if she is, I have no objection; that's all," his father interjected speedily.

"Oh I see…thanks," the other replied, feeling rather embarrassed.

Frank smiled to himself, stretched out his long legs in front of the fire, and arms folded across his stomach, settled deeper into the armchair.

A crepuscular gloom was already sifting into the valley as the pair of them strolled hand in hand up the lane, and although it was unseasonably mild for the time of year, the damp air felt cold and clammy after the warmth of the farmhouse. They passed beneath huge bare looping limbs of one of the massive hedgerow beeches. Its uppermost branches clawed at the darkening sky like some manic old crone's wizened bony fingers. A grey squirrel was darting this way and that amongst them, chattering bad-temperedly as it constantly chastised them for disturbing its peace, all the while its fluffy tail twitching and jerking in annoyance.

"I think we've spoilt his afternoon," Susie commented, stepping deftly over a small rivulet pulsing in tiny wavelets across the lane.

"It's okay; I don't think tree rats celebrate Christmas."

A sudden gust of wind blew through the trees, buffeting the walkers and whisking dead leaves into the air from the sides of the road. It went as quickly as it came, the leaves flitting like butterflies back down to earth again. "Looks like there's more rain on the way," Dan said, peering up at the threatening black clouds rolling across the sky from the west. "We'll just go the top of the lane shall we? Then head back?"

"Suits me."

By the time they reached their objective, the wind had got

up, the heavy hostile clouds now scudding darkly above them. Occasional drops of cold rain flecked their faces, blown in on the strengthening gale. Hurrying back down the road in near darkness, they were nearly home when the downpour started in earnest. Wind whipped at their faces and legs as they hurried onward in the dark, smacking them mercilessly with sheets of rain whilst drops of water fell persistently from overhead boughs, splattering on their heads and shoulders. In a very short while, they were both soaked and it was with a good deal of gratification that they crashed through the farmhouse door and escaped from the deluge.

"Give me your coat, and I'll hang it by the range with mine. My God, you're soaked through!"

"Oh it's not so bad, I'm sure I'll soon dry out."

"Why don't you go upstairs and take that wet top off? You can have one of my shirts and jumpers for now." He frowned. "Don't think my trousers will fit you though."

"Oh, well maybe I should be getting back then."

Dan felt a sudden sharp stab of disappointment in the pit of his stomach. He could hear his father softly snoring in the front room.

"Do you want a cup of tea first?" he asked lamely.

"Er…"

"Look, do you really want to go back? I mean, I can drive you down to the pub now, and you can get some dry clothes and perhaps stay here the evening. We can have a few drinks and maybe a stupid game of Trival Pursuit or something, and…"

"And shall I pack my toothbrush as well?" she broke in impetuously. "Sorry, I didn't mean to…"

"No, no, that's alright. Yes, I'd like that." He took her palms in his and kissed her cold lips. He noticed a sparkling drop of rainwater fall softly from her hair onto her shoulder, dissolving into the soft fibres of her Cashmere sweater.

"Come on, into the kitchen and dry your hair," he ordered. "I'll just change out of these wet things and tell Frank what's going on before we go."

"Oh, I'd forgotten about him, will he…" she asked anxiously.

"Mind? No; not at all. He's already said."

"One, two, three." Frank triumphantly placed his mover, full of wedges, into the centre of the board, and emptied his glass. The three of them sat on the floor. Several empty wine bottles and one of whisky adorned the mahogany side-table by the door. The fire in the hearth had by now dwindled to a crumbling pile of soft red embers nestled in a bed of fine grey ash.

"What shall we give him, Susie?"

"Orange, definitely orange, he's not so good at sports."

"Right." Dan extracted a card, squinting at the words. "What's the crucial card in the game of Hearts?"

"You've got me there; I've no idea. The Queen of Spades."

"You jammy…"

"Was that the answer? Ha! Well it just goes to show I'm not quite as stupid as you two thought."

"Yeah, but you had your fair share of luck: and anyway, how were we supposed to know some of those answers? All those films and songs were about way before we were even born."

"Never mind, it's only a game."

Dan sighed. "Still, at least we can still whop you Brits at cricket, that's the main thing."

"You could be right, but I'm not going to start on that one.

In any case," he added, stifling a yawn, "it's time I was in my bed." He rose a little unsteadily to his feet. "Either of you two want a nightcap, just help yourselves." Shutting the door behind him, he crossed the hall and clumped wearily up the stairs.

"Well, shall we have another?"

"Not for me thanks. I've had quite enough for one night."

"Okay," he replied, trying to quell the feeling of anxiety growing in his belly. "Shall we go up?"

Dan undressed speedily and slipped between the sheets. He lay on his side whilst his girlfriend carefully peeled off her clothes and stacked them neatly on the chair beside the bed before flicking off the bedside lamp and sliding between the sheets. He rolled over to face her. They shared a lingering kiss. When their lips finally parted, he was fully aroused. She reached a willowy arm downwards, and wrapped her long fingers firmly around him.

"Perhaps we'd better not, eh?" he whispered. His voice had an edge of panic which she failed to notice.

"Only Frank's just across the way, and the walls are very thin. He's probably not asleep yet."

"Fine." Susie released him from her grip and rolled over on her side, presenting him with her back.

"Good night," she said coldly.

"Good night."

Unsettled as they were, the pair of them nevertheless fell fast asleep within minutes.

Dan woke with a jolt. Consulting his digital clock, he noted it was a quarter to four. He could see nothing in the Stygian darkness, but could hear his father snoring on the other side of the house, as well as his girl's light breathing beside him. He turned to her, placing his forearm around her ribs, his palm on her soft stomach. His insistent erection pressed against her buttocks. Drowsily, she murmured something and rolled onto her back. He kissed her tenderly on the lips, then again more urgently. He edged on top of her and a lifetime's angst fled him as he slowly and languorously made love to the woman of his dreams.

The rapping on the bedroom door wrenched Dan from his slumber.

"I've brought you up a cup of tea. Are you decent?" Frank asked.

"Hang on a sec." Dan hastily slid on his jeans and poked his head around the door to see his father at the far end of the landing, about to descend the stairs after having deposited two full mugs on the bare boards by his son's bedroom door.

"Thanks."

"You're welcome. I'm just popping out to get the paper – won't be long. Do either of you want anything from the shop?"

"Oh, no thanks. I'll get some breakfast on the go in a minute."

"No rush, whenever you're ready." Frank trotted downstairs. Dan picked up the mugs and kicked the door shut with his bare foot. As he turned, he noticed Susie had woken, and was sitting up in bed observing him.

"Mmm, room service. I *am* spoiled," she purred.

"Yep, and I'll do you some breakfast while you drink it too, if you like. What do you fancy?" Bending over next to her, he carefully placed the mug on the bedside table.

"What do I fancy? Let me see." Reaching out a long arm, she deftly popped the steel rivet at his waistband. Nimble fingers gripped his zipper and pulled it downwards with studied care.

"I fancy that breakfast can wait a little while, don't you?" She grinned mischievously.

The Christmas wreath tacked onto the Post Office door was slightly askew. Inside, a line of coloured fairy lights had been looped along the top of the window and its Georgian panes were speckled with spray snow. A pathetic plastic Christmas tree, laden with gaudy baubles and far too much tinsel, stood sulking in the corner.

"Good morning Frank, had a good Christmas?" Anne enquired politely.

"Yes thank you, very nice. And you?"

"Oh, don't ask! My useless husband's spent the most of the festive season so far tucked up in bed, coughing and sneezing."

"Oh dear, poor chap."

"And so I've spent most of the time pandering to his needs," she continued, completely ignoring his response. "Silly old fool."

"Yes, well, just the paper please. Oh, and I'd better have some baccy as well."

That undeniably disapproving look crossed her features as she plucked a pouch of tobacco from a cardboard container on the shelf behind her.

"There. Must make a nice change for you - not being on your own, I mean. Mind you, I wouldn't mind if I was, not this year at any rate." Frank opined that her long suffering husband probably felt the same way, and not just at Christmas.

"Yes, it's nice to have a bit of company."

"Susie's such a nice girl. It's a shame about...well, I suppose that's all in the past. We all make mistakes, don't we?"

she remarked pointedly. "Still," she ploughed on, denying Frank the opportunity to comment, "she seems to be happy with Dan now. Perhaps she's turned the corner." She looked at him questioningly.

"I really couldn't say Anne. They've only been seeing each other for a short time."

"Yes of course. I don't wish to pry; I just hope the girl finds someone suitable."

"Quite." He gathered his shopping. "Thank you, and I hope Gerald feels better again soon. Give him my best wishes, won't you?"

"Oh I will, I will. Along with all the others he's been sent," she added sardonically.

CHAPTER ELEVEN

"I've got in touch with some estate agents in London," Dan said. It was the end of January, and he was the only person at the bar. Save for an elderly couple cuddling the fire, the pub was empty. Susie placed his refilled pint in front of him.

"It's time to get gran's house sorted out. I want to put it on the market at Easter, or at least shortly after. I've been recommended a couple of firms to do the house clearance, but I want to get up there and see them myself. I also want to go through her things, just to keep a few mementos for Jane and me."

"That's nice. When were you thinking of going?"

"Well I don't know. In a week or so? Thing is, I was rather hoping you might keep me company."

"Oh; well I'll have to ask Pete. It should be alright, we're hardly rushed off our feet at this time of year."

"Ask Pete what?" A large man sporting a voluminous black beard appeared behind her.

"Dan's just asked me if I could go with him up to London."

Pete frowned. "When?"

"Next week, or maybe the week after?"

"For how long?"

"Probably three or four days," Dan interrupted.

A broad grin spread across the landlord's ruddy rotund face. "Of course you can go – but only if you make sure you enjoy yourselves!"

Ten days later, and Dan was in his grandmother's house with his girlfriend. He'd instructed a firm of estate agents to sell the property, and had commissioned a furniture dealer to clear the house of its entire contents, save for a cardboard box of personal effects which he'd found in the loft and a few family photographs dotted around the place.

"What's that you've got?"

"At a guess, I'd say old letters and some more photos," he answered, plonking his burden on the kitchen table. Let's go back to the hotel and sort through it, shall we? It'll be warmer there. Then once Newman's lot have taken everything else away, we'll come back and give the place the once over."

"Sounds like a plan."

A short while later, they sat on the warm soft red carpet of their hotel bedroom, the contents of the upturned box scattered before them.

"Looks like old letters mostly. Blimey, she kept every one my mum wrote from Australia, looks like."

He pulled an envelope at random from one of several bundles secured neatly with a thick rubber band.

"She must have written this one soon after getting there. Listen. *I'm finding it hard getting used to the intense heat and flies but am settling in well to the Aussie style of life. Ben's family are very kind and attentive, as of course is he, will write again soon. Big kiss for dad…*

Ben's my dad," Dan explained. "Blimey, she must have been pregnant with me then. That feels kind of weird."

"Is this her, do you think?" Susie held up an old photograph of a pretty girl, casually dressed in jeans and a white T-shirt.

Dan felt as if he'd been kicked in the guts. "Oh mum…" His was filling up as he tenderly took the picture from her and studied the smiling face. A tear popped out of the corner of his eye and tracked down his face. It dangled precariously from his clean-shaven chin.

"Oh I'm sorry," Susie exclaimed, "I didn't mean to…"

"It's okay, it's just…" He could go no further, and started to sob soundlessly, letting the photograph drop to the floor.

"Hey, hey, it's alright." She wrapped her arms around him and drew him to her, cradling his head against her chest. After a while he stopped crying.

"Sorry about that," he sniffed.

"Don't be silly," she soothed.

"Come on, let's leave this for a while. What say we go out and grab a bite? Then I'll take you to the British Museum like I promised."

"Good idea. Do you fancy Italian?"

"Anything you like," he smiled. "I'll go with the flow."

Frank was ensconced in his chair by the fire, watching television when Dan entered the sitting-room a few days later carrying the cardboard box.

"Do you want to have a look at some of this stuff? I think you'll find a few of the photos interesting."

"What? Oh," his father answered a touch irritably: he was enjoying one of his favourite programmes. "Alright then." He switched the set off.

"I've sort of got most of it in order and there's loads of pictures of mum – right from when she was a baby. These are the more recent ones. Do you recognize her?" He handed him a photograph. Frank immediately felt whisked back in time.

"God yes. I'd forgotten how beautiful she was: I must have been mad to dump her," he added wistfully.

"Yeah well, water under the bridge and all that, eh?"

"I suppose."

"Look at this one, that's uncle Ned on her left and dad on her right. I remember that, we'd just finished rounding up some of the cattle for dosing."

"Uh-huh."

Frank dutifully examined the pictures presented to him over the next hour or so, making appreciative noises every now and then, when he thought it appropriate to do so.

"Well that's just about the lot," Dan remarked, carefully placing them back in the box. There's loads of letters of course that I've not read through yet."

"Right, well I'm not sure I want to be privy to them – that's your prerogative."

"Okay, that's fine."

"There is one thing that strikes me as a bit odd…"

"Odd? What do you mean?"

"Well, your grandmother kept all those photos and all those letters from your mother right back to when she was little…"

"When she was a baby in fact," Dan broke in.

"Quite. But there's not a single reference to your uncle… what was it?"

"James. Yeah, but I told you, they'd fallen out."

"But to destroy all trace of him, even in her most personal possessions: it's like she wanted to pretend that he never existed. He must have done something really heinous for her to take that sort of drastic action."

"Yeah I guess. Maybe I'll find a clue in her letters."

"Perhaps. Changing the subject, are you going out tonight?"

"No, it's a bit late now; besides, Susie's working."

"Good, there's something I need to talk to you about."

"Oh, that sounds a bit ominous."

"Pour me a drink and get yourself one, then I'll explain. It's alright, you needn't look so worried."

Armed with a tumbler generously charged with whisky a few minutes later, Frank started to talk.

"You obviously heard about Tom."

"Bob's son? Yes, of course. He shot himself, didn't he?"

"Oh yes, no doubt about that. I just wondered, you know, if you'd heard anybody saying anything else about him."

"Well, yes actually. But I don't take any notice of rumours, so I'd rather not say."

"But your natural father had already sired one illegitimate child, so why wouldn't you think him capable of doing it again?"

"Hey steady, no, not at all! Right, okay, I did hear that there was a tale going round that you and Bob's wife…"

"Elizabeth."

"Alright, Elizabeth – I didn't know her name – were seeing each other…"

"And that during that time she fell pregnant with my child," Frank finished for him.

"Well yes."

"So were you going to question me about it?"

"God, no! It's none of my business! Like I said, I've no intention of listening to malicious tittle-tattle," Dan replied indignantly.

"Or were you afraid of what may have come out?"

"Of course not. Christ man, why are you having a pop at me?"

An uncomfortable silence followed. Frank took a mouthful of whisky, swallowed noisily and started again.

"Alright, I'm sorry; I don't know where that came from. Thing is…" He paused while he considered the best way to put it. He emptied his glass. Dan dutifully replenished it, and once Frank had it safely in his grasp again, he continued.

"Lizzie, I mean Elizabeth and I were mutually attracted. And when I say that, I don't just mean I wanted to get her into bed: it was more than that. Trouble was, I was a bit slow off the mark, and before I knew it she'd married Bob. I never expected that, him being so much older and everything. To my shame, even after they were wed, I tried to make her change her mind. I only succeeded in upsetting her. She told me that I was too late, she was married to him and loved him, and that was the way it was going to stay."

"And Tom?"

"Tom was Bob's boy. There's no doubt about it. You see, we were only that intimate on a couple of occasions, and that was way before she fell pregnant. Once she was, then that dashed any hopes I might have still stupidly harboured of her leaving him for me."

"Did her husband suspect anything?"

"No, I don't think so. He may well have realized we were drawn to one another, but once she'd married him he felt secure. He trusted her, and she was trustworthy. She was that sort of girl. There was nothing physical between us once that ring was on her finger. So there you have it, straight from the horse's mouth. Anything else you hear from those blabbermouths in the village is pure fiction, malicious fiction at that."

A stultifying silence ensued, during which neither of them could think of anything further to say. Then Frank scrunched out his cigarette in the ashtray and drained the last drop from his glass.

"Right, I'm ready for bed," he announced decisively.

159

"Me too, I reckon. Thanks for telling me, but I meant what I said. I really don't think it's any of my business."

"Fair enough, but I'm glad you know the truth now – I don't want you thinking I'm a bigger bastard than I really am." With a wry grin, he rose stiffly from his chair. "Good night boy," he said over his shoulder when he'd reached the door, "sleep tight."

"Night, you too," his son rejoined.

"Oh, and you ought to get some of those photos framed. You can put them anywhere you like around the house; don't keep them squirrelled away."

"Thanks, I'll do that." Dan placed the guard in front of the dying blistered embers of the fire, and gathering up the box headed upstairs.

Over the next few weeks, on the few nights he found himself alone in bed, he read through his mother's letters. Mostly they contained the usual mundane details of his family's life, what the weather was like, how he and his sister were doing at school, etc. As he ploughed his way through the months and years, there was no mention of his uncle at all. It was not until one wet February night, when he breached the last neat bundle, that he found any reference to James.

...of course I understand that you want to put your affairs in order now that dad's passed away, but I'm not sure about cutting him off completely. Although I was only a child when it happened, I still think that maybe I was partly to blame. I'm sorry, I know that'll make you very cross, but I can't help the way I feel. I still hate him for what he did, and never want to see him again as long as I live, but I'm uncomfortable about having his inheritance. Couldn't you please at least leave him some money? I'm frightened he might try and do something otherwise. Please give it some thought.

Your loving daughter,
Sally.

Dan read through the letter again, but clearly there was no clue as to the nature of his uncle's misdemeanour. All he could garner from it was the clear distress his mother felt when her brother was mentioned. What a pity she never kept the letters she had in reply. Slipping the missive back in its envelope, he put it on the bedside table and turned off the light. As the first warm waves of sleep slipped over him, he wondered if Susie might see something that he'd missed in the message, and determined to show it to her the next day.

"Well she was clearly frightened of him because of what he did to her," she said, after some thought. Susie was propped up on his bed, legs tucked underneath her, scrutinizing the letter.

Observing her, an inexplicable feeling of dread started to slither around Dan's stomach like an oily serpent languidly uncoiling itself.

"You said he was quite a bit older than your mum, didn't you?"

"Yeah, there were a good five, maybe six years between them."

"Mmm. You know, I'm not sure if I should say what I think…"

"Go on."

"It's only an idea and I'm not saying it's right – at all."

"Okay fair enough, just tell me," Dan replied impatiently.

"I think he may have, well, *interfered* with her."

"What? Christ! Why?"

"I'm just saying that's what it looks like: to me, that is. Do you have any clue as to how old your mum was when this happened?"

Dan racked his brains. "I know that once he left for university she never saw him again."

"So he would have been what, eighteen? And your mum thirteen," she added thoughtfully. "Plus, she felt partly to blame, didn't she? That's classic. It would also explain the drastic action taken against James, wouldn't it?"

"I guess it might."

"You're right of course. *Might* is all we've got; unless you uncover the secret in one of letters you've not yet been through, or ask him yourself."

"No, no way – I never want to see the guy. Anyway, what would be the point?"

"Exactly." She slipped off the edge of the bed and kissed him on the cheek. "Best forget all about it. And anyway, I'm getting hungry. Where's that supper you promised?"

Three evenings later, and Dan finished reading the last (he assumed) letter his mother had written to his grandmother. There had been no further reference to his uncle. Sighing, he neatly returned it to its place and slid the box under the bed, vowing to banish all thoughts of James and his crimes from his mind and to move forward with his new life.

CHAPTER TWELVE

"In like a lion out like a lamb - and vice versa," Frank pronounced wisely. He was sitting on the dry ground, his back against the smooth grey trunk of a tall ash-tree, legs drawn up to his knees. His crumpled shirtsleeves were pushed up to his elbows as he studiously rolled a cigarette between grubby fingers. The early March sun was beaming down benevolently from a cloudless blue sky and the gentlest of warm breezes occasionally stirred the pale yellow blooms of primroses densely clustered in the sheltered hedgerow bottom. Pregnant black buds dotted the ends of the branches high above his head, impatiently waiting to burst open, nodding occasionally in the light wind. Somewhere in a distant blackthorn copse pigeons cooed softly and lovingly to one another, the soothing sound floating enchantingly across the sun-soaked valley towards him. It was one of those magical mornings when the air was thick with the promise of rebirth - when spring was truly just around the corner.

"What was that?"

A lighter flamed as Frank lit his smoke. "It means if it's dry at the beginning of the month, it'll be wet at the end: if it starts cold, it'll finish warm, and vice versa. See?"

"Oh, and is it true?"

"Is it true?" He exhaled a plume of blue smoke that hung lazily in the air before slowly dissipating. "Yes, I think it probably is; on the whole."

"On the whole?" Dan laughed. "Right." He tapped a staple into a freshly planted post, securing the barbed wire tightly in place. The harsh sound of hammering rang out rudely across the still countryside.

"That's that one done. Are you going to help me unroll the next stretch, or are you going to just sit there being prosaic?"

Reluctantly, Frank extricated himself from his comfortable seat.

It was after lunch that same day, and Frank was perusing the weekly farming section of the regional newspaper. "There's some cattle for sale here might be worth a look at," he muttered, more to himself than to Dan, who stood by the range, pouring boiling water into two mugs.

"Are you thinking of buying some then? I thought you were going to wait 'til the grass started to grow a bit. There you go." He placed one of the steaming mugs at his father's elbow. "Don't spill it."

"Thank you. Yes, you're right, I *was* going to leave it for a while, but if I buy some now it could work to my advantage. March is sometimes known as the hungry month. That is, stocks of hay and silage start to run out and everyone's anxiously waiting for the grass to grow. Unless there's plenty of fodder about, cattle prices are depressed: and there's a shortage of feed this year after the dry summer…"

"…but we've still got plenty of old hay in the barn to see us through well into April," Dan finished for him.

"Exactly." Frank took a tentative sip of the scalding coffee. "Right, I'll give the fella a ring now: strike while the iron's hot so to speak." Clutching the folded newspaper, he pushed back his chair and went in search of the phone. Dan could hear a few muted mutterings from the hall and then his father was back in the kitchen. He tossed the paper onto the table and picked up his tobacco tin.

"That sounds quite promising; I said we'd go and see them tomorrow morning."

Dan retrieved the paper. "Are these the ones?" he asked. "Genuine dispersal sale of twenty-three mainly Aberdeen Angus cows warranted in calf to Charolais bull. Will split if preferred."

"Yep, that's them." Frank licked the edge of his cigarette paper, and stuck the resultant roll-up up in the corner of his mouth. "Seems like he's desperate to get rid of them as well," he added, reaching for the lighter.

"Why doesn't he just take them to market then, and be done with it?"

Frank shrugged his shoulders. "I don't know, could be because he wants to find them a good home together. Some farmers hate the thought that their stock might fall into the hands of a dealer and maybe get lugged halfway across the country. More likely, he thinks he can get a better price by selling privately rather than risk the vagaries of an auction. Either way we'll find out tomorrow, won't we?"

"But didn't he tell you how much he wanted for them?"

"He gave me a figure, yes."

"A fair one?"

"I would say so. It's difficult to tell without seeing the animals. And then, I'm sure I'll be able to grind him down a bit too. He needs to sell."

"Right."

Dan wished fervently that his father would go on his own the following day; he had no desire to witness another occurrence like the car-buying episode.

165

The next morning was just as pleasant as its predecessor. Once again the sun shone down from a cloudless sky, with merely the gentlest of breezes tickling the uppermost branches of the tallest trees. Dan slammed the door shut, and sat down in the front of the Land Rover next to his father.

"Do you know the way?"

"Yup, I reckon. Anyway, I've got the map in my pocket, just in case." A few early season flies were buzzing annoyingly on the dusty windscreen, the unusually mild weather fooling them into thinking it was summer already. Opening his window, Dan whisked them outside with the back of his hand.

"Right, what are we waiting for then?" Frank started the engine and they set off, leaving a cloud of blue exhaust smoke hanging noxiously in the clean air. After an hour, and having only taken one wrong turn, they reached their destination. Frank parked alongside a stone wall which flanked a large, mainly cobbled farmyard behind and above which sat an imposing Victorian farmhouse. At the top of the yard, an ornate cast-iron gate opened onto a few brick-built steps which climbed to a cinders path scything through a rangy lawn to the farmhouse door. There was a narrow border against the house that contained several neatly clipped shrubs and clumps of daffodils dotted the grass, their bright yellow and orange flowers bobbing prettily at the end of sappy emerald stems. Frank carelessly flicked his cigarette butt into the road and wound up his window.

"This is it, Higher Barton. I wonder where everyone is." As if on cue, the farmhouse door swung open and a man of around sixty appeared. He waved cordially before making his way towards them. Introductions over, he led them up the lane a short way to a modern cattle barn where the animals were housed for the winter.

"You see," he explained, "I realize now that the work's become too much for me. Loathe as I am to sell them, I have to face facts. I don't think I could cope with another calving season, not with my arthritis."

"Well Mr. Harvey, I have to say they look good; you've done them well."

The farmer smiled at the compliment. "Thank you."

"But they're not *quite* what we're looking for. You said on the phone that you wanted to sell them in one batch?"

"Preferably, yes…"

"Only we didn't really want to buy so many."

"Oh."

"Even so, they're nice cattle, and none of them very old, is that right?"

"Yes, the oldest is seven I think. I've got all the paperwork inside if you want to go through it," he added helpfully. "It would help me a lot if you took them all."

"Yes of course, I understand that," Frank replied sympathetically. "What do you think, boy?

Oh no, don't drag me into this, for Christ's sake. "Erm," Dan started unhelpfully, "well I suppose we could take them all – at a push. Could we?"

"Just about eh?" Frank leaned on the shiny metal gate and rolled a cigarette. He decided it was time to look pensive. "Did you say you still had last year's calves?"

"Er, yes, but like I said, I want to keep them another month or two. Trade will be better then."

"Yes, should be. Would you mind if we had a look at them?"

"No, I suppose not. They're back at the farmyard, but I really don't want to sell them yet."

"No, no, I quite understand. Can we have a closer look at these before we go back?"

167

After a detailed inspection of all the livestock, Frank made his offer. He was willing to buy all the cows for a little less than was asked for them on the condition that he could also purchase all eight heifers born the previous year. Mr. Harvey, now known to them as George, wasn't happy about selling the heifers and had gone indoors to consult his wife.

"What do you think?"

"It's your decision, dear."

"I know, but you must have an opinion."

"Alright, but don't bite my head off. He's not far off with the price on the cows, is he?"

"No."

"And he'll take them all. And look after them by the sounds of it too."

"Ye-es."

"And nobody else has phoned to show interest."

"No-o – apart from Toby."

"Well *he* won't give you anything like what you want, will he?"

"Shouldn't think so."

"So there's your answer. And you'll still have a nice bunch of steers to sell in a month or so, and plenty to feed them with…and," she went on, preventing him from responding, "you know what father always said…"

"Yes dear, I know. Never be afraid to take a profit."

Satisfied, she nodded and picked up a kettle from the side. "Why don't you invite them in then? I'll make us all a nice cup of tea while you sort out the paperwork."

For something that was his decision, he thought wistfully as he pulled on his wellingtons, his wife certainly had a lot to contribute.

Barely half an hour later, Frank and Dan were on their

way home again. "I'll give Phil a ring this evening, see if he can fetch them up on Saturday; if he takes the big lorry, he'll get them all in two loads. Can you get the covered yard ready for them tomorrow? I'll give you a hand to put up the feed barriers – they weigh a ton."

"Yeah sure. What about the young stock?"

"We'll put them in the lean-to on the far end; there's plenty of space in there for those few."

"Sounds like a plan." In an uncharacteristic display of contentment, Frank started tapping his fingers on the steering-wheel and humming vaguely as the old Land Rover trundled noisily along.

"Well," he smiled, after they'd been travelling for a short while, "what do you think of our new acquisitions?"

"Oh they're lovely cattle, aren't they? And I can tell you're pleased."

"Absolutely. And the heifers, well they were just a steal, a real steal. Now listen, will you go down with Phil and pick them up?"

"Yes of course, but I thought you'd want to go…"

"No, I'm entrusting you, so make sure that you get all the passports for them. George said he'd write a bill of sale on receipt of the balance owing. So don't leave without that. You know how much that should be, because you know how much I've already paid him – right?"

"Right."

"Good, then I'll leave it all up to you. And Phil will sort out the movement forms for you."

Once the cattle had arrived and were happily settled in, the whole ambience on the farm changed. The sense of emptiness and abandonment seeping from the deserted forlorn buildings was replaced immediately by one of companionable warmth and serenity. Frank found himself one evening, as he often did, leaning on the rails watching his cows eating their way steadily and dreamily through still vaguely scented bales of silver-green hay that Dan had broken up and thrown in wads in front of the feed barriers. He drank in the balmy bovine fragrance that drifted towards him from the comfortingly warm golden bed of straw in the building behind them. The sense of purpose that had re-emerged from his battered mind when he'd discovered the existence of his son was now suddenly reinforced by the establishment of his new beef enterprise. With a pang in his heart, he suddenly realized that if his boy were to ever leave him on his own, that he could all too easily slip back down the well of despair that had nearly cost him his life just a few short months earlier. That was a frightening thought, and one he was keen to quickly dispel. He sighed heavily and took one last drag from his cigarette. The tip flared a cherry red, like coals blown in a forge and he dropped the butt and shredded it under his heel against the concrete as he exhaled the soothing smoke. One of the cows raised her head from her food and a pair of dark limpid eyes followed him as he turned around and ambled back across the yard to the house, his slender shadow stretching out in front of him.

Suddenly it was snatched away, the westering sun brutally blotted out by bulbous rain-gorged clouds ballooning across the sky.

By the following morning, rain was teeming from an angry dark cloud-choked sky. By the evening it had cleared and a blustery cold north wind had set in, blowing heavy showers of rain and sometimes hail across the countryside. This cruel wintry weather lasted until April, forcing spring to wait in the wings. Frank was right: March roared itself out like a lion.

And then suddenly, almost overnight it seemed, the wind swung round to the south and lessened once again to a benign warm breeze. The waterlogged pastures quickly started to dry out in the warming sunshine. At daybreak birds began to sing with gusto in the trees and hedgerows where engorged buds split open one after the other, revealing feathery pale soft leaves. In the winter-weary pastures, a green sheen spread indiscriminately as fresh new growth started to appear. As if in response to all this manic fecundity, the cows began to bag up, their udders swelling, filling with rich milk in anticipation of the arrival of new life and consequently new hope for the farming business.

Now, with the change of seasons well under way, it wasn't long before there was enough grass to turn the cattle out into the lush green pastures. Both Frank and Dan were eagerly awaiting the arrival of the first addition to their new herd. Frank would rise with an eager sense of anticipation at first light, hoping in his heart that he'd be the one to find the first calf. Equally, his son would wander down to the field at dusk with the same objective; and if she wasn't working, Susie would accompany him.

It turned out that Frank discovered the first calf to be born, on one chilly but fine morning a week after Easter: on April 20th, to be exact.

Although not yet fully light when he latched the heavy farmhouse door behind him and stepped out into the cold traces of the night, the dawn chorus was well under way with a raucous and frenetic urgency. The birds' singing immediately reminded him of Mervyn, the local character who many years previously came every month to record the cows' individual milk yields for his father in the happy days when the dairy was in full swing. On a fine summer's morn, his greeting was ever the same.

"'Tis a bootiful day and all the birds is singing lovely."

Smiling inwardly, he made his way across the yard and traversed the slightly frosted pasture where the cows sat like ghostly grey statues in the soupy half-light. As yet unwilling to rise from their nocturnal resting-places to welcome the new day, they seemed half asleep, dozily and hypnotically chewing the cud as their warm breath roiled out in steamy clouds before them in the still air. Walking towards them, he counted their still forms carefully, as he did every morning, and found he was one short. He stopped and counted them again. One short. Trying to rid his mind of the picture that suddenly leapt into it of a cow lying dead and bloated in a ditch, he went in search of the missing animal, starting systematically along the field's north boundary. He breathed a sigh of relief when he found no corpse in the drainage ditch that ran alongside the overgrown hedge, and turned his attention to a small thick frowzy copse of tangled blackthorn in the lower slopes of the field that had encroached into the pasture from an untended corner. Experience had taught him that cows chose the most bizarre and unsuitable spots to give birth. Crouching slightly to avoid being lacerated by the sharp thorns, he ventured inside, following a muddy trail of bovine footprints winding their way between swooping branches laden with white blossoms. Some of the flowers had shed already, lying like abandoned confetti amongst numerous gnarled and twisted stems corkscrewing from the pungent earth. A little way in, in a muddy trampled area less choked with growth, he saw the cow. She stood proudly over her calf, which seemed oblivious of his presence and was curled up like a contented cat. She, however, was well aware of him; no doubt aroused by his clumsy stumbling approach through the scrub. She lowered her head at him as if issuing a warning – which he chose to ignore.

"Alright dear," he said softly, "I only want to see that your baby's okay." As he ventured slowly toward the calf, with the intention of dragging it out of its hazardous resting-place and into the open field, the cow tossed her head at him. He was beginning to think that his plan might be flawed.

"It's alright dear," he repeated, this time with far less assurance. "Can I just see your baby's okay?"

At that precise moment the cow lunged at him, catching him square on the chest with her shaggy black head as he tried in vain to back off. He was flung unceremoniously against the trunk of one of the larger thorn trees, landing flat on his bottom with his long legs stretched out in front of him.

"Now then," he muttered shakily, "you didn't mean that, did you?" The cow once again shook her head at him, but this time pawed at the ground for extra effect. Fear made him angry.

"Right then you bugger," he addressed her loudly, hoping he sounded a good deal braver than he actually felt, "you can bloody well stay there for all I care: I was only trying to help." Pushing himself up on his palms, he scuttled crab-like backwards until he considered himself to be well out of range, then turned and walked from the thicket. To preserve some dignity he tried to demonstrate that he wasn't in too much of a hurry, whilst with trembling fingers he rolled a cigarette. When he reached the farmhouse Dan was in the kitchen making tea.

"You've been a while; everything okay?" he asked. Frank appeared around the door.

"Christ, look at the state of you! What have you been up to, mud wrestling?"

"Yeah, very funny. I slipped in that shitty copse at the bottom of the field, that's all. Where, incidentally, I found our first calf."

"Great! What have we got, a boy or a girl…?" Dan noticed that Frank looked a little dazed and was rubbing his ribs.

"Well, I didn't really get close enough to see."

"Oh." He passed him a mug of tea. Frank noticed the queer look he was giving him.

"Alright, she had a pop at me; biffed me in the chest actually."

"Are you okay? Did she hurt you?" Dan asked with genuine concern.

"No, just bruised me a bit I think. I'll be fine."

"Still, it must have shaken you up a tad, eh?"

"Nothing a cup of tea won't sort out: then I'll phone the surgery, make an appointment to see the doctor."

"So she did hurt you then?" The anxiety was once more apparent in Dan's voice.

"Maybe bruised a rib or two perhaps. No, the reason I want to see the doc is so's he can give me a note: I can claim on my personal accident insurance then, should be worth a couple of hundred quid or so." Frank put his tea down on the table, pulled up a chair and with a grin sat down and popped the lid off his tobacco tin.

Dan informed Susie of the morning's events later that evening as they sat under the buttery glow of the wall lights beside the crackling fire in the Maltsters Arms.

"So he's alright really, then?"

"Yeah, he's fine now – it just shook him up a bit, I think."

"I'm not surprised. Well let's hope the rest of them are a bit quieter."

Dan stretched his legs out in front of him and sitting back in the wooden settle wrapped his sinewy arm around her shoulder. "It's one of those things, any cow can get funny when they calve – it's just natural protection. Anyway, she did warn him to back off."

"I suppose. You'll be careful though, won't you?"

"You've no worries on that score. Another glass of wine?"

"That sounds nice; then I've got something to tell you."

Dan fetched the drinks and handed her hers. "Thanks." She took a sip and carefully placed the glass on the small table beside her. "Daddy came to see me today."

"Oh?" He couldn't think of the best way to respond to this, and left her to continue in her own time.

"He wasn't very happy."

"Really?" Dan answered. "What was he unhappy about?"

"About us."

Dan felt the hairs on the back of his neck stiffen. "What's it got to do with him? I thought he'd disowned you."

"Well yes, he did, but he said he was worried."

Dan knew how her father had treated Susie after her foolish affair with a married man. He had no regard for any man who could behave in such a cruel way to his own child and who was unable to show any compassion towards her, let alone try to forgive the girl for her mistake. He'd also heard some pretty unsavoury talk about him. Local hearsay had it that he was arrogant and a bully and he recalled Frank speculating about him knocking his wife around as well. Christ, maybe he'd even hit his daughter on the odd occasion.

"Dan?"

"Sorry, but he's got no right to be worried, not after the way he treated you. Anyway, what's he got against me?"

"Look, don't be so offended: he's only being protective. Truth is, he's never liked Frank and..."

"Oh I get it," he interrupted heatedly. "Frank's a bad influence on me and so I'm bound to be a bad influence on you. What a bloody nerve! He's not exactly spoken highly of himself, is he?"

"What's that supposed to mean?"

"You know, what he did to you, kicking you out and all that…"

"Oh no, come on Dan, what else have you heard?"

"Alright, I'll tell you," he continued, anger spurring him on. "There was a rumour going round that your father hit your mother."

"So?"

"Oh, you don't seem very surprised."

"I work in a pub Dan. I hear all sorts. Like I said before, I don't take any notice of idle chitter-chatter. And let me tell you, your father's been the subject of many a tall story, but I wouldn't give any of them credence."

He said nothing in reply.

"Oh I see, so you still think my dad's a wife beater, do you?"

"Hey, I never said that."

"No, but you suspect it, don't you? You won't believe he isn't unless I prove it, will you? But why stop there?"

One or two heads at the bar turned their way with mild interest at her raised voice.

"What do you mean?"

"Oh you know exactly what I mean. You're wondering if maybe he hit me as well, aren't you? You think I'm perhaps some pathetic victim of domestic violence – that I'm frightened of him."

"I never thought anything like that, honestly."

She swallowed the rest of her wine in one hit. "Just take me back to the pub will you?"

"But…"

"I don't want to talk about it for a minute longer."

He dutifully drove her back to The Golden Fleece. They parted in stony silence.

When Dan returned to the farmhouse, Frank was in the front room with the telly blaring.

"Is that you Dan? You're back early." Seeing his son enter the room and sensing something was wrong, he turned off the television. "Everything alright?"

"No, not really."

"Oh. Lover's tiff?" he ventured cautiously. Dan didn't answer. "More than that?" Still no answer. "Want a drink?"

"Yeah, why not."

Frank poured him a generous measure of Scotch, taking the opportunity to top up his own glass at the same time. "Do you want to tell me about it? I don't mind either way, but you never know - I might be able to help."

Dan took a swig of whisky while he considered this. Then he spilled the beans, recounting the conversation between him and Susie.

"Bloody hell, boy; you really shouldn't have gone that far. No wonder she got so mad at you."

"But it was you that told me you thought he knocked her mother around!" Dan objected.

"It was only a suspicion! I didn't expect you to go blabbing it out."

"No…fair enough: but I was angry at her after what he said to her about me and you."

"Okay, well at least you didn't tell her it was me who planted that seed in your mind – which, incidentally was very wrong of me. Thinking about it since, it was a spiteful stupid remark from a man who'd had a few beers. Don't get me wrong, the bloke's a number one arsehole, always has been. He's arrogant, selfish and self-important. Having said that, I can't honestly think he's a wife beater."

Dan groaned. "Shit, what a mess. What can I do now?"

"I know what I'd have done at your age. I'd have dropped her like a hot potato."

Dan looked desperately shocked. "But I don't want to lose her."

"No, of course you don't, because you're a better man than me. However, remember that if you do manage to get back with her – and that's one hell of a lot of humble pie – you'll still have daddy to contend with."

Dan smiled ruefully. "Faint heart never won lady fair, eh? Humble pie here I come."

"Exactly. Incidentally, if it's of any consolation to you, my opinion, for what it's worth, is that you're making the right decision. She's one in a million that one."

"Right, I'll talk to her tomorrow evening then; that is, if she'll see me."

"Oh I think she will; just don't cock it up, for Christ's sake." He rose from the armchair and placed the guard in front of the dying embers of the fire. "Time for bed."

"Yeah, me too. I'll just wander down and check the cows before I turn in, shall I?"

Dan nervously dialled the number of the pub the following morning, hoping that his girlfriend would pick up the phone. In the event, it was the landlord who answered.

"Oh hi Pete, it's Dan. Is, er, Susie about by any chance?"

"Hello mate. Yeah, she's in the bar I think. Do you want a word?"

"If I could please."

"I wish you bloody well would, she's moping around with a face like a smacked kipper. Have you two had words?"

"Sort of, yeah."

"I don't know - young lovers! Hang on then, I'll see if I can find her for you."

The phone clattered down, and Dan heard Pete clump off. A door opened. "Susie, are you in there? Your boyfriend's on the phone!"

He heard footsteps approaching, followed by a scrabbling sound as she picked up the receiver.

"Hello?" She sounded like she'd been crying, but her tone also seemed reproachful and defensive.

"Hi. Susie, look I'm sorry about last night. Can we talk?" He said this in a rush, spitting out the words.

"Go on," she replied icily.

"I don't mean over the phone. Can I see you?"

Apart from some crackling on the line, there was silence. "Susie?"

"Yes alright, but not here. I'll meet you by the bridge at eleven."

Dan glanced at his watch. It was nine forty-five. His heart gave a small bird-like flutter.

At the appointed time, he pulled his car into a wide layby on a sweeping corner by the bridge and cut the engine. There was no sign of Susie. He clambered out, slipping the ignition keys into his trouser pocket, and was almost immediately bowled over by an exuberant black Labrador bounding out into the road from a footpath running alongside the river. The dog had obviously been in the water, for after this enthusiastic greeting, the animal shook itself vigorously from tip to toe, speckling his jeans with the resultant arc of spray.

"Bruce, *Bruce! Come here! Heel!*" Anne appeared, somewhat out of breath after staggering up the muddy path from the riverside, a blue nylon lead dangling lifelessly from her right hand.

"Oh hello, Dan," she gasped, "I'm *so* sorry, has he soaked you? I only let him off the lead for a swim – he does *love* the water so – and he just shot off. Come *here* Bruce." She lunged at the dog, managing to grab his collar, and clipped on the lead. "There. It's such a lovely morning I simply had to get some fresh air so I left Gerald in charge of the shop: do him good I say."

"Ah right."

"Have you come down here for a stroll? Get away for a while? Clear your head maybe?" She probed.

"Er, well no; not really."

"Oh I see; some clandestine meeting is it?"

"No, no."

She laughed. "It's alright, I'm only teasing. It's none of my business, and I've no wish to pry. Come on Brucie, we'd better get back to the shop and check up on my fool husband. Goodbye Dan, say hello to Frank for me, won't you?"

She disappeared up the road, the unruly Labrador straining at his leash, almost choking himself in his efforts to drag her away. Dan wandered over to the old stone bridge and gazed down into the fast-flowing translucent brown waters as they tumbled boisterously over and around large limestone rocks and swirled alongside grassy banks which in places had become undermined by the winter torrents and had collapsed like crumpled cliffs into the river.

"See any fish?"

He started. Turning round, he saw Susie. "Er, no, I haven't…do you fancy walking along the river for a bit? It's such a nice day…only if you've got time, I mean."

She shrugged noncommittally. "If you want."

"Look Susie, I'm really sorry. I should never have said those things about your father. I know he's not like that. I was just angry at him for having a go at me – and Frank."

"You really upset me."

"I know. Will you let me make it up to you?"

"Are you sure you want to?"

"Yes of course, why wouldn't I?"

"Maybe there's no point, I mean how long are you going to be around for? For all I know, you might decide to flit off back to Australia any time."

"I've no plans to at the moment."

"I know that, but what if you fall out with Frank, or you decide you don't want to stay? You said yourself that he's not the easiest man to rub along with."

"I don't know what else to say, except that at the moment we're getting along okay and well...I don't want to lose you. Please believe me, whatever happens in the future I really want you to be with me."

"Blimey! That almost sounds like a proposal."

"I'm sorry; I didn't mean to be so heavy."

"No, don't be so silly; I'm not trying to tease you."

"Do you want to split up then, I mean if your fath..."

"No, I don't want that at all. Look, I'm not stupid; I know daddy's got his faults: nor does he do himself any favours when it comes to getting on with people. But there are reasons for his sometimes difficult behaviour that go way back to his childhood; and he's still my dad and I love him."

"Yes of course you do...then we'll just have to try and convince him that I'm not such a bad fella after all, won't we?" he added with a wry grin.

CHAPTER THIRTEEN

Dan was feeling very nervous: the laid-back Australian side of his character seemed to have completely deserted him. However, as he was about to meet his girlfriend's father for the first time, this was hardly surprising. He trotted downstairs and entered the kitchen where Frank was sorting through a pile of cattle ear tags assigned for the newborn calves.

"I'm going to go down to the meadow and tag those two that were born yesterday," he said, the cigarette pinned between his lips flecking the table with flakes of grey ash as it bobbed up and down. "Hopefully they'll be sound asleep and I'll be able to sneak up on them and do the deed before they realize what's happening."

"I'll come with you if you like," his son offered. Frank squinted at him through a thin curl of smoke drifting in front of his eyes. He grinned, inhaling a good lungful before removing the butt and extinguishing it lavishly in the ashtray.

"Better not boy: we don't want you to be late for your date, do we?"

"Yeah, very funny."

"Don't look so worried! Douglas loves the sound of his own voice. All you've got to do is sit there and nod politely now and then. You can do that, can't you?"

"Yeah, but I've got this awful feeling I'll drop myself in it somehow. What if he asks me if my intentions towards his daughter are honourable?"

"The man's a prick, like I told you. But I doubt even *he* could be that pompous. He'll just bore you stiff with his life story and his career *in the city.* You've nothing to worry about."

"I wish I could be so sure. Anyway, I suppose I'd better make a move."

"But you're not meeting him for another good half-hour, are you?"

"No, but I want to get to the pub first: I don't want him getting the drop on me."

Frank, hiding a smile, pocketed a couple of tags and rose from the table. "Right, well I'm away too. Best of British luck."

The bar in the Maltsters was deserted at this early hour. The fire, having just been lit, was crackling away merrily, tongues of dancing yellow flames leaping and cavorting up the chimney as the dry kindling quickly caught. There was a faint clean aroma of furniture polish hanging in the air.

"Hello Dan, don't normally see you in here this time of day. What can I get you, love?" The buxom landlady smiled warmly at him.

"Pint of lager please. I'm er, meeting someone actually." He smiled a little shiftily. "Susie's dad."

"Douglas? He's not one we see very often. There you go, have that one on the house."

"Thanks, but…"

"That's alright. I expect you need a bit of Dutch courage."

Dan took his drink and sat at the table furthest away from the bar. He'd barely settled before the door swung open and a man entered. He was in his fifties, about five foot six, and overweight. From Susie's description, this bloke was clearly her father. Dan smiled at him and uneasily rose from the table, catching the edge of it and slopping some of his drink onto its recently buffed shiny surface.

"You must be Mr. Willis. Hi, I'm Dan."

He held out his hand. The other regarded it as if it were something he'd picked up on the sole of his shoe, but nevertheless shook it weakly. Dan felt the cold puce palm in his with some disgust.

"Can I get you a drink?"

"Thank you, I'll have a half of bitter please: I'm not really a lunch-time drinker." He glanced disapprovingly at Dan's pint.

The two of them sat down awkwardly. The landlady brought the beer to them.

"There you are, Douglas," she said. "How are you keeping? And how's Audrey?"

"We're both well thank you," he replied coldly, making no attempt to elaborate. She turned and left the bar.

"Er, Susie told me that you worked in the city," Dan said after a short stultifying silence. He hoped he sounded a lot more interested than he actually felt. "I don't think I could do that, I'm pretty much a country boy really."

"Yes, Susan did say." He took a careful sip of beer. "Not everyone's cut out for a professional career in business."

Dan felt his hackles rise already, but boldly continued. "Yes, I guess it must be pretty stressful. I can see it takes a certain type of guy to cope with it. I mean, you must have to be pretty gritty, don't you? All those important business decisions, high level meetings and man management stuff – I couldn't do it."

"No, well it does take a particular type to handle all that pressure, it's true," he uttered pompously.

Gee, this guy really is a prick. "But that's by the by; I came here to talk about Susan, not myself."

Dan's heart sank. "Yes, of course. What about her?"

"We, that is her mother and I have been, well, a bit *worried* about her – especially after that unfortunate business with the er…well I'm sure I don't have to spell it out to you. Thing is, like all good parents, we just want the best for our child and…"

"…and you don't think that a farm boy from Australia is a suitable match." Dan concluded for him.

"I wasn't going to put it quite like that. I only want you to be aware that she's been hurt in the past, and I wouldn't want it to happen again."

"No, nor would I."

"So the two of you are serious, then?"

"Put it this way Doug…Mr.Willis, the last thing I'd want to do would be to hurt her in any way; I can assure you of that."

"That's easily said young man, but what are your plans for the future? I don't wish to be offensive, but at the moment you're just a farm labourer, aren't you? And if I know Frank, that's what you'll remain if you don't get away. And if you were to leave, what of my daughter?"

Dan was becoming angry. If the guy didn't wish to be offensive as he put it, he was going a bloody strange way about it. He took a swallow of lager to try and steady himself.

"If I leave, Susie'll come with me – if that's what she wants."

Douglas blanched. "What? You'd take her to the other side of the world? We'd never see her again!"

"Mr. Willis, I've got no plans to go anywhere, least of all back to Oz. And you're wrong about Frank: he wants me to stay and work the farm *with* him, not *for* him. I honestly don't know what else to say."

Dan hurriedly drained his glass.

"Would you like another?" Douglas asked grudgingly.

"No thanks, I'd better be getting back - we're calving at the moment. It's nice to meet you." Stifling a burp, Dan stood up and extended his arm. Once more he felt the cold lifeless hand feebly shake his.

"Likewise, I'm sure: oh by the way, just one more thing." Dan tensed.

"My wife would like you both to come to lunch on Sunday, any time around one."

"Oh, right thanks, I'm sure that'll be fine - I'll look forward to it," he added, failing hopelessly to convey any feeling of enthusiasm or gratitude.

Frank was in the kitchen crudely hacking off thick slabs of bread from a large farmhouse loaf.

"Is that you boy?" he shouted, hearing the door slam noisily shut. "Do you want some bread and cheese?"

Minutes later, the pair of them sat at the table eating.

"Well, how did your meeting go?" Frank enquired, failing to prevent a broad grin from spreading across his face. Didn't Duggy buy you lunch?"

"Yeah very funny. You were right though, the fella's a complete dick. He got right up my nose."

"I trust you didn't upset him."

"No, but it came bloody close."

"And did he bore you rigid with stories of his glittering career in *the city?*"

"Thankfully not. He was more concerned that I wasn't a suitable match for his daughter."

"And did you manage to convince him that you were one of the good guys?"

"I'm not sure."

"Well," Frank opined, picking his teeth with the corner of a cigarette paper pack, "I think you did well not to fall out with the obnoxious twit. Mind you, I suppose he's not entirely to blame for being how he is."

"Oh? How's that?"

"Apparently his father was a bit of a disciplinarian."

"But how can anyone know that? He's only lived down here a few years, hasn't he?"

"Yes, but you're forgetting the superhuman capabilities for gleaning information that our dear postmistress is endowed with. By all accounts, he was raised in a house where definitely children should be seen and not heard, and as he was the only child, he had a pretty desperate upbringing: especially when you consider his mother died when he was only eight years old. He hardly ever saw his father – he was a diplomat or something, I think. His life only improved marginally when his father was posted overseas and he was dumped in one of the less prestigious boarding schools. In holidays, he stayed mostly with one or other of his friends: his papa seemed to simply forget all about him. When he left as soon as he could at sixteen, he lodged with an aunt he'd hardly ever met before and got a job in a bank, where he spent the rest of his working life and where he met his future wife. He'll tell you that he took early retirement and moved down to the South West, which isn't quite true. He lost his job. After years of loyal service, he was booted out through no fault of his own, in favour of some spotty nerd fresh out of university, no doubt. Fortunately for him, at more or less the same time his father died, leaving him enough to comfortably retire on."

"His father must have been a fair age then."

"In his nineties by all accounts."

"And his son never saw him in what, forty years?"

"At least."

"Did the father ever remarry?"

"I have no idea."

"I wonder if Susie knows."

"Susie? Don't even think about asking her. As far as she's concerned, her father's retired on a hefty pension and I suggest we leave it like that, don't you? Are you seeing her tonight?"

"No, she's working. I'll see her Saturday – before my next appointment with Duggy on Sunday."

"Sunday? What's happening on Sunday?"

"I've been invited to lunch, to meet Mother."

"Lucky old you!" Frank laughed. "Oh well, perhaps you'll hear all about his illustrious career this time. I tell you, once he gets going, you'll never get a word in edgeways."

The idiotic grin was once more plastered across his face as he went about the task of rolling a postprandial cigarette.

"There is one consolation, I suppose."

"Oh yes, and what's that?"

"I won't have to cook you a roast."

Susie was pleased that her boyfriend's meeting with her cantankerous father had gone, if not well, then at least not badly, and told him so on Saturday evening as they cosied up together on the familiar wooden settle by the fire in the bar.

"He's really not as bad as people think; once you get to know him," she declared, in an attempt to put him at his ease. Dan thought gloomily that his life would be far easier if he could avoid getting to know the man at all.

"Cheer up, mummy's a marvellous cook, and you'll like her, I promise. Come on, I'll buy you another – but don't be too long drinking it, I've got plans for tonight. She drew her hand up from its resting-place on his knee and slipped it provocatively between his legs.

On Sunday morning, any sense of comfort she'd provided the night before had dissipated like morning mist on the meadow. The warm spring sunshine streaming through the open window did little to brighten his dark mood as he lay there, hands behind his head, listening to his girlfriend's soft breathing and watching the curtain flutter lightly in the gentle breeze. Pulling back the sheet, he sat on the edge of the bed and tugged on his socks. Susie murmured something intelligible, then turned over and went back to sleep.

Downstairs in the kitchen, Frank was hugging a cup of tea and perusing yesterday's newspaper.

"Morning boy, you're up early. Do you want a cup of tea?"

Dan yawned. "Sounds like a good idea."

He dragged a chair from beneath the table and sank onto it.

"It's a gorgeous day," Frank lyricized, "and I found another calf - that puts me well ahead in the finding calves stakes."

"Yep, I won't catch you now. What's that, two left to go?"

"Three."

"Mind you, I never had a chance really."

"Why?"

"Come on, everyone knows there are more births around dawn. It's natural, to avoid predators."

"Really, funny that. Only, I haven't seen many lions or tigers around here for a while."

"You know exactly what I mean."

"Well if that's the case, you should've taken the dawn patrol – instead of the graveyard shift."

"And deprive you of your beauty sleep? Which, incidentally you are clearly very much in need of."

"Oh yes, very good."

"And I may not have won the finding the most calves stakes," Dan continued, clearly on a roll, "but I definitely won the not getting beaten up by any cows stakes."

"Yes okay, very droll." He drank the last of his tea and banged his mug down onto the table. "Right, well as much as I enjoy all this banter, I've got work to do – we can't all go off on a jolly just because it's Sunday."

"Some jolly. Anyway, what have you got to do that's so urgent?"

"I'm going to put the fertilizer spreader on the tractor, and get them both ready for action. By which time, I trust you'll have been able to prepare me a suitable breakfast. Then while you're out enjoying yourself, I'll top-dress the fields we've laid up for silage. Because, contrary to popular opinion, grass don't grow much without a bit of encouragement."

Dan felt a touch disappointed; not only had he looked forward to carrying out that particular task himself, but he also felt envious of his father tootling around in the sunshine whilst he was stuck indoors trying to make polite conversation with Susie's parents.

"And then," Frank continued, pausing briefly to light his roll-up, "I'll probably wander down to The Golden Fleece for a well-earned jar or three."

"Rather you than me, I'd sooner avoid that loud Sunday lunch-time crowd."

"Oh they're only in the pub for an hour or so while their dutiful wives cook the roast: most of them will have gone by the time I get there."

"You hope. Do you want me to give you a hand with the spreader?"

"No, I'm sure I'll manage thanks. You just concentrate on breakfast."

"Right, I'll take Susie a cup of tea; then I'm on the case, alright?"

Nearly five hours later, Dan drove up to the white-painted wooden gate standing adamantly shut at the entrance to the property. The house name was stencilled boldly along the top bar in black lettering.

"The Laurels – how very appropriate," he mused, observing the neatly clipped laurel hedges that bordered the neat gravel drive leading up to the pink house. Susie jumped out of the car.

"Go on. I'll shut the gate behind you – daddy doesn't like it left open." Dan drove up the short driveway, turned the car round, and neatly parked to the side of the front door.

"What did you do that for, a quick getaway?" Susie laughed as they scrunched their way across the immaculately raked chippings. Dan grinned. He was just about to rap on the polished brass knocker, when the door suddenly swung in before him to reveal a small, slight not unattractive young-looking woman dressed in a rather lacy blouse and a tidy tartan skirt. He could see that she'd recently had her hair permed.

"Come in, come in, it's so nice to meet you at last Dan; Susie has told me *so* much about you." She leant forward slightly and rather self-consciously he gave her a peck on her proffered cheek.

"It's a pleasure to meet you, Mrs. Willis," he replied smoothly.

She giggled coquettishly. "I have to say, I do like your Australian accent…"

"Thank you, it's taken years to perfect."

"…but please just call me Audrey."

"Audrey! Don't prattle on the doorstep for heaven's sake! You'll let all the cold air in! Show our guests through!"

"Sorry Douglas!" She ushered them inside somewhat nervously. "You look nice, Susan darling. Is that a new top you're wearing? I saw one similar in m & s last week but I couldn't make up my mind whether to buy it or not. I must say, it does rather suit you. Anyway, you'd better go and say hello to your father while I organize some drinks. We aren't big drinkers Dan, but Douglas and I always have a glass of sherry before lunch on Sundays: it makes the day a bit more special, we think. Can I get you one?"

"Er, that'd be lovely."

"I think he'd prefer a lager mummy, if you've got one," said Susie, attempting a rescue.

"Oh yes of course. How silly of me. There are a few tins somewhere I think, left over from Christmas. Let me go and have a look."

Douglas carefully folded up his Sunday paper and laid it on the deep pile of the cream carpet by his side, before wrenching himself from his comfortable armchair as they entered the immaculate sitting-room. A small coal fire burned brightly in the grate and a large fluted glass vase brimming with yellow chrysanthemums had been placed centrally on a spotless white doily atop a polished round mahogany table to the side of the door. Floral curtains hung in the large bay window, gathered in the middle with neat tie-backs fastened to white walls. There were a couple of old stern-looking photographs of presumably family members on the mantelpiece. A mirror hung above these, flanked by two wall lights. On the other walls were a couple of sentimental prints depicting two syrupy-looking landscapes. One was of an orchard whose trees were smothered in an inordinate amount of sickly pink and white blossom, whilst the other depicted some charming little children picnicking in a sun-kissed meadow of tall wild grasses and flowers of every conceivable hue. The room to Dan appeared lifeless, cold and formal. They were ushered onto the settee, where they sat in silence, both wondering desperately how to start a genial conversation.

"It's a nice house you've got here, Mr. Willis," Dan said after a bit, trying to sound more at ease than he was. "Have you er, lived here long?"

"A few years now, I suppose. I took early retirement, you know. I worked in the city for many years, but when my chance came to retire, I grabbed it with both hands. They didn't want me to leave of course, but there you are. Like I told them at the time, nobody's indispensable. I'm sure they found someone to fill my shoes eventually."

"Right." He glanced at Susie hopefully. She, however, had no idea how to butt in and change the subject.

"Like I said to you before Dan, a career in business is not for everybody. You need a pretty thick skin, not to mention a razor sharp mind, nerves of steel and the ability to…"

"Here we are!" Audrey arrived, carrying a small round tray with the drinks. I've got Stella or Foster's, Dan. Which would you prefer?"

"Stella please."

"Right you are." She placed the tray carefully on the table beside the flowers. "Do excuse me, but I must see to the lunch." She scooped up the unwanted can of lager and scuttled from the room.

"Anything I can do to help, mummy?" her daughter called after her.

"No thank you darling, I've only got to make the gravy - everything else is ready," came the distant reply. For a while, the three of them engaged in small talk about the weather and other trivia and then they were summoned to the dining-room. This was another impeccably tidy area whose furniture consisted of a long oval mahogany dining table in the middle of an oak-planked floor, with a sideboard along one wall and a Welsh dresser against the end wall. Rather attractively, there were French windows to the side leading out to a freshly mown lawn surrounded by recently pruned shrubs. To his horror, Dan noted a few garden gnomes dotted about in the borders.

"It must be nice in here in the summer, with the doors open," he said politely.

"Oh yes it is," Audrey replied fervently, "and the room faces west, so we get the evening sun as well."

"Just the place for a barby, then."

"Oh we don't bother with all that," Douglas broke in. "I mean, sitting outside, getting chilled, in a pall of smoke eating food that's burned on the outside and raw inside, warding off all manner of insects. That's not for us, is it Audrey?"

"Well I don't know…it might be rather fun," she contradicted bravely, emboldened by her preprandial intake of sherry.

"Yeah? I'll tell you what, when the weather's a bit warmer I'll do one up at the farm. And I promise you, it won't be burned – or raw."

"Oh I don't know that we really…" Douglas started doubtfully.

"That sounds lovely Dan," his wife interrupted, "we'll look forward to it." Her husband scowled at her.

Susie's assertion that her mother was a good cook was verified. The roast beef was perfectly undercooked, and the apple crumble presented for pudding faultless. As they ate their way through the meal, Audrey seemed to become increasingly effusive, and demonstrated great interest in Dan's background and the current goings-on at the farm.

"It must be a real joy for Frank to have a herd of cattle again; after all he's been through."

"Yes I think it is. It's amazing what a difference it makes to a place, having some animals running around in the fields."

"Yes I'm sure…" she said dreamily. "I sometimes think I'd have loved the life myself."

"Humph, no money in that," Douglas muttered dismissively before shovelling another spoonful of crumble topped with a large yellow dollop of clotted cream into his mouth. A small globule of cream remained trapped between his lips.

"Just look what happened after all that Foot and Mouth fiasco, eh? How many farmers gave up completely and retired happily with a big fat cheque? No, they weren't so daft, they took the money and got out while the going was good."

"But it must have been terrible for them, daddy," Susie objected. "Some of the herds killed out represented decades of breeding and generations of work, not to mention irreplaceable blood lines; so who can blame them for losing heart, and who can say it won't happen again?"

"I still say it gave them a good opportunity to get out," her father replied stubbornly, "with honest taxpayers' money," he added provocatively.

"Well now," Audrey interjected, seeing the conversation might be about to get heated, "has everyone had enough to eat?"

A little while later, having hastily taken coffee, Dan thanked Susie's parents for their hospitality, but said that they really should be going, mumbling some excuse about having to check on a cow that was on the point of calving.

"Are you really worried about her?" Susie asked, as Dan drove back in the warm spring sunshine.

"Sorry?"

"About the cow."

"Oh no, not really. I just thought it wise to quit while we were ahead, before the conversation spun back round to Foot and Mouth, or the bank. Why, do you mind? Do you think I was rude?"

"Not at all, I thought you were very well-behaved. If anyone was going to lose it, it would have been me. Daddy has an uncanny knack of winding me up."

"I think your daddy has an uncanny knack of winding everybody up, don't you?"

"Yes probably." She smiled. "Anyway, at least we're talking again, and you've broken the ice. Things'll get better now."

"Do you reckon? I'm not so sure that he considers me a suitable suitor, if I can put it that way. He'd much rather you were seeing somebody professional with prospects, not some old farmhand."

"Look, he might think that now, but once he gets to know you a bit better, he'll change his mind."

"Will he?"

"Why shouldn't he? He may be all sorts of things, and God knows he's far from perfect, but once he realizes that we're happy together he'll approve, believe me. He only wants the best for his daughter, like any good parent."

"I suppose…I liked your mum."

"And she liked you too."

"Yeah?"

"Yeah, definitely! Which is good because she'll badger him as well."

"She didn't seem the type to me – to nag, I mean."

196

"Well perhaps badger's the wrong word, but she has her ways of getting through to him, despite appearances. They've been married a long time, after all."

Dan parked by the farmhouse next to the Land Rover. "I thought Frank'd still be in the pub."

At that moment his father appeared from the old dairy, calving ropes slung over his shoulder.

"Good, I'm glad you're back; I could do with a hand. One of the cows is calving, and she's been at it a while. She doesn't seem to be making any progress so we'd better see if we can pull it off for her. We'll have to try where she is I think, I doubt if we'll manage to get her into a box."

"Give me a minute, I'll get changed." Dan trotted into the house.

"Shall I come as well?" Susie asked.

"If you don't mind – we may well need you."

Minutes later, the old Land Rover was rollicking over the lush green pasture, its occupants jostling about inside. A blue plume of smoke twirled from the frayed end of the exhaust pipe.

"There she is, in the corner. Stop here," Frank instructed. As they neared the beast they saw that she was flat out on her side, oblivious to their approach, flanks heaving with her frantic but fruitless efforts to give birth. Two frighteningly large bloody mucous-covered hooves protruded from her swollen vagina. She suddenly raised her head, twisting it round in an attempt to see what could possibly be causing her so much distress. Her sides billowed out once more as she made yet another huge and heroic bid to rid herself of her crippling burden. To no avail, and her head fell back to the ground with a defeated groan of despair issuing pitifully from her open maw. Her long pink tongue lolled from the corner of her frothy mouth, tickling the growing blades of grass. Seeing the

197

animal's obvious pain and suffering, Susie immediately wished she was somewhere else – anywhere else.

"Right, let's get the ropes on its legs. At least it's coming out the right way, that's something." Having secured both front feet, Frank passed the ropes to his son.

"Just hold them for a minute while I try to find the head; don't pull, but keep them taut, ok?"

Dan nodded. Frank thrust his arm into the cow's vagina with a grunt. Blood and amniotic fluid bubbled around his elbow as he strove to penetrate deeper.

"I can feel the end of the nose," he panted, "that's good. There's nothing wrong with the presentation, the bloody thing's too big, that's all."

"What about a caesarian?" Susie suggested helpfully.

"I don't think that would help: the calf's too far forward." He took one of the ropes from Dan.

"Right when she strains, pull – as hard as you can."

After a few back-breaking attempts to get the calf free, it was plain to both of them that they were getting nowhere. A bead of sweat trickled from Dan's forehead and ran down his nose to drip off the end.

"This is no good, and the poor old girl's getting knackered - we'll have to try something else," he panted.

"Then it's the Land Rover," replied Frank.

Susie was aghast; the situation was going from bad to worse. Surely they weren't going to rip the poor thing out with the Land Rover. Dear God.

"Susie, back up the Landy."

"But…" she started to object.

"Please, just do it, it'll be alright," Frank cut her off shortly. A little while later and the ropes from the calf were secured to the ball hitch.

"Right, jump in and pull forward a bit...slowly."

It took a few seconds before Susie realized that Frank was addressing her. "Me? But I can't..."

"Please Susie, I need Dan this end. Just put it in the lowest gear and take up the tension on the rope. Don't worry, I'll shout when I want you to stop. Hang on, before you do, have you still got that bar of soap?"

"Yes."

"Good girl. Let me have it, would you?"

To say that she reluctantly climbed into the cab would be a huge understatement. Nevertheless, climb in she did and edged forward at a snail's pace, aware that the slightest slip could spell disaster.

"Whoa!" Startled, she stopped at once, yanked up the handbrake and switched off the engine.

"That'll do. Well done."

She jumped out and looked at the rope. It looked tight enough to play a tune on. Once again Frank's long arm delved into the cow's insides, this time he clasped the bar of soap in his hand.

"When I reach the head," he explained, "I'm going to try and push the soap over it, give us a bit of lubrication. When I say, boy, put all your weight on the rope, see if that'll shift it."

Holding the soap in the tips of his fingers, Frank, huffing and puffing and with his shirt now stuck to his back with sweat, managed to poke the soap over the calf's forehead. With greater effort, he carefully tried to push the inside velvety lining of the vagina back over as well. There seemed to be no room at all. It felt as though the calf's head was swathed in an enormous tight rubber band.

"Go on Dan," he grunted. Dan leant all his weight on the

already rigid rope and suddenly the head shot forward. "Grab a leg!"

Now, with a leg apiece, they pulled the calf out. Once the head was clear, the rest of the body quickly followed, sliding slickly, almost gracefully out onto the grass. The calf immediately began to make desperate and frenzied attempts to draw breath. The skin rippled on its ash-grey flank, testimony to a strong heart beating beneath.

"My God, what a monster!" Dan exclaimed excitedly. "I've never seen anything that size, alive that is. What a beauty! Come on then, big fella." He massaged the animal's chest and dug his fingers into its mouth to clear the airways before untying the ropes from its legs. Once the calf was sitting up and breathing normally, they turned their attention to the cow, who was lying, totally exhausted, on her side.

"Poor thing, she's totally wiped out. Do you reckon she'll be okay, Frank?"

Without answering, Frank yet again pushed his arm up inside her. He held it still for a few seconds before withdrawing it.

"I hope so – leastways she's not bleeding internally, so fingers crossed. Let's give her a minute before we try to get her on her feet, eh? Give her a bit of space."

Dan drove the Land Rover a bit further up the field and the three of them sat in the cooling air as the warmth of the early spring sun began to be usurped by the encroaching cool air of dusk. After Frank had wiped the worst of the gore from his hands on the grass in a desultory sort of way, he lay on his back and balancing his tobacco tin on his flat belly, rather to Susie's disgust, casually rolled a cigarette. The calf unexpectedly emitted a loud indignant bellow. The cow's ear twitched. The calf then repeated the performance. The cow lifted her head, then with a huge effort rocked into a sedentary position. She looked around, seemingly wondering what that strange object behind her could be. Another bellow brought her unsteadily to her feet. She stood, swaying slightly for a minute or so before tentatively walking drunkenly across to her newborn, where, still a bit wobbly on her pins, she started to lick it all over. As the minutes passed, the licking grew more enthusiastic and she appeared to become more stable. The calf now began to try to raise itself onto its shaky legs.

"There, I think we can leave them to get on with it," Frank said, with a good deal of self-satisfaction. "One of us had better come back in an hour or so though, just to make sure they're okay."

They remained there a few minutes longer before he scrunched out his smoke into the soft earth and got to his feet.

"Must be time for a cup of tea."

Back at the farmhouse, Susie filled the old enamel teapot with steaming water from the freshly boiled kettle. Her boyfriend and his father were at the table, having cleaned themselves up at the old Belfast sink. A faint whiff of coal tar hung in the air.

"Did you get to the pub?" Dan enquired.

"I had a couple of pints, yeah. Once I saw the cow was going to calve, I didn't want to leave her too long. Besides, the loud crowd had practically taken over the whole bar. I know I said I thought they'd have been gone by the time I got there, but they'd just all been on a jolly skiing holiday, and were determined that everyone should know about it. Anyway, how was your lunch?"

Dan glanced fleetingly at his girlfriend before answering. "Yes, it was very nice actually. Audrey's a very good cook."

"Good."

"Have you had anything to eat, Frank?" Susie asked.

"Well not as such, no."

"Would you like me to make you a sandwich?"

"No, there's no need to go to any trouble."

"It's no trouble, what do you fancy? Ham and pickle? Cheese and pickle?"

"Ooh, I don't know. What about all three?"

"Coming up, and if I've got a few minutes later, maybe I'll bake a few buns as well."

"Hey, now you're talking."

"What?" Dan expostulated, "since when have you been Mrs. Bun the baker's wife!"

"You may mock, but just you wait."

An hour or so later, with Frank dozing in his favourite armchair and Susie up to her elbows in flour, Dan dawdled down to the field, his shadow stretching out behind him as he walked directly towards the lowering sun. Somewhere in the valley bottom, which was beginning to shroud over with mist, he thought he heard the muted mellifluous call of a cuckoo. Shading his eyes, he looked across to the spot where they'd last seen the cow. She was sitting in the pasture, moist breath rolling out in front of her, chewing the cud dozily. A silvery grey object was tucked up by her side, apparently fast asleep. Mindful of his father's experience, he moved cautiously towards her. She rose hurriedly to her feet when she saw him getting nearer. He could make out that one of her teats was not swollen and dripping milk like the other three, but in fact was clean and shrunken. Correctly ascertaining that the calf had obviously had a good feed and was now sleeping it off, he wisely determined discretion to be the better part of valour, and turned back.

"Well, what do you think?"

Frank shot a glance at his son, looking for help. "They're okay; a bit, I don't know, stodgy."

"Stodgy?"

"I mean, they don't seem to have risen much."

"No," Susie agreed disappointedly, "it must be the range – I'm not used to cooking on it."

"You *did* use self-raising flour, didn't you?" Dan interjected.

"What? Yes…" a frown creased her forehead, "that is, I think so. I used that one…"

"Ah, that explains it," he said, looking at the packet. "Never mind, you'll know next time."

CHAPTER FOURTEEN

"Have you heard?" Anne asked Frank, in hushed tones of barely concealed excitement. He gathered up the tobacco pouch and multi-pack of cigarette papers and stuffed them into the top pocket of his faded Barbour jacket. Then he neatly folded his newspaper and stuffed it under his arm.

"Heard what?" he asked indifferently.

"Bob's selling up."

"What are you whispering for, Anne? There's nobody else here."

Somewhat embarrassed, she cleared her throat and spoke aloud. "Well have you?"

"Yes actually, since you ask. He told me himself; just a week or so ago."

"Apparently he's going to move into one of the cottages down by the old mill."

"Yes, he told me that as well."

She looked crestfallen. "Who do you think'll buy the farm? I mean, I suppose the land's worth something, but the house needs a bit doing to it, doesn't it?"

"So I believe – updating is probably how the estate agent would put it." He made his way to the door. As he pulled it open he said over his shoulder, "We'll just have to wait and see won't we?"

"Oh Frank!" she called after him, "Be a love and latch the door back, will you? It's such a lovely day."

The postmistress was certainly not wrong there, Frank thought as he walked back to the farm in the warm spring sunshine. May was now upon them, and the banks beside the lane were festooned with wild garlic and bluebells. Tall foxgloves stretched skyward amongst the rich green foliage, and here and there the odd clump of pale primroses was still defiantly in bloom, not yet swamped by the rapidly growing hedgerow grasses. Swollen green seed-heads of daffodils long since flowered stood defiantly on stiff stalks, their jaundiced leaves collapsed in a tired tangled mass beneath. The air was filled with enthusiastic birdsong, and the trees were dusted with a fresh green haze of emerging new foliage. He lifted his face to the heavens to feel the warmth of the sun on his grizzled features. Arriving at the narrow stone bridge over the river, he stopped and rolled a cigarette, leaning over the parapet as he did so to appreciate the tinkling clean water chuckling around the shiny washed rocks and over brown pebbles on its shingly bed. He was in no hurry to get back to the farm, happy instead to linger and enjoy the rarity of such a stunningly glorious morning. He was so wrapped up in his thoughts in fact, that he never heard the car pull up beside him and nearly jumped out of his skin when a voice greeted him from its interior.

"Morning Frank, how's things with you?" Bob asked with genuine interest.

"Christ, Bob, I didn't hear you pull up, I was miles away; I nearly fell head first into the river."

"Sorry," the other replied quietly.

"No, don't be daft, it's my fault. I sort of got lost in my own thoughts; you know how it is sometimes."

"Yes, I certainly do," Bob answered wistfully. "Talking of which, have you come to any decision about what we discussed?"

"Not as such. Like I said, I need to sound Dan out about it."

"Of course. I'll leave it with you: just don't take too long, okay?"

"No, I'll let you know as soon as I can."

"The auction date's fixed for the third of June, so if you're interested you need to move soon." He pulled away, and Frank raised his hand in acknowledgement before sending his cigarette butt spinning into the fast-flowing waters. He sauntered home, his brain fully occupied in trying to find a way to make the purchase of Bob's farm a worthwhile and viable proposition. By the time he pushed open the farmhouse door, he reckoned he had the answer.

"You timed that right - I've just made some coffee!" Dan shouted from the kitchen. "And I've got some good news!"

Frank peeled off his jacket and draped it over a hook on the back of the door. He came into the kitchen, pulled back a chair and dropped onto it. He placed his tobacco tin on the table, popped open the lid, and began to studiously fashion a cigarette.

"So, do you want to hear my news?" Dan asked as he put a mug of steaming coffee under Frank's nose.

"Me first."

"Sorry?"

"There's something I want to talk to you about; that I should have already mentioned, actually." He ran his tongue along the pasted strip, before carefully rolling the paper over it, sealing the cigarette.

"Oh? Sounds intriguing. You'd better spill the beans then." Dan retrieved his coffee and sat in the chair facing his father.

Frank stuck his smoke in the corner of his mouth and lit up. He clipped his lighter shut with a metallic snap and placed it carefully on the table. He inhaled deeply before extricating the roll-up and flicking the ash off its tip into the clean ashtray. "You know I told you about Bob selling up?"

"Yes."

"What I didn't tell you was that he gave me…well, sort of first refusal, if you like."

"Come again?"

"He asked me if I wanted to buy the farm, before it went to auction. In fact," he continued before his son could react, "the price he's asking seems very fair."

"Oh, but…I mean, can you afford it?" Dan queried, rather at a loss as to how to respond to this bombshell.

"Not exactly, no. But there may be a way forward. If the bank'll lend me some of the money then I reckon that if I bought it, did up the farmhouse and sold it on, I'd get the land for very little."

"But why would you want to take it on? I mean, it'd be a lot of extra work…"

"Actually, for once I wasn't thinking of myself."

"Eh?"

"Come on Dan, there's no need to be so coy. If you don't want to stay here, that's fine: and before you say it, I also know that you've only been here a few months and you've probably not thought that far ahead, but I'm afraid I can't help that. The thing is, this is a once in a lifetime opportunity and it needs serious consideration. You must realize as well that if you want to settle down some day and do all the normal things like raising a family, then this farm, as it is, will not provide you with enough income to achieve a decent standard of living."

"Hang on a minute, you're going way too fast here. Are you telling me that you want to hand down the farm to me?"

"Lock, stock and barrel – if you want it. What did you

think I'd do? Leave the lot to the bloody Donkey Sanctuary or something?"

"Well I don't know…I hadn't given it any thought; it's not like you're an old man or anything. And like you said, I've only been here five minutes."

"Right, okay, fair enough." Frank considered this for a little while before continuing. "I don't want to put you under any sort of pressure, and God only knows what might happen in the future, so I'll go ahead and buy the place and we'll take it from there, shall we? In any event, it's got to be a good business move for me; wherever you decide your future may lie."

"I guess…but it's a big lay out, isn't it?"

"It'll be alright so long as I can sell off the farmhouse reasonably quickly. Like I've told you, this is the sort of opportunity that may only come around once in a lifetime: I intend to grab it with both hands."

"Fair enough."

There followed an uneasy silence during which Frank vigorously rubbed out his stub in the ashtray, smearing the clean glass with a dirty trail of smutty ash. Dan somehow felt that he was being unfairly pressurized, and could think of nothing further to say.

His father meanwhile, oblivious to his son's concerns, rolled yet another fag. He dropped the finished cigarette into his tobacco tin. "So what's your news then?"

"What? Oh, I've had an offer on the house."

"Good. Are you going to accept it?"

"Er, yeah, I think so; it's a fair offer – only a bit short of the asking price."

"It's none of my business of course," Frank snorted, "but if I were you, I'd get straight back to the estate agent and refuse it. Let 'em sweat a bit for a couple of days, then ask for a bit more; after all, the place hasn't been on the market very long, has it? And prices are rising all the time."

"Oh I don't know - it'd just be nice to be rid. I don't think I can be bothered with the hassle." Then, as an afterthought, "…and it's the only offer I've had."

"Well it's up to you of course, I'm only saying what I'd do." With that, he collected his tobacco tin and stood up.

"Right, I've got a few phone calls to make. Do you need a hand moving the cows?"

"No, I'll be fine."

"Frank, before you go…"

"Yes?"

"Well, I feel a bit sort of…awkward."

"Awkward? Why so?" he asked, failing to hide the note of irritability in his tone.

"Well, you saying about the farm and everything…I mean, I don't want you to think me ungrateful or anything, but…"

"Look it's alright, I do understand. You haven't offended me if that's what you're worried about."

"Good." A prickly silence followed.

"Is that all then?"

"Yeah, I guess. Look, maybe I could help a bit, you know, with the money from the house."

"No, I wouldn't want you to do that."

"But if it helps…"

"No, not unless you're sure that's what you want; and you aren't, are you?"

"Well, not exactly, no."

"So we'll leave it like it is then."

"But what if the bank won't lend you the money?"

"If that happens, and if you can commit yourself to making your home here, then I may consider it. If not we'll just carry on as we are until you decide otherwise, okay?

"Okay."

"In the meantime, there is one thing you can do for me."

"What's that?"

"Move those poor cows into the lower meadows before they decide to break down the hedge and move themselves."

The sun beamed down benignly on Dan as he strode through the cropped grass where the cattle were currently grazing towards the lower meadows. The lightest of winds stirred the pale green leaves at the very tops of tall alders rooted on each side of the babbling brook that sliced through the meadow. Orange dung-flies flew buzzing into the warm hazy air as he walked by, disturbed from their feasting on the numerous sloppy green pats that lay dolloped haphazardly across the tightly grazed pasture. Catching sight of him as she raised her glossy black head in a rare break from feeding, one of the more vociferous cows bellowed loudly and indignantly in his direction. Half chewed grass shot from her maw as she shouted. Having said her piece she stood looking at him accusingly, mouth agape, a long string of saliva dangling from one corner, swinging gently in the breath of the breeze like some silvery remnant of a broken spider's web. As if to further enforce her point, she lifted her tail and fired a volley of loose green shit that splattered noisily onto the turf behind her, creating a pile of dung whose consistency for some strange reason or other reminded Dan of his mother's cake mixtures.

"Come on then!"

At the sound of his call, the other cows in turn raised their heads, and realizing that they were about to be moved into pastures new, started to hurriedly walk towards him. The calves, all of whom had up to now been fast asleep in a heap in the middle of the field, sensed the agitation and began to charge around excitedly. Tails held aloft they dashed about, darting between their mothers and kicking up their hind legs with pure exuberance. The cows, infected by this joie de vivre, were becoming increasingly spirited and started trotting, then cantering, then galloping in Dan's direction. He was thinking that perhaps he should have called them when he was a bit nearer to the gate, rather than here in no man's land. He had no option now but to run – and he did. Having got to the gateway into the lower meadows, he wasted no time in nipping behind it. The cattle were hot on his heels and travelling too fast to stop at the gate, they overshot it and came skidding to a halt a few yards further down beside the hedgerow.

"Right…just…calm…down…" Dan panted. The herd circled and began once again to move briskly up to the gate whilst he tried to count all the calves. Content that he had them all there, he unlatched it and swung it wide open. The beasts trotted through the opening and finding themselves in fresh grazing charged en masse to the far end of the field, legs flailing and udders swinging. Once they'd reached their goal, they charged all the way back again before spreading out more sedately to pluck at the grass, ignoring their more agile offspring who continued to frolic in the sunshine. Latching the gate, Dan, who was still recovering from his sprint finish, leaned against the warm wooden rails and took in the idyllic scene unfolding before his eyes. The steady crisp noise of the grazing animals, the lazy swishing of their tails and the sun's rays on his face had a wonderfully soporific and calming effect on him. After a few minutes spent watching the calves playing, he straightened himself up and wandered back to the farm. As he strolled along, his thoughts were of his natural father, and where the future lay for them both. Was everything moving just a bit too fast?

He voiced this very concern to his girlfriend that same evening as the two of them walked hand in hand alongside the stream through the pasture just vacated by the cattle. It was becoming one of their favourite spots for a stroll. As the cool night air began to steal over them, one or two early damselflies dipped and danced above the sparkling water, their gauzy wings now and again kissing the surface tenderly.

"I don't get it," Susie said. "I mean, he told you that he'd still try and buy the farm whatever your plans for the future might turn out to be, didn't he?"

"Yeah, but I still get the feeling that he's only doing it for me, and that I should feel grateful. Instead I feel like I'm chucking it back in his face. I'm worried he's pinning his future happiness onto me, and that makes me very uncomfortable."

"He didn't say that…"

"No. I know he didn't *say* that," Dan interrupted tetchily, "but did he *mean* what he said?"

"How the hell should *I* know?" she retorted angrily; then with a sigh added, "Look, you'll have to take him at his word, won't you? Go with the flow, see how things pan out."

"I suppose. Sorry, you don't need me rabbiting on."

"That's alright." They continued in silence for a little while, passing a mass of midges crazily darting in all directions through the dying slanting amber rays of the setting sun like frenetic fireworks or manically charged electrons suddenly bursting into life in some bizarre school physics experiment. Susie then decided to grasp the nettle.

"Can I tell you what I think without you biting my head off?"

"Of course," Dan replied, feeling a touch offended.

212

"Well it seems to me that you're feeling all this unnecessary guilt because you're actually becoming quite fond of the old bugger."

He stopped, turned, and looked at her thoughtfully for a moment. A smile slowly crept across his features. "You might be right at that," he laughed. "You might well be right."

They continued on their way, their dark shadows lengthening before them, the chill air now creeping into their bones. "Shall we go out for a drink?" Dan asked suddenly.

"If you like – unless you just want to crash by the fire."

"Do you?" He asked with unnecessary graciousness.

"No, I mean I don't mind really…" she trailed off with equal civility.

The Maltsters Arms was unusually busy that night when they sidled round the door. "Oh, looks like it's darts tonight, I forgot it was Tuesday," Dan uttered apologetically. "Let's go into the lounge."

The lounge bar was all but deserted and armed with their drinks, they settled into a quiet corner.

"So are you going to accept the offer on the house?"

"I was thinking I would, but Frank reckons I should hold out for a bit more. He's probably right, thinking about it." Susie regarded him quizzically. "I mean, it's not been on the market long, and house prices are moving up every day."

"Hmm. And a bird in the hand is worth two in the bush, and the longer it lies empty the more it's costing."

"That's true for sure." He looked pensive for a while. "I must admit, my first inclination was to accept: until Frank sowed the seed of doubt, that is."

"Well, it's up to you."

"I know. Either way I'll let them sweat for a day or two." He noticed she was grinning broadly. "What?"

"Listen to yourself! Talk about a chip off the old block."

"Do you reckon?" He laughed. "I can't be that bad. Another beer?"

"Blimey, you soon got that down your neck. What's the rush?"

"No rush," he grinned. "Are you, er, staying tonight?"

"Do you, er, want me to?" she retorted teasingly. He gave her hand a squeeze.

"Of course I do."

"Then you'd better get me another drink – or is that the plan, eh? To get me inebriated so's you can have your wicked way with me?" She slid her hand between his thighs.

"Steady!" he whispered loudly, deftly removing it. "Those two old biddies are watching us."

"Oops," she giggled flirtatiously and smiled broadly directly towards the offending women. Scowling, they simultaneously dropped their eyes in a feeble attempt to deny they were spying.

"Anyway," he went on, "since when have I needed to get you drunk to get you between the sheets?"

"You cheeky bugger!" she laughed.

CHAPTER FIFTEEN

Frank was unaccustomed to feeling nervous. In fact he was trying to ascertain, as he waited to see his bank manager - or rather *business* manager, when the last occasion might have been. Even on his wedding day he had no nerves, at least nothing compared to the butterflies that fluttered around his stomach now. He concluded that the last time he experienced this sensation was whilst waiting outside the headmaster's study prior to receiving his one and only caning. In the event, the anticipation was far more frightening than the physical punishment. At the time, he'd sensed that the teacher was far from comfortable with his task, embarrassed even, and the whole thing was over very quickly, with hardly any lasting pain. Furthermore, the episode awarded him a badge of honour among his schoolmates. Bringing his thoughts back to the present, he regretted that his previous contact had been moved on. John was the antithesis of a bank manager, a warm friendly and helpful man who appreciated a glass of single malt and was genuinely concerned with his clients' welfare. No doubt, Frank opined glumly, he'd been moved on for being too pally. He visibly jumped when the door in front of him swung open, and a tall young man in a dark pinstripe suit strode through. Frank sprang to his feet and the manager clasped his hand in a firm, almost brutal handshake.

"Mr. Anderson, pleased to meet you. William. William Farnsworth."

The said William then ushered Frank into his office, directing him to a shiny black faux leather chair in front of his tidy desk. He pulled up his own plush executive office chair, and unclipping the button on his jacket, placed his forearms on the table. He sat with pale hands clasped together, holding Frank in a serious, earnest and rather unsettling gaze.

"Now, you wish to purchase a farm - is that right?"

"Yes." Frank wriggled uncomfortably on the plastic chair. "I need to borrow some money."

"Yes, I see. And the idea is to sell on the house, after renovating it; is that it?"

"Well it doesn't need renovating, just updating really. You know - new kitchen, bathroom, lick of paint, that sort of thing."

"And how are you going to fund this enterprise?"

"Oh, I've got enough squirrelled away for that."

"You have no other liabilities?"

"Sorry? Oh, no, no mortgage or overdraft or anything. In fact, I only need two hundred and fifty thousand: I can find the rest."

"I see," the young man grinned. "That's still a considerable amount."

"Yes," Frank interjected quickly, "but I should be able to sell the house and a few acres for around five hundred thousand."

"And is that your own estimation of its potential worth, or have you sought professional advice?"

"Oh no, I've had valuations from three different estate agents. And the housing market's going up all the time, isn't it?" he added encouragingly.

"It seems to be, yes. But for how long?"

"Long enough for me to do the place up and sell it on, for sure. Look, my own farm's got to be worth what? Seven hundred thousand? Eight? Surely that's enough collateral to guarantee a loan of two and a half hundred thousand pounds, isn't it?"

"On paper, yes: but we don't lend money just on the premise that we'll be safe, Frank. For your sake, it has to be a sound proposition."

Frank thought this rather unlikely, but decided to keep his opinion to himself. This turned out to be a wise move, for he came out of the office half an hour later having secured the loan for what he considered to be very advantageous terms. Finding himself in an uncharacteristically frivolous mood, he slid into an off-licence on his way back to the car park and bought a couple of bottles of champagne. He briefly considered a pint or two on the way home, but decided against it. He would get back, tell Dan the good news, then after a bite to eat, go and see Bob: strike while the iron's hot was definitely an adage with which he enthusiastically agreed. To his disappointment however, when he reached the farm his son was not there. More importantly, Dan hadn't prepared him any lunch. After storing the champagne bottles in the door of the fridge he morosely hacked off a chunk of bread, adorned it with a thick slice of cheese and tucked in with gusto. Leaving his empty plate on the table together with the unwrapped cheese and savaged loaf, he rolled a cigarette whilst waiting for the kettle to boil. When he phoned Bob a while later, there was no reply. Ten minutes after that, there was still no answer. Barely had he returned the receiver to its cradle when he heard the outside door shimmy open and judder against the wall.

217

"Dan, is that you? Where've you been?"

"Me? Oh, I've just been for a nice walk." The reply came embellished with a hefty dose of irony.

"Eh? What do you mean?"

Dan appeared in the doorway, looking more than a little bit hot and bothered. Golden stubble glittered on his unshaven red face, and his fair hair was plastered in sweaty ratty locks across his forehead. "The heifers decided to explore the wood; it took me ages to find them. Right down the far end they were, in that thorny copsy bit. Can't we stop them going in there? It takes such a long time to track them down."

"I tell you what, why don't you run the electric fence alongside? That'll keep them out of the wood for now, until we can get something more permanent sorted. All the gear's in the old dairy - I'll give you a hand if you want."

"Right; thanks. How did you get on at the bank?"

"Better than I thought I would, I have to say. I mean, the bloke looked like he'd only just left school for God's sake. What the hell would he know about a good business opportunity?"

"So, did you get the loan or not?" Dan asked a tad irritably as he stuck the kettle under the cold tap and started filling it through its spout.

"Well yes, he arranged a loan for me; at quite good terms actually," Frank conceded grudgingly.

"So he wasn't all bad then?"

"No, but I'd sooner have dealt with John. God knows why these people have to change everything around every five minutes."

"Don't ask me."

"Any joy with the house?"

"I've told the estate agent the offer's not enough, but they haven't got back to me yet." Just at that moment, the phone rang.

"There you are boy, that's probably them now."

Dan went to it, returning a few minutes later. "You were right, that was them."

"There you go, what did I tell you?"

"They said our buyer was disappointed we didn't think his offer enough, and that he could not consider increasing it. In fact, he's turned his attention to a similar property and had an offer accepted."

"Oh dear - I'm sorry, I should have kept my nose out."

"Oh it doesn't matter. Anyway, I didn't have to listen to you, did I? And I expect somebody else'll come along soon," he added with a confidence he did not feel. "Can you give me a few minutes for a coffee and a sarnie before we go and sort this fence out?"

"Ah, I really wanted to go and see Bob this afternoon, get this sale sorted out a.s.a.p. in case he has a change of heart. I don't suppose you can put it up on your own, can you?" Frank asked sheepishly.

"Yeah sure, you go ahead. I'll manage."

"Good…erm, I'll just see if I can get him on the phone again." Frank sidled out of the kitchen.

Still feeling uncharacteristically tetchy, Dan clumped the kettle down onto the hotplate. He cut a couple of doorsteps from the ragged remains of the loaf and wedged a generous slab of cheese between them. As he waited for the kettle to boil, he tackled his sandwich hungrily. He could hear his father talking rapidly in the hall.

"Do you want one?" he asked, waving his sandwich at Frank when he returned a minute or two later.

"What?" Oh, no thanks: I'm going straight over to see Bob." He lifted his waxed jacket off the back of a chair, and shuffled into it, then tapped the pockets to confirm the presence of his tobacco tin and lighter.

"I'll see you later." As if an afterthought had suddenly struck him, he took a green trilby from a hook behind the door before leaving the house.

"Good luck then!" Dan shouted after him.

Frank was about to climb into the Land Rover when he decided to shrug off the jacket he'd only just donned. He hurled the hat across the seats, where it came to rest inelegantly on its side against the passenger door, and threw the coat unceremoniously after it. Blue smoke wafted across the yard as he started the engine, then spiralled from the tailpipe as he drove quickly along the lane, the noisy polluting diesel engine blasting up the hill, drowning out the heavenly sound of birdsong on that perfect sunny spring afternoon. After only a couple of miles or so, he turned off the lane and continued up what Bob laughingly called his drive, which was in reality a rough dirt-track. As he bounced towards the house veering left and right to avoid the mostly unavoidable potholes, Frank felt grateful that the road only continued for two hundred yards or so. He pulled up by the house and yanked on the handbrake. Once the engine was stilled, a cloud of dust which had been trailing the vehicle wafted over it, settling on the faded paintwork. With a deep breath Frank got out, slammed the door shut, and strode purposefully up the garden path. Again, garden was a bit of an exaggeration; it being more an extension of the field opposite with a track jagging through it. *Still,* Frank thought, *it's only cosmetic. Nothing a bit of tidying up won't put right.*

He attempted to depress the button to ring the bell, but it

was seized solid. Instead, he rapped loudly on the door with a balled fist. From its neglected peeling surface, flakes of ancient red paint fluttered to the floor like the desiccated wings of long-dead insects.

"Alright, alright, I'm coming! You don't have to make so much noise!"

As Bob wrestled with the door, its bottom scraped the faded Victorian floor tiles in protest.

"Hang on Frank, the bloody door's a bit stiff. It doesn't often get opened, you see. I normally come in the back."

Frank entered the dingy hall, noting the tired wallpaper and dirty decaying skirting-board. Bob ushered him into the sitting-room, where he tried to make himself comfortable in one of a pair of elderly armchairs sitting sullenly in their washed out tatty linen covers. The springing was so poor that he felt as if he was practically parked on the floorboards. Tapping the pudgy arms lightly with his fingertips, he was amused to see little puffs of dust rising into the air.

"Scotch?"

"Yes, why not?"

Bob disappeared to the kitchen, returning after only a minute with two generously filled glasses. He handed one to his guest and collapsed into the other chair.

"Cheers!"

"Cheers!"

There was a moment's silence while they both savoured their drinks.

"So," Frank ventured, "the farm. I'm still interested."

"I gathered that." Another short silence. "Old Wakeham thinks I should see what it makes at auction."

Frank chuckled. "Old Wakeham wants his commission; of course he wants to hold an auction. Are you telling me you've changed your mind? I've got the money by the way: we can proceed as soon as you like."

Bob thoughtfully took a sip of whisky before letting out a deep sigh.

"If you don't want to sell it to me for the price you said, I understand. I'll take my chances at the sale. Course, I may get it for less on the day."

"…Or you may have to pay more."

"Indeed."

A frown creased Bob's brow as he once more became pensive. The truth of the matter was that up to now there'd been very little interest in the property. The estate agency had sent a few people around, but Bob could see their interest dwindling as he showed them around. In some cases it was the steepness of the land that he could tell was putting them off, in others the state of disrepair of the farmhouse. Actually, he considered gloomily, it was probably both of these factors in the majority of cases. Going to auction was going to be something of a gamble. No, he really didn't have a choice.

"I've not changed my mind."

"What, so do we have a deal then?"

"If you're happy."

"Yep, I'm happy."

"Don't you want a survey on the house done?"

Frank had considered previously that a survey might provide him with some peace of mind, but had rejected the idea for two reasons. The first was of course money; he hated the notion of parting with a thousand or so pounds for a so-called professional's labour for a few hours. The second was he knew the history of the property and that it was basically sound; he'd noted that on his previous visits with the three other estate agents who'd provided him with valuations for the bank.

"No, I don't need to do that. I've had a good look round myself."

"Well, that's it then. Blimey, I wish everything was as simple." With an effort, Bob extricated himself from the depths of his chair. "Top up? To seal the deal?"

"Thank you." Frank handed over his empty glass and pulled his tobacco tin from his pocket. Resting it on the wide arm of the chair, he popped the lid and busied himself rolling a cigarette as his host went in search of the whisky bottle.

Twenty minutes later he wrenched himself from his chair and scrunched out his second cigarette in the ashtray. The two shook hands and Frank left with an assurance from the other that he would withdraw the farm from the market. For his part, Frank promised to immediately instruct his solicitor to carry out the conveyancing. He glanced at the clock on the mantel as he left the room; ten to four.

"I'll phone him as soon as I get back," he said, "he should be in his office still – that is, if he hasn't slid off for a round of golf or something."

Dan was not about when he returned to the farm, and assuming that he was putting up the electric fence along the woodland edge, Frank bumped across the fields in the Land Rover to join him. Arriving at the wood, he saw him unwinding a large reel of plastic orange wire. Enthusiastically he jumped down from the vehicle, leaving the driver's door hanging dejectedly open.

"How'd it go?" Dan shouted across to him in an effort to stop his words being whisked away by the strengthening wind that no more than an hour or so ago had been a pleasant breeze. Previously gently rustling leaves began to whip about in the disturbed air with increasing violence. Frank visibly jumped as the Land Rover's door banged shut behind him. Grinning broadly, he gave his son the thumbs up then trotted across to help him. A short while later the fence was up with the power unit ticking rhythmically. The wind was gusting ever stronger, and angry black bulbous clouds were scudding across the sky, blotting out the sun as they piled in from the west. As the Land Rover descended the fields to the farmyard, a few ominous drops of rain splattered onto its dusty windscreen.

"Looks like we got that done just in time," observed Frank as more raindrops obscured his view whilst others clattered heavily onto the aluminium roof of the cab. He switched on the wipers. Their wet rubber blades smeared the accumulated dust across the glass, almost completely obscuring his vision before the increasing rainfall washed it clean as they manically clacked back and forth. With the vehicle parked in the yard, the two of them leapt out and ran across the already puddly concrete to the sanctuary of the farmhouse.

"Looks like it's coming in properly now," Dan said as he leaned over the sink to fill the kettle.

"You know what they say," his father replied, "a wet and windy May fills the barns with corn and hay."

"Is that right? Anyway, never mind all that. Tell me how it went. How long will it be before the farm's yours?"

"Well it was all pretty straightforward really," Frank explained as he casually rolled a smoke. "I agreed to his asking price - mind you, I did think for one sticky moment that he'd changed his mind. As for how long it'll take, that's up to the solicitors. Hopefully about eight weeks: we both want it sorted soon as."

"Great. Fingers crossed then...I guess we ought to celebrate," Dan added. "Fancy a few pints tonight?"

"Let's just keep it under our hats for now, shall we? I don't want all those nosey buggers knowing my business. We'll celebrate properly once we've exchanged contracts, okay?"

"Fair enough…"

"Mind you," Frank continued, "that doesn't mean that we can't have a few jars later anyway, does it?" He grinned conspiratorially at his son.

The unsettled weather continued as May slipped imperceptibly into June. The calves grew fat on the rich plentiful milk greedily suckled from their mothers, and the cows in turn remained sleek and contented on the abundant supply of sweet fresh grass. Contracts were exchanged, rather to Frank's surprise, as soon as the middle of the month, and a completion date set for 8th August. At the same time, the rainy weather cleared and the sun broke through once more, turning both Frank and Dan's thoughts towards conserving some grass for the long winter months. The workload over the next couple of weeks promised to be demanding. It was also a busy time in the village shop now that Anne knew Bob had sold his farm, and more importantly, who had bought it.

"It hardly seems fair to me," she said to Mrs. Manning. Her voice had a sharper more malicious tone than usual. "I bet he bullied that poor man into selling the place to him; you know how devious Frank can be."

Mrs. Manning nodded knowingly.

"I mean, it's only a few weeks since Tom…well, you know."

"Oh yes I know, but Bob seemed happy with the deal; he told me so himself. I don't suppose his heart was in it any longer, and who can blame him?"

But Anne remained doggedly sceptical. "That's as may

be," she grunted, "but there's not much I wouldn't put past that Frank Anderson. I mean, first a son he doesn't even know he's fathered appears, and now this. And what does he want with another farm, eh? He can't even look after the one he's got, can he?"

"Well, I don't know. But he has tidied the place up a bit recently, what with all new fencing and suchlike."

"Oh yes, I know," scoffed the postmistress. "But who's doing all the work – and probably for a pittance too? His long lost son, that's who."

CHAPTER SIXTEEN

It seemed as though half the population of Devon had turned up for Bob's machinery sale on that drizzly morning in early July. Soft curtains of rain drifted across the green landscape and the leaves on the trees shivered tremulously in the warm breeze, dripping water onto the ground below. Neat regimented rows of everything from half-used rolls of rusting wire and buckled metal gates to modern farm implements were laid out in the wet grass. People wandered up and down, occasionally poking through a box of various old tools or stopping to appraise the condition of some plough or other. Some carried Styrofoam beakers of steaming tea or coffee or munched on a bacon sandwich from the catering van which, even at this early hour was doing a brisk trade. Dan, with his arm casually around his girlfriend's waist, was strolling up the field, glancing with only mild interest at the various lots they passed.

"I didn't think there'd be *this* many people here," he commented as he looked at the cars, trucks, Land Rovers and tractors still streaming into the makeshift car park in the neighbouring field.

"No, nor did I," Susie agreed. "Mind you, it's a wet day I suppose - a good excuse for a day out."

"Morning, you two." Anne had suddenly appeared. She was brandishing a bacon and egg bap, unaware that the soft yolk had burst and was spattering her jeans with yellow glutinous guano-like globs. "Where's Frank? I thought he'd be sniffing out a few bargains."

"Oh, I expect he'll be here soon. Do you, er, have your eye on anything in particular?"

"Me? Heaven's no. I just thought I'd come over and have a bit of a nose. I've left Gerald in charge of the shop, so goodness knows what disasters will be waiting for me when I get back!" With some difficulty she took a bite from the sizeable roll. Another dollop of yolk fell from it and flumped onto her denims.

"Right, well we'd better get on, eh? Nice to see you." Dan and Susie hastened away while the postmistress continued her valiant struggle with the bacon and egg roll. When they reached the top of the field, they saw Frank scrutinizing a mower in the next row. He looked up as they approached.

"Don't look too bad," he observed, as much to himself as to them.

"Are you thinking of buying it?" Dan asked.

"Well only for the right price. Mine was making a horrible noise that last field I cut, and we've still got all of Bob's ground to knock over; or most of it."

"Yeah, I suppose. There's loads of people here, though - there might be a lot of interest," his son added dubiously.

"That's true, but then I expect that most if not all of them have finished their harvesting by now."

At the bottom of the field the auctioneers had appeared. One of them lustily rang a handbell as they strode over to the start of the first row.

"No doubt we'll soon find out," Frank added. Brushing the water off the shiny red paintwork, he settled himself on the machine. Balancing his tobacco tin on his lap, he nonchalantly began to roll a cigarette. Once lit, he inhaled deeply, letting the smoke trickle from his nostrils as he exhaled slowly.

"It's quite sad really," he pronounced with feeling. "It's like the bare bones of the whole of the man's life are laid out here in rows, exposed to the elements, to be picked over by vultures."

Neither Dan nor Susie could think of an appropriate reply.

Like a cluster of insects, the crowd slowly made its way from one lot to the next, following the auctioneers in their brown stock coats. Barely three hours later, the fun was all over and the field cleared as people went off clutching their booty or wandered away empty-handed. Later still, when Dan arrived on the tractor to pick up the mower successfully snaffled by his father, the place was deserted. The caterers and auctioneers were long gone, and the only evidence left of the event were a few disconsolate lots lying unclaimed, trampled grass sporting the occasional crushed or discarded Styrofoam mug, and various tyre tracks criss-crossing the site. With the machine attached, he drove out of the field before hopping off to shut the gate. For a moment he surveyed the scene, his father's words echoing in his head. Then he jumped back into the cab and drove off down the lane.

That evening, he was in an ebullient mood as he chatted to Susie while she worked behind the bar.

"It's been quite a good day really," he remarked cheerfully. "Frank got his bargain at the sale, and later this afternoon the estate agent from London phoned to say I'd had another offer on the house."

"Good for you; is it a better one than you refused before?" she asked laconically.

"Marginally, yes."

"So are you going to accept it this time?" He noted the terseness in her tone.

"Yep, I've learnt my lesson on that one I reckon."

"Good."

He took a swig of lager. "Are you okay?" he asked cautiously.

"Yes, why shouldn't I be?" she retorted sharply. "Sorry... I didn't mean to snap, I'm in a bit of a bad mood, that's all. It seems like I've been behind this bar all day, and it's been so quiet the time's really dragged by. I like it much more when it's busy. And I know what'll happen tonight, it'll be dead 'til about half past ten when Maurice will come in for his regular couple of pints and he'll hang on long after I've called time."

"Oh well, at least you'll have me to keep you company until then, won't you?" he smiled.

If Dan's girlfriend was in a grumpy frame of mind that night, then his uncle's mood could only be described as foul. He hated this time of year, being sent out to cover stupid village charity events, pointless fêtes, or one of the many trivial local small shows that regularly took place as the summer progressed. On the rare occasions lately when something newsworthy had occurred, like that lad who'd shot himself in the woods, he hadn't been sent to get the story; no, it was always blue-eyed boy Sandy who got the best scoops. His editor obviously had it in for him he thought sourly as he knocked back his drink and gestured to the barman to refill it. And how many years of service had he devoted to that rag? Bloody nearly twenty-five, that's how many. And what thanks did he get? Bloody Sweet Fanny Adams - that's what.

"How do, Jamie boy?" A tall gaunt man with thin silvery

hair hanging in wisps from a bald pate pulled up a stool beside him. "What've you been up to?"

"Oh, evening Arnie." Arnold Murray was the sports correspondent on the paper, and a commentator at some of the more important matches transmitted by the local radio station as well. He'd been at the Advertiser almost as long as James. "I've had an absolutely cracking week actually. Didn't you read my piece on the new toddler group in Halwell? Worthy of an award, I thought." There was a slight slur in his voice.

"Can't say I did, old chum. Still, got that to look forward to, haven't I?"

James regarded him bleakly.

"…And if you look at me like that, I've a good mind not to tell you the good news."

"I'm sure I can survive without hearing it."

"I'm sure you can, old thing, but you never know, it might just cheer you up."

James sighed heavily. "Go on then, tell me; then perhaps you'll consider leaving me in peace."

"Well, it would appear that your favourite member of our happy team is moving on."

"By that I assume you mean Golden Boy."

"The very same - Sandy Cobden himself."

"Where's he going?"

"He's accepted a job with The Western Herald: chief reporter apparently. I don't think the boss is too happy about it." With a slightly tremulous hand, he raised his brimming pint to his lips.

"So I suppose that means we'll get lumbered with another Dick once he's gone. How's that good news?"

"Ah, but you're not quite right there, dear boy. Thing is,

our Lord and Master wants to hire a trainee reporter which means…"

"Which means," James concluded for him, "that he'll be covering all the crappy assignments that I've had to do up to now, and I'll get the more interesting ones."

"Quite; or at least that's the theory. Just one thing old chap, word to the wise and all that, eh? Try and lay off the sauce a bit - during working hours at any rate. And smarten yourself up as well. I mean, how many years have you had that tatty old sports jacket you're always wearing?"

James was about to object, but his friend hadn't finished. "These things get noticed old fella, believe me."

It was pretty much out of character for James to take any advice from anyone about anything, but the one person to whom he sometimes listened was Arnold. He took time out the next morning to visit the barber's for a tidy up before furnishing himself with a new jacket. He spent the morning in the office, expecting the editor to call for him in order to inform him of his promotion. By half past twelve, the anticipated meeting had not happened, and James was beginning to think that Arnie had got hold of the wrong end of the stick. He was also beginning to think that a pint or two wouldn't go amiss before he went off on his next assignment at three o'clock, to report on the official opening of a new branch of Sainsbury's; as if there weren't enough bloody supermarkets littering the town already. He switched off his computer, rose from his desk and plucked his new jacket from the back of his chair. At that moment an overweight man in his late forties with obviously dyed jet-black curly hair springing off his rounded shoulders, popped his head round the door.

"Ah there you are, James. Could I have a quick word in my office before you dash off? Won't take a minute."

Dan surveyed the scene gloomily, noting with discomfort the peeling mildewed wallpaper and rotting window frame in the front room. Even the glorious late summer sunshine pouring through the grubby glass did little to lift his mood. A few bluebottles bashed the panes angrily, in a noisy and futile attempt at escape. He strolled over and attempted to open the casement. Reluctantly the window opened part-way before the bottom rusty hinge snapped off, leaving it dangling precariously at a lopsided angle. Hastily he tried to close it again, managing only to partly jam it into its weathered frame. As he did so, one of the small Georgian panes, long since robbed of most of its securing putty, fell onto the overgrown lawn. It was 10th August, and Frank had left him to "make a start tidying up" while he undertook the far lesser task of mowing some of Bob's overgrown hayfields in the sunshine. Dan could hear the mower humming along happily somewhere in the distance. He left the lounge and made his way to the kitchen along the dark hallway. The state of this room was even worse; it would have to be gutted and all the units replaced as well as all the plumbing. Upstairs was no better. Plaster on the ceiling sagged and in some places had fallen off entirely to reveal bowed ancient wooden lathes. The bathroom needed a total new suite and all the pipework needed to be replaced here as well.

Clattering back down the stairs he tried to think positively. At least *they* were sound, and the roof seemed in good enough order from the outside; one or two slates had slipped, but that was no problem to fix. He forced the door open to the cupboard under the stairs. He looked at the electricity meters and the wiring with growing dismay. '*Strewth, the whole bloody lot looks like it came out the ark.* And his father wanted the house finished and put on the market by the middle of September!

He stood up and stretched his back, deciding that his first task would be to rip out the worn carpet on the stairs, and to throw out any other floor coverings before hacking out the stained and chipped kitchen units. Then he'd need to turn off the water and disconnect and dispose of all the sanitary ware in the bathroom and downstairs cloakroom. By the time he left at around six that evening, he'd made good inroads.

Delicious smells wafted towards him as he closed the farmhouse door. Unable to conceive that his father might be actually bothering to prepare a meal for him, he assumed correctly that Susie was there.

"Hello darling," he greeted her before pecking her on the cheek, "I didn't expect to see you tonight; I thought you were working."

She grabbed him by the shoulders and kissed him full on the lips. "There, that's more like it. Pete gave me the night off. It's been that quiet lately, and it hurts him like hell to have to pay me for standing around."

"Well, I've got no objections. Is Frank about?"

"In the front room, nursing a glass of Scotch and glued to that telly he hates so much." She reached into the fridge and pulled a bottle of cold lager from the shelf. Popping the top, she poured it expertly into a glass and handed it to her boyfriend. "There you go."

He took a long draught. "Lovely, that certainly hit the spot. Hey, cold lager and a cooked meal when I get in from a hard day's toil - domestic bliss. Just think; if you gave up work I could get this treatment every night."

"Don't even go there, I'm not about to let myself slip into a life of drudgery looking after you and your dad's every need. Now go and get in the shower, you look a right mess."

Later that same evening, in the comfort of the front room

and after he had diplomatically done the washing up, Dan tackled his father.

"There's more to do than I first thought; it'll take a while to get it all finished."

"It won't take that long – I'll give you a hand in a day or two; once I've finished haymaking."

"The whole place'll need rewiring, and most of the windows are rotted out. When I opened the one in the lounge, the glass fell out."

"Fell out?" Frank exhaled a plume of blue smoke and tamped his butt out in the crowded ashtray.

"Yeah, the hinge just snapped, it was so rusty. Then one of the panes fell out into the garden."

"So why did you open it?"

"Eh?"

Dan noticed a grin spreading over Frank's face. "Look, it's not a problem. I'll go round with you first thing tomorrow and we'll make a list. It's easy enough to get replacements. As for rewiring, that won't be a problem either. Steve said he'd do that for cash – he's already given me a price."

"Some of the plaster's falling out as well, and some of the bedroom ceilings don't look as if they're going to stay up for much longer."

"That's not a problem either; Bill can tidy them up when he fits the windows…"

"I think some of them need a bit more than just tidying up…"

"No, they'll be fine. Blimey boy, you start talking about ripping out ceilings and replacing them, then you're talking real money…"

"And then there's the damp in the hall and kitchen…"

"Well that's definitely one can of worms that we won't go

235

into. I'll get some Damp Seal, just bung that on before you paint the walls and it should keep the damp back for as long as we need; especially at this time of year. Now is there anything else worrying you?"

"The plumbing's a bit dodgy, there're all sorts of botched repairs and add-ons, and I haven't even dared to look in the roof at the header-tank."

"Are there any leaks anywhere?"

"No, I don't think so, but…"

"Then forget about what's going on in the roof space; we'll leave the pipework for the next incumbent to sort. Anything else?"

"No, only there's not much time to get everything done – I mean, the garden alone's going to take some sorting."

"You just concentrate your efforts on the house; I can get one of the lads from the village to get the garden straight. Young Adam's always keen to earn a bob or two. And I'll get a load of stone delivered too; he can fill in the potholes in the road while he's about it."

"Adam Thorne?

"Yes…why? Do you have something against him?"

"No, no, of course not…only he's not the brightest firework in the box, is he?"

"Bloody hell, Dan! He's only got to do a bit of manual graft. How would you put it? *It's not rocket science, mate.*"

"I suppose, but you must have heard about Arthur's sow?"

"I didn't know he'd worked for Arthur."

"Well he did – only for a couple of weeks mind," he added portentously.

"So what happened?"

"He spread a nice fluffy bed of straw around the pig while she slept."

"So what's wrong with that?"

"The sow wasn't asleep."

"Eh?"

"The sow was dead."

"Oh."

"Then there was the slurry tanker incident a few days after."

"Go on then, tell me."

"Having diligently filled the tanker with a nice load of smelly pig slurry from Arthur's store, young Adam trundles up the lane to spread it in the field as instructed. Unfortunately for him, he'd not switched the valve over properly so by the time he got there the tanker was empty, having coated the highway with a generous layer of piggy poo."

"Oh dear. Still, I'm sure he'll be able to do a bit of gardening without any great disasters. Just keep an eye on him, that's all."

"Don't worry; I'll be doing that alright."

The pair of them went round the house the following morning, Dan making a list as they did so of materials that would be needed for the refurbishment.

"Right," Frank said as they stepped outside into the bright sunshine. "Now before I go and turn the hay, I'll get hold of Bill. We'd best get those windows in and plastering done as soon as, then you can start sloshing some paint about. Steve's coming round later to see what's needed to sort the wiring."

He snapped open his tobacco tin and teasing some strands of golden tobacco free, deftly rolled a cigarette.

"Can you get rid of those old units in the kitchen and all the wall tiles, and the rest of the rotten skirting in the hall today? Then if you've got time, finish disconnecting the bathroom suite - I'll give you a hand to take it out in a day or so after the hay's done. We'll go out together to find a replacement, and some new units for the kitchen, so make sure you measure them up accurately. And if you've still got some time left, take down all the disgusting old curtains and fittings." He paused to light his smoke. "We'll put up some nice new poles, so make sure to measure the windows accurately as well, okay?"

"Sure, no worries." *Why don't you stick a broom up my arse and I'll sweep the floor as well.*

Frank exhaled, and a thin plume of smoke was whisked away on the rising breeze. "And if you do all that, you can make a start on stripping the wallpaper."

He gazed thoughtfully into the blue heavens. "That wind's getting up, I hope it's not going to rain…"

Luckily for Frank, the rain held off for the next few days, although the skies became increasingly cloudier and a cold westerly wind set in. Just a couple of hours after the local contractor, a small and generally cheerful man called Les drove off in an enormous green tractor, the matching green round baler bouncing happily behind him, the rain started in earnest. By this time Frank had made his way down to his new farm to see how work on the house was progressing.

"Oh," he said with feeling, "you've got all the units out of the kitchen and the bathroom; I was going to give you a hand with those."

"Oh yeah, Adam helped me. He may not be that bright, but he's as strong as an ox."

With a splintering crack, Dan prised the last length of decaying skirting from the wall and stood up, stretching his back. Frank wandered outside to inspect the garden. The grass had been cut short, and although this gave the whole area a rather yellow and jaded appearance, the overall result was a vast improvement on its former condition. The overgrown shrubs had been tidily trimmed back, and the border under the window dug over and weeded. The edges of the path, before little more than a narrow dirt-track to the front door, had been squared up and the turf removed to be replaced by crunchy fresh grey gravel.

"Well this is much better, I must say!" Frank shouted cheerfully over his shoulder. He regarded the scene happily as he leaned against the front door jamb to roll himself a smoke. Dan appeared in the doorway clutching the piece of old boarding. "You see," his father continued, "I told you he'd be alright. He's done a good job, hasn't he?"

"You're absolutely right, the garden's a whole lot better – and there was only one little blip."

"One little blip? What was that?" Frank, his forefinger and thumb pinching the cigarette, brought it to his lips and inhaled sharply.

"I told him the fuel for the strimmer was in the red can, and the petrol for the lawn mower was in the green one."

"Oh no, don't tell me he got them mixed up."

"Yeah, 'fraid so. I just happened to spot him through the window with the mower belching smoke out all over the place."

"That's not so bad, just empty it out and replace the fuel. A bit of oil in the mix won't seriously hurt, so long as he didn't…"

"…get it the other way round? Sorry, but he did: the engine's seized solid. Looks like we're going to have to put a new strimmer on our shopping list for tomorrow."

"Oh for God's sake." Frank irascibly scraped out his barely smoked fag on the stone step and flicked the ragged remnants down the path. "I thought you said you'd keep an eye on him!"

"Hey, don't blame me - I haven't got eyes in the back of my head, you know!"

"Alright, okay, fair enough." Frank took a deep breath and slowly expelled it. "Come on, let's go back inside and check what we need to get for the kitchen. How's Steve getting on anyway?"

"He seems happy enough, although he did say it might be a good idea to replace the hot water cylinder while he's about it."

"Yeah, well *he* might well think that, but then he's not the one paying for a new one, is he? There's nothing wrong with it is there?"

"No, not exactly, although there's some staining around the inlet which probably means it'll need replacing sooner rather than later. I think he just thought that while we're doing the place up, we might as well do that as well, make a proper job of it."

"Well I wouldn't worry about that, it's fine as it is for now."

Dan considered it wise not to contradict his father, as he was clearly now not in a receptive frame of mind for any remotely critical comment. "Still," he remarked, trying to lighten the mood, "at least the hay's all baled up safe - that was pretty good timing."

"Yeah," Frank conceded begrudgingly.

"How many did you get?"

"One hundred and eighteen – minus three that took off down the hill. Honestly, you'd think by now that Les'd know how to drop 'em without that happening," he added bad-temperedly.

Dan thought that given the steepness of some of the ground it was a credit to the man that he hadn't lost several more. "Did they all end up in the wood?"

"Yep, we won't get them out of there."

"Oh well, something for the wildlife in the winter then. If anybody asks, you can say you've done your bit for nature conservation now."

Frank failed to see the funny side.

CHAPTER SEVENTEEN

Dan could tell immediately from her shocked expression that there was something very wrong when Susie came back from the shop clutching her crumpled carrier bag.

It was now early September, and Bob's old farmhouse was very nearly ready to put back on the market, due mainly to the young man's hard work. In fact, the only task left for him to do was to decorate the dingy hall and fix the new curtain rail in the sitting-room. He'd started the day in a tired but contented frame of mind which quickly dissipated when he saw her anguished state.

"What on earth's the matter?" The concern in his voice was all too obvious. "Are you alright? Has something happened?"

She slumped into a chair and dumped the bag of shopping on the table, her soft eyes glassing over.

"What is it Susie? Tell me for God's sake – you're worrying me."

"It's Bob," she sniffed. "He's died."

"Died? But how?"

"That bitch Anne was broadcasting it in the Post Office, telling all and sundry and loving every minute of it. From what I could gather, Mrs. Manning found him this morning when she went down with his eggs and milk. Just slumped in the armchair, he was. She said he looked for all the world as if he was just asleep."

242

Dan crouched down beside her and hugged her closely for a while. He kissed her damp cheek tenderly and wiped a tear from her chin before rising stiffly to his feet.

"Come on, I'll make you a cup of tea; then I'd better find Frank."

"Oh, you should have heard her Dan; she was being a right cow. She said it was all Frank's fault for pushing him out of his farm. She said it gave him nothing left to live for."

"Look, don't let her upset you – you know what she's like. And anyway, Frank didn't force him to do anything did he? He decided after he lost Tom that he'd had enough of the place. That Anne's just a poisonous old windbag."

"Yeah, I know, of course she is. I should know what she's like by now, shouldn't I?" She blew her nose noisily and wiped her glistening cheeks with the back of her hand. "I hope Frank doesn't let her get to him."

"Let *who* get to him?"

Without the pair of them noticing, Frank had come in to the house and now stood framed in the kitchen doorway. "What's going on exactly?"

"I'm afraid Susie's just heard some bad news. It's Bob. It seems he passed away some time in the night. Mrs. Manning found him this morning - when she went round to his cottage," Dan added, by way of an explanation.

"Oh dear, poor old chap, he hadn't…"

"No, apparently he'd slipped away in his sleep," Susie interjected. "There's no suggestion that he, well, you know... not like Tom," her voice trailed away.

"You don't need to say any more, I get the picture. No doubt the whole bloody lot of them think it's entirely my fault; is that right?" Frank asked vindictively.

"It's just Anne, you know what she's like," Dan broke in, "I wouldn't take any notice…"

"I've not been taking any notice of that malicious cow for years, that's the trouble!" Frank hissed angrily. "She's got a nasty little mind: it's high time I had a word or two with her."

"Oh please don't!" Susie suddenly interrupted. "It wouldn't do any good."

"Maybe not, but it might make *me* feel a whole lot better."

"No," Dan said forcefully. "If you do that, it'll only make matters worse. Don't say or do anything - it'll all blow over in a few days' time."

Fuming, Frank dragged back a chair and sat down. He then pulled his tobacco tin a little shakily from his torn jacket pocket and went about the familiar task of rolling himself a cigarette.

"Does he have any family anywhere?" Susie enquired quietly. "I mean, who's going to arrange the funeral and everything?"

"There's no family," Frank answered shortly. He stuck his smoke in the corner of his mouth, where it jerked up and down as he spoke. "He asked me some years back if I'd act as joint executor to his will; I could hardly say no, it wasn't as if there was anyone else he felt he could trust. So I suppose I'll be getting a call from his solicitor any time soon."

Robert Stanton, editor of the South Hams Advertiser these last seven years, leaned his not inconsiderable frame forward in his comfortably upholstered office chair, flung the open manila folder that he'd been reading onto his shiny mahogany desk and pressed a chubby finger onto a button on his intercom.

"Sandra? Is James in yet?"

"No, I don't think so; it's only *just* gone nine," she answered in silky tones.

"Well send him in as soon as he graces us with his presence, would you?"

"Of course."

"Thank you." He released the button and raised himself onto his feet. Sandra was a nice girl, uncomplicated and efficient. When she'd first started working at the paper he'd thought it possible that she might be cajoled into having a discreet affair with him. He'd rapidly reached the conclusion, however, that this was an absurd fantasy. How could a young girl like that possibly find him in the least bit attractive? Reaching down, he shimmied the few sheets of paper from the folder and read through them once more before replacing them inside. He'd barely done so, when there was a timid knock at the door.

"Come in!"

James edged round the door. Pulling up his own chair, Stanton beckoned him to sit at the table facing him.

"So what's this all about, then, eh? Why have you dug all this up again? I thought Sandy had already covered every angle."

"Well he did, more or less." James cleared his throat. "I think there's a bigger story here. You see, Sandy covered the boy's suicide, but there's more. Apparently, his mother had died of cancer when he was young, and now his father's just died suddenly as well. I want to write a piece charting the father's tragic life: how possibly he died of a broken heart sort of thing."

"Hmm. He died of a broken heart. Yes, I like the sound of that. Okay, get up there, see what you can find out, not just about him but about his wife and boy. And keep me informed."

"Right."

"Go to the funeral, that's a good a place to start as any."

"I'd already thought to do that," James replied a little irritably. "Unfortunately it's a private cremation. But I'm sure I'll get a good story out of it if I dig deep enough. I've got a good feeling about this one." And he truthfully did. He honestly believed that this could be his big break. After all these years of crappy assignments, he at long last had the chance to prove he could produce a good piece of journalism. He was determined to put all his effort into it. He even dared to think that his stagnant career may finally be on the up.

"Can I take Colin along?" Colin Trimble was the paper's resident photographer.

"Colin's pretty busy this week, we've got all those events at the Naval College to cover don't forget. Get me the story first, eh? And depending on what you find out, we can decide then if we want any pictures, and of what."

"Fair enough: I'm on my way."

Although it was past midday when he arrived in the village, James resisted the temptation and drove past the pub. He rightly figured that a good place to commence his research would be the Post office, and Anne proved more accommodating than he could have possibly hoped in providing him with information.

"So his wife passed away, when?" he enquired in as sensitive tone as he could muster.

"Well, let me see. It would have been when poor Tom was about six, I think. We weren't in the village at the time, but naturally we heard about the sad circumstances later."

"Naturally."

"Breast cancer it was, took her very quickly by all accounts. Terribly sad, she was so young – a good deal younger than him, actually."

"Yes, life doesn't seem fair sometimes, does it? But they were happy together were they? So far as anyone knew?"

"Oh yes, of course…although she was a bit of a flirt I believe, before she married, that is. I'm sure it was nothing more than that," she added teasingly. "Then of course poor Tom…but you know all about that I expect."

"Oh yes, tragic, absolutely tragic. In actual fact, I sent my junior up here to cover the story."

"Of course! Sam somebody wasn't it? I remember speaking to him."

"Sandy."

"That's it! Sandy. He was a nice man, very polite and professional. I don't expect he'll stay your junior for long!"

"No, I don't suppose he will. Erm, this might seem a silly question, but how did Mr. Sanger take his son's death?" James asked, eager to steer the conversation in a more relevant direction.

"Hard to say really. Bob was not one to wear his heart on his sleeve, you see. He kept himself very much to himself."

"So he had no close friends to confide in?"

"No, nobody in particular." She paused thoughtfully. "That's rather sad, isn't it? When you think about it."

"Oh yes, very." A touch of irritation crept into his voice; he really wanted to get on. "What about family?"

"Sorry?"

"Did he have any family living nearby? Or anywhere, come to that?"

"Not as far as *I* was aware."

And you would have known if there were, for sure. "He must have had some friends though, didn't he? Even if they were just people he had a pint with occasionally."

"Well I suppose you could talk to Frank."

"Frank?"

"Frank Anderson, up at Willow Farm. I mean, I know he used to be friendly with his wife," she remarked suggestively. "And I happen to know that Bob appointed him as an executor in his will. He sold his farm to him too. Some would say for too little money – not that I'd be one to judge."

"Really? Why would he do that?"

"Why indeed? But like I say, it's only what *some* people think."

"When you say he was friendly with his wife…"

"Look you'd better draw your own conclusions on that one. Like I told you, it was before my time and only hearsay…"

"But there was more to it than that, wasn't there? How long after their marriage was Tom born, eh? Not too long, I bet."

"I really couldn't say." Anne was beginning to get flustered.

"But that was it, wasn't it? People reckoned this Frank was the boy's father."

"No, I mean…"

"Thank you for your time, Anne. I think I'd better go and have a chat with the man myself." He pulled a dog-eared card from his pocket and put it on the counter. "Anything else you think I should know about, just give me a call." Smiling, he turned and left the shop. He closed the door, bell tinkling, carefully behind him.

As he made his way back to his car, his imagination started to run away with him. If he was right, and the boy's father was this Frank bloke, then why had Sanger been friendly with him?

How about this? Maybe the boy hadn't committed suicide at all, and he'd been shot either deliberately or by accident by the man he took for his father, and maybe Anderson knew this and was blackmailing him. No, that was too far-fetched.

Or maybe the two men had been in cahoots. Perhaps they both wanted rid of the simpleton. He considered that if he trod carefully, he would be able to learn more at Willow Farm. Sadly for him, in that respect he was way off the mark.

Frank had just nodded off when he heard the knocking on the door. A siesta after lunch was not something he usually afforded himself, but he'd been working hard lately and he reckoned he merited one; especially since this afternoon he was on his own, Dan having gone shopping for a birthday present for his girlfriend. He reluctantly pulled himself from the snug depths of his armchair. There was another rap on the door.

"Alright, I'm coming!" he shouted irascibly as he shuffled on his slippers.

"Yes?" He squinted at his unwanted visitor, standing in the bright sunshine.

"Mr. Anderson?"

"Yes, what do you want? If you're selling, I'm not buying."

"No, no, I'm not a salesman. My name's James Ward, I'm senior reporter on the South Hams Advertiser."

James Ward! Frank hid his surprise well, responding nonchalantly. "South Hams Advertiser? You're a little out of your catchment area, aren't you?"

James ploughed on regardless. "My, er, colleague covered the story of the poor lad who shot himself a couple of months back – you may have spoken to him. His name was San…"

"No, I definitely did not. I don't speak to reporters," he interrupted rudely.

"Oh, well never mind. Thing is, now with his dad sadly passed away as well, I thought I'd come up here myself, you know, to get the human angle on it." Looking at Frank, James felt very uncomfortable. The man seemed to be studying him in a most peculiar manner.

"What exactly do you mean by *human angle*?"

"Well he's obviously had a pretty tragic life - my readers would be interested and would want to empathize with him. You knew him probably better than most, didn't you? What was he like? As a human being I mean."

"Who told you that? Oh don't tell me, you've been in the Post Office asking questions. Well I wouldn't take too much notice of what our postmistress has to say, she's far too fond of a good gossip to let truth get in the way."

"I did get that feeling, I must admit. So how long had you known Mr. Sanger? Was he a bit of a recluse?"

"I've already told you I don't talk to reporters," Frank answered unhelpfully.

"I understand completely," the other replied obsequiously, "but if you were his friend," he persisted, "then perhaps if I heard your side of the story, I could paint a truer picture of the man."

"My side of the story? Just what kind of diatribe are you thinking of writing?"

"I only want to print the truth, and show sympathy and…"

Frank cut him off angrily. "Bollocks, you want to write a story that'll sell your paper and put you in the limelight more like - bugger the truth."

"That's a bit harsh, after all we all have to earn a living somehow," James whined.

"Quite, which reminds me, I've got better things to be doing with my valuable time than gassing to you all afternoon, so if you don't mind…"

"But if you could only…"

"Let me make it plainer: Sod off!" The door slammed shut in the reporter's startled face. James wisely decided to postpone any further sleuthing until the following day.

When he returned home, before heading to the pub to

spend the evening perched on a bar stool as was his custom, he spent a good hour putting what he'd heard, and his subsequent conclusions, down on paper. Only once he'd finished did he grab his coat and go for a drink.

"You off already, old boy?" his friend asked barely an hour later.

"Yep, you should be pleased Arnie - I'm following your advice."

"I'd be happier if you did so before my round, old fruit, instead of before yours. I must say, you seem pretty chipper. You got your teeth into a good story at last, or have you miraculously fallen headlong in love with some poor unfortunate female?"

"No lady, old mate, but you could be right about the scoop." James slid from the stool and patted his colleague on the back. "Take care, Arnie."

"I told you yesterday, I need Colin up at the college, and that's all there is to it." James' editor leaned forward in his chair and made a show of perusing some documents on his desk.

"That's not until this afternoon. Look, this is an ideal opportunity. We can get some pictures of the farmhouse and the land, including the exact spot where the lad shot himself and the cottage where his father died."

"I'm not sure. I mean, I'm not comfortable with this… subterfuge."

"It's hardly that, all I did was phone the estate agents and arrange a viewing. How many people do that who aren't serious buyers?"

"It's hardly the same thing," Robert replied as he leaned back, brushing his curly locks from his blue eyes. The firmly upholstered chair creaked ominously under his weight. He sighed deeply. "Go on then, take him with you if you must, but on your own head be it."

James grinned and turned to go.

"Just make sure you get him back here for two-thirty," he added. "On the dot."

"No problem."

"There'd better not be, or it'll be the last assignment of any interest I put your way."

When James and Colin arrived at the farmhouse, Sarah, an attractive slim brunette, was already there waiting. On seeing them, she climbed out of her car clasping a couple of glossy sale brochures which she thrust at James as he shut his car door behind him.

"Good morning. Mr. Ward?" she enquired politely, extending a hand. "Here are the property details."

Ignoring her invitation to shake hands, he took the papers, holding on to one, and handing the other to his colleague. "Yes, thank you…"

"Sarah."

"Sarah." His attempt at a friendly smile came across more like a salacious leer. "I'm pleased to meet you. Oh, this is my friend Colin. Would it be alright if he took some photos as we go round?"

She smiled. "Of course, please do. Shall we start with the house? Then I'll show you the garden and paddock."

"Fine."

"Ask me anything you like during the viewing, and I'll do my best to answer any queries you may have. Could you tell me what your position is at the moment? The office hasn't given me any details."

"I'm sorry?" James was perplexed.

"I mean as regards your property search."

"Oh, right. At the moment, we're just looking really. We've got a nice town house, but we've always wanted to move to the country."

"Well I hope the two of you find this one suitable; there aren't that many period country houses on the market just now." Holding her head slightly to one side, she smiled sweetly at them.

James was horrified. "Oh no, my wife and I," he spluttered, "my wife…er Maria and I want to move."

"Oh I see. So are you looking for a family home in particular?"

"Well," James was getting into deeper and deeper water. "We don't have any children at the moment, although we might later, we're just looking for a change of direction."

"And do you have a property on the market?"

"Oh no, not quite yet – but it will be soon, when we've tidied it up a bit…you know."

"Right. Well if you like, I'll put you on our mailing list and we'll be able to send you details of any other properties in the same price bracket that may be of interest."

He noticed in the corner of his eye that Colin was grinning like a Cheshire cat.

"There's no need, really. I'd rather we looked around ourselves - thanks all the same."

"Okay, but if you change your mind give us a call – we're here to help." She smiled amiably. "Shall we go inside then?"

James was relieved when the tour of the property was over, and he was driving away. "It should be along here somewhere," he said.

"What should be?"

"The spot where the lad Tom did himself in; Sandy said it was in the woods not far from the house. There was an old tumbledown barn just inside the gateway. The body was found behind it, on the other side of a small stream. There, what's that?" He pulled the car up by an overgrown entrance. Just inside the woodland was a derelict barn; what remained of its old cob walls were completely smothered in ivy and the roof had collapsed inwards. Rotting timbers and rusty corrugated sheets, buckled and twisted, lay on the ground, holed and here and there grown through with straggly elder bushes.

"This must be it: come on, I want a piccy."

They scrambled through the undergrowth, coming out at the back of the barn. The stream beyond was practically invisible, enshrouded by a choking new growth of snaking brambles and tall nettles.

"They must have found him somewhere around here."

Colin felt somebody walk over his grave. "Are you sure we're in the right place?"

"We have to be near." James examined the area. "Look, over there!"

"Where?" Colin was beginning to get irritated: he'd been stung by nettles, scratched by marauding brambles, and now was being nibbled by midges.

"On that ash sapling over there. Is that what I think it is?"

"Police tape." A small length of the blue and white plastic tape remained tied to the trunk of the small tree.

"Right, take the photo and then let's bugger off out of here."

Back in the car, James glanced at his watch. "We'll go down to the village and you can take a few shots of the cottage where the old man was found. We should have enough time for a quick pint before we head back as well."

"Now you're talking my language," Colin rejoined amicably.

Pete was stacking glasses when the two of them came into

the bar. "Good afternoon, gents, you're just in time. What can I get for you?"

"Bass alright, Colin?"

"Lovely."

"Two pints of, please."

Pete carefully poured their drinks.

"We've, erm, just been looking at a property near here," James ventured in an attempt to engage the landlord in conversation as he pulled up a stool.

"Oh yes."

"Yes, Springfield Farmhouse."

"There's been quite a lot of interest in that one, or so I'm led to believe."

"Rather a sad story though." Pete regarded him blankly. The reporter soldiered on. "You know, with the boy's suicide and all that…"

"Yes, I suppose. Five pounds exactly, please."

James gestured to Colin who reluctantly slid off his perch, dug deep in his pocket, and handed over a crumpled ten-pound note.

"Will you join us?" James offered.

"Thank you, I'll have a half if I may."

"Cheers."

"Cheers."

"Did you know Mr. Sanger well?"

"No, not that well. He was a man who kept himself pretty much to himself – we didn't see a lot of him in here."

"What about Mr. Anderson?"

"Why the interest?" Pete asked, a note of suspicion creeping into his tone.

"Oh, no reason," James replied lightly, "just being nosy, that's all."

"Like you were in the shop yesterday?"

"Ah yes. Fair enough. Guilty as charged."

"Mr. Ward, we're a very small community here and people don't have much to talk about – do you understand?"

"I'm not sure I do."

"Let me explain. Stories get exaggerated, embellished if you like. People imagine situations that don't exist."

"Sure, but Anderson and Sanger – I sense there's something not being said…"

"Well I'm sorry, I can't help you. You'll have to speak to Frank about that."

James sighed. "I've already tried that. Come on, what's the secret?"

"No secrets that I know of. Now if you don't mind, I'd like you both to drink up please; it's time I closed the pub."

James swung the car left out of the car park and headed for the main road. "You know, I think that man knows something."

"How do you work that one out?"

"Oh, just a gut feeling."

"I see, well if he does, he's not about to tell you, is he? So you might as well let it drop." Colin belched pleasantly.

"Let it drop? That's hardly good investigative journalism, is it?"

"Bloody hell mate, this is The South Hams Advertiser, not Private Eye."

"Maybe," he conceded, "but the principle's the same. I think perhaps I ought to have another little chat with the Post Office lady; if anybody's going to spill the beans, she will."

"Whatever." Colin settled down in his seat and closed his eyes.

The next morning found James sitting at his desk trying to piece together an article from the various bits of information and innuendo he'd gathered in the village. He stopped writing on his word processor and having saved his work, leaned back pensively in his chair, hands clasped behind his head. He was wondering whether it would be worth his while to drive up and have another chat with Anne. The phone on his desk suddenly burst into life, its shrill ringing yanking him from his contemplation.

"Hello?"

"Oh, er, hello. Am I speaking to James?" The voice sounded uncharacteristically reticent.

"The very same."

"Oh good. It's Anne here, from the Post office in Littleham."

"I thought I recognized the voice. How can I help you?"

"Well I wanted to stress to you that what I said the other day, well...a lot of it's only hearsay. I wouldn't want to be implicated in any malicious gossip. I'm sure you realise what these small communities are like – people have to have something to talk about."

"Of course, I quite understand. Rest assured, anything you've told me will be treated with the utmost discretion," he replied smoothly. "Actually, I was just about to phone you myself."

"Oh really?"

"Yes, only you seem such a reliable and trustworthy source of information, if I might put it that way."

Flattery was definitely the way to Anne's heart. "I do try to see things squarely, that's true."

"Then perhaps you could help me with a couple of bits of information so I can sort of see the whole picture – make sure I've got it all clear in my mind."

"Of course, if I can."

"Mr. Anderson bought Mr. Sanger's farm privately; you

told me before that you thought he'd got it cheap. Do you know how much was paid it?"

"Neither of them would say, but…" She thought for a moment. "It was rumoured that Frank paid as much for the farm as he's asking for the farmhouse and a few acres – give or take."

"Really? So he's set to make a nice tidy profit, then?"

"By all accounts, yes. Mind you, he's spent a bit doing the old place up - although if I know Frank, he'd have done it on the cheap."

"Ah, okay, that's interesting. The other thing is you said that you couldn't really gauge the state of Mr. Sanger's mind after he lost his son because he kept himself to himself. Is there nothing you can recall? He must have come into the shop at some time. Is there anything at all you remember?"

"I'm sorry, I hardly ever saw him in the weeks after the tragedy. But after he moved to the cottage, well I heard how he was because Marge, that's Mrs. Manning, saw him most days; she took him fresh eggs - and milk and bread too if he needed it."

There was a slight pause as she gathered her thoughts. James sat tensely, the phone clamped to his ear.

"She said he was distant. He'd always been aloof of course; that was in his nature. But Marge could see he'd changed. She said he seemed to be sinking into himself. Like a little boy lost, that's how she put it."

"I see," James said pensively. "Thank you very much Anne, you've been a great help. I appreciate it."

"Not at all." Smiling, she put down the phone. Gerald's head appeared round the door.

"You just can't help yourself, can you?" he accused her loudly.

"What do you mean?" She was shocked by the aggressive and angry tenor of his voice: something she was certainly not used to.

"You were talking to that bloody reporter again, weren't you? After all you promised yesterday!"

"There's no need to swear, Gerald. I merely phoned him up to inform him, as we agreed yesterday, that what I rather irresponsibly divulged to him was in the main part speculation, and…"

"In the main part! That's rich."

"Gerald, please don't shout. Goodness, I can't think what's come over you."

"Maybe," he uttered exasperatedly, "maybe I'm getting tired of your constant prattling and gossiping."

"Oh, thank you very much. So, prattling is it?"

"Look, it's one thing having a bit of harmless tittle-tattle going round the village, but this is different. That guy's a reporter and you've managed to fire his imagination with all kinds of salacious and groundless allegations."

"Oh nonsense, dear. I've explained the situation to him and he's assured me of his discretion…"

Gerald moaned. "Discretion? Oh Anne, how can you be so naïve? Come on, oh God I hardly dare ask, what else have you told him?"

"Nothing!"

"Really?"

"Well nothing important. He wanted to know how much Frank had paid for Bob's farm…"

"…which you couldn't tell him because you don't know."

"Absolutely, though we all know roughly the amount, don't we?"

"Anything else?"

"He asked about Bob's state of mind before he died which

I *do* know, because Marge called round nearly every day…and there's no need to look like that."

"I just hope for your sake that none of this rubbish is ever published."

"Oh don't be so melodramatic. It can't hurt Bob or Tom, can it?"

"No, that's right, well thought out. But what do you think Frank's reaction will be, eh? He's hardly going to thank you for dragging his name through the mud and besmirching his character, is he? For God's sake, woman, have you never heard of slander?"

CHAPTER EIGHTEEN

"They're late," Douglas muttered irritably. He emptied his sherry schooner, waving it pointedly at his wife who sat opposite him in the other armchair. She ignored the hint, choosing to concentrate instead on her crochet.

"It's only just gone seven dear; they'll be here in a minute."

"Well I'm not going to wait – do you want another drink?"

Before she could answer, there was a soft chime from the front door.

"That'll be them." Audrey carefully placed her needlework on the thick pile carpet and stood up.

"It's alright," Douglas muttered huffily, "I'll let them in - you see to the drinks, will you?"

It was two days since Frank's unwelcome visitor, and was also Susie's birthday. Douglas had hoped that by now she might have settled down with a suitable man. He was disappointed that his daughter was still with that Australian fellow: not what he would have planned for her at all. Still, he kept his opinion wisely to himself, annoyed that everybody else appeared to like the boy. More annoyingly still, his daft mare of a wife seemed to dote on him.

"Come in, come in!" he gushed with false bonhomie. "Happy birthday, darling!"

"Thank you, daddy."

"So how's the farming going?" Douglas asked Dan stiffly, once they were all seated in the front room. "I hear Frank's extended his empire."

"Er, yeah, that's right. We've been pretty busy, what with that and doing up the old farmhouse to sell on."

"Oh yes. Have you had much interest?"

"Fair bit – there've been lots of viewings."

"Any offers?"

"No, not good enough ones, anyway."

"Mmm, perhaps Frank's asking too much. This property boom can't last forever, you know: I think the bubble's got to burst soon."

"There's no sign of that at the moment though, is there?" Dan countered. "And anyway, the house hasn't been on the market that long. I sold my gran's quite quickly – and for a good price."

"Ah yes, but that's in the city. It's totally different."

"Really? Surely there's a knock-on effect; the estate agents say that a lot of people buying in the countryside now are coming from London, looking for a change of lifestyle."

"I suppose old Wakeham told you that, did he? Like he'd know, I don't suppose he's ever been out of the county," Douglas scoffed dismissively.

"Never mind all that, dear; it's Susie's day. Now open your presents, then we can eat." She picked up two packages from the table, neatly encased in pink birthday paper and tied with gold ribbon, and handed them to her daughter. Susie carefully peeled off the wrapping and thanked her parents for the blue top, and yellow checked skirt.

"I hope they're your size; you can always change them if they don't fit, or you don't like them – I've got the receipts in my bag," Audrey said anxiously.

"They're lovely mum, I'm sure they'll be fine."

"Good," she replied with relief.

"So, did you get anything else nice?" her father asked pointedly, glancing at Dan.

"Haven't you noticed?" Susie brushed back her hair to reveal a pair of gold drop earrings, each clasping a single pearl.

"Oh, they *are* pretty," her mother enthused as she put on her glasses. "Come over here, let me have a closer look." Susie dutifully knelt on the floor next to her. "Oh, aren't they gorgeous? You *are* lucky, having a man who spoils you like that." She beamed at Dan. "Where did you buy them?"

"That antique jeweller's in Queen Street."

"Oh I know the one; they've got some *lovely* stuff in there."

"I wanted to get her a pearl necklace," Dan said with a grin, "but the ones in that shop were a little too expensive."

Susie suppressed a giggle.

"Oh no, Dan; you definitely made the right choice," Audrey pronounced.

"Certainly did," Susie agreed. "After all, anybody can have a pearl necklace, can't they?"

Douglas fidgeted uncomfortably in his chair. "How's the supper coming along? I'm getting rather hungry."

As ever, Dan was relieved when he escaped from Susie's father and was on his way home.

"Do you fancy a quick one in the pub?" he asked, "I could do with a nice pint of lager to wash away the taste of that wine your father served up with supper."

"How rude! I didn't think it was that bad."

"Perhaps not, but seeing what he pays for it from that wine club of his, I reckon it ought to be a lot smoother than that."

"Oh yeah, and since when have you become an expert on fine wines?" she laughed.

"Ever since you've been an expert on jewellery. What was all that about a pearl necklace?"

"You started it!"

"Yeah, okay. Let's hope they didn't get the joke."

"They didn't - trust me."

The bar of The Maltsters was, as usual, pretty quiet. There were just a few locals settled on stools at the bar and a young couple at one of the tables, deeply engrossed in conversation. Susie made herself comfortable at a corner table while Dan fetched their drinks.

"There you go." He placed a large glass of white wine under her nose and sat down opposite, slopping his pint of lager on the polished surface as he did so.

"Cheers."

"Cheers." He took an appreciative swallow and wiped his mouth with the back of his hand, setting his glass carefully on a beer-mat.

"I need to talk to you about something," he ventured.

"Okay," she replied, somewhat fearful at the serious timbre of his voice. "What is it?"

"You know that reporter I told you about; the one that pestered Frank?"

"Yes of course; he came in The Fleece too, Pete told me about him. He said he was probably the most obnoxious man he'd ever had the misfortune to serve in his pub."

"Yeah, well I can believe that alright." He took another swig of lager.

"And…?"

"Well I sort of knew him before…"

"What are you saying, Dan? Either you know him or you don't." A hint of annoyance had crept into her voice.

"Okay, I know who he is…"

"We all know who he is, Dan: a creepy backstreet journalist."

"No, you don't understand."

"Well explain it to me then!" she urged, frustrated with his obtuseness.

"He's my uncle."

She stared at him for a moment or two before speaking. "Your *uncle.*"

"Yes, mum's brother," he answered quietly.

"Talk about a small world," she muttered. "So did Frank recognize him; or did he recognize Frank?"

"Oh no. I told you before; they never met."

"So there's no way that James could have realized…"

"Who he was talking to? Or that his nephew was living under the same roof as his sister's ex? No, no way at all."

"Not just his sister's ex though, is he? He's his nephew's father as well."

"Absolutely. Er, there's something else I haven't told you about him."

"What's that?"

"He wanted to contest the will."

"Whose will? Your mother's?"

"No, no, gran's."

"How did you find that out? Did your sister tell you?"

"Jane? No, my solicitor had to let me know about it."

"So what happened?

"He was advised against it, and didn't proceed. He did, however, get in touch with Mr. Hutchison, my solicitor, to see whether I might see my way to giving him some money once the house was sold."

"What a bloody cheek! Dan? You surely didn't, did you?"

"No of course not, I'm not that bloody daft."

"Because if you did, you'd never get rid of him; he'd always be pestering you for more."

"I know, I know. I just felt sort of sorry for him I suppose – and guilty."

"Guilty? Honestly Dan, what am I going to do with you?"

She leaned across the table and planted a kiss on his lips.

"Forget all about him, if anyone should feel guilty, he should."

"Yeah, I already decided that some time ago."

"Good."

Despite his obvious faults, James possessed a journalistic talent that had been deeply hidden for a long time, buried beneath his feelings of self-pity and suppressed under a numbing shroud of alcohol. Now he'd found himself presented with a story that could enable him to show his true literary prowess, he tackled it with fervour, banishing all other considerations from his mind and forsaking all booze until he'd finished the piece. It took him the best part of a week to complete and edit to his satisfaction, but when the extended article was written, it was indeed a work of splendid journalistic quality, worthy of a much wider coverage than the local rag could possibly provide.

"I must say, James, this is a very good piece of investigative journalism. I have to say I'm surprised: I honestly didn't think you had it in you. However, I was clearly mistaken – well done."

Once more, Robert tested his chair's strength to the limits by leaning his large frame back in it. Once more it creaked in protest. "I've read it carefully, and am happy to put the entire piece to print: as you are no doubt aware, that doesn't happen very often in this game."

"No; thank you."

"We'll run it next week, centre spread with pictures of the spot where the boy shot himself and the cottage where the old man died. Might get one in of the farmhouse as well, okay?"

The article was duly published, and something happened that convinced James that his star was truly in its ascendancy. A well-known journalist, who happened to be on holiday in the area at the time, read it and subsequently wrote a shorter version of the story which appeared in one of the national Sunday newspapers a couple of weeks later. This was of course spotted by the eagle-eyed Anne. Curiously enough, nobody in the village had seen the original piece, the South Hams Advertiser not being their local paper: nobody that is, save the postmistress. She had bought the previous two editions and had scanned each page with nervous trepidation, fearful of what she might find. When she saw the centrefold in the following week's edition, her stomach lurched unpleasantly. When she read through it, she was horrified at the nasty innuendo and rumour that leapt out at her. That bloody journalist had twisted everything she'd told him to produce a sensational and scandalous story. And now here it was, for the whole world to see, splashed across the sixth page of a major national paper! Biting back tears, she'd shown her husband.

"How can they print such tripe! I never said anything like that," she wailed.

"I did try to warn you. Bloody hell, when will you learn to keep your mouth shut, Anne! I mean, spouting off to a journalist for Christ's sake!"

"But he's twisted everything I said! Oh God, what will Frank say when he sees it! It's obvious it's about him! Can't we sue the bloody paper or something?"

"I can't see how. He's mentioned no names; it's merely insinuation and speculation; rather a clever piece of journalism actually."

"Gerald!"

"Okay, okay. Look, it'll probably blow over. Nobody else around here's seen this, have they?"

"Not as far as I know."

"Well then, just sit tight. Today's newspaper's tomorrow's fish and chip wrapper and all that."

But now the whole story, or at least a condensed version of it, had been exposed to national coverage and while Anne was worrying about Frank's reaction, Douglas was feeling rather chipper.

"It proves what I've thought all along," he pontificated to his wife.

"Really? What's that?"

"Well it's obvious, isn't it? Surely even you can work it out," he added meanly.

"Work *what* out, exactly?"

"What sort of man he really is."

"All I can *work out*, as you so eloquently put it, is that some grubby malicious backstreet journalist with an even grubbier mind has written a malicious article containing nothing but repugnant and malevolent innuendo in order to sell his paper and no doubt further his career."

"Is that so? My God Audrey, you're so bloody naïve sometimes…"

"Am I really, Douglas? Well maybe I am, but it's better than being vindictive and small-minded!" she hissed.

"I see, so that's how it is, is it? I suppose it'll be up to me to sort this out then."

"Sort what out? What are you talking about?"

"I am not going to stand by and let my daughter become a laughing-stock by carrying on with that man's bastard son for a moment longer. I'll have a little chat with Susie and tell the girl a few home truths."

"Don't you dare start meddling again! Look what happened last time."

"Meddling? I suppose it didn't bother you that she was having an affair with a married man?"

"Of course it did, you stupid man. But what did you achieve, eh? You succeeded in ostracizing her when she needed our support most...you bloody *abandoned* our daughter!"

Douglas, momentarily stunned by this vitriolic outburst, could think of no immediate response.

Audrey, now on a roll, ploughed on.

"We've only just got her back and I won't stand by and watch you pull this family apart: if you insist on sticking your oar in where it's not wanted, then you'll get no support from me. In fact, I'll bloody well leave you to stew in your own juices – I mean it, Douglas. This particular worm has finally turned."

She picked up her knitting from the arm of the chair and in the tense atmosphere all that could be heard for a minute or two was the furious clacking of the metal needles as she manically continued with her work.

Douglas was aghast. His wife had never spoken to him in this manner before and for a while he said nothing, but merely sat fuming, staring with unseeing eyes through the window at his perfectly tended garden.

"Well I've heard it all now," he muttered eventually, "and after everything I've done for this family." Audrey offered no response; she merely carried on knitting.

"Fine," he said crossly, "we'll just stand by and let her get on with it, shall we? We'll watch as she ruins her life."

Audrey had said her piece, and wasn't about to rise to his anger. "That's the whole point though, isn't it?"

"What is? What are you gassing about now?"

"It's *her* life," she replied levelly.

"And you're perfectly happy for her to remain involved with a...with a...country hick like that."

"Oh don't be such a prig, for heaven's sake! Dan's a good, kind, well-balanced boy, and I for one have no problems with him seeing our daughter. In fact, I haven't heard anyone say a bad word against him. You're the only one who's taken a dislike to him, and we know why that is, don't we?"

"For God's sake, woman, he's an Australian farm labourer. I want better prospects for my daughter than that."

"But that's just you being snobbish and bigoted, isn't it?"

"Snobbish? Bigoted? There's nothing wrong with having standards, and...and values...and ideals," he added swiftly.

"If that's how you see it, then frankly dear, you're on a hiding to nothing and like I said, I'll have no part in it. It's clear to me that the two of them are in love, and nothing you or I may do will change that. Perhaps it would be better if you resigned yourself to it – for all our sakes."

"Really? Well, we'll see about that," he retorted angrily and rose from the chair.

"Where are you going?" Audrey asked anxiously.

"I'm going for a turn around the garden – the atmosphere in here is a little cloying for my taste."

Without further comment, she carried on with her knitting.

As he paced across the immaculate lawn towards the shrubbery at the far end, Douglas was still fuming. However, after a while he started to calm down. He glanced approvingly at the neatly clipped shrubs. The buddleia was still in bloom, attracting a myriad of bees to its sweet blossoms, as well as several butterflies flitting enthusiastically from one flower-head to the next. He sat down on the rustic wooden bench beneath the rustic wooden gazebo. The rambling rose that wound around its timbers was still in flower, although most of the blooms had gone over, spilling wilted pink and brown petals onto the grass. A faint whiff of their delicate subtle perfume still lingered in the warm summer air, mingling with the syrupy scent of honeysuckle whose tough fibrous tendrils snaked around the branches of the old apple tree just below him on the boundary of the property. He was quite shocked after his wife's outburst: he'd never, in all their years of marriage, witnessed such behaviour - and the things she'd called him!

But as he mulled everything over in his mind, he could perceive no way in which to persuade his daughter to discontinue this relationship. He reluctantly came to the conclusion that Audrey was right; the two of them were in love and there was nothing he could do about it. He groaned quietly; it was times like these that he wished he hadn't given up smoking his pipe. He could do with a calming bowlful of tobacco.

Sighing, he got to his feet and tried to look on the bright side. Perhaps the lad wasn't that bad after all – even though that would be unlikely seeing who his father was. But then he might, with any luck, have more of his mother in him. And he might, with any luck again, settle down and inherit Frank's farm. That would provide a secure and reasonably prosperous future for Susie. Oh God, why couldn't she have moved away from the village, met some steady chap with a civilized job in the city, and settled down to an urbane existence with a secure future?

Whilst Douglas was having an increasingly bad day, just up the road from him Bill was leafing through the pages of the Sunday tabloid provided by Pete for his customers. He sat quietly by the black empty fireplace, his dog in his customary position on the settle beside him. There was nobody else in the pub, and Susie was behind the bar, distractedly inspecting her nails.

"Well, well," Bill muttered under his breath. Susie looked up.

"Is there something interesting in the paper, Bill?"

"Mmm, you could say." He neatly folded the page and passed it to her. She read with increasing anger.

"What a load of rubbish! Listen - *Outward appearances can be deceptive. But dig deeper under the veneer of this sleepy little Devon village and you'll uncover all manner of intrigues, misdeeds even maybe blackmail and serious wrongdoing…* it's obvious where this came from and who it's about. Frank's going to go ape."

At that moment Pete came up from the cellar, armed with a full crate of clinking soft drink bottles.

"Who's rattled *your* cage?" he asked, noticing the barmaid's angry expression. Susie waved the article under his nose. He put his clattering burden on the floor and pulling a pair of spectacles from his top pocket, peered at the print through their smudged lenses. "Bloody hell, that's a bit rich."

"I'll have to go and show it to Frank," Susie said, her voice etched with concern.

"But you've only just got here!" Pete objected, "We're fully booked for Sunday lunch."

"I know, but they won't be here for a while yet. Can't you manage without me for half an hour?"

Pete sighed heavily. "Oh go on then: but I want you back here by a quarter to one – no later."

"Thanks Pete." She snatched the paper from him and trotted off to collect her handbag.

Frank was surprised to see Susie waiting for him as he drove into the yard, the dung spreader bobbing along behind his muck-splattered tractor on its broad flotation tyres.

"What's this? I thought you were working today. Have they given you the push?"

She thrust the paper at him. "I thought you should see this."

"Oh. My glasses are inside – you coming?"

"No, I've got to get back or I really will be sacked. I'll be down about two."

"Right, see you then; don't work too hard!"

Once in the kitchen, Frank flung the paper onto the table and gave his hands a cursory wash under the cold tap. He sat down and rolled himself a cigarette. Having lit it, he picked up his glasses which he'd earlier abandoned on the tabletop, and studiously read through the article. Then he read through it again, now and then angrily flicking the ash off his cigarette into the ashtray. Dan came into the room.

"Well, all the heifers seem happy enough, lying there in the sunshine dozily chewing the cud. It's alright for some, isn't it?"

Frank barely noticed his presence.

"Something up?"

Frank irately tamped his butt-end out. "Your bastard of an uncle, that's what's up. Take a look at this." He passed the newspaper to his son. "I'm going to carry on with the muck spreading." He pushed back his chair and got to his feet. With a face like thunder, he strode out of the house, slamming the door behind him. He stomped across the yard, climbed into the tractor cab and drove away at speed, trailing the bouncing spreader.

273

Having read the offending article, Dan could not help but be worried. He became even more anxious when Susie returned later and Frank had not come down for his lunch.

"I think perhaps I ought to go and see what's happened to him," he muttered. "It's nearly three o'clock."

"Did you tell him lunch was at half past?"

"Yes of course I did," he answered irritably.

"Okay, no need to bite my head off. Go on then, I'll finish doing the gravy if you like."

Dan slipped out of the door and crossed the yard. Just as he was about to walk up the track leading to the higher pastures, he heard the tractor coming down. After a minute or so it came into view. Frank swung into the yard and parked up. He killed the engine and stiffly climbed out of the cab.

"I was about to come and look for you, we thought you'd got lost," Dan said lightly.

"I thought I'd finish the job while I was about it," the other replied gruffly.

"Oh, right. Anyway, lunch is ready."

"Good." Frank forced a smile. "I'm hungry."

His son continued to try to introduce a touch of levity to the situation. "Did you manage to get any of it on to the field?"

"What?"

He gestured at the tractor which now was completely plastered in rich well-rotted black manure. The light lenses and windows were almost totally obscured. It seemed the only glass which remained at all transparent was the windscreen, where the wipers had provided a small but smeared area through which to peer out.

"Oh yeah. Well the wind was blowing all over the place up top. I couldn't help getting the tractor a bit shitty."

The meal followed in stilted silence, with Dan and Susie

274

exchanging occasional worried glances. The uneasy atmosphere was eventually broken by Frank. "You two are very quiet, is everything alright?"

"Sorry Frank, it's just…" Susie trailed off unhappily.

"Look, if you're bothered about that load of old rubbish in the newspaper, don't be. I'm not."

"Really?" Dan was clearly doubtful.

"Yes. I can't say I wasn't mad at first, but it's okay, I'm over it."

"But he implied such horrible things; nobody could blame you for being upset," Susie offered sympathetically.

Frank's laugh was hollow.

"Yeah, I know: but there's nothing I can do about it now, and if I let it get to me then the little sod's won, hasn't he? Besides, in a couple of days everyone will have forgotten all about it, and I'm sure I can stand the glances and gossip until then. After all, it wouldn't be the first time tongues have been wagging about me. So can we all just put it out of our minds and move on?"

"Yeah sure," Dan replied with a good deal more conviction than he felt.

"Good." Frank pushed his knife and fork together on his empty plate. "Now, if I'm not very much mistaken, I believe I can smell an apple pie in the oven."

Frank had indeed calmed down in the last couple of hours or so – at least outwardly. He was nevertheless still seething with anger inside, and all the while was considering the best way to deal with Mr. Ward. He'd never been a vindictive or spiteful man, but there was no way on God's green Earth that he would allow these foul accusations, however veiled, to be levelled against him without some form of redress.

He would pay the man a visit, he decided – but not for a day or two; he'd wait until he'd cooled down a bit. After all, what was the old adage? *Revenge is a dish best served cold.* Yes, he liked the sound of that. Having eaten his dessert, he cracked opened his tin and carefully teasing out some strands of tobacco, rolled himself a nice relaxing smoke.

CHAPTER NINETEEN

The rain drummed maddeningly on the aluminium roof of the old Land Rover, sending rivers of water cascading down the windshield. The wipers swished frantically back and forth in a losing battle to clear the screen. It had seemed, in the last few days that summer had abruptly come to an end. Frank rubbed the glass with the back of his hand in an effort to clear the haze slowly spreading across it. The vehicle's de-mister was in no way coping. Flicking on his indicator, he turned left onto the road to Dartmouth. Dan and Susie had gone away for a short break in the Cotswolds, and Frank had decided this absence would afford him the opportunity to visit the boy's uncle. James was surprised to hear from him the previous day, and even more surprised when the man said he wanted a meeting.

"To be honest," he'd told him over the phone, "I thought you'd be mad at me after you'd seen the piece; it wasn't too complimentary, was it?"

"That's precisely it," Frank had answered, stifling the urge to shout abuse down the line. "You see, I'd like the chance to put my side of the story, tell you what's really been going on."

James' ears pricked when he heard this, and he invited him to come to his office.

"No." Frank was emphatic. "I'll meet you by the quay, opposite the Royal, about twelve."

James agreed.

Now, strolling alongside blue-painted metal railings that ran the length of the quayside, Frank spotted his man sitting on one of the benches looking out across the water. Seeing his quarry approach, James leapt to his feet and flung his half smoked cigarette to the ground, grinding it beneath the grubby sole of his unpolished shoe.

"Hello Frank, good to see you again." He held out his hand. Frank ignored it.

"Shall we sit down? Just watch out for the seagull shit."

"I'd sooner go for a stroll, if that's okay with you."

"Sure, of course, why not? Now the rain's stopped," he added. Noting Frank's expression, he was starting to become a little nervous.

"So what was it you wanted to tell me?" he prompted, after they'd gone a short way.

Frank stopped and turned to face him. James' feeling of unease increased.

"That's pretty easy. I want you to know that if you ever write any crap like that again about me or my friends or family then I'll personally come down here and tear your fucking head off."

"Hey hang on a minute: you can't threaten me like that!" he squeaked, fear rising like hot bile in his throat.

"Oh yes I can, you little shit." He took a gamble. "You see, I know all about you and your dirty tricks. Not only that, I know what you did to your sister all those years ago."

"My sister! What are you talking about?"

"What am I talking about? Sexual abuse of a minor, that's what. Not only that, your own sister, for God's sake. How disgusting is that? Mind you, it'd make a good story…"

"It's not true! And anyway, who'd believe you? Where are your witnesses?"

"You're looking at him."

"What? What do you mean?" he blustered.

"I mean, you revolting little man, that I was dating Sally just before she went away; I don't know where you were, university or somewhere I guess. She told me what you did."

"You don't know what she was like, her and her friends! They taunted me, all of them! And they were all a bunch of prick teasers as well - leading all the boys on all the time. But she was the worst, she was always tormenting me!"

"Tormenting you? For Christ's sake she was what, thirteen at the time? And you were seventeen, eighteen?"

"That's not the point, she acted like she was a lot older; it was obvious to me the little slut wanted it."

Frank momentarily saw red and grabbing the man by his throat, pinned him hard against the railings.

"Get off me!" he protested hoarsely as his face began to redden, "I can't breathe…"

Frank relaxed his grip. "So," he said, pulling James upright before releasing him, "you raped her."

"No, no I didn't!" With disgust, Frank noted that he was on the verge of tears.

"I didn't rape her," he reasserted, "I just…"

"What? Had a bit of a fiddle, did you?"

"She wanted it! Anyway, she must have got scared because she started to fight me off; so I let her be."

"And she told her mother what you'd done, and that's why you were disinherited."

"How do you know?" The surprise in his voice was palpable. "She'd never have talked to you about it."

"Are you certain about that? I mean, are you willing to risk losing your career over it?"

"I'll deny it all if you do, say it's the ramblings of a jealous man, something like that. After what I've already discovered about your dubious character, people will be happy to believe me instead: and I'll have you up in court for slander before you know it," he added desperately.

"Is that right? And what if Dan backs me up?"

"Dan? Why should he? He doesn't know you and you can't tell me Sally would have told her precious son about it, because there's no way she would have."

"But he does know me actually: he's been in touch you see."

"You're lying."

"In fact, he told me what you've been up to," Frank carried on confidently, " trying to coerce him into handing over some cash when you realized that your pathetic idea of contesting his grandmother's will was doomed to failure. My God, what a nasty piece of work you really are!" He paused for a few seconds. "I suppose that you *could* deny everything, but you'd still have to explain your disinheritance: it could get very messy."

"If you know where my nephew is, you've got to tell me – he's the only family I've got; I've a right to know."

"Like hell you have, sonny. He knows that you exist, but he certainly has no desire to meet you, let me assure you of that. The best thing you can do is to forget any ridiculous ideas you may have entertained of a nice lump of cash coming your way, and crawl back under whatever stone you slid out from…"

"But that's not fair…"

"Shut up, I'm talking. I'll not tell him what you did to his mother for his sake - not yours. Finally, just in case you didn't get my gist before, if you ever pester me again, or try to contact the boy, or write any more crap like that, I will come and find you - understand?" He glared at James.

"Yes."

"Good. Right, I think that's all. For your sake, you'd better hope our paths don't cross again." Frank turned on his heel and strode off to the car park without a backward glance.

James, his feathers more than slightly ruffled, scuttled off to one of his favourite haunts: he was sorely in need of a drink.

"I just don't get it Arnie," he moaned. "I mean, why on earth would the boy even know of that old bastard's existence? And why would he get in touch with one of my sister's ex-boyfriends anyway?"

He waved his empty glass at the barman, who approached frowning deeply. "Okay, James, make this the last one will you? I've already told you to watch the language."

James was swaying slightly on the stool; hardly surprising since he'd been in the pub all afternoon.

"Okay, okay. Keep your hair on." He smirked crookedly. "Well Arnie, you're a worldly and wise sort of chap, what do you think?"

"I honestly couldn't say old boy; I only popped in here for a quiet drink after work. I don't know the fellow, do I? Maybe your sister still held a torch for him, or…"

"Bloody crap," James interrupted him brutally, "nobody in their right mind would carry a torch for a sod like that. Sorry, sorry, didn't mean to swear."

Arnold hurriedly downed his beer. "Right, that's me done. Must dash, old fruit." He slipped from his stool and quickly left the bar, leaving James staring morosely after him.

The barman leaned across the counter and addressed him quietly. "Come on James, time you drank up, there's a good chap."

"Alright Mark, marky marky. I'll be two ticks." He sat

quietly while he finished his beer and having done so, climbed carefully from his seat and tottered to the door. He was sure he would be received with a good deal more warmth in one or other of his less salubrious hang-outs.

At almost the same time Frank finally finished battling with some ridiculously complex paperwork from the Ministry. It had taken the best part of a couple of hours, and he considered that a pint or two might be in order. As usual this early in the evening, Bill and his dog were the only punters in the bar of The Golden Fleece.

"Evening Frank, pint of Guinness is it?"

"Sounds good." He nodded a brief greeting to Bill, and pulled up a stool. "Nice and quiet in here," he observed happily.

"It is now," Pete agreed, placing the foaming drink in front of him, "but I've got twenty-three meals booked for later - and my staff's on holiday with your son."

"I'm sure you'll cope." Frank busied himself with rolling a cigarette.

"Have you er, been in the Post Office lately?" the landlord asked delicately.

"If you mean *'Have I torn Anne off a strip for blurting out all that malicious gossip to that low-life reporter?'* then the answer's no," he replied bluntly.

"Well yes, I suppose you could put it like that." Pete was clearly taken aback by Frank's brusque response.

"Look, as far as I'm concerned the matter's finished, okay?"

Before the other could reply, the door swung inwards and the lady in question entered, her husband trailing behind. "Oh no," Frank muttered under his breath. Seeing him at the bar clearly disturbed her.

"Good evening, everyone," she said nervously, avoiding eye contact with any one of the small gathering. "I'll have my usual please, Gerald dear." She sidled up to Frank and spoke softly in his ear. "Might I have a word?"

"Of course," he answered, making no attempt to lower his voice, "what about?"

"Can we sit over there? I don't want everybody to listen in," she explained.

Frank moved to the chosen table, and she sat down opposite him. "I just wanted to say," she started, "I just wanted to put the record straight about that stupid article in the paper. That horrible man deliberately misconstrued everything I told him."

"Oh? And what was that?" Frank was beginning to enjoy himself.

"Sorry?"

"What did you tell him that he deliberately misconstrued?"

"Nothing! At least, nothing about anyone, I mean you, in particular. He just twisted everything I said."

"So why did you talk to him at all?"

"That's exactly what I asked her," Gerald butted in, placing their drinks on the table.

"Gerald, please, this doesn't help."

"You couldn't help yourself, could you?" he reproached her. "And now, because of your irrepressible appetite for tittle-tattle, you've done some serious damage."

"Gerald please, I'm trying to apologize to Frank."

"Go on then."

"What?"

"Apologize."

"Gerald, dear, I was telling Frank, before you rudely interrupted, that that man from the paper totally misrepresented

283

me. I most certainly did not imply half the things he wrote…"

"No," Frank said calmly, "but come on Anne, you can't deny that you have a certain tendency to, what shall we say… fabricate?"

"I should tell it like it is if I were you Frank," Gerald intervened. "What he means, Anne, is that you make up stories, spread malicious gossip, slander people even."

Frank inexplicably and uncharacteristically suddenly felt sorry for the postmistress.

"Yes," she conceded, "you're probably right dear. I'm sorry Frank: but please believe me, I didn't want all that to be spread across a national paper, I didn't think…"

"Maybe that's your trouble, you don't think what effect your inane chit-chat's going to have on others."

"Alright Gerald, I think your wife's got the message. Let's forget about it now, shall we? Water under the bridge and all that."

"Thank you. Can I get you another?" Anne offered.

"There's no need really…"

"Please, I'd like to."

"Okay, thanks." He drained his glass. Anne glanced at her husband who, with a barely perceptible raising of the eyebrows stood up, grabbed the glass, and went to replenish it. The three of them then sat rather uncomfortably for some time, Anne trying to disguise her feeling of distaste as she watched Frank scrub out yet another filthy dog-end in the ashtray in front of her.

"So," she enquired, lifting her gaze from this spectacle, "when do Dan and Susie get back from the Cotswolds?"

"Friday," came the terse reply.

"Gerald and I had a lovely break up there several years ago, didn't we dear? *After* we were married of course."

"As far as I can remember, it rained most of the time and the place was swarming with American tourists."

"Yes but it's a lovely part of the world; and anywhere near Stratford's bound to be full of Americans, isn't it? I mean, they don't have a culture of their own, do they? Where are the two of them staying?"

"Some hotel in Moreton-in-Marsh."

"Oh we stayed in Stow - it's a bit more expensive, but worth the extra of course."

Of course.

Frank was starting to get irritated. He said nothing, instead concentrating his efforts on creating yet another cancer stick.

"Any luck with the house?"

"Sorry?"

"Bob's old house; has there been any interest at all?"

"We've had several viewings…" Frank submitted cagily.

"But no offers?"

"Not as yet, no."

"Oh well, I'm sure you'll find a buyer soon," she said, although Frank definitely caught a whiff of cynicism in her reply. "These things can take time."

Frank, trying not to appear in too much of a hurry, wolfed down the rest of his pint and set the empty glass down on the table. "Right, that's me done. Thanks for the drink." He got up and with a feeling of relief soon found himself outside in the fresh air. Anne turned to her husband.

"Well he doesn't change much; it's like trying to get blood out of a stone. Mind you, there's one thing I know. Gerald?"

"Sorry, what's that?"

"I reckon we'll be hearing wedding bells soon."

"Oh yes, and who might they be for?"

"Honestly! Dan and Susie of course."

"I don't think that's very likely; she's hardly going to leap into marriage after all she's been through, is she?"

"That just goes to show how little you understand the female mind. Now please get me another glass of wine, and make sure it's a large one this time!"

Mrs. Manning practically ran up the road in her urgency to reach the shop. She threw the door open, making the bell jingle-jangle manically in distress. "Anne? Are you in there somewhere?"

The postmistress's head appeared around the corner from the private part of the premises. "Goodness Marge, what on earth's the matter? I was just making myself a quick coffee."

"Oh, thank you, that would be lovely," the other woman replied, clearly misunderstanding. "Have I got some news for you!"

"Shut the door then, and come in the back for a minute."

Anne studied her friend expectantly from the other side of the kitchen table. Mrs. Manning's podgy fingers clasped a steaming mug. She took a tentative slurp of the hot liquid.

"Well?"

Marge put down her mug. "I've just come back from taking Mr. Harris his eggs," she began. Anne said nothing; clearly her friend was building up to something and she would have to be patient.

"Do you know who his neighbours are? Or should I say neighbour?"

"Well, as he lives on the edge of the village, he's got fields on one side and if I'm right, The Laurels on the other."

"Exactly: or to be more precise, Douglas and Audrey Willis." The plump woman smiled conspiratorially.

"So what juicy gossip can you possibly have about the two most boring people in the South West? Don't tell me Mrs. Mouse has finally plucked up the courage to murder him and dump his body in the river."

"No, but she's left him." The smug smirk remained glued to Mrs. Manning's tubby cheeks.

"Never! After all these years! Are you sure?"

"Yep. George told me all about it. Apparently they had a big bust-up because Dougy flipped when he heard his daughter had gone off for a mucky few days with Frank's boy. Said he'd disown her, and that he wouldn't ever talk to her again and that he demanded Audrey do the same." She paused to take a mouthful of coffee. Swallowing noisily, she continued. "Anyway, Audrey was having none of it. She said... she said that if he thought she was going to kowtow to him for the rest of his miserable life, then he was sorely mistaken. She said he could keep his pompous bigoted opinions to himself and stick them, well, you know..."

"Marge, how do you know all this?"

"Because they were yelling at each other in the garden – George heard every word," her friend replied triumphantly.

"Wow, go on."

"That's about it, really. She finished by telling him in no uncertain terms that their marriage was well and truly over."

"I'm sick of it Douglas... that's what she said... I'm sick of it and I'm sick of you. I'm leaving, and don't expect me to come crawling back to you. I've had enough - I never want to see you again."

"And so did she carry out her threat?"

"Yes, she went yesterday evening."

"Does anyone have any idea where she's gone?"

"She told George, but he wouldn't say other than she's

staying somewhere not far away. I suppose she wants to see her daughter when she gets back tomorrow."

"Yes," Anne replied thoughtfully, "I suppose she does."

But when she returned from the Cotswolds, her daughter wasn't particularly keen to see her.

"Honestly mummy, aren't you both a bit too old for all this melodrama?" Susie rebuked her, the telephone pressed hard against her ear.

"I'm certainly not being melodramatic, dear. I've put up with his bullying ways and bigotry for far too long, and I'm telling you that I've had enough. It's about time I had a bit of a life for myself."

"But what are you going to do? Where are you going to go?"

"I've no intention of going anywhere at the moment. Your father can go back to London; he's done nothing but moan since we moved here anyway. I'm sure he'll be delighted to get back to his stuffy friends."

"Are you sure you know what you're doing? It's a big step, and…"

"Yes it is," Audrey interrupted curtly, "and one I should have taken a long time ago."

"Do you want me to talk to him?"

"You can do what you like, Susan. But like I said, our marriage is over."

"Alright mummy, I'll talk to you soon." She replaced the phone in its base unit and went back into the kitchen.

"Well?" Dan asked, handing her a glass of wine.

"She's adamant she's not going back," Susie sighed. "I don't know what to do."

Frank exhaled a plume of blue smoke and ground his cigarette butt aggressively into the ashtray with a grimy thumb.

"If you want my opinion, you can't do anything - they're grown-ups, let them sort it out between themselves. Your mother's better off without him I reckon," he added under his breath.

Dan threw him a disapproving glance.

"Look, I'm sorry you're upset Susie, but just leave them to thrash it out, eh?" He gave her a brief hug before shuffling on his jacket. "I'm going to move the young stock; won't be long."

"He's right you know," Dan ventured once they were alone.

"But…"

"They're your parents, and you love them both, and you don't want them to split up," he finished for her. "Thing is, if you try and mediate between them I just think you'll end up getting hurt. You've got to let them decide." He kissed her lightly on the cheek.

"Okay, fine: I'll just have a chat with daddy tomorrow to get his side of the story, and if I think I can't help, I'll leave things well alone."

She sensed that Dan couldn't quite take her word for it.

"I promise - okay?"

It was a beautiful late summer's day as Susie scrunched up the clean gravel drive of The Laurels. The short grass in the lawn was bejewelled with countless small spiders' webs cradling the fresh morning's dew. Deep green leaves on the shrubs shimmered in the benevolent sunshine, and the leaves on the aspens and silver birch whispered to one another softly and soothingly as the barely perceptible breeze kissed them as it stole by. Somewhere up in the cloudless blue heavens, a young buzzard wheeled and soared on the thermals, its piercing cry sounding forlorn and lonesome. She took a deep breath and pressed the doorbell.

"Oh, it's you," her father observed. "How did you get here? I didn't hear a car."

"No, it's such a lovely day, I thought the walk would do me good," she replied cheerily.

"You'd better come in I suppose; but if your mother sent you to plead her case, I'm not interested."

"She doesn't know I'm here."

Douglas stiffly invited the girl to sit in the front room, and brought her a cup of tea. He sat himself in the armchair facing her. "Well? What is it you wanted to say to me?"

"Oh daddy, I just don't want you and mummy to split up. Isn't there any way you can patch things up?"

"Patch things up?" he asked, his anger already rising. "What would you suggest?"

"Me? I don't know…"

"I've done everything I could for this family, God knows - and especially for you. And how do you repay me? I'll tell you how, shall I? Despite all my efforts, and money spent on your education and upbringing, what have you turned out like?"

"You're blaming *me* for mummy leaving you?"

"Well, why not? It all started with your stupid demeaning affair with an older married man, and not having learned from that particular monumental misjudgment, you debase yourself further by going away for a dirty weekend with your farm boy without a thought as to how me or your mother would feel about it!"

"Debase myself! Farm boy? Is that what you honestly think of me and Dan?"

"You have to admit, Susan, he's hardly a suitable match."

290

"You really are priceless, daddy," she said quietly. "I always knew you were opinionated and prejudiced, but I never realized you could be so cruel and hurtful."

"Oh, I see. Now we're getting to the nub of it. How dare you accuse me, after the way you've behaved, showing me no respect and taking me for a fool! Well you're probably right," he rushed on, "I probably am a fool for marrying your mother and expecting that she and you might treat me in the way I deserve."

"What! Mummy's done nothing but pander to your every need: she's had no life of her own!"

"Her life's with me! To love, honour, and obey!" He was almost ranting now, and spittle flew from his lips as he spat out the words.

"I think I'd better go, I'm not doing any good here."

"That's right, you go. Go on, abandon me as well!" He glared at her.

She carefully placed her untouched teacup back in its saucer and rose from the chair. Grasping the ceramic round doorknob, she turned and looked him straight in the eye.

"I'm truly sorry you feel like that."

Once outside in the warm sunshine, she found herself choking back tears. She walked quickly up the road, her vision blurred, hoping not to bump into anyone she knew before she could find refuge in the distant farmhouse. The lone buzzard still circled way overhead, only now its mournful keening appeared even more desolate and woeful to her. When she reached her destination, thankfully encountering no one on the way, she slipped through the door, shutting it firmly behind her. She made her way into the deserted kitchen, and pulling out a chair, slumped onto it. Dropping her head forward onto her clasped hands, Susie let the tears flow freely.

After a little while she stopped sobbing. Feeling better, she dried her eyes and blew her nose noisily. She then decided to busy herself with some housework.

When Dan came in at lunch-time, he was greeted by the raucous sound of the hoover vibrating through the floorboards from somewhere above him. He kicked off his boots and went to the foot of the stairs.

"Susie, is that you?" he shouted. "How did it go?"

"Hang on, won't be a minute!" she yelled back. "I've made some soup for lunch; it's on the side – just needs heating up!"

He put the saucepan on the hotplate at the same moment as the noise from upstairs ceased.

"Have you been crying?" he asked her tenderly when she appeared. "What happened?"

She could feel her eyes hazing over again. "He was really horrible: he's never said such nasty things to me - ever. I had to walk out."

"Never mind, you tried." He came across and hugged her. "Don't be too upset, I'm sure he didn't mean what he said; he's just angry I expect."

"No, you were right," she sniffed. "I shouldn't have interfered: it's my own stupid fault."

CHAPTER TWENTY

October, and the dying slanted rays of the setting sun burnished the dark sullen edges of angry-looking bulging brooding grey clouds as it sank below the black horizon, smearing the sky a bloody red. It had been raining on and off all day, heavy showers hurriedly blown across the landscape on chilly blustery winds. Frank noted the wistful smells of autumn in the sharp air that even now whisked him straight back to his childhood: the aroma of wet fallen leaves and distant wood smoke reminded him that winter was just around the corner. He was leaning on the gate looking at his cows bunched around a couple of round feeders, tucking into bales of fragrant meadow hay which he'd dropped in for them. The only sounds were the contented munching of the animals and the steadfast dripping from trees whose overburdened branches gratefully shed water from sopping tired foliage.

He stuffed a cigarette into the corner of his mouth and lit it, appreciating the scene in front of him. As a trail of tobacco smoke drifted lazily away from him in the still air, he reflected upon all the events that had reshaped his life during the last twelve months. He shuddered to think that this time last year he'd been on the brink of suicide, and now look where he was! He'd got his son back, he'd got his farm back on its feet and expanded it, and in the last week the sale of Bob's old house had been completed. With a sudden stab of fear, he realized that to be left on his own again would be too much for him to bear. Speedily dismissing that uncomfortable thought from his mind, he cast his eye once more over his cattle before climbing into the tractor cab and heading back to the yard in the gathering darkness.

After her upsetting confrontation with her father, Susie had wisely decided to leave her parents to resolve their problems on their own, although her mother remained adamant that she wanted a divorce. This outcome seemed increasingly likely now Douglas had scurried back to London, where he'd ensconced himself, permanently it would seem, in a small flat in Bayswater, leaving Audrey to take up sole residency at The Laurels.

"It's getting a bit nippy out there now," Frank commented as he entered the warm kitchen, "we'll have to think about bringing the cattle in soon if it keeps on raining." He noted with pleasure that his son's girlfriend was in the house. She'd spent a good deal of time with Dan recently, and he was hopeful that she might move in permanently in the near future. As it happened, Dan was thinking along the same lines, but had yet to pluck up the courage to broach the subject with her.

"Well the sheds are all ready for them; all I've got to do is spread a bit of straw round."

"Good. I'm for a bath. What's for supper?"

"Shepherd's pie," Susie replied breezily, "it'll be ready in half an hour."

"Perfect," he said smiling. At that moment the phone began to ring. "Won't be for me," he quipped, "I'm not expecting anyone." With that, he trotted off up the stairs.

"It's probably mummy, I'll get it."

Following a lengthy conversation in the hall, whose tone Dan could not decipher due to the tuneless singing emanating from the bathroom, Susie came back.

"That was mummy. She said she's started divorce proceedings."

"Oh. Is she okay?"

"Okay? Yes, she's fine. In fact, I don't think I've ever heard her sounding so happy; she says she's looking forward to being single again - 'with any luck by Christmas,' to quote her exact words."

"Right, well I suppose it's good that she feels quite upbeat about it all."

"Good?" she retorted tersely.

"Well, not good, but…you know; at least she's got an eye on the future."

She sighed. "It's funny, but I'd never dreamed they'd split up, not them. Mummy always seemed so *settled*. Do you think that she's been unhappy for a long time?"

He pondered this for a several seconds. "I think that she's suddenly realized that she doesn't need him any longer: she's discovered that she can stand on her own two feet. In fact, it sounds as though she relishes the prospect."

"So did she stay with him for my sake?"

"I think she stayed with him simply because she didn't consider any other option. She was a good, loyal wife who only went against him when he ordered her to sever contact with her daughter. That was too much to ask," Frank offered. With a bath robe clinging to him, he pattered across the room, leaving a trail of wet footprints. He grabbed a pair of woollen socks and a shirt that had been drying on a rack above the range. "I'm sorry Susie, but your father couldn't have asked for a better wife. She put up with his bullying belittling ways for years. Any other woman would have left him a long time before. And yes, she might have put up with him partly because she didn't want to upset you, but then she wouldn't have been the only woman guilty of wanting to protect her children, would she? So don't blame yourself, and I'm sorry: I know he's your father and you love him."

"I'm not sure that I love him much at the moment," she answered, before changing the subject completely. "That shirt's not been ironed yet. Why don't you get one out of the airing cupboard?"

"I like this one; anyway it's only for work." And before either of them could object further, Frank left the kitchen, whistling tunelessly as he padded up the stairs.

"Right." Dan opened the fridge. "Glass of wine?"

Despite her recent serious faux pas with James, Anne was once again in full flow. "Yes, Marge told me only this morning. *He's* shot off to London, and *she's* obviously taken full advantage of the fact. She's back at The Laurels, and apparently she wants rid of him - *for good,*" she added meaningfully.

"I never would have guessed she'd have had it in her," Sally replied, "not in a month of Sundays!"

"Quite," Anne broke in, denying her friend any further comment. "She always seemed such a mouse!"

"I suppose she must have just had enough…who would have thought it…?" she trailed off.

"Apparently they had a hell of a row," the postmistress continued, warming to her subject. "George - that's their neighbour - heard every word."

"Really? How extraordinary!"

"In fact, he said some of the language even made *him*

blush, and he was in the merchant navy for the best part of forty years!"

"Good heavens!" If Sally was expecting any further juicy details, she was about to be disappointed.

"There. Now is there anything else today? Do you need any cheese? We've got some nice tasty cheddar in."

"Er, no thank you dear, I think I'm alright for cheese." The truth was, the last time Sally had purchased cheese in the shop it had proved to be pretty tasteless, not to mention rather past its best. Since then, she'd bought what she needed from the supermarket in town. Not only was it cheaper, but it was also tastier and fresher.

"Have the Hobsons been in yet?"

"Who?"

"I think that's the name - the people who bought Springfield."

"Oh yes, I mean no. At least, *she's* been in. I've not met *him* at all; although I've seen him from a distance - he goes jogging, you know; of all things." She raised her eyebrows.

"Oh. He's a doctor or something, isn't he?"

"Chiropractor or Osteopath I think. I wouldn't know the difference," Anne declared dismissively.

"I believe Chiropractors are mainly concerned with the spine and vertebrae, whilst Osteopaths take a more full body approach to healing. You know - diet, the condition of the blood etc. Of course, they *are* very similar professions, both being holistic healers."

"Of course." Anne was staring blankly at her friend.

"So what's *she* like, then?"

"Oh I don't know, let me think. I didn't really take much notice." She thought for some seconds. "About forty, I should guess – maybe a bit younger. Long fair hair – natural, not out of a bottle, just a hint of grey here and there. Light blue eyes, nice complexion. About five foot six, fairly slim, still attractive. Obviously takes good care of herself and probably a stunner in her time. She talks with traces of a south London accent. That's about it. Oh, and she's got a grown-up daughter from a previous relationship; she's been married for five years. She met him on holiday in Italy with her daughter. He proposed to her six months later at the top of the Eiffel tower. She's got an elderly mother who's in a home, his parents are both dead. She is an only child, he's got a brother who he doesn't communicate with – I don't know why. He works in Torquay, she's a supply teacher but is looking for a permanent position in a local Primary school, and they bought the house down here because they both fancied a move to the country. By all accounts, she wants to have a small herd (or is it flock?) of alpacas, and he's always fancied a life of at least semi self-sufficiency. They're both avid gardeners and share an interest in local history and archaeology. She did tell me, but I can't for the life of me remember his or her daughter's name."

"Never mind, I'm sure it'll come to you." Sally picked up her wicker shopping basket from the counter and hooking it on her forearm headed for the door. Stepping outside, she noticed unhappily that it was raining again. As she struggled to unfold her umbrella, a voice shouted after her.

"Neville! That's the husband's name!"

Smiling inwardly, and firmly clasping the handle of her brolly, she strode briskly homewards beneath its protective blue canopy.

Around the end of the month, on an uncharacteristically cold evening for the time of year, Susie and Dan were cuddled up on the settee watching television. Frank had gone to bed, moaning that there was nothing worth viewing.

"This is nice, just you and me and rubbish on TV." He sat up and drained his wineglass. "Oh dear, looks like I need to get another bottle." He reluctantly stood up and went in search of one. He soon reappeared and replenished their glasses.

"Cheers, happy days."

"Cheers."

Armed with Dutch courage afforded him by the rich burgundy, he began. "I've been thinking…"

"Really, is that a new experience for you?" she giggled.

"No, seriously Susie."

"Go on then, I'm all ears."

"It's just that…well, you spend a lot of time up here and…"

"You're not going to ask me to chuck my job in again, are you? Because we've already been through all that."

"No, I'm not. If you stop interrupting me, then maybe I can tell you what's on my mind."

"Oops, sorry, won't say another word."

"I was wondering if we'd, that is if you'd move in here permanently." There, he'd said it.

"Live together, you mean."

"Yes, why not?" he replied tetchily. Suddenly his good humour was beginning to evaporate.

"Well at least you didn't ask me to marry you," she said quietly.

"What? Oh well, lucky escape then, eh?"

"Dan, don't be so touchy."

"Well I'm sorry, but I don't know how else to react. I thought we were getting on fine together. I thought it was time we, you know, took the next step. Obviously I was wrong."

"Oh don't be like that."

"So how should I be? I mean, are you telling me that this is as far as we go? What is it? Are you afraid of commitment or do you just not want us to become a proper couple?"

"Dan, please, I can't do this right now. And you know I think a lot of you, but I'm not ready for this, you're moving too fast."

"Susie, I love you and I want us to be together properly," he said with a note of exasperation. "And if you feel the same, what's the problem?"

"You *know* the problem! I've been hurt before, I don't want to get into a deep relationship…"

"…because you're frightened of being hurt? I'd never hurt you: and in any case, we've all had relationships go wrong, it's part of life. You've just got to, I don't know, shake yourself down and get on with it. Besides," he continued, a little more subdued, "from the moment I saw you I knew you were the one for me, don't ask me how or why, I just did. And if you wanted me to, I'd marry you tomorrow."

Susie didn't respond; she just sat on the edge of the sofa, hands clutched together, looking at her feet.

"There, now you know how I feel."

"I don't know what to say, only that I can't do what you ask, not yet."

"Not yet. So when might you? Some time never?" He was becoming angry again.

"I don't know."

"You don't know," he echoed softly.

"We can still be friends…" she offered.

"No, I couldn't do that, you mean more to me than that. If you don't want to commit, then I'd sooner not see you at all, it would be too painful."

"Oh, I suppose that's fair enough. I'm sorry, I'd better go."

"I'll drive you back," he answered far too quickly.

"No it's okay, I can walk."

"Not this time of night. Come on, I'll drive you."

"But are you alright to drive?"

"Of course, I've only had a few glasses of wine." With that he stood up with an almost indiscernible wobble, and went into the kitchen to retrieve his car keys.

Frank was already up when Dan, feeling slightly muzzy-headed, appeared in the kitchen the following morning. "Tea's in the pot," he said cheerfully as he busied himself making his first smoke of the day. Dan picked a mug off the draining-board and poured some tea into it, before adding a splash of milk.

"Are you not making one for your girl? Is she having a lie-in?"

"I don't know Frank, she didn't stay last night."

"Oh." He noted the unhappy tone of his son's voice, and could see the melancholy in his face. "You two fallen out?"

"You could put it that way. We've split up, actually."

"Oh dear...oh well," he continued lightly, trying to convey a nonchalance he in no way felt, "I'm sure you'll make up again, we've all had tiffs before."

"It's a bit more than a tiff."

"Ah." Frank was beginning to feel ill at ease; he did not relish playing the role of agony aunt. "Do you want to talk about it?"

"Nope, there's no point really."

"Fair enough," Frank replied with a measure of relief. "But it might help if you did." *Why did I say that?*

Dan slumped onto a chair and gazed mournfully into his brew. "Okay, I asked her to move in. I didn't think it was that big a deal, but apparently it is. She said she's not ready. I got angry, and she left. That's the bare bones of it."

"Ah," Frank uttered again. He lit his cigarette and took a deep drag. A mistake, for the first one of the day inevitably made him cough.

"You ought to pack that in," his son observed.

"Yes, I expect you're right," his father spluttered. He drank some tea to quell the hacking. Once it had stilled he spoke again. "Remember what I told you about her, before you started going out together?"

"What, you mean about her being fragile and damaged?"

"Well I don't think I went *quite* that far."

"No alright."

"You're hurt because you think she doesn't have the same feelings for you as you do for her, right?"

"I suppose."

"Did she say that to your face?"

"No, not in so many words, but…"

"But nothing," he sighed. "You may think I'm a silly old fool, but I've seen you together, and I can tell you that she loves you every bit as much as you do her."

"Well she's got a funny way of showing it."

"She's a woman, boy. Don't ask me to fathom out what goes through their minds, but listen: it'll turn out right, just give her a bit of time."

"She can have plenty of that as far as I'm concerned," came the cross reply. He swilled the rest of his tea, and got to his feet. "I'd better get the yard sorted out if we're bringing the cattle in later."

"Aren't you having any breakfast first?"

"I'm not hungry." He noted the anxious look in his father's face. "Don't worry, I'll rustle you up something before I go."

302

A couple of miles down the road, Susie was pouring her heart out to her mother; something until very recently she would never had envisaged doing. "But mummy he wouldn't let me explain - he just went off on one."

"Oh really Susan," Audrey replied with a forcefulness that shocked her daughter, "what did you expect? You more or less told him that you didn't want to be with him."

"That's not what I meant!"

"Well *I* know that, but does he?"

"That hardly matters now, does it? Now we're finished. And that's probably a good thing, especially with my track record."

"What nonsense! Everybody makes mistakes. Hopefully we learn by them."

"I think perhaps I'm better off on my own," Susie said tearfully.

"You love him though, don't you?"

"Is that enough?"

Audrey thought for a moment. "I think yes, for the most part."

"But what about you and daddy; splitting up after all those years? You must have loved him when you got married, didn't you?"

She considered her response before replying. "Actually, I'm not sure I did."

"Oh." Susie was rather taken aback.

"Don't get me wrong, your father and I certainly shared a mutual attraction back then, and he was, well, different. He was funny and charming - good company. But did I love him? I don't think so, not in the real sense of the word. Then as the years passed, life seemed to sour him. To be honest, whatever he might have said to people about his exciting job

303

in the city, I honestly think he was bored and frustrated; he expected to get much further up the ladder before he was put out to grass."

Her daughter was regarding her quizzically.

"He didn't take early retirement you see, he was made redundant."

"But he should have said!"

"Oh no, he couldn't have done that. Not after telling all and sundry how indispensable he was to the company."

"Poor daddy."

"Yes, in a way I sort of agree with you; although he did rather dig his own grave."

"I hope he's not too miserable…"

"I don't think he's miserable now he's back on his own patch. In fact, I believe he's been offered some part-time consultancy work. Anyway, that's by the by: we were talking about you. You need to talk to Dan - properly."

"What's the point?" she asked despondently. "We'd only start arguing again. I think we both need a bit of a breather, give us time to think."

"From what you've told me, it's *you* who needs to think things through."

"Alright, you're right! I'm the one with the problem!"

"I didn't mean that at all, as well you know; and there's no need to raise your voice. I've had quite enough of that from your father over the years."

"I'm sorry mummy. Oh why did he have to ask me to move in with him? Things were great between us until then."

"Susie, darling, sometimes in life you just have to grasp the nettle. I know you've been badly hurt before, and so does he. Nobody can guarantee that if you both commit yourselves to each other that life will be plain sailing for evermore. But if you don't trust your feelings, then you'll end up a bitter and twisted old spinster. You can't go through life worrying what might be around the next corner."

Susie sighed heavily.

"I can't do what he wants, not just yet. I just can't. He'd be better off with somebody else, somebody without all my emotional baggage."

"But he doesn't want anybody else, does he? He wants you."

"Then I'm sorry." She dabbed at her eyes with a tissue, and glanced at her watch. "Thanks for listening, mummy, but I've got to go now – I promised Pete I'd open up."

Standing on the front doorstep, Audrey watched her daughter disappear around the bend in the driveway. When she heard the gate gently latch, she went into the kitchen and made herself another cup of coffee. What could she do to help her daughter other than offer her advice? By nature, she was not one to interfere. She could have a quiet word with Frank, or she could hope that Dan and Susie would find their own way to resolve their differences. Maybe that would be her best option. In her limited experience, sticking one's nose into other people's business, even if one of those people happened to be one's own daughter, rarely resulted in a satisfactory outcome.

CHAPTER TWENTY-ONE

The cows stood in a neat line in the open yard, their shaggy heads thrust through the steel feed barriers, tucking into the sweet silage. Behind them, their calves charged gleefully around the bedded area, making most of the space vacated by their mothers. Amidst their swirling bodies, Dan forked fresh golden straw around. Normally, the spectacle of the young animals frolicking about in this way would lift his heart, but today he was under a dark cloud. Even the unseasonal sunlight warming the cows' black backs failed to lighten his mood.

"I'll go on up in the Land Rover!" Dan jumped; huddled under his dark shroud of gloom he'd failed to notice his father approaching.

"Alright!" he shouted back, "I'll come up on the tractor when I've finished here! Be about ten minutes!"

Frank acknowledged this by giving the thumbs up. He turned away and left his son to it. As the old Land Rover rattled up the stony track, trailing its customary plume of acrid smoke, he started to worry again. It had been nearly two weeks since his boy had split with his girlfriend, and there had been no contact of any sort between them. During all that time Dan had been wandering about in a blue funk with a face like a wet weekend. He told himself that his son was old enough and ugly enough to sort his own love life out, but he didn't seem to be managing very well. He was clearly miserable without Susie, but seemed at the same time to be determined not to make the first move at any sort of reconciliation.

The pair of them need their bloody heads banging together, he thought angrily as he slid back the blurred side window and flicked his cigarette butt out. Perhaps he should have a word with Audrey, see if she had any bright ideas. But deep down inside him he realized that interfering would achieve nothing. He'd just have to hope that the two of them came to their senses, and soon. Or at least, if they really were finished, that Dan would be able to move on and find somebody more suitable to share his life with.

Of course, what really worried Frank, worried him sick in fact, was the possibility that Dan may decide to move on to pastures new and leave him on his own – that didn't bear thinking about, so he hastily dismissed the frightening thought from his mind.

He soon pulled up alongside a massive overgrown hedge, cut the engine and clambered out. This was going to be some job, he thought as he walked the length of it, observing the tangle of large blackthorn trees, their twisted branches and limbs entwined around each other, their thick top-heavy ivy-choked crowns stooping downwards, almost touching the ground in some places. Corkscrewing their way skyward through this unruly tangle were massive tall briars, their thorny stems almost as thick as a man's wrist. To add to the chaos, the remains of an ancient metal fence ran through the middle, whose broken and bent rails lay either half buried in the bank, to protrude here and there at crooked angles, or had become embedded in the trunks and boles of the growing trees.

Frank ambled back to the Land Rover and lifted the chainsaws from the back. It was certainly an unseasonably beautiful day he mused as he unscrewed the fuel cap from one and reached over for the can of two-stroke mixture. Having topped up the fuel and chain oil in both machines, he adjusted the chain tensions and ran a file across them both, ensuring a good cutting edge. He leaned on the bonnet and popped the lid off his tobacco tin. As he pulled appreciatively on his cigarette, he surveyed the scene around him. The sky was a cloudless expanse of blue, and there wasn't a breath of wind. Despite a hard frost blanketing the countryside that morning, there remained only faint traces of it in the lee of the dense tousled hedge shaded from the sun. He felt its benign warmth on his back, and ripped off his tatty jumper to get the full benefit. Most of the leaves had fallen, but there still remained a few, crinkled and dried and very dead that clung determinedly onto the ends of gaunt bare branches. As he watched, some of these reluctantly gave up the struggle and fluttered sadly toward the ground where they came to rest, unmoving and disconsolate.

The sound of the approaching tractor broke the peace. Dan jumped out of the cab, slamming the door noisily behind him.

"Looks a bit of a challenge," he commented, casting his eyes over the neglected wild growth. "When was the last time someone gave this any attention?"

"Christ knows; twenty years ago at least, I should think - maybe more. It's just one of those jobs that, well, that me and dad never got around to."

"Ah; so what's the plan of attack?"

"Here, catch." Frank lobbed him a pair of gloves. "Grab a saw and fight your way inside."

Dan looked dubiously at the seemingly impenetrable

growth of wicked thorn and briar. "If you cut 'em off on the bank, we can pull 'em out and I'll take out anything we can use for firewood. What's left can be dragged into a line and when it's dry, heaped up with the loader and burned."

"Right. So it's one of those nose down tail up jobs then, is it?"

"That's it - oh, and watch you don't catch the fence, there's bits and pieces of it buried and grown in all over the place."

"Great, it just gets better."

"I'm just saying be careful; that's all. That's a nearly new chain on that saw and I don't want to have to fork out for another one just yet."

Without replying, Dan dropped the visor on his safety helmet, clamped the defenders onto his ears, and gave the cord start a vigorous tug. The chainsaw immediately barked into life, shattering the peace and spewing out milky blue exhaust fumes. By lunch-time the two of them had made a good start on the hedge, and by the end of the day they were both tired and aching. Frank shut off his saw and settled it gratefully on the grass. He yanked off his helmet and lobbed it into the back of the Land Rover.

"That's a better noise," he declared, as, hands on hips he swayed from side to side to ease his stiffening back. Wisps of steam snaked from his sweaty forehead and rose into the increasingly cold winter air. He then retrieved his jacket from the seat of the Land Rover and rummaged around in a pocket for his tobacco tin. "I didn't think we'd do so much today." Leaning on the bonnet, he carefully rolled a cigarette.

"Dan?"

His son was approaching, with two saws in one hand and a can of fuel and one of oil in the other.

"What?"

"I said I'm pleased with how far we've got with the hedge from hell today."

"Oh, right." He dumped his burden in the butt and bent to unzip his safety leggings.

"I think we deserve a pint or two, don't you?"

"Oh, I don't really fancy going out. You go if you like, I just want to get in and have a bath; then I'll get the supper on the go."

"Okay, if that's what you want; but you can't hide forever."

"I'm not hiding; I just don't want to go to the pub, alright?"

"Okay, okay, whatever you say. I'll go on my own: it makes no difference to me."

They drove back to the yard in uneasy silence. The all-encompassing depressing darkness of another cold night falling around them did nothing to brighten the mood.

"Do you want a hand to feed up?"

"No, you're alright, I can manage."

"I *know* you can manage boy…oh never mind." Frank reined in his sudden feeling of irritation. "I'll erm, I'll just have a quick shower, then the bathroom's all yours."

It was with some relief that he found himself an hour or so later in the cosy atmosphere of the public bar of The Golden Fleece. Frank was also thankful that the place, for now at least, was quiet. The only other occupant of the bar was Bill – and his dog of course.

"Evening Bill, how goes it?"

"I'm fine Frank, and yourself?"

"Yeah, good thanks."

"Haven't seen Dan for a while."

"No, well we've been quite busy; he's fine though."

"That's good."

Frank felt no compunction to elaborate, turning instead to address Pete. "Well, here we are then; another Christmas almost upon us. And not one," he added quietly, "that I'm particularly looking forward to."

Pete smiled. "No change there then Frank."

"You know what I mean: Susie and my boy."

"I know what you mean. But there's nothing we can do mate; they'll have to deal with it between themselves."

"So is she…? Does she *want* to get back with him?"

"Christ knows. If you were to ask her, she'd tell you it was all over. But I'm not so sure that's what she wants, she's so bloody miserable. I tell you, a face like that could turn my beer."

"Dan's exactly the same. Moping about, not talking - he's starting to do my head in. Christ man, there must be some way of getting them to see each other, if only to bang their heads together."

"I doubt that would help: Susie's a stubborn one when she wants to be."

Frank gloomily lit up. "I thought of having a word with Audrey," he said nonchalantly.

"The Merry Divorcée? I'm not sure about that."

"No, nor am I, not sure at all."

A short silence followed.

"There is something might be worth a try."

"Oh yeah, and what's that?"

"Well there's a darts match tomorrow night - away at The Swan. If you tell him we're a player short, I'm sure he'll step into the breach."

"He might," Frank conceded, "but how does that help?"

He slid his empty glass across the bar. The landlord picked it up and held it at an angle under the Guinness tap. Black velvety liquid poured thickly down its inside, settling at the bottom. As the level rose, the dark porter swirled and broiled beneath a steadily rising creamy head of froth.

"If you make sure he doesn't get here 'til half eight, I'll be gone with the team by then. Susie's manning the bar tomorrow; the place should be pretty quiet and with any luck the two of them will talk to each other." Pete placed the replenished pint on the bar.

"And she'll tell him how sorry you are, but that he's no longer needed."

"Exactamundo."

"I suppose there's a chance it'll work."

"Do you have any other bright suggestions?"

"No, I don't."

"Well we'd better give it a try then, hadn't we? Before the two of *them* drive the two of *us* completely round the bend."

Frank smiled laconically and raised his drink to his lips. "Cheers. Here's to it."

He returned home, suitably refreshed, about an hour later to be greeted by the comforting sounds and smells of sausages sizzling in a frying-pan on the range. His son was poking them around disinterestedly.

"It'll be few minutes yet, the spuds aren't quite done."

"Fine. Have you got a drink?"

Dan waved a half empty can of lager at him, before turning his attention back to his cooking.

"Quiet down there tonight," Frank commented. "Bill was the only customer in the whole place."

"Oh."

"No one else at all. Pete was behind the bar, before you ask."

"I wasn't going to."

"He erm, he wondered if you would help him out actually," he continued cautiously.

"Me? Why, what does he want?"

"He's a player down for the darts match tomorrow. He thought you might be able to make up numbers. It's only at The Swan," he added, as if this would make any difference.

"Oh I don't know, I'm not sure I can be bothered…"

"Go on, it'll do you good to get out - and I'm sure Pete'll appreciate you helping out," Frank replied, playing on Dan's good nature.

"What time?"

"Half eight."

"That sounds a bit late for a darts match."

"Well that's what the man told me."

"Go on then, tell him I'll be there."

"Good. I'll give him a bell now, while you're mashing the spuds."

The only person in the pub when Dan appeared the following evening was Susie. She stood behind the bar, drying glasses. "Oh hello," she greeted him coyly, "pint of lager?"

"Erm, well I just came to make up the numbers for the darts actually. Where is everybody? Am I early or something?" he asked.

"No, no." She was beginning to feel embarrassed. "Pete said to thank you for coming, but he's got a full team - and they've gone. He would have phoned you, but guessed you'd be on your way already."

"Oh well, never mind," he replied disconcertedly. The atmosphere suddenly seemed very thick.

"So…would you like a pint?"

"I don't really think…"

"On the house?"

"Well alright then, thanks."

"Do you want to sit by the fire? I'll bring it over."

"Oh right, okay." Now you could cut the atmosphere with a knife. Dan tried to act nonchalantly, casually slipping off his jacket and hanging it on the back of the door. He turned and watched the girl carefully pouring his drink. He took a deep breath. "I don't suppose…"

"Sorry?"

"I don't suppose you'd like to join me, would you? I mean, just for a quick drink."

She surveyed the deserted bar. "Yes alright," she smiled. "We don't seem to be that busy at the moment."

A minute or two later, Susie brought their drinks over and sat down on the other side of the table to him, next to the crackling fire. "So, how have you been keeping?" she asked politely.

"Oh fine, thanks…"

"And Frank?" she broke in, before he could continue.

"He's fine too. Look, I'm sorry that I went off on one, I really am, but I don't want us to…"

"No, *I'm* sorry, I know what I said was hurtful."

"It's okay," he chirped with false bonhomie. "It was my fault. I shouldn't have overreacted like that. I understand if you don't want us to well, you know…" he trailed off.

"No Dan, it was me that was in the wrong; I realise that now." Before he had time to respond to this unexpected revelation, the door shimmied in and Bill's Jack Russell trotted into the bar, his master hard on his heels. The dog tripped across the faded carpet, leapt onto his customary position on the wooden settle, and sat there wagging his tail, surveying the scene with pointed self-assurance. Susie stood up and made her way back behind the bar. "Pint of the usual, is it Bill?"

"Yes please. I think I might have a bite to eat as well: you doing food?"

"Of course, the Special tonight is chilli con carne, prepared by my own fair hand."

"That sounds nice, is it good and hot?"

"Yep, but I can always make it spicier if you want."

"Oh no, no, I'm sure it'll be fine; don't want to blow my socks off." The thought of Bill's unwashed socks parting from his unwashed feet turned Dan's stomach.

"Does it come with rice?"

"If you want - or chips."

"Can't have a little of both I suppose, can I?"

"For you Bill...anything." Susie smiled sweetly at him, gave him his beer and disappeared into the kitchen. Bill took a sip, then came over and sat beside his dog.

"Evening Dan."

"Bill."

"Haven't seen you about for a bit, are you two back together then?"

"No," Dan answered quickly, "not really."

"Oh." A long silence followed, during which Bill appeared to be collecting his thoughts. "You know," he finally continued, "I've never really understood women."

"Really?" Dan rejoined, feigning surprise.

"Yes, they're different from us; they think differently, don't they? You're much better off with one of these." He stroked his dog affectionately as the animal looked lovingly into his eyes. Dan hastily drained his pint.

"Are you going to have another?" Bill nodded at his empty glass.

"Erm, well I was thinking of getting off, actually…anyway, there's no one behind the bar at the moment." As if by command, the landlady popped her head around the door leading from the kitchen. "You boys alright for drinks?" she asked. "Susie's just doing your chips, Bill."

"Thank you," he replied. "Can you replenish this one's glass?"

"Of course."

Margaret had barely refilled Dan's pint when the door burst open and in rolled John Chester with one of his cronies. "Good evening everybody!" he boomed, unwinding a long woollen scarf from around his neck and draping it haphazardly on a coat hook. "Blimey, it's quiet in here tonight!"

"There's a darts match - away at The Swan," Margaret informed him.

"Oh. I see Dan's here though. How's farming Dan? All muck and magic still, is it?"

"Er, yeah, something like that."

"What can I get you, John?"

"What do you think Charles? Director's do you?"

His companion smiled meekly. "That'll be fine, John."

"Lovely. Two pints please Margaret – then we'll have to shoot, the memsahib's cooking supper and I'm under strict orders not to be later than nine: only got a pass out because Charlie's staying for a couple of days." He chuckled at his own pathetic joke.

"You'd better get your skates on in that case, it's nearly a quarter to now."

Concerned that the man would try and drag him into an unwanted and one-sided conversation, Dan turned to address Bill.

"So how's the summer been for you? Busy?"

316

"Yeah, not too bad. I've had a few commissions for garden tables and the like - in fact I made up a couple for Pete, with benches as well."

"Oh, good."

"Things'll quieten down now though. Actually, I quite like the winter, even when it's freezing cold in the caravan: people don't hassle me you see – I don't like being hassled."

"Well no mate, you don't need that sort of stress."

"No I don't. There's too much of it nowadays in my opinion; and it doesn't do anybody any good all this rushing about."

"I'm sure you're right."

"I mean, you don't achieve anything by tearing around like a blue-arsed fly, do you? People should chill out more."

Before Bill could expound further on this, Susie appeared at the table carrying in one hand a plate groaning under the weight of a tumbling heap of white rice alongside a huge dollop of steaming chilli, whilst in the other clutching a plastic basket piled high with golden chips.

"There you are Bill, put yourself outside of that."

"Thank you."

"Right," Dan interjected, "I'll leave you to your food then. Nice chatting to you Bill."

Susie retrieved her abandoned wine and spoke quietly in his ear. "Come into the lounge, we can talk in there if you want." Meekly he followed her from the bar.

"Oh what it is to be young and in love!" John's booming voice rolled after them. "Come on then, Charles, the smell of that food's got me feeling hungry." He swilled the rest of his pint down his fat gullet with ease. His companion struggled to swallow the remainder of his drink, eventually admitting defeat and leaving the last third of it on the bar as his friend slipped out into the night without bothering to wait for him.

Once again, Susie and Dan were by themselves.

"So, where were we?"

"Where *are* we might be more appropriate," Dan replied.

"Yes, I suppose that's right."

"Look, if you don't want to discuss this now, we can always…"

"No, it's okay. We won't be interrupted, Margaret's manning the bar now."

"Right."

"I've had some time to think now and…and I don't want to lose you."

He sighed heavily. "But what does that mean?" He drained his glass.

"Let me get you a refill."

"Susie, just tell me…"

But she was already up and on her way to the bar with their empty glasses. When she'd returned with the drinks, she sat down opposite him, taking his hands in hers. She squeezed his fingers and looked him straight in the eye. "It means, stoopid, that I want us to be together."

He gazed at her blankly.

"I want us to be an item, I want to be with you: that is, if you still want to be with me."

"Are you sure?" he asked softly. "You see, I've been thinking as well, especially about what you said about coming on too strong…"

"Dan, listen, I've had time to think, okay? Now do you want us to go on seeing each other or not? It's a simple enough question, isn't it?"

"Yes of course I do!" he blurted out. "You know I do!" His

eyes were beginning to fill up. She leaned across the table and kissed him lightly on the lips, her large hooped earrings rocking slightly as she bent forward and twinkling as they caught the light. She then gently released her grip on his hands and sat down.

"I meant what I said about not giving up working here though," she asserted. "For now, anyway…"

"Of course, that's fine." They sat in companionable silence for a little while.

"Do you still want me to move in with you?"

"Well, yes. But only if you really want to…only if you think it'd make you happy."

"Hmm, that's a difficult one."

His heart missed a beat. "What do you mean, difficult?" he asked, suddenly panicked.

"Well, would I rather listen to Pete snoring through the wall, or your father?"

"Oh yes, very good." The relief in his voice was tenable.

"Anyway," he added, "Frank's two walls away."

"Oh, then I suppose that decides it for me - your place it is."

319

CHAPTER TWENTY-TWO

Despite James' conviction that at long last his true worth as a journalist was going to be recognized and his hitherto hidden talent would lead to a prestigious career working in Fleet Street, since he'd had that unnerving meeting with Frank back in the summer his fortunes were once again plummeting. He had written a few articles which had been published in some of the more respected periodicals of the day, but unfortunately for him they'd not received the acclaim he thought they'd rightly deserved, and any opportunities for him to work as a freelance dwindled to nothing. Without the stimulus this extra work provided he found himself slipping back into his old ways, and by the end of autumn his drinking was seriously interfering with his work as he slid ever deeper into the black hole of self-pity he'd dug for himself. It seemed he'd had his fifteen minutes of fame.

"So what's going to hit the headlines this week, old boy? War declared in the Balkans? Hitler alive and well and living in luxury on the Costa del Sol? Or, I know, let me guess. Supermarket plan for village ousted? No? Rural bus services to be cut? That's always a good one. Ah, what about this? Mayor in twinning visit success with somewhere we've never heard of."

~~Frank~~ James glowered at Arnie. "You can be a real pain sometimes: you know that?"

320

"Absolutely, old thing, but at least I'm not a stupid prick like you."

"What?"

"You heard."

"Oh I heard alright, I'm just not sure you said it. Christ, I thought you were my friend."

"Quite, and friends tell it like it is."

James said nothing in reply, but merely knocked back his drink and rapped the empty glass on the bar.

"Refill, is it?"

"Yes please John, and make it a large one this time."

"It was a large one last time."

"Oh," James grinned stupidly. "Are you going to have another, Arnie?"

"No, I'd best get going."

"Go on, have another drink with a stupid prick!"

"James, I…go on then, a quick one."

"Another large one if you please, John."

Arnie picked up the Scotch. "Thanks old boy, cheers."

"Cheers me dears!" James chinked his glass so brutally against his colleague's, that it was a miracle neither of them shattered. "So, why am I such a prick, then? Eh, old fruit?"

"Look, now's probably not the time, I didn't mean…Oh hell. I did *try* and warn you, didn't I? About the booze I mean? It's a slippery slope old chap."

"You're right old friend, you're right! In fact," James slurred, putting his arm around Arnold's shoulder, "you're always right. Mr. bleeding Perfect, that's what you are!"

Arnold, sensing there might be trouble ahead, hastily emptied his glass. "Well thanks for the drink, but I really must be on my way. Can I put one in for you?"

"That's uncommonly civil of you old bean," James

replied, his tone full of bitter mockery. "Thank you very much - it's a real privilege to have had your company."

"Yes, well, I'll be off then. Er, John? Would you mind?" Leaving the exact amount for the drink, he quickly stuffed the remaining loose change in his trouser pocket and slipped off the bar stool.

"Toodle-oo, Arnie. Be sure to give my regards to your wife, and all the other members of your happy little family!"

Arnie raised his arm to acknowledge this dubious farewell gesture without turning his head, and made his way swiftly out into the street.

Prick, if anyone's a prick around here it's you, Arnold bloody perfect Murray, James reflected scornfully, before turning his attention to the important business of tackling his freshly poured glass of whisky.

When he arrived at work the following morning, unshaven, the sour smell of spirit still lingering on his stale breath and a quarter of an hour late, he found a memo on his desk from his editor. Brief and succinct, it merely said *See me as soon as you get in.* He looked around the newsroom.

"Anybody know anything about this?"

Some of the members of staff failed to meet his gaze and carried on with their work as if they'd not heard him, others shrugged their shoulders noncommittally.

"Great, that's all I need," he muttered under his breath as he pulled a grubby comb from his pocket and ran it quickly through his greasy hair. He buttoned up his jacket and strode purposefully from the room, trying to ignore the nagging thumping behind his temples that his earlier intake of paracetamol had spectacularly failed to dispel.

"The thing is," his editor explained a few minutes later, "there are going to be some changes to the paper. Circulation's been steadily dropping for the last, well, few years probably and unless some remedial action is taken soon, we'll be in real trouble."

"Does that mean redundancies? I suppose," James continued before any reply could be forthcoming, "we could do without some of the girls in the office, and our young trainee's only been with us a short while, I'm sure I could cover his work."

"The first thing that's going to happen," Robert resumed, as if he hadn't heard a word his chief reporter said, "is we're going to merge with the Kingsbridge Times."

James' jaw dropped. "Merge?" he bleated, his hangover suddenly forgotten. "But that's a bit drastic, isn't it?"

"I'm afraid it is, but needs must and all that: and yes, there *will* be redundancies."

"Oh, so do you want me to break the news to young Nick and the others?"

"Er, no, that won't be necessary."

"Right." James was feeling increasingly uncomfortable. His palms were sweaty and his head had started banging again. "So, do you know who's getting the boot?"

"I'm sorry James, but…"

James suddenly felt sick to his stomach.

"Oh no, don't say it! But I've been with this paper for years! And I'm chief reporter!"

"Look, I really am sorry, believe me. But the decision's been made. I'm afraid we've all had to make compromises."

"Oh, is that right! So what compromises have you made then, Mr. Stanton? Tell me."

The other man sighed. "The editor at the Times has decided to retire actually…"

"Oh, I see, so you're sitting pretty then, you'll still be in charge."

"Yes, but I'll have a lot more work for no more money, if that's any comfort."

"Well no actually, it isn't. It's no bloody comfort at all! What am I supposed to do now? I'm finished."

"You'll receive a generous amount in severance pay - that should tide you over until you can find another suitable position."

"Another suitable position? Fat chance at my age."

"Well maybe you could get some freelance work or something."

"Oh come on, we both know that's not going to happen. Why me anyway? Young Nick's only been here for a few months; why don't you give him the heave-ho? He's young enough to start somewhere else."

"It would appear that young blood is favourably looked upon, and…"

"Young blood? Don't all my years of experience count for anything?"

Robert looked at his chief reporter, taking in his dishevelled appearance. Christ, the man looked more like Columbo, but at least the fictional detective didn't ooze the sour smell of stale alcohol from every pore. "I've got to say I've been most impressed with Nick's work since he joined us. Not only is he diligent and punctual, he has shown excellent communication skills and his journalistic abilities seem to come naturally. I think he's got a great future ahead of him."

"A new broom always sweeps clean," James commented bitterly.

"Maybe, although I'm positive there's more to the young fellow than that."

"So that's it then."

"I'm afraid so. You know, it pains me to say this James, and I do so only in the hope that it may help you in the future; but you have rather let yourself down in the last few months. After that excellent piece you wrote that went national, I expected better and brighter things of you. What went wrong, do you think?"

"What went wrong? I don't know, I just sort of….ran out of steam."

But they both knew the real cause, and that of course was the man's fondness for a drink. When his successful article had failed to be followed up by another of comparable quality, he had, as usual sought solace in the bottle, and again, as usual, that led to more mediocre journalism and heavier drinking. Now, with the loss of his job, he had reached his nadir.

"I think we both know the real reason for that, don't we?" Robert asked. James made no comment. "Okay then, I'll have to formally give you a month's notice. We'll take it from the end of the week, shall we?"

"Fine, whatever you say."

"And like I said, there'll be severance pay on top."

"Right." James couldn't be bothered to ask how much that might add up to, although one thing was for sure: it wouldn't keep him in beer for that long. An urgent and overwhelming fearful feeling of claustrophobia engulfed him. He had to get out of this place, and although it was barely nine-thirty in the morning, he was desperate for a drink.

"Are you alright? You look a bit peaky. Look, take the day off, there's nothing much happening. I tell you what, as it's Thursday take the rest of the week off; it might give you a chance to see what's out there, eh?"

"Yeah, thanks. I'll do that."

"And once again, I'm sorry to be the bearer of such bad news."

Heaving a sigh of relief to find himself outside in the fresh air, James pulled the door shut behind him and turned the grimy collar of his coat up against the rain. Water gurgled noisily as it tumbled down the cast iron downpipe beside him to course along a drain under the pavement before being disgorged to join an effusive bubbling stream that raced away along the gutter beside the kerb. After a few metres, this rushing flood plunged suicidally between the bars of a large metal grid, cascading into dark and cavernous storm drains beneath. Spray fanned across the road from the tyres of passing cars as they sped past, their dark windows streaked with rain, while fat, heavy raindrops pummelled the shiny surfaces of umbrellas under whose flimsy protection wet and miserable pedestrians scuttled by on the puddle-strewn asphalt.

What to do now? James decided to go home and get some sleep. His head was pounding worse than ever; he'd feel better after a bit of a lie-down. He'd stop at the off-licence on the way, get a bottle of vodka or something - just to help him relax, that's all. Then later on he'd be in a fit state to consider his options.

At three o'clock that afternoon, he woke up: four hours after he'd dropped off to sleep. His headache had gone, or at least had been anaesthetized by alcohol, for although he'd thought to have just a couple of drinks to send him off, the litre bottle of vodka now stood on his bedside table only a little more than half full. He lay there for a minute or two, gathering his thoughts. Then the horrifying reality of the morning's events hit him. He groaned. There must be some way ahead. He wondered if he could attempt to track Dan down. He was sure he'd be able to wheedle some money out of him. But no, he daren't try it, for although Frank's threat to destroy his career was obviously now irrelevant, his promise to come and find him and deal with him was still very much alive. James' cowardly side of his nature far outweighed his greedy side: he'd have to think of something else. He glanced at the clock; another couple of hours and Arnie'd be in the bar. Perhaps the man could give him a few pointers. He had to admit to himself that this plan offered little chance of success, but Arnie did have contacts and in any case he had to start somewhere.

Just before five, having showered, shaved and changed (and having knocked back a couple more large vodkas) James left his dingy depressing flat and headed out to find his colleague. Unfortunately for him, Arnold knew of no vacancies that might be suitable, nor could he suggest any publication that might be approached with freelance work.

"I'm sorry old chap, I really am. But everybody's in the same boat these days it seems. Anyway, if I *do* hear of anything I'll let you know at once."

So finding himself left to his own devices, he spent the rest of the long evening drowning his sorrows, and on returning to his flat the wrong side of midnight, downed the rest of the vodka straight out of the bottle before passing out.

CHAPTER TWENTY-THREE

"Well I'll be…"

Anne let the half-eaten piece of toast fall from her hand and thrust the paper under her husband's nose, jabbing with a buttery finger at the small column in the margin. "Look, read that."

With a sigh, Gerald painstakingly folded his own paper and placed it neatly on the table. He peered at the text.

JOURNALIST FOUND LIFELESS

The body of James Ward, a reporter working for this paper, was discovered on Sunday morning on the bedroom floor of his flat by police who broke in, having been alerted by a friend said to be concerned for his welfare. It is believed that James passed away in his sleep sometime during Thursday night and police are not treating the incident as suspicious. See Editorial, page 6.

He regarded her over the top of his glasses.

"Well go on then, find the Editorial!" she urged impatiently.

Gerald trawled through the pages until he found what he was looking for; he carried on reading out loud:

> *"It is, of course, always a terrible tragedy when someone close dies unexpectedly. All of us here at the South Hams Advertiser were therefore deeply saddened and shocked to learn of the passing of our associate, James Ward. James had been with the paper for many years and had only recently been promoted to chief reporter. He was a valued member of the team and will be deeply missed by his colleagues. All of us here send our sincere condolences and commiserations to his loved ones and wish them to know our thoughts are with them at this sad and difficult time.*

Not much of an epitaph, is it?" Gerald muttered. "It can't have taken any thought at all to write that blurb."

"Well, it's not surprising I suppose," Anne replied. "He did turn out to be rather obnoxious, didn't he? Underneath that charming exterior, that is."

"I think it was only you that found him charming my dear and…"

"Alright, alright, there's no need to drag all that up again."

"No, and better not speak ill of the dead, eh?"

"Quite. I wonder how it happened. Do you think he had a heart attack? Or perhaps he suffered a massive stroke; maybe he choked on his own vomit. He was a bit of a drinker, wasn't he?"

"For God's sake Anne, I'm trying to eat my breakfast! Anyway, does it really matter? The poor bloke's gone and that's the end of it."

"Yes, you're right: there's no point in speculating." In spite of this remark, her mind was whirring. "Perhaps he was onto something big, and he was got at!" she enthused, unable to quell her lively and vivid imagination.

Gerald groaned. At that moment the doorbell rang loudly

and petulantly. "I'll go," he said, "I don't seem to be hungry anymore."

Of all their regular customers, perhaps the one he least wished to see at that moment was Frank; but it was he nevertheless who was waiting behind the cluttered shop counter. "Morning Gerald, must be almost time you strung those chic Christmas decorations up again, isn't it?" He smiled wickedly.

"Er, yes, it will be soon I guess," he replied distractedly, the jibe flying right over his head.

"I'll just have my usual two ounces of baccy please - oh and better have some papers as well; a couple of packets of green ones if I may."

He noticed several copies of The South Hams Advertiser in the display. "You don't usually have this one on the shelves."

"No, they're free this week, some sort of promotional offer."

"Anything exciting in it?"

"I don't know, probably the usual stuff," Gerald answered awkwardly.

"Oh well, I'll take one anyway if they're giving them away. I can always use it to light the fire."

Gerald smiled weakly. "Right, that's six pounds sixteen altogether then please." He took the ten-pound note offered and gave Frank his change.

"Lovely, see you then Gerald." Frank turned on his heel and strode out of the shop.

Anne came through the door. "Didn't you tell him?" she hissed, noticing with disgust that her latest customer had left a trail of boot prints across the floor bearing the unmistakable hue and distinct aroma of cow dung.

"I didn't have a chance!" he protested. "Anyway, he bought the paper so he'll soon find out, won't he?"

"Oh yes, brilliant!"

"What?"

"Ye Gods Gerald, you make me wonder sometimes, you really do!"

By lunch-time that same day, everybody in the village had heard or read the news. Not many of them were overly saddened of course. Dan, however, felt a degree of sympathy for his uncle.

"I should like to go to the funeral," he announced as he speared another carrot.

Frank eyed him critically.

"What?"

"Nothing: if you feel you ought to go, then you'd best go."

"Yeah, well he *was* my uncle, after all. Do you want to come with me?"

"Look boy," Frank replied irritably, "if you want to go, that's fine; but don't ask me to go along with you."

"Okay, okay, no worries."

"I'll go with you," Susie cut in quickly.

"You don't have to, I don't mind going on my own." Dan shot a meaningful glance at his father.

"No, I want to."

"Good. Thanks. I'll phone the paper after lunch, find out what the arrangements are."

Frank had nearly finished his coffee when Dan came back into the kitchen. "That was all rather sad."

"What was?"

"Well, I phoned the paper, and then I spoke to the undertakers. They want the cremation to take place next

Thursday, but they want me to put together the service. I'm the only family he had, apparently. To be honest, I don't know what to do. How could I? I didn't know him." He sounded exasperated.

"So was there a will, or anything that James said that might help you? You know the sort of thing, favourite songs, stuff like that."

"Not as far as I know. One of his work colleagues told them that in no way would he have wanted a church service, that's all."

"Well why don't you phone the paper back, and speak to the guy? Better still, go down there yourself and talk to everybody who knew him. And while you're in Dartmouth, go to the printers and get some orders of service knocked up."

"But what if nobody has any suggestions? What do I put in it?"

"Surely somebody where he worked will have some idea: I mean the man was there for years."

"I suppose," Dan replied, not sounding the slightest bit convinced. "And who's going to conduct the funeral?"

"Someone at the crematorium, I suppose." Frank answered disinterestedly.

"I don't know if he'd want a priest to do it."

"He's hardly in a fit condition to object, is he?" Frank muttered under his breath.

"Frank, honestly!" Susie interjected.

"Well, I can't see what else you can do," Frank retorted grumpily. *Nor why you'd want to bother.*

"No," his son answered gloomily, "nor can I."

As it turned out, Dan managed to get some idea of his uncle's preferences by talking to his colleagues. He laid out an order of service which included a Cat Steven's song as well as one by James Taylor. Arnold Murray very decently said he'd deliver a short eulogy. Arnold also suggested providing refreshments afterwards at one of James' regular watering-holes, which suited Dan.

On the day of the funeral, there were barely a dozen people present. The whole ceremony had a feeling of being rushed: a couple of the funeral directors stood at the back of the small chapel, occasionally glancing at their watches and exchanging anxious looks. After the brief service, the gathering in the pub was equally lacklustre. Members of staff at the paper huddled together in one group, whilst the others who consisted solely, as far as Dan could make out, of James' drinking buddies, stuck resolutely together in another. They seemed doggedly reluctant to even converse with each other, let alone anyone else present. Dan very soon made his excuses, and with Susie on his arm, gratefully headed home.

"Not much of a turnout," he muttered darkly as the car climbed the long hill out of the town.

"No, still Arnold seemed very nice, didn't he? And he gave a good eulogy."

"Yeah, I suppose. I still think Frank should have come, though."

"Mmm."

"What does that mean?"

She sighed. "It means I'm not sure I agree with you. The only connection he's got is through your mum - and she disowned her brother remember."

"Yes, and I get the feeling he knows why that happened."

"Oh Dan, does it really matter? Look, they're both gone now, don't you think it's time to move on?"

"Water under the bridge and all that, eh?"

"If you like: anyway what good would it do to trawl it all up again?"

He considered this for a moment or two. "I guess you're right - as usual." He smiled across at her. "I was just curious. But I'll let it go; we should be concentrating on the future after all, shouldn't we? Not the past."

"Absolutely." Susie leaned over and kissed him, leaving a cherry red smudge of lipstick on his freshly shaved cheek.

James had, of course, died intestate and so after some time Dan became sole beneficiary of his estate, since he was his only living relative. This matter was finally resolved barely three weeks before Christmas. His legacy from his uncle was however paltry. Apart from several dog-eared books, his inheritance included a pile of scratched and warped vinyl records, a few hundred pounds in the bank, and the contents of the man's flat: that is, stained and battered furniture fit only for the local council tip, a mish-mash of domestic porcelain and cutlery surely destined for the same end, and an ancient television and music centre that nobody could possibly have been interested in, however desperate.

"Not much to show for a man's life," Dan observed laconically.

Susie looked around the squalid kitchen. "No, it certainly isn't. It's beyond me how anyone can live like this."

"I guess that's what happens when you piss all your money up against the wall."

"I suppose - still sad though, isn't it?"

"Very. Come on, let's get out of here. I'll get the place tidied out after Christmas. The money in my uncle's account will just about cover the cost of redecorating as well as another month's rental while we do it."

"We?"

"Well, me then."

"Don't be silly, I was only kidding; of course I'll help you with it." They gratefully turned their backs on the mess and skittered down the stairs.

On the way home, they discussed their plans for Christmas. "I'm working on Christmas Eve, and then thankfully I'm off 'til the twenty-eighth."

"That's good."

"Yeah, God I'm really glad I've got Boxing Day off. That twerp Mike Chester's always there at lunch-time, sporting his compulsory new Christmas jumper and jollying it up loudly to impress his friends."

"What a lovely picture that paints."

"Quite."

"What about your mum?"

"My aunt's invited her over - though I don't think she's that keen. She may even stay at home."

"Why don't you ask her to come up to the farm?"

"What?"

"Well why not?"

"I don't know, the thought just never entered my head. What about Frank?"

"What about him?"

"Well, will he mind?"

"Mind? Why should he? But if you like, I'll ask him tonight."

But he would have no need to. Earlier that morning, barely half an hour after Dan and Susie had left for Dartmouth, Frank was chuntering along in his smoky old Land Rover about two miles from Littleham on his way back from collecting a few things from the local farming co-operative, when he happened upon Audrey standing at the roadside disconsolately examining a very flat tyre on her car. He pulled up with a shrill squeal of brakes and cut the engine.

"Morning, you look like you could do with a hand."

"Oh, Frank, would you mind? I'm sorry; you must think me quite pathetic!"

"Don't be silly." He climbed out of the cab and flicked his half smoked cigarette casually into the bottom of the hedge. "You've got a spare I hope?"

"Well, I *assume* so. I've never had a puncture before, you see."

"Oh, lucky you. Well never mind, it's only flat at the bottom!" He scrabbled around in the boot and located the wheel brace, jack and spare wheel. Swiftly he loosened the wheel nuts, got the car in the air, and changed the wheel.

"There." With the vehicle lowered to the ground, he returned the tools to the boot. "I'll chuck this in the back of the Landy, shall I? Then I can take it into Dave's for you in the morning if you like. You don't want to be without a spare do you?"

"Oh would you? That would be kind."

"Of course, it's no trouble." He picked up the wheel and heaved it into the rear of the already crowded vehicle.

"Would you like to come in for a coffee on your way back?"

"Thank you, but there's no need to go to any trouble."

"It won't be any trouble at all."

"In that case I will; I could certainly do with one."

Frank let her drive on ahead before clambering into his vehicle and following on behind. He pulled up by the gate leading to the gravelled entrance to the house and got out. Slamming the door firmly shut, he dusted down his jacket and trousers and scrunched up the path. The front door stood ajar. "Hello?"

"Come in, come in," a voice called from the direction of the kitchen, "don't stand on ceremony." He closed the door behind him and walked along the spotlessly clean Victorian tiles of the immaculately presented hall.

"Come and sit down," Audrey invited him when he popped his head round the door. "How do you like your coffee?"

"Oh, er, black with two please." He pulled out a pine chair and she thrust a sparkling glass ashtray under his nose. "Please smoke if you want, I really don't mind."

"That probably puts you in a minority these days," he quipped.

"Yes, probably, but don't you think the world's going madly health conscious? I mean, a little bit of what you fancy can't do any harm."

"I completely agree." Frank flipped the top of his lighter open and lit his cigarette. Inhaling pleasurably, he flicked ash from its glowing tip into the ashtray.

"There." She placed a steaming mug in front of him and sat down on the other side of the table. He took a tentative sip: the coffee tasted strong and good.

"I can't tell you how happy I am that Dan and Susie have patched things up, I really do think they make a lovely couple, don't you?"

"Yes, they certainly seem to get along pretty well together," Frank concurred easily. They've actually gone to Dartmouth today to try and sort out Dan's uncle's affairs."

"Oh, right." She held out a plate. "Would you like a biscuit?"

"Oh, no thank you."

"A sad business – but then, he didn't know him well, did he?"

"No no, not at all. There was some falling out between his mother and James; Dan never clapped eyes on him, even when he came here snooping around after Bob died."

"Oh yes. That must have been very hurtful: what he wrote about you, I mean."

Frank shrugged nonchalantly. "Sticks and stones and all that."

"Still, you must have been angry with him."

"Angry? Yes I suppose I was; for a while anyway."

"So you went to see him."

Frank was taken aback by her bluntness. "How do *you* know?"

She smiled. "My sister lives in Dartmouth. I was staying with her when I saw your Land Rover parked on the quay - it is rather, how shall I put it? Distinctive. I put two and two together."

"And you made four. Okay, I'll tell you the whole story, but I must ask you not to repeat it to anybody."

"Not even my daughter?"

"*Especially* not your daughter."

"Alright."

Frank ground his cigarette butt in the bottom of the ashtray. "Sally, Dan's mother…"

"…and James' sister?"

"Exactly. Sally and her mother had washed their hands of their brother and son respectively for an offence he committed against his sister when she was just a teenager."

Audrey was listening attentively.

"He erm, he molested her, sexually."

"Oh."

338

"Sally only ever told her mother, no one else ever knew."

"Oh," Audrey uttered again, inadequately. "So, you and Sally…?"

"Sally and I were an item once, if I can put it that way. A short while after we split up, she moved to Australia and married. I had no idea she was pregnant at the time, and her husband had no reason to suspect that Dan wasn't his own son. The boy only discovered the truth after his parents were both tragically killed in that road accident, and that's why he got in touch."

"So she kept her secret to protect her husband - and her child?"

"Exactly: she put them first, they didn't need to know the truth. She was a good woman and I was a damn fool to let her go. Still, I paid for it later when I married that Isabel, big time."

"You don't resent her for not telling you that the child was yours?"

"No, not at all; what would that have achieved at the time? Nothing but heartbreak, that's for sure. Besides, I was young and selfish; I wouldn't have wanted to know."

He finished the rest of his coffee and placed the empty mug carefully on the table.

"More coffee? Or perhaps you'd prefer something a bit stronger? Whisky's your tipple, isn't it?"

"Well perhaps just a small one; to keep out the cold."

"I won't be a tick - it's in the dining-room." She rose from the table and left the kitchen. Frank heard the sound of a cabinet door opening, followed by the unmistakable soothing glugging noise of a decanter being poured. A minute later Audrey reappeared with a large crystal tumbler a quarter full of Scotch. "Anything with it?"

339

"Same amount of water please." Frank rolled a smoke whilst Audrey topped up the drink under the cold tap. She then handed it to him.

"Thanks. Aren't you going to join me?"

"Well, it's a bit early for me. Oh what the hell! I'll have a small sherry." Once more she disappeared into the dining-room.

"Cheers!"

"Cheers!"

They chinked their glasses cautiously. "So, do you think I'm right?"

"What, not to tell Dan about his uncle?"

"Yes."

"I do. What would be the point? It wouldn't do any good."

"That's what I thought. But I've got a feeling he thinks I know something about it: and I know he resents me for not going to the funeral."

"It'll blow over in time; he'll probably put it down to your churlish nature and general bad temper."

"Oh thanks," he grinned.

"Tell me, how did you get the truth from James? I mean, it's hardly a thing anyone would readily admit to."

"No, but it was quite easy really. I merely made out that I already knew what he'd done: he was only too willing to put his own side of the story, and in doing so spilt the beans."

"So what was his version?"

"That she was, excuse me, a prick...I mean that she led him on..."

"A prick teaser? I have heard of the expression, you know."

"Sorry." Frank felt uncharacteristically embarrassed by her candour.

340

"What a despicable man."

"Quite. Sally was only thirteen at the time."

"Good grief."

"Anyway, it's all done with now. You won't say anything, will you?"

"Of course not. You did the right thing for the right reasons."

He regarded her quizzically.

"To protect your son? You see, you're not all bad."

He made no reply, and still feeling a little embarrassed, sought to change the subject. "We were chatting a couple of days ago, about Christmas?"

"Christmas?"

"Yes, we all wondered if you'd like to come and join us at the farm. There'll be plenty of everything to go round."

"Oh I don't know, I hadn't really thought. I *was* going to stay with my sister."

"Oh, okay."

"But I have to say that, well it's not that we don't get on or anything, but we really don't have anything in common and Roy, her husband, well he really is a most dreary man…"

"Is that a yes, then?"

"Thank you, yes. Yes it is. I'd love to - but on one condition."

"What's that?"

"That you let me provide the turkey and ham."

"But it's already ordered!"

"Then I'll pay for it. No arguments."

"Fine, if you insist - but there's really no need." Frank took a sip of whisky, enjoying its comforting warming tendrils spreading through him.

"Good. I look forward to it. It'll certainly make a change!"

"Yes, I suppose it will. Are you finding it hard, you know, getting used to being on your own?"

"I found it hard at first. Actually," she added pensively, "I think it was more strange than hard. You see, Douglas always dealt with life's little day-to-day concerns while we were married, and I was always grateful for that. But since he's been gone, I've discovered it's actually very easy to cope by oneself: I feel totally liberated, I never thought I'd have such self-confidence. I realise now just how much my life was a drudge, and what a miserable sod he really was most of the time."

Frank, in mid-swallow as she said this, very nearly choked on his Scotch.

"Oh dear, are you alright?"

"Yes, I'll be fine. It just went down the wrong way, that's all," he gasped. When he stopped coughing, he wiped tears from the corners of his eyes with a grubby handkerchief hastily excavated from his jacket pocket. "Well I'm glad you're okay; loneliness can be a terrible thing."

"Yes." She smiled across at him with such warmth and benevolence that it made him feel rather uncomfortable, although oddly enough at the same time aroused.

"You'd be speaking from experience, I take it."

He suddenly felt unnerved. "You could say." He drained his glass. "Anyway, I'd best be off. Thanks for the drink. I'll pop the wheel back later tomorrow, alright?"

"That'll be fine, and thanks for being my knight in shining armour."

"Any time."

As the Land Rover rattled along the lane, its customary curl of blue smoke corkscrewing behind it, Frank was wondering what on earth that had all been about. Was Audrey coming on to him? Or had the whisky fuddled his brain? No, that would be daft, she was just being nice. She'd only comparatively recently escaped from a long and, by her own admission, mostly unhappy marriage. Why on earth would she want to be involved with another man now that she had her freedom? He caught a glimpse of his careworn face in the shuddering rear view mirror: especially a rough old bugger like him.

Mind you, she was still an attractive woman. With a jolt, he suddenly realized that he'd always found her appealing; alluring even: and he knew they were about the same age. Douglas would have been a good ten years older than her, probably twelve, as Anne was only too fond of reminding people from time to time. *Not that there's anything wrong with that- I'm only saying.*

CHAPTER TWENTY-FOUR

Smoke mushroomed from the pile of spray in thick grey roiling clouds, great churning plumes occasionally being whipped and flicked around by the swirling and strengthening wind, like the huge billowing sails of some immense ship straining against the rigging in a turbulent Turner seascape. Frank pulled back on the hydraulic lever, lifting another load high into the air and approached the fire, dumping his burden satisfactorily on top of the smoking heap. After a moment's hesitation, angry grey smoke belched skyward, darkening the already sombre afternoon sky. Seconds later, with a mighty crackling and snapping, a long orange tongue of flame leapt upwards, licking the air hungrily and banishing the smoke. Half burned glowing twigs and foliage were hurled upwards in the intense heat, drifting down to earth some way off like sooty snowflakes.

The hedge from hell, as it had been appropriately dubbed, was now cut back and steeped neatly and Frank was enjoying the task of burning up the overgrowth he and his son had cleared. Thanks to an uncharacteristically dry February, he was able to drive the tractor into the field without tearing the ground up. He reversed the tractor up, swung in behind the neat row of hedge parings, and dropped the loader to the ground. He surged forward and lifted another load into the air on the forks. Once again he dumped it smack on top, momentarily dousing the fire and causing a thick pall of smoke to balloon upwards, blotting out the sky, before surging feathered flames, in incandescent rage, burst ferociously through again. In less than an hour all the spray had been heaped onto the fire and Frank backed up and turned the engine off. He climbed down from the cab and sat on the front wheel. Although he was some way from the inferno, he could feel its intense heat on his face. He rolled a cigarette and watched the ferocious fire die down whilst he smoked. In a very short time, there remained only a heap of glowing embers in the middle of the bonfire. With the wind still gusting erratically, occasional puffs of hot ash spun into the air, disgorging red sparks like fireworks. Frank got up from his perch, stretched and clambered back into the cab, slamming the door behind him. He pushed the unburned edges in with the loader, before heading for home in the gathering gloom. The first drops of rain were spattering onto the tin roof of the lean-to as he jumped out of the tractor and walked across the yard towards the house. He noted with some satisfaction that Audrey's car was parked beside his tatty old Land Rover.

Audrey had been spending quite a lot of time at Willow Farm since December. Frank told himself that she was merely here to see her daughter; and that if he suspected she had any other motive, he was clearly mistaken. Still, all four of them had passed an enjoyable Christmas together, and he had to admit that he felt relaxed and happy in the woman's company. In fact, wasn't he pleased to see that she was here again now? It was no good fooling himself, that warm feeling that had overcome him on Boxing Day evening when they were all playing silly parlour games by the fire: when had he last felt contentment like that? Had he *ever* felt like that? If he was honest, he probably never had; at least not in his adult life.

Warm air assailed him as he opened the door, along with the mingled homely aroma of a freshly baked cake and the faint tang of wood smoke. He could hear Susie and her mother chatting happily in the kitchen.

He flicked off his boots, hung his precious donkey jacket on a hook on the wall, and joined them.

"Cup of tea, Frank?"

"Oh yes please. Something smells nice."

"That'll be my Victoria sponge," Susie pronounced proudly, pointing to her creation which stood, dusted with icing sugar and oozing strawberry jam, on a plate on the side.

"Looks delicious - any chance of a slice?"

"It's only just come out of the oven!"

"Even more reason."

"You'll have to wait 'til Dan gets in, I want him to admire it first."

"Oh Susie really, cut the poor man a piece!" Audrey berated her.

"No, no, it's alright...I'll wait. He'll be in soon."

As if on cue, the back door opened and a moment later Dan appeared in the kitchen. "Has your mum been baking?" he teased.

"No, it's all my own work." She picked up the plate to show him. "Do you want to try some?"

Dan looked dubiously across at his father. "Well, I'm not sure...after the last time."

"Ha-ha, very funny. I've used self-raising flour this time, if that's what's bothering you. Still never mind, if you don't want any I'm sure Frank and mummy will have some."

"I was only kidding. Go on, I'd love to try it."

Susie replaced the plate on the side and retrieved a large knife from the drawer.

"This really is very good," Frank complemented her a few minutes later, launching the odd crumb across the table from his half full mouth as he spoke.

"Thank you."

"And the sponge is so light," Dan added, determined not to be left out.

"And the jam's good too."

"Oh yes, the jam's delicious."

"Well you've got mummy to thank for that, she made it herself."

"Mmm. I can honestly say that's the best cake I've tasted in a long while." Frank wiped his mouth with the back of his hand and smiled broadly at Audrey. "I tell you what, why don't we all go out for a bite to eat later? My treat," he offered congenially, in a rare show of generosity.

"It's a nice idea, but I'm afraid I'm working tonight," Susie replied.

"Yes, and I stupidly promised Pete that I'd play darts," Dan said somewhat ruefully.

"Never mind, another time then. Unless...Audrey, perhaps just you and me?"

"Are you inviting me out on a date?" Audrey enquired mischievously.

"Oh no, no," Frank hastily replied, feeling uncharacteristically flustered. "I er....it's just an idea. We can all go another time, if you want."

"It's alright, I'm only teasing. Where shall we go? The Captain's Table?"

A feeling of panic, bordering on horror, washed through Frank. The Captain's Table was a ludicrously expensive and some would say spectacularly pretentious restaurant serving reasonable dishes at far from reasonable prices: and it was French-themed. Frank didn't do French.

"Well," he began weakly, "if you like…"

"Mummy, stop it!" Susie chastised her.

"Oh, I see," said Frank, noting that Audrey was once again winding him up. "Very good. Shall we go to The Maltsters then? Rather than just down the road?"

"Yes, that would be nice. Right, I'd best pop back home and freshen up."

"I'll pick you up about seven, shall I?"

"Perfect."

After Audrey had left, Dan flipped his car keys off the hook by the door and chucked them on the table in front of his father. "Here, you'd better have these."

"Eh?" Frank regarded him quizzically, a half-rolled cigarette lightly balanced on the fingers of his right hand.

"Well you're not going to take her out in that filthy old Landy, surely?"

"Oh no, I suppose not." Frank replied vaguely. "But don't you want your car if you're going out as well?"

"Nah, we're at home tonight: besides, *I'm* not the one with the hot date."

"Oh yes, very droll."

Frank pulled over by the wooden gate to the entrance of The Laurels. He felt inexplicably and to his mind ridiculously and unnecessarily nervous. He angled the rear view mirror towards him and peered into his freshly washed and shaved face. Combing a couple of loose hairs back behind his ears, he reflected that he didn't actually scrub up too badly. He climbed out of the car, tugging the collar of his jacket up around his ears in a feeble attempt to protect himself from the rain, which by now was hammering onto the road and teeming along the verges in muddy rushing torrents. Scrabbling with the latch, he swung the gate open and dived back into the car. He drove sedately up to the porch which was illuminated by a welcoming coach light. He turned the car around, stilled the engine, extinguished the headlights, and still feeling like an anxious teenager on his first date, hopped out, took a deep breath, and rang the bell.

"Come in, it's open!" A voice called from inside.

Frank rigorously wiped his feet on the **welcome** sign daubed on the doormat, went inside, and softly closed the substantial glossy white heavy door behind him.

"I won't be a sec, pour yourself a drink!" came a shout from somewhere upstairs. "The whisky's on the sideboard in the dining room in the decanter! And while you're there you can pour me one too - I'll have a gin and tonic please; you'll find ice and lemon in the fridge!"

"Righto!" He shouted back. He shrugged off his jacket and hung it on the mahogany coat stand. He'd barely finished making their drinks before he heard her trotting down the stairs. She was wearing a knee-length snug-fitting blue skirt and a cream lacy sort of blouse. A light blue cardigan was draped nonchalantly across her shoulders. Her hair was pinned up at the back in a small bun, with odd escaped auburn wisps kissing the soft nape of her neck. Frank thought she looked rather charming. Actually, he hastily reconsidered, she looked absolutely gorgeous.

"Is that mine?"

"Er, yes." He handed her the glass. Ice tinkled merrily as he passed it over, bubbles playfully fizzing around the slice of lemon bobbing on its surface.

"Cheers!"

"Cheers!" she rejoined. "Mmm, that's nice. I'm sorry to ask, but you couldn't do something for me, could you?"

"Of course, what is it?"

"Well it's this damn zip - I can't quite do it right up: I've been struggling upstairs with it for ages. Would you mind?"

"No of course not," Frank flustered. "Ermm…"

He carefully put his whisky on the side and with as much care as if he was handling a piece of rare porcelain, placed one palm lightly on her hip and pulled up the zipper. "There you go."

"Thank you, it's virtually impossible to do on your own."

He smiled weakly at her. "I'm glad us men are of some use then."

The incessant rain was still pouring out of the pitch-black night when they left the house. "Blimey," Frank observed once the two of them were safely ensconced in the shelter of the car, "I hope it lets up soon or we'll have floods to contend with."

"Will your animals be alright?" Audrey asked.

"Oh they'll be fine, they're all inside this time of year - and the water's never got high enough to get into the buildings, nor the house come to that: not in my lifetime anyway." He chuckled softly. "There was one time when we had a bit of a problem, though. My father was alive then, but I think we'd all realized that, well…that he was beginning to go downhill. Anyway, he'd got a small flock of sheep because by that time I pretty much ran the dairy single-handed. It was about this time of year. No, it must have been later because they had young lambs with them. Anyway, it had been raining all night and carried on through the morning. The sheep were in the pastures bisected by the stream and some of the ewes and lambs had got separated. The stream was by now a swollen muddy torrent threatening to burst its banks. I managed to get across and pen up the stranded sheep, carrying the lambs across the water to safety. I then opened the pen to allow the ewes to swim across to their babies whilst I stood in the swirling flood to make sure they weren't washed downstream."

"Gosh, that all sounds very exciting."

"I suppose it was: you wouldn't believe how a normally benign brook could change so fast."

"So did you save them all?"

"Yes."

"And the sheep actually jumped in the water of their own accord?"

"Yes, at least most of them did. Even stupid old sheep have a pretty strong mothering instinct. The only casualty in fact was my dad."

"What?"

"Well, he saw me and my mother struggling and heroically came to help. Unfortunately, the current was too strong for him and he got bowled over."

"Was he alright?"

"Oh yes, we managed to drag him out, but he lost his Falklands' hat."

"His what?"

"His Falklands' hat. It was a battered old trilby he wore that his dog had chewed holes in a few years back, at the time of the Falklands' conflict. Hence the name: we often wondered where it ended up."

By the time they pulled into the car park, the heavy rain had diminished to a thin drizzle, although the wind appeared to be getting stronger, buffeting the pub sign on its hinges as it swung bad-temperedly back and forth. Curiously enough,

Audrey chose to sit at the table most favoured by her daughter whilst Frank got their drinks and grabbed a couple of menus from the neat stack propped against the stone pillar at the end of the polished bar.

As they worked their way through the meal, the conversation naturally turned towards their children. "I think that Susie has at last managed to put the past behind her," Audrey said, delicately slicing through her tender sirloin. Blood oozed around the serrated edges of her knife.

Frank eyed her over a forkful of chips. "Yes, I think you're right; although," he added with a note of caution, "it's early days yet."

"Oh yes, I totally agree." A brief silence followed, as each of them concentrated on their food. "And there's been no further mention of James?" Audrey emptied her wineglass.

"Not a dicky-bird. Can I get you another?"

A short while later, they had eaten their fill and were both feeling very relaxed in each other's company. The wood fire crackled merrily beside them, adding to the general sense of well-being and comfort.

"I must say, this place has certainly changed since I was here last," Audrey commented.

"Yep, it was a bit rough I must admit."

"I remember coming in here with Douglas, not long after we'd moved to the village. The landlord - oh what was his name?"

"John."

"John, that's it. Well, he just glared at us when we came in as if we were something he'd just scraped off the bottom of his shoe."

"He was definitely a strange one, I must agree; not really landlord material."

"When we asked him if he was doing food, he gruffly conceded that he could provide a ploughman's or a pasty: and if we wanted a pasty, he'd be willing to warm it up for us in the microwave – at no extra charge!"

"Yes, well times have changed since then."

"They certainly have. Do you know what happened to him? He wasn't married, was he?"

"No, he was never married. I've an idea that after he sold the pub he went to live in Scotland with his sister. But I'm not sure."

"Was he Scottish? You wouldn't have thought so by his appearance, he was rather a weedy man as I remember."

"I think he had some Scots ancestry from way back. He used to sport a kilt on New Year's Eve; it was about the only time the miserable bugger cracked a smile." Frank scrubbed out his fag-end in the bottom of the ashtray. "Right," he said decisively, "I suppose it's about time we made tracks."

Audrey smothered a yawn. "Yes, I suppose it is: time to drag ourselves away from the fire and face the wild elements again."

Outside the drizzle had fizzled out to leave a chilly dank night shrouded in thick mist. Frank drove slowly back through the murk, the narrow beams of the car's headlights valiantly but ineffectively striving to pierce through the pearly blanket of fog.

"Would you like to come in for a nightcap?"

"Well, I don't know…" Frank wavered, glancing at his watch.

"It's not that late yet, and a whisky'll keep the chill out."

Frank was not one to readily turn down a glass of Scotch.

"Isn't it strange," he remarked thoughtfully, "how so

much can change in such a short period of time? I mean, take my life over the last eighteen months or so; it's been turned right around."

Settled comfortably in Audrey's plush armchair, he drained his glass and stretched his feet out luxuriantly. "I mean," he continued, the benign effects of the alcohol loosening his tongue, "I was at a pretty low ebb before I found out I had a son, what with everything that had happened before."

"Yes, well that's quite understandable, isn't it?"

"I suppose so. Thing is, and this might sound daft, I've got used to having the boy around - and Susie, come to that. I'm not sure how I'd cope if I were ever on my own again. I didn't realise how totally miserable I was until I tried to…"

"But that's all in the past now," Audrey cut in hastily. "It's over and done with. Now, would you like a top up?"

"No, I'd better not; I don't expect Dan would appreciate me depositing his new car in the ditch."

"Don't risk it then."

"What?" He regarded her blankly.

"Do I have to spell it out to you? Stay here the night. Now do you want another drink or not?"

CHAPTER TWENTY-FIVE

"I don't know what you're grinning about," Frank growled.

"Me?" Dan asked, feigning innocence. "I'm just happy to be alive I suppose; and so were you earlier. Didn't I hear you actually singing this morning, when you were feeding the cows?"

"What? That was nothing," he blustered. "It was just some silly catchy tune that happened to come on the radio."

"Oh, I see. Nothing to do with your date the other night then," he teased. "When you stayed out - all night."

"I've already explained that; I didn't want to drive home after I'd had a bit to drink, especially in your car. Now can we drop it please? It's becoming a bit tedious," he added haughtily.

"Okay, okay, I'll say no more about it - but you had a good time, didn't you?"

"Yes, yes, I told you before, we had a very enjoyable evening," Frank replied tetchily. "But never mind all that - there's something else I wanted to talk to you about, while I've got you on your own so to speak."

"Oh?" The kettle was boiling away merrily, steam jetting from the puckered lips of its stainless steel spout in a thick straight column. Dan lifted it from the hotplate and filled two mugs. He gave them both a brief and rapid stir, before passing one to his father.

"Thanks. You and Susie, you seem to be quite settled now. Is that right?"

"Well yeah, we're getting along fine."

Frank drew on his cigarette thoughtfully and tapped ash off its glowing end into the crowded ashtray. "Good, only I was thinking: would it perhaps be better if you had your own place?"

"How do you mean? Do you want us to move out?"

"No, no, of course not. I only thought, we could divide the house up, it wouldn't be difficult to do. We could easily convert the old dairy and store at the end into living accommodation; that'd give us all plenty of room."

"I suppose. But wouldn't you…I mean that'd sort of leave you on your own. Wouldn't you mind?"

"Mind? No of course not. Besides, we'll be in the same building for heaven's sake: and I'm sure you'd take pity on me from time to time and poke a pie or something round the door."

"Of course - maybe even the odd cake or two as well. Right, I'll mention it to Susie as soon as she gets back - if you're sure."

"Positive. Besides, you two need your own space, and it'd also give me a chance to watch what I like on the telly without being frowned at."

"How do you want us to pay for the conversion?"

"It's my house so I'll pay for the building work - so long as you don't want anything too elaborate. You can fork out for whatever furniture and fittings you need afterwards. Does that sound fair?"

"Perfectly fair - more than fair actually."

"And if you're agreeable to the idea, I want to make you a junior partner in the farming business, just to give you a bit

356

of security, and as a supplement to your meagre and pitiful wages."

Dan felt that all his Christmases had suddenly come at once. Frank noticed the look in his eye and felt a little uncomfortable. "It's erm, it's not that big a deal; it's mainly for tax purposes," he added gruffly. "The less money I'm forced to stuff into the arse pocket of that thieving chancellor, the better I'll feel."

"So what do you think?" Dan was perched on a bar stool, watching his girlfriend as she emptied the washer and stacked the sparkling glasses carefully on the deep shelves behind her. "It's only really an idea, we can leave things as they are for now if you want," he added, trying to sound casual about the whole proposal. She pushed the bare rack into the machine and shut the door on it. "Is that what you want?"

"Me? Hell no, I think we should have a place of our own; don't you?"

"Yes," she smiled. "I do."

"Good, well the next step is to see what we want to do building-wise, before we get an architect in to draw up some proper plans. Hopefully, if we do everything right, we'll get the necessary permissions from the council in a few weeks, and we can start work as soon as the weather gets a bit better." He could sense that something was wrong. "What is it?"

"Oh Dan, it's a lovely idea, but I don't know if I can be well, comfortable with it." His heart sank. "I mean, I haven't got that much money, and I wouldn't want you to pay for it all; it doesn't seem fair."

He reined in his sudden feeling of annoyance. "Look, I'm not paying for it, Frank is. At least, he's paying for the building work. And," he continued before she could object further, "it's something that will benefit the three of us; after all, the house is his."

"Probably more like the four of us."

"Eh?"

"So you haven't noticed."

"Noticed what?" He looked at her blankly before it dawned on him. "You don't mean…you're not…?"

"No not that! You've got the wrong end of the stick: I'm talking about mum!"

"You've lost me."

"And Frank?"

He still looked bemused.

"Your father has been popping in to see my mother practically every time he's found himself passing her door, and that's been most days lately."

"I didn't know. At least, I'd noticed he wasn't his normal grumpy self recently; but that's all."

"Well there you have it. So you see, his generous offer to do up the house gives him just as much privacy as us."

"But you can't think…"

"That he and mummy will get together? Actually yes, I do; strange as it sounds, it seems that's exactly what's going to happen - sooner or later."

"'Strewth, that's a kind of weird thought."

"Absolutely, but it's a kind of weird thought that we're probably going to have to get used to."

"So where does that leave us?"

"I suppose it leaves us one end of the house, and them the other. Now listen, Dan," she said, swiftly changing tack, "I know you've got all that money from your grandmother, but I don't want you spending masses on turning the place into a palace."

"I wasn't about to do that, not when it isn't really ours."

"Quite, we don't need much to start with. And I want to do my bit; I'll decorate the place when it's ready."

"Fine, you can decorate it completely how you want it, I've got enough to do on the farm without sploshing paint around indoors."

"And it isn't as if Frank pays you much, you may well need that money later on, if we…" she trailed off.

If we what? Get married? Have kids?

"Yes I may; although he did actually mention that himself," he conceded. He watched her as she tilted his mug under the lager tap, and expertly filled it with the frothing bright yellow liquid, slowly bringing it upright when it was nearly full. She presented it to him crowned with less than half an inch of foaming head, a single drop of golden lager tracking down the outside of the chilled, rapidly misting-over glass.

"What? You mean he's giving you a pay rise as well?" Susie asked. Dan couldn't fail but to notice the heavy dose of irony in her voice.

"Well not exactly, no. He, er, he wants to make me a junior partner."

"Oh?" Susie's undisguised cynicism was swept away by an overpowering surge of genuine surprise.

He noticed the look of consternation that had suddenly appeared on her face. "I don't think it's entirely philanthropic, he said it was mainly for tax purposes."

"Tax purposes? Partly maybe, but I don't think that's the real reason. No, I think that he's made a very generous gesture: very generous," she added thoughtfully.

"…And that's not all," Anne continued, delighted not only to have Mrs. Manning but also Sally as her captive audience. She paused for dramatic effect.

359

"Well?" Mrs. Manning asked brusquely, "are you going to tell us or not?"

The postmistress drew a deep breath and carried on. "It seems that Frank has been seeing rather a lot of a certain recently divorced woman in the village of late."

Her eyes darted between the two gossips, wondering which one of them would put two and two together first. They both looked absolutely clueless.

"Well come on, it can't be that difficult!"

Mrs Manning went to open her mouth.

"Well Marge?"

"Well there's only one woman matching that description that I know of living around here…"

"And that's Audrey!" Sally broke in triumphantly.

"Exactly."

"Tosh," Mrs. Manning piped up vehemently. "You can't seriously be suggesting that a refined woman like that would want anything to do with a…with a *character* like Frank Anderson."

"Well they do say that opposites attract," squeaked Sally.

"Yes, but that's taking it to extremes. No, I'm sorry Anne, but you must have got your wires crossed this time."

"Oh I don't think so," she insisted. His Land Rover's been seen parked by her gate *and* by the front door on several occasions in the past few weeks, and they've been spotted out together - on their own, and not just once or twice, either."

"Well what does that prove? Nothing," scoffed Mrs. Manning. "Except perhaps that they may occasionally enjoy each other's company," she unwillingly acknowledged.

"Oh I think it's a bit more than that." The postmistress decided to unleash her main weapon. "He stayed with her all night a fortnight or so back."

"How do you know?"

"George saw them go out together - in his boy's car, and he heard them come back again. That car was parked there until half past seven the next morning, when Frank sneaked back to the farm. No doubt he thought he'd not been spotted, but George doesn't miss much."

"No, evidently not."

"Where've they been seen then?" Sally asked. "I haven't noticed them together in the village."

"Well, no Sally dear, they wouldn't be that obvious," Anne replied condescendingly. "They've been spotted cozying up together in the Maltsters a couple of times, and in town."

"Oh." Sally looked rather crestfallen.

"I still find it hard to believe," Mrs. Manning said. "I mean, what could possibly be the attraction for her? I know Douglas was a bit of a - well, you know, but even so…"

"Tosser?" Anne offered.

"Anne!" Sally objected, trying to hide her embarrassment.

"I'm not wrong though, am I?"

Neither woman contradicted her. "Anyway," she added dismissively, "never mind him, he's yesterday's news. I suppose you both know about the building work that they're going to do?"

"Of course," Mrs. Manning replied indignantly, "everybody saw the planning application in the paper."

"And the notice at the top of the lane," Sally rejoined helpfully. "But that's so Dan and Susie can have a place of their own; she told me so herself."

"Ah yes, but it also leaves Frank his own place as well, doesn't it? You see, it cuts both ways. I wouldn't be at all surprised if we didn't have a wedding before much longer." She paused for dramatic effect. "Maybe we'll even have two."

361

"Now I really think you're in cloud-cuckoo-land," her friend said dismissively.

"We'll see Marge, we'll see. Stranger things have happened."

"Not round here they haven't," she snapped dismissively.

Their conversation was rudely curtailed by the jangling doorbell and Mrs. Hobson appeared before them, looking rather windswept.

"Oh good morning, Louise, how are you?"

"Fine thank you." The other ladies politely nodded to the newcomer. "That is, I will be when Neville gets his own car back on the road; I must admit cycling does have its disadvantages as a mode of transport, especially when it's as breezy as it has been the last few days."

Anne smiled courteously. "And how are you all getting on up there? How are the alpacas?"

"Oh, we're all well, thank you; although we keep finding more work needs doing on the house; the plumbing is rather inadequate I'm afraid, and there seem to be patches of damp popping up where we didn't notice them before."

"Oh dear, well I suppose that's the risk when you move into an older property." *Or one renovated by Frank Anderson.*

"Never mind, I'm sure we'll get it how we want in the end."

"Of course. Any luck finding a job?"

"Yes, actually. I start in the autumn, down at Kingsbridge Primary for six months."

"Oh that *is* good news. Now, what can I get you?"

Mrs. Hobson had in fact come to the shop for some cheese, but having noted the sorry, tired and sweaty state of the cracked cheddar block, rapidly changed her mind. The yellowing stilton looked little better. "Erm, I'll just have a few slices of ham if I may and a couple of those pasties; oh, and a small sandwich loaf."

"Certainly."

When they once again had the place to themselves, the women resumed their gossiping. "She's a bit of a funny one," Anne said. "Nice enough, but a bit funny all the same - a bit of a health freak I think. I believe her husband is as well. Last time she came in here, she asked me if we ever stocked organic produce, and gluten free, whatever that is."

Mrs. Manning was keen to have her tanner's worth. "I'm surprised they've lasted so long as they have, I don't think country living's quite what they imagined it to be."

"I haven't seen much of them," Sally commented, "but they seem very nice."

"They've got wind chimes in their garden," countered Mrs. Manning. "And not only that, I heard he's a vegetarian. *And*" she added with emphasis, "he told Pete he wanted to take up morris dancing; I mean, I ask you!"

The summer sun beamed down benignly from a cloudless sky. It was the end of June, but already the rich green pastures of a month before had faded to a jaundiced yellow. So far, it was the driest summer Frank could recall since the drought year of 1976. Still, he was not unduly concerned. With the extra acres afforded him by his purchase of Bob's ground, and a surfeit of hay and silage from the previous season, he was well placed; even if he had to start feeding the cattle in a week or so. From his vantage point atop an old elm stump above them he admired his herd, their glossy black coats shining, a picture of bovine health. The cows stood bunched beneath tall bank-side alders, half asleep in the heat of the day and dozily flicking at the buzzing flies that constantly pestered them. Their calves lay flat out, motionless save for the occasional twitch of a tail here and there, their silky flanks rapidly rising and falling as they rapidly breathed the hot air in and out. He noted, as he had in former dry seasons, that cattle always seemed to do well despite the lack of fresh grass.

The building work was finished on the house, and all the harvesting was over unseasonably early. Susie was busy decorating, and, a little reluctantly, her boyfriend was helping her. Frank exhaled pleasurably before scrubbing the butt of his cigarette out between his legs on the wooden seat that had once been a mighty tree before it succumbed to the ubiquitous Dutch elm disease. As his workload was now lighter, he had uncharacteristically decided that a holiday might be in order and consequently had invited Audrey to accompany him on a week's break to Jersey. She had accepted this offer enthusiastically and they were due to fly out the following day. As he got to his feet he reflected, not for the first time, how circumstances had so dramatically altered over the last couple of years. Casting his eyes over his beautiful herd one more time, he also realized how lucky he was to have everything he now had. He turned his back on this heart-warming sight, unlatched the gate, and headed home under the burning rays of the midday sun.